Tuppence Ha'penny Is A Nickel

by

Francis X. Atherton

Fitzhenry & Whiteside

Tuppence Ha'penny Is A Nickel

©Fitzhenry & Whiteside Limited 1987

Fitzhenry & Whiteside
195 Allstate Parkway
Markham, Ontario L3R 4T8

Printed and bound in Canada

Canadian Cataloguing in Publication Data

Atherton, Francis X
  Tuppence ha'penny is a nickel
ISBN 0-88902-916-4

1. Atherton, John Joseph — Fiction.   2. Atherton,
Mary Louise — Fiction.   3. Canada, Western — Social
conditions — Fiction.   4. Canada, Western —
Emigration and immigration — Fiction. I. Title.
PS8551.T44T86 1986   C813'.54   C86-094343-7
PR9199.3.A83T86 1987

Author's Note

This is a story about real people and real events. It is about a generation of people now gone, and of the age of innocence in which they lived. I mention this at the outset, so that those of you who may be in the mood for a lusty tale of intrigue or shock may put this aside for a more propitious moment; a moment when, I hope, you may enjoy a tender and whimsical look at the decades that immediately preceded and followed the turn into the twentieth century.

The story is about my mother and father and their eldest children, and about their early lives in England and Canada. It is a tale that has long demanded release from the lockup of my mind; not only because their lives and interests were quite dissimilar to ours, and their standards and morals formed by a far different environment, but because their story is a revelation of lives changed and shaped in the disparate worlds of Britain and its Dominion, as they existed at that time.

The book covers the period from 1889 to 1909, which was before I existed. Still, since I too am a product of the age of innocence, and had the memories of my family to draw on, I hope I may have captured the flavour of the times and of the generation. Most of the characters are real, and the events true, and even chronologically correct, on occasion. I had to lean on my imagination for the reactions, thoughts and words, which would result from such characters and events. Arthur Weldon and Conrad Archer, being villains, had to be created Out Of The Whole Cloth, which is a Victorian way of saying they are figments. The other people, or people like them, did exist. If they are distorted, the fault is mine, and is the result of impressions received from, but not necessarily intended by, my mentors. At any rate, the persons are all human, and if they had shortcomings, I hope that they may be forgiven.

Francis X. Atherton

CHAPTER ONE

Arundel, 1888-1889

The tearful parting with her aunts had come as a surprise after the years of antagonism and resentment between the women and the young girl. She sat, eyes wet and unseeing, as the train moved out of Brighton Station, then as the train left the squalor of that part of town and passed through a suburb of better dwellings and small farms, she began to recover her composure. When rolling hills appeared, crests bathed in sunshine under a fall sky, her anticipation of the journey, and its ending, returned. She dabbed resolutely at her eyes and began to sort out her feelings.

To be sure, she was more than vaguely aware of the sacrifices the aunts had made for her and for Margaret. Her oldest sister's rebellion, when she had run away, must have been a great blow to their pride and confidence. And if she and Margaret had resented the exile from their own family and the austere lifestyle of these maiden ladies, how much more had the aunts been dismayed at the disruption of their lives by the pair of children suddenly thrust upon them.

Her guilt was short lived however, and she dwelled with no little pleasure on the sweetness of the parting. It had been so *romantic* and sad! With the resilience of youth, she accepted her newfound rectitude with a final sniff and dab at the moisture in her eyes. She wondered briefly whether Margaret had actually become an actress as threatened, and decided that her own life would be just as exciting. Savouring the changes to come, she then dismissed all tail ends of melancholy and buried herself in her book.

In the girl's preoccupation, and enjoyment of her novel, the only other occupant of the coach was able to study the young passenger. Ingenuous reading for a fifteen, possibly sixteen, year old — Lewis Carroll's *Through the Looking Glass* — but then, the good lady thought approvingly, an indication of proper upbringing. Pretty as a picture, she tallied; straight nose, lively brown eyes below dark brown hair, a pointed chin of character. Decently, but not expensively, dressed; from an upper lower-class family, she'd guess. The good dame rather fancied herself a

1

precise judge of people, and having thus placed the young girl in an approximate economic and social class, she lost interest, and turned to her own reading.

The elderly traveller had made a shrewd appraisal of her companion in the second class coach. The girl's father, John Heffernon, was extremely conscious of his status as a Master in the goldbeater's guild. In the Victorian order of things this put him somewhere between a successful small tradesman and an impoverished medical practitioner. His wife, Patience, was a seamstress with some claim to a stylish clientele in London.

Their daughter in the railway carriage was the third of five children. At the time of the birth of the fifth child, Jinny, both mother and the new baby were sickly, and the family had been divided as a result. Two of the children went to the sisters Lawrence in Brighton, the second oldest girl, named Jess, to an uncle and aunt in Yorkshire. The two youngest children, Will and Jinny, remained with their parents in London.

Subtle differences resulted from this scattering of the family, and one not a bit subtle. Will and Jinny retained the London twang of their neighbourhood, while Jess developed the Yorkshire dialect of the relative who raised her. The two sisters in Brighton, schooled by their aunts, had developed a softer, more genteel sound; but whether of London, Brighton, or Yorkshire, all had been brought up within the narrow confines of thought common to their time.

A change of trains at Littlehampton gave the younger passenger an opportunity to tidy herself for the coming reception at Arundel, some five miles away. Some nervousness set in. Jess's friend, Mrs. Carr, had said she would make her welcome. Did that mean she would be met at the station, or would she have to walk to the castle by herself?

As the train rumbled through the South Downs, she caught glimpses of the River Arun, and most of her misgivings gave way to the pure pleasure of the scene. Even greater delight came as the carriage rumbled through the final curve of track, and Arundel Castle burst into view.

Set prominently on a slope above the village and the Arun River, its towers, battlements and walls of brown and grey stone sparkling in the sun, Arundel Castle was all, and more than, she had expected. Its shapes and shadows filled her vision, making it the perfect setting for every knightly romance she had ever read. She, Polly Heffernon, was to be a part of this!

It was Cecelia Carr, housekeeper to His Grace, the Duke of Norfolk, who met her at the train, welcomed her warmly, and brought the enchanted girl to the castle by way of the tiny village. Together, they climbed the hill to the Barbican tower gates and into the enclosed compound which had once been a jousting yard.

She put the girl at ease as they went, explaining the origins of the various walls and buildings, and finally led her through an inconspicuous door in the courtyard to the servants' wing and the small bedroom she was to share.

"Sit down, dear," she told the newcomer, sitting herself on the one wooden chair in the room. The girl sat on one of the two cots, relaxing with her back against the wall. Mrs. Carr's correction was as kind as it was firm. "Sit straight, Polly," she said. Polly's education had begun.

"You are sixteen, Polly?"

"I will be in three months, Mrs. Carr!" The girl's eyes beseeched acceptance of her maturity.

"A little young," Mrs. Carr smiled, "but I think you'll manage. You are to be a maidservant, Polly," she told her. Then, "Polly?" she murmured to herself. "What are your other names, dear?"

"Mary Louise, ma'am, but my family call me Polly."

Mrs. Carr smiled. "You see, we have two Pollys and three Marys on staff, my dear. Do you mind very much if we call you Louise?"

The girl detested the name Louise with a loathing that only a young maiden can invoke. With dismay, she could see herself doomed to a lifetime of being "Louise," someone she was sure she wouldn't like. Polly was a name that suited her. She liked it for its perky, informal sound; but Louise!

With a burst of inspiration, she looked at Mrs. Carr pleadingly and said, "Please ma'am, if you don't mind, I'd prefer to be called Alice."

And so it was that Mary Louise (Polly) Heffernon became Alice, like the heroine of Lewis Carroll's devising. Most fitting too, as this new Alice, in the romantic setting of Arundel, felt herself truly in Wonderland.

There were other changes that the castle would work upon the girl, and a significant one began the following morning, when a chuckle from the other cot in the room revealed a plain-faced girl propped on her elbow, red hair tumbled. Mary Sweeney, out of Dublin by way of Liverpool, grinned cheerfully at her new roommate. "Are you awake, then?" she wanted to know.

"Oh yes, and after a lovely sleep!"

"Then shake yourself, Miss," she said, bounding out of bed. Alice needed little urging.

After she washed and dressed, Alice looked at herself in the tiny mirror with approval. Fifteen buttons on the bodice from waist to neck prevented any unseemly gaping, and a demure round collar circled her throat. The skirt of her uniform was generously proportioned and ankle length. Over it, her new friend tied a half apron, fastened with a large bow at the back, and placed upon her head that badge of servitude, the maid's cap. It was not demeaning to Alice, who wore it and her uniform as proudly as any new recruit in the army.

"I'm off to Mass now," said Mary Sweeney. "You can wait for me here, or come along, whichever your little heart desires."

Having been dimly aware that the Dukes of Norfolk were Roman Catholic, Alice had not considered the possibility that the servants might be Catholic as well. Now Mary's invitation to attend Mass in the chapel started a tug-of-war in her mind, between her half-felt fear and distrust of the "Romans," and the magnetic lure of mystery.

Her impulsive agreement to attend the Catholic service that morning was to mark the start of her life at Arundel; to introduce a factor of compelling force in her life and growth; and to stretch thin the tenuous bond joining her with her family.

Alice's first year at Arundel was a kaleidoscope of colourful events and people. From the housemaids, responsible for the care of the common rooms, she learned the procedures of dusting and polishing, under taskmasters even more meticulous than her aunts. The care of furniture, floors and silverware was not too arduous, though rug beating was a heavy task, and a duty drawn regularly because of her lack of seniority. Even this hard work, however, couldn't dampen her spirits. The atmosphere of the backstairs and downstairs of the castle was lively and uninhibited, and kept her in a state of bliss that frequently brought indulgent smiles from the older staff members.

She loved the atmosphere of the huge kitchen, the headquarters and social club of the house servants. Here they assembled for meals, and from here they were summoned to their various duties. The kitchen had its own social order. Age and seniority were respected with a reverence that might be expected in the House of Lords. The *family* was never discussed in the kitchen, except in terms of utmost respect, although senior staff members appeared to be allowed a certain fondness, though not familiarity, with individual family members.

Beyond an occasional kind word in passing from the master of Arundel, Alice had little communication with His Grace. She soon, however, became his admirer and, typical of her age, even a little in love with him. He was held in high regard by his staff for his unfailing courtesy, and for his dedication to duty.

Cecelia Carr was a confidante of the Duke in all domestic matters. She ruled his household with style, efficiency and a loving hand; while unbeknownst to her, everything she was and did was unconsciously being copied by Alice Heffernon, in this developing year of her life. The woman hidden in this artless young girl was growing to maturity in vastly different circumstances than she had ever known.

She now knelt in the chapel beside Mary Sweeney without the strangeness of a year ago. She was able to follow the service with understanding, to stand, kneel, or sit as required; activities which at first had seemed too frequent and confusing. She was able to pray without distraction, and she regularly thanked God for the friendship of Mary Sweeney, for the kindness of Mrs. Carr, and for the Duke and the young Earl. She also belatedly prayed for her parents, her brothers and sisters, and her aunts, and hoped that they too could find such happiness.

Alice celebrated her seventeenth birthday shortly before her second Christmas at Arundel. What should have been a euphoric day for her was shattered by the news Mrs. Carr brought to her. Her mother had requested her presence at home for Christmas. To go home and miss the excitement of Christmas at Arundel was unthinkable for Alice, and her dismayed reaction was plain to see. Cecelia Carr's own response to the girl's dismay was surprise and disappointment in her protege. Her reproachful look had to be answered.

"I'm sorry if I seem ungrateful, ma'am. You've been most kind to me. You see," she continued, "I have not been close to my parents since I was little. We haven't quarreled, ma'am, but I just don't know them very well, having spent most of my life with my aunts." It sounded lame, even to her. "Of course I'll go home if they want me," she said. "I should make an effort to know them better, and if your offer of leave is still open, I'll accept it with thanks."

Cecelia Carr was relieved, but had no idea that her intended generosity had taken the elation out of her protegee's birthday.

CHAPTER TWO

London and Arundel, 1889-1891

London was dark, wet and very unChristmasy when Alice's cabby finally found the street where her parents lived. From previous visits with her aunts, she recognized the house and shop, and the sign above the door.

JOHN HEFFERNON, ESQ.

Master Goldsmith

Below the lettering was the colourful symbol of the Goldbeaters' Guild of the City of London.

They were waiting for her in the shop. It had been two years since she had seen her immediate family, and her parents were understandably reserved with this new and grownup daughter. Poor Will, her brother, taking his cue from his parents, was restrained in his greeting, but there was no lack of warmth in the embrace and welcome of her sister, Jinny.

Patience, the seamstress, led the way into her home, through the curtain dividing it from the shop in front. Her mother was smaller than Alice remembered; thin, small and astringent, as if her very tissues were drawing in to shut out the corruption of a naughty world. Her dark hair was drawn back into a bun; her clothing, drab and unimaginative, showing nothing of the style of her fashionable clientele. She and John were members of a small and restrictive congregation, where any frivolity of dress or deportment was discouraged.

"Well then, Polly," said her father, with forced heartiness, taking her portmanteau as she removed her hat, cape and gloves, and sat beside her excited younger sister. She turned then to her father with not a little regret. They were as strangers.

"How are you, Father?" she asked dutifully.

John Heffernon was of medium build and fair complexion. His rather nondescript features were framed inside whiskers that dipped from his temples to his jowls, then rose again to meet his full and drooping moustache. His hair was otherwise sparse, and combed sideways across the top of his head. For the occasion, he had donned a rusty black suit with a lapelled waistcoat, and wore a wing collar, around which he had tied a dark cravat.

"I'm well enough, Polly," he admitted, almost with reluctance.

"And how are *you* feeling, Jinny?" Alice turned to search her sister's face. Jinny's cheeks were thin and coloured by an ever present fever that racked her. Her eyes glowed with an intensity only partly due to excitement. Alice impulsively put her arms around the girl, worried by the thin body and frail shoulders.

"Oh, I'm just fine, Polly. It's so good to have you home. You look so grown up and fashionable."

"You mustn't excite yourself, Jinny." The tenderness of Patience Heffernon's tone and expression transformed her. Alice saw a concerned mother, wrapped in a love of her ailing daughter. She saw it with a sense of loss for herself, but with relief and joy for Jinny.

Alice's older sister, Jess, was built to match the bigness of her heart. The tinkling bell that signalled her arrival could scarce announce the energy with which she bounced into the room, to envelop her sister in a giant bear hug. "Polly!" she yelled, with loud delight. Half a head taller than the younger girl, and much stouter, Jess held Alice at arm's length. The white midwife's uniform she wore was loose and uncorseted like Jess herself, practical and without frills. "It's good to see tha', lass," she said, "and don't tha' look bonny!" Jess's speech was pure Yorkshire. She pulled Alice down on the sofa beside her. "Are you liking Arundel and all?" she wanted to know, but did not wait for an answer. "Have tha' met the Dook yet, love? And isn't Mrs. Carr a dear?"

"Yes, yes!" laughed Alice. If Will or Jinny lacked confidence, dear Jess had enough for the both of them.

Christmas Day in London fared badly for Alice; church, for starters, being a dull affair at the storefront chapel. The preacher read the Nativity story from St. Luke's Gospel, but followed it immediately with a sermon devoted to the godlessness of people who profaned the birthday of Jesus with strong drink and gluttonous appetites. Home was not much better. The listless and leftover Christmas tree which Jess had purchased at the last minute, was set upon by John Heffernon.

"It's a pagan thing, Jess," he said heavily.

Jinny was ecstatic, and none had the heart to spoil her delight in this only concession to Christmas frippery. They even managed smiles of appreciation for the happiness she had been given.

Will looked at his parents, and ventured to say, "Merry Christmas, everyone!" and for a while, at least, the determined little spirit that had been struggling for survival all day was released into the room.

It was Will, too, who unintentionally precipitated the argument before bedtime. "I passed by the Roman church last night on the way 'ome," he said with a chuckle. "They was getting ready for their Midnight Mass. Place all lit up, it was, and people going in and out to confess their sins to the priest."

John Heffernon snorted. "They've got lots to confess, poor fools, but not as much as the priest who takes advantage of 'em."

Alice challenged him. "How, Father?"

"Well for one thing, Polly," he told her, "they take money for forgiving sins." He nodded his head wisely. "Only God can forgive sins, and He doesn't charge for it." Mary Sweeney had said nothing about paying to go to Confession, but she let her father continue.

"I've heard there's goings-on too, between . . ." but he was interrupted by his wife.

"Father!" she said warningly.

"Well, be that as it may," said John Heffernon, "it's always been an evil organization, and it's bent on taking over the world."

"And how would they go about that, Father?" Alice was becoming nettled. She was confused about some of the things she had discussed with Mary, but nothing she had seen at Arundel fitted with these assertions.

He was a little stumped. "Well, I suppose by gettin' into governments and kingdoms. They have a lot of influence in some foreign countries, you know." The thought carried him on. "You see, Polly, if you are a Catholic then you have to give complete obedience to Rome. If you are a king or prime minister in one of them countries, the Pope calls the tune."

"That may be in some countries, but certainly not in England." Alice was shocked and indignant. "The Duke of Norfolk's a Catholic, and he doesn't seem to be under anyone's thumb!"

John Heffernon's lips tightened. "I know he's your employer Polly, but you steer clear of him. It's said he's in league with Rome, traipsing over there regular to no good purpose."

She was astounded. "I don't believe that! There isn't anyone kinder. Everyone at Arundel loves and respects him." In her protectiveness, finally she became incautious. "Why, in the chapel," she said, "there's no one more humble or prayerful than His Grace." The silence that greeted this remark emphasized Alice's indiscretion. Will looked stricken and Jess wagged her head at her sister in exasperation. Only Jinny missed the import of what Alice had said.

"What do you know of the chapel at Arundel?" Her mother's voice had an edge that boded no good.

"I've been there a few times," she said.

"You've attended services in a Catholic chapel?" John Heffernon was shocked.

"Yes, Father." Alice was scared, but held her ground.

"What was Cecelia Carr thinking of to let you attend their . . . their Mass?" Her mother accorded the word its true diabolical wickedness. By now Jinny understood the trend of the conversation, and sat with wide open eyes, fear on her face.

"Mrs. Carr's a Catholic, too," Alice told them. "But it isn't her fault. She didn't encourage me, or discourage me for that matter. She seemed to think it was all right." She gathered her courage. "And I think it's all right too." She looked to Jess for support, but received no sympathy there. Jess's compressed lips told Alice she had brought this on herself with her loose tongue.

"You think it's all right to attend Catholic services, do you?" John Heffernon's voice was deceptively mild.

Alice knew her answer would not be well received, but it was honest, and her tone respectful. "Yes Father," she said, and waited for the storm to break.

She departed for Arundel the next morning, in an atmosphere of discord and distress. Poor Jinny and Will were stricken by the heat of their parents' tirade and appalled, as well, that their sister had held her ground. Jess obviously thought Alice should have left well enough alone, while Patience and John Heffernon believed their daughter doomed to perdition. They had raged at her with texts from the Old Testament and passages from the Apocalypse, and named the Church of Rome the modern Babylon, its Pope the Antichrist.

Through it all Alice had maintained only that the people and services at Arundel were not like that at all. She was shaken by the confrontation, and sorry that the spark of warmth kindled that Christmas afternoon had been quenched so quickly, and by her own indiscretion.

Away from them, her resentment returned. What right had they to direct her life after ignoring it for so long? She was not a child anymore, she told herself with fine indignation. She earned her own living, and was able to manage her own directions.

"I baptise thee in the name of the Father and of the Son and of the Holy Ghost." With these words the chaplain of Arundel Castle and pastor of St. Philip's in the village brought Alice Heffernon into the embrace of Holy Mother Church.

Fourteen months had elapsed since the girl's bitter parting with her family. Fourteen months begun with resentment and determination to deny her parents any vestige of control over her.

Upon her return to Arundel that Christmas, she had gone to Father Burke with the disturbing conversation with her parents fresh in her mind. In an England just emerging from the tyranny of the Reformation, Father Burke was used to handling touchy as well as nonsense questions. He was a skillful apologist, with his own interpretation of a harsh Catholic canon law. His answers soothed Alice's fears and, as she continued to seek information, he permitted her to join a class of instruction, with the understanding that she would make no commitment until she was eighteen.

She continued, defiantly at first, then with an increasing peace of mind, to attend daily Mass in the chapel. There was an appeal to her romantic nature in the ritual and colour of the services, as well as an atmosphere of peace and quiet when she slipped into the chapel to pray by herself.

Now, just as she had rebelliously associated the stifling presence of her parents' home with their religion, so did she begin to equate the grace and kindness she had found at Arundel with the Roman Catholic faith. Her models were Cecelia Carr, the Duke, and even light hearted Mary Sweeney.

In the year that went by, great changes took place in the girl's makeup. Day by day she was shaping, physically, emotionally and spiritually, into a semblance of the mature woman she would be. She was aware that men found her attractive and, while she did nothing in particular to get attention, her features drew the approving glances of the men around the Castle and the young parishioners of St. Philip's. Her brow was wide and high in the romantic tradition of the era. High cheekbones emphasized calm brown eyes under wide and slanted eyebrows. Her dark brown hair was piled loosely at the back of her head; drawn back from her face and brow, it revealed a straight nose and a wide and generous mouth, and exposed small and finely chiselled ears.

Upon her reception into the Church she experienced no surging feeling of elation, but rather a perception of peace, a rightness about her conversion and a sense of fulfillment.

The tidings of their daughter's adoption of the Roman religion was received without undue shock, but certainly with an increase in bitterness towards Alice, by Patience and John Heffernon. From this time onward, Alice was out of favour with her parents and, though she attempted to retain a measure of contact with them, she was generally rebuffed, and discouraged from any real reconciliation.

Her dear sister, Jess, unmarried and still living in London, wrote to Alice in a friendly and understanding way. Privately, she couldn't conceive that Alice would be drawn to Catholicism, but was broadminded enough to think her sister sufficiently mature, and with every right to make her own decisions. In later years, when one of her own children would wonder why their family was Protestant, and their cousins Catholic, Jess would explain and fondly reminisce in her homely Yorkshire fashion, "Our Polly was always sneaking off to the Italian church to see all the performance and carryings-on."

So Arundel Castle, and the people who dwelled in it, imposed their changes on the girl from Brighton. From the Duke, and from Cecelia Carr and Father Burke, she acquired high standards of loyalty and service; from Mary Sweeney, the gift of laughter and the saving grace of a good sense of humour. She was to draw deeply upon these resources in the life that lay ahead of her.

CHAPTER THREE

Beccles, 1891

One hundred and fifty miles northeast of Arundel in Sussex, and separated from it by an array of counties, customs and dialects, is the village of Beccles in Suffolk. It is a town whose venerable origins are earmarked by a gaunt and crumbling tower, once on the sea, but with the changes wrought by time upon both sea and coastline, now a mile or more inland.

In 1891, there were two other imposing buildings in Beccles, both of Gothic design. One of them, the pre–Reformation church occupied by the Anglican community, was authentically old and hoary. The other was just recently constructed, with stones unmarked by wind or weather, lacking even a strand of ivy to give legitimacy to its classic lines. It was the brand new St. Benet's, built by the Catholics.

On a particular Sunday morning in May, the Anglican services being somewhat later than the Catholic ones, all foot and vehicular traffic seemed to be headed for St. Benet's where the pastor of a few weeks stood at the top of the steps greeting his flock and savouring the morning.

Hugh Edmond Ford, a Benedictine in his first posting as a parish priest, was tall, energetic and outgoing. An academic who had taught in boys' schools throughout most of his ecclesiastical service, parochial duty was a new experience for him, but one he was tackling with interest and enjoyment. Like his brand new church, Hugh Ford was untried but abounding in promise.

Father Ford turned from an elderly couple to a newcomer. Puzzled for a moment, he broke into a broad smile as he held out his hand.

"Hey! I know you, young fellow. You were the juvenile lead in the play last evening! Welcome to St. Benet's."

He was looking at a young man just into his twenties, a little showily dressed perhaps, but with a smiling face and a direct gaze. He grinned impudently at Father Ford as he acknowledged the recognition and took the offered hand.

"I'm Joe Atherton, Father." The youth's frame was wiry to the point of thinness, but he filled his clothes well and wore them with the easy confidence given to tall men. His airy mien changed to mock sorrow. "So you saw it then; our glorious Final Performance." The failure of the touring theatrical company was not daunting him a bit, Hugh Ford could see. An engaging scamp, he decided.

"Are you busy today?"

"Not me, padre."

"Then come and have breakfast with me after Mass."

"Thanks," said Atherton, "I'll do that, Father!" His easy acceptance showed no embarrassment at this latest rescue by the clergy.

With a wave to the priest, the youth passed into the church's interior. Signs of its newness were seen in temporary furnishings like the small pressed metal holy water font, and the thin runner down the centre aisle, more to keep down the dust from the new concrete than to decorate. In contrast, the altar was new and grand with carved gilt in great profusion. No expense had been spared in the installation of the pipe organ which, even as he entered, sent soft music from the choir loft.

It lent a suitable note to Joe Atherton's entrance. He was sure that many of the congregation must be aware of him as the recent star of the ill-fated Fauntleroy production, so his every movement became stagey. With dainty grace, his fingers slipped into the holy water font, and with suitable reverence, he blessed himself with broad and dramatic gestures. He chose the centre aisle to give the greatest impact to his progress into the church, then selected a pew close to the communion rail at the front.

As he knelt in the pew and faced the altar, his attention to the religious aspect of his church attendance recovered momentarily, and with a little guilt for his shameful pride, the young man remembered to give his thoughts completely to the usual pre-Mass prayers for himself and his family.

"Do hurry, girls!"

The mistress of Gillingham Hall tapped an impatient toe for the tardiness of young ladies and glanced once more at her brooch watch.

"Girls!" she shouted again warningly, and they clattered down the broad staircase in a chorus of apologies, resplendent in light summer clothing and fashionable headgear. Any irritation Mary Kenyon might have felt vanished in her pleasure at the girls' appearance.

Margaret's white linen and flounced dress, in keeping with her thirteen years, was of calf length, displaying white stockings and high white boots which clattered as she dashed out the front door.

Mary Kenyon's look of pride at the older daughter on the stair was mixed with a little misgiving. Was the full length dress too old for a seventeen year old? She had not the heart to refuse Mary when she had implored, "Please Mummy, Alice has a long dress!" Now young Mary looked so grown up! The new, demure and grownup elder daughter hurried to the waiting coach.

With brief regret for the loss of her Mary's girlhood, Mary Kenyon turned her attention to the most recent arrival at Gillingham Hall, its newest staff member. With approval, Mary Kenyon noted that Alice Heffernon was dressed simply and in good taste. The lines of the pink gown followed the girl's figure, accenting the bust line as it curved to a slim waist. A frothy eruption of lace cupped a pointed chin and framed her smiling face. A narrow brimmed straw sailor hat balanced precariously atop her piled and pinned hair and tipped ever so slightly over one sparkling brown eye.

"My dear, you look beautiful!" Mrs. Kenyon's cry of approval made Alice blush with pleasure. It was a warm compliment to come from a lady, herself tall, patrician, and lovely.

"Come along then, my dear," said Mrs. Kenyon, and picked up her own long skirt and swept out of the house and into the waiting carriage. "Sit beside me, Alice," she said.

It had all happened so quickly. She had gone about her duties at Arundel, only vaguely aware of the handsome couple who were guests of His Grace, until she had been called by Mrs. Carr to meet John and Mary Kenyon.

Each had offered a handshake and a warm smile to the startled Alice who, in her confusion, had managed a small curtsey even as her hand was held, and a murmured response to their greeting.

Their invitation was a bombshell. Would she like to 'come and live with them'? It was a novel method of offering employment but, as she was to learn, typical of the Kenyons. Simply, they needed a companion for their two older daughters and Alice had been unhesitatingly recommended by Mrs. Carr. The offer was the more unnerving to Alice because she had been entirely content with her life and situation at Arundel. Not once had she considered the possibility of leaving.

She had been given a little time to respond to the Kenyons, and gradually came to the conclusion that change was inevitable. Mary Sweeney had recently become engaged to be married and had already started to drift away from her close association with the younger Alice. It was obviously too good an opportunity to miss; a thought shared by the housekeeper of Arundel. Gratefully, Alice accepted.

On the day of her departure, Mrs. Carr had given a speech of farewell in the kitchen on behalf of the staff, and embraced the girl with a hug and kiss. With all the embraces and good wishes that followed, Alice was to remember forever this warm tribute from a dignified and proper lady.

Mr. Gillespie, the Gillingham coachman, pulled up at St. Benet's with a flourish and jumped from his seat to hand down the ladies. He reserved a special reassuring smile for the newest employee of the Kenyons, still in a daze over her new status.

Riding in the carriage, indeed! Alice smiled brightly back at Mr. Gillespie, sharing her elation with him.

John Kenyon arrived on foot as the ladies stepped down from the carriage. He had volunteered to walk on this spring morning, the younger children having accompanied Nanny and other servants to an earlier service. The master of Gillingham Hall was a tall good looking man in his forty-seventh year. He greeted his family affectionately.

"Now aren't you all a treat for these poor old eyes!" he exclaimed extravagantly.

"Indeed," agreed his wife with some satisfaction, then glanced toward the priest at the top of the steps. "Come along, all of you. We're keeping poor Father Ford waiting."

Greetings and the introduction of Alice to the pastor over, the Kenyons led their family into the church, down the centre aisle to their pew. That a young man was praying in the aisle seat was not, in itself, alarming to Mary Kenyon, but she had no intention of clambering over him with her entourage. Her genuflection to the altar, followed by a firm nudge on his shoulder, apprised Joe Atherton of this fact.

Joe was startled from his brief devotions. Haivng thus dislodged him, the determined lady directed the girls, led by Alice, into the pew, thereby crowding the stranger over to the side aisle position.

Joe Atherton had a brief flash of the loveliness pressing him to the end seat, and retreated in confusion. A burst of organ music signalled the entry of Father Ford and his acolytes from the vestry, and Joe's natural insouciance began to return. He deftly outmaneuvered Alice in reaching for the nearest prayerbook, thereby leaving her the choice of sharing his, or that of young Mary on her other side.

Alice was not as unaware as she appeared. Nor was young Mary Kenyon, who slyly watched for her new friend's reaction to the interesting young man by her side. When Alice turned to her, she found Mary studiously reading her copy of the book, with no intention of helping Alice put the young man in his place.

Alice had seen him at his prayers before his dislodging by Mrs. Kenyon. She had taken his age to be near her own, and in a fleeting glance had noted his medium brown hair, prominent features and interesting, if not handsome, face. She had been quite impressed when he hurriedly stood and revealed his height and wiry figure. She had been amused at his discomfiture when pushed to the end of the pew, but was now in the position of having to snub him completely or accept the offer to share his book.

She held out for a while, then turned towards the book, primly assuring herself that she really should follow the celebration of the Mass. During the service she kept the most insecure of grasps on the book, to signal her lack of claim to ownership, and as the Mass ended she removed her hand and attention so promptly that Joe had to swoop quickly to catch it.

As organ and choir exulted in the recessional hymn, Joe Atherton turned to the attractive girl beside him, hoping for some sign of recognition. He had stolen many looks in her direction during the service and was smitten as never before. His interest continued to be challenged by her indifference as she turned her back on him to follow the Kenyon family out of the pew. He was determined to see her again. The thought grew as he followed the family up the aisle and watched their exit from the church.

The rectory of St. Benet's was new, but its furnishings sparse. Father Ford had brought his books and a comfortable chair to make his study habitable, but his parlor and dining room were like those of all other religious dwellings. Plain wooden chairs, bare tables and decorations only of a religious nature, pictures, statues, and Hugh Ford's rosary, hung over a hook in the entrance hall where he could grab it on his way to Benediction. The house was no better and no worse than other priestly dwellings Joe had visited. Impersonal, bare and severe.

"Come into the kitchen, my friend, it's more comfortable there," Father Ford said, as he led the way through the rooms to the rear of the house.

Here, the ladies of the parish had given the room some small warmth, adding a rug to its oil-clothed floor and cheerful curtains at the windows. A checkered tablecloth spread with dishes and cutlery was ready for the priest's breakfast.

"Sausage and eggs sound good?" asked Father Ford as he busied himself in the pantry. "Here, make some toast," he added.

"Will I now!" said Joe. He had not eaten since suppertime the night before and that meal had been insubstantial. The girl in the church was still on his mind. "That family in the pew near the front . . . " His casual approach didn't fool the priest.

"Ah, the family with the lovely girl who sat next to you."

"That's the one!" Joe looked up eagerly to find the priest looking at him with a smile. Joe gave an appreciative chuckle at being found out, but he wasn't disconcerted. "Pretty, isn't she?" he challenged.

"As a picture," agreed the priest, volunteering no other information as he stabbed holes in the fat farm sausages.

"Local gentry, I suppose?"

"Yes, the Kenyons of Gillingham Hall, and your toast is burning."

He hurriedly turned the toaster before too much damage was done. "Oldest daughter?" he asked, paying elaborate attention to the toast.

"No."

"Come on, Father!"

"All right," the priest gave up the sport with a chuckle. "She's just as new around here as yourself. Her name is Alice Heffernon and she's employed at Gillingham as a companion and sort of mother's helper." His next remark was half serious. "Mind you, I'm not anxious to expose my flock to you travelling fellows, so perhaps you should forget that particular young lady."

The tantalizing smell of breakfast drove further questions from Joe's mind as he sat at the table. Father Ford noted the zeal with which the young man attacked the food, and wondered what the next move would be for his guest.

"Will you go home, Joe?"

The young man considered, between mouthfuls. Beccles wasn't such a bad place, and he'd sure like to get to know Miss Heffernon. He made up his mind quickly. "I may try to get work here."

The priest was astonished. "But you're an actor."

"I'm also the best da'. . . the best printer in England!"

"You mean printing as in typesetting, press operating? How old are you?" He passed more toast to his famished companion,

"Twenty in a couple of weeks, as a matter of fact, but I started to learn the trade when I was thirteen. Got lots of experience, can always get a job." In spite of his boastful words, the priest believed him. An amazing young man, he thought.

"I'm also a professional runner," Joe said, spooning jam onto his toast.

"WHAT!"

Joe laughed at the look of incredulity on Father Ford's face. "Haven't done any running recently. Prefer the stage, but I've been in meets all over the country. Quarter mile mostly. Not very profitable though; the owners rake off the cream and the runners get only the glory. Still, I've a championship of Northern England." He took an appreciative gulp of his host's fine tea.

Hugh Ford shook his head in wonder. "Do you have a home and family?"

Joe laughed aloud. "Indeed I have. A father still going strong, and a mother who has borne fifteen children and raised twelve of us!"

"Good God!" said Hugh Ford, with more awe than reverence. He recovered to ask, "What does your father do?"

"Well, my brother William, who is studying for the priesthood, says that our father is a sanitary engineer. Actually he has a plumbing establishment, but then William is a little stuffy."

"Do you think priests are a little stuffy?"

"No, I think William's stuffy. As the first born in the family, he feels his responsibilities very heavily. I'm the second son, thank goodness, so I've always been able to relax."

"Evidently," said the priest drily, and Joe responded to the look of amusement with a chuckle at his own expense.

"What part of the country do you come from? I don't place your accent."

"Garn . . . cant'cher naow?"

Hugh Ford laughed. "Don't try to tell me you're a Londoner."

"No, from the North country actually. Parents from Lancashire. I was born in Norwich. I guess my travels and stage experience account for the way I talk. I've been told I sound like a Yank at times."

The priest got up from the table, picking up his own and Joe's plate. "Well, I may be able to help you find lodgings if you really want to stay in Beccles, and there's a busy printshop in the village."

Joe rose in a hurry to help. "That would be wonderful, Father. I'd just as soon not creep home with my tail between my legs."

Hugh Ford paused briefly and raised an eyebrow at his guest. "Somehow," he said pointedly, "I just don't see you doing that under any circumstance."

CHAPTER FOUR

Beccles, 1891

In the weeks that followed her arrival in Beccles, Alice was too involved in her new life to give any thought to the young stranger who had shared his prayerbook with her. Not that she was overworked, but each day brought a new and captivating aspect of Gillingham and the Kenyons. The atmosphere at the Hall was loving and lively, as informal as Arundel Castle had been precisely formal. Mr. and Mrs. Kenyon were without any pretence, their children wonderfully bright and alive. The younger Kenyons were frankly curious about the newcomer and deluged Alice with questions about herself and her life at Arundel.

There were six children at home and an older brother at University. Those at home were all girls, with one exception, Joseph, an eight year old who had fought his way to an undisputed place in a family of outgoing females.

Although not wealthy by Victorian standards, the Kenyons, with the inheritance of Gillingham Hall only a year or so earlier, were able to live in comfort and some style. They were served, in addition to Alice, by a butler, a cook, a parlor and a kitchen maid, a coachman-groom, the usual nanny, and a gardener who employed casual help as needed from the tenant farmers.

Gillingham itself had been built by the father of Sir Francis Bacon in 1610. A square mansion, more Georgian than Tudor in appearance, it had interior charm and roominess that belied a rather austere exterior. Trees, shrubs and gardens softened the stark outlines of the house, and a hedge-lined driveway leading to the coach house added distinction to the home of the Kenyons.

The household was unique in its stress upon the equality and dignity of the individual. Almost Quakerlike in its recognition of personal worth, the children were never allowed to talk down to servants, tenants or villagers. John and Mary Kenyon, as well as their children, addressed the butler as Mister Churchward, and the coachman as Mister Gillespie; but even with this small formality, a degree of intimacy existed between the staff and family quite unprecedented in Alice's experience. Boldness of nature by either servant or child was frowned upon in the household, and liberties were not taken, simply because each person felt at ease, and part of a tremendously successful establishment.

Alice helped with the youngest children, assisting Nanny while the older Kenyon offspring attended their studies with a lady in the village but, since the younger charges still kept up the custom of an afternoon nap, she was encouraged by Mrs. Kenyon to get out of the house for a while every day.

She became familiar with the village and the rolling Suffolk countryside nearby and, one sunny afternoon in June, she had stopped on the High Street to contemplate the old and forbidding tower. It did not appear to have any connection with the buildings near it, all obviously of a more recent vintage. A voice behind her startled her for a moment, and she turned to see the pastor of St. Benet's.

"I'm sorry if I frightened you, Alice." Hugh Ford held out his hand to his young parishioner. "I was just asking if you knew about our Norman tower."

"Oh, hello Father," Alice replied as she took his hand. She looked at the tower again. "No, I didn't know it was Norman. I should have recognized it; the stonework is similar to the Keep."

"Do you miss Arundel?"

"I think of my friends there often," said Alice, "but the Kenyons have been so kind and the feeling in their home is so happy that I haven't had a chance to become homesick. You were about to tell me of the Tower," she reminded him.

"Oh yes. It is the oldest structure around here. The reason that it stands alone is because it was once a watchtower and lighthouse on the seashore."

"So far away?" protested Alice.

"It wasn't, eight hundred years ago," said Hugh Ford. "It is hard to believe that the sea has receded so far." He looked at his watch. "Have you a half hour for a guided tour?" he asked.

For the next while they walked and talked together, Father Ford pointing out the town's few other landmarks, while they gradually learned about one another's lives and interests, and enjoyed their communion. He was old enough to put her at ease in his company, but young enough to appreciate her freshness and youth.

Finally they came to the original church, the one serving the Anglican community. It was gray, worn and ivy covered; its pitted stone walls attesting to the church's antiquity. The churchyard beside it was enclosed in an iron fence and was heavily treed; low branches swooping over the broken and leaning gravestones, threatening to hide the markers entirely. Patches of sunlight filtered through the shrubs and trees, relieving the murky shadows.

In one such open spot, as the priest and the girl walked through the cemetery, they came to a low tomb on which was seated a young woman, engrossed in a book.

"Hello, Annie," said Father Ford softly, and the girl scowled as she raised her head, resenting the intrusion upon her solitude. Her face assumed a less resentful aspect as she recognized the priest, but there was no welcome on her face.

"Hello, Father Ford," she answered respectfully, and rose immediately.

"Alice, may I present Annie Pipe; Annie, this is Alice Heffernon, who is at Gillingham Hall with the Kenyons."

Alice saw a girl of her own age, somewhat taller than herself, with a direct gaze that looked at her with curiosity, but without any apparent compulsion to be pleasant to a newcomer. She had good even features, and beautiful dark hair which flowed down her back from the loosely tied ribbon at the nape of her neck. Her speech, as she acknowledged the introduction, reflected the Suffolk dialect, but with an evident striving for a more fashionable accent. Alice remembered her own early Londonese, now almost undetectable in her conversation, and her conscious efforts to correct it.

"How do you do," Annie Pipe replied, nothing in her manner encouraging familiarity. Nevertheless, Alice felt drawn to this dark and brooding girl, and wanted to know her better.

"Do you come to this place often?" Alice asked.

"Yes."

"May I see you if I come this way tomorrow?"

"If you like," she replied indifferently, and as Father Ford had started to walk on a few steps beyond the girls, Annie Pipe returned to her book.

"Goodbye," said Alice, as she started after the priest.

"Goodbye," echoed the other girl, with only a short glance up from her reading.

Alice and Father Ford continued their walk, and although Alice was eager to know more about the girl, the priest volunteered no information. They parted company at St. Benet's, and Alice turned towards Gillingham with the resolve to seek out Miss Annie Pipe on the morrow.

The Kenyon children's tutor gave lessons in her own home on the High Street. School was over for the day as Alice neared the neat cottage, with its flower filled garden. The Kenyon girls came out of the garden gate.

"What have you been doing?" Mary asked, as she tucked her arm in Alice's and fell in step.

"I had a lovely walk with Father Ford. He showed me around, and after we had seen the Tower and both churches, we met a young lady in the churchyard."

"Annie Pipe," announced Margaret.

"How did you know?" asked Alice curiously.

Margaret tossed her head. "Oh she's always there, so she won't have to talk with anyone!" It was obvious that the girl did not have a great regard for Annie Pipe's wish for solitude. Mary was a little more tactful.

"Annie is entitled to her own company if she chooses, Margaret. There're lots of times when you don't want to be bothered with anyone, you know that."

"But all the time?" asked the gregarious Margaret. It was incomprehensible to her that anyone might possibly prefer her own company for more than half an hour at best.

"Well, Annie is a little different," Mary acknowledged, "but if she wants to be alone that's up to her."

"Doesn't she have to work?" asked Alice practically.

"She is a sales clerk in the mornings at the ladies' shop in the village," said Mary, "and she does the books for her father, who is the bootmaker here. The family goes to St. Benet's," Mary added.

"Except Mr. Pipe," Margaret amended. "At least he doesn't go on Sunday, says it's bad for business, but he goes every Monday without fail."

"That is just gossip!" Mary rebuked her younger sister. "The Pipe family is, well, interesting!" she told Alice. "They don't care what people say about them, and so, a great deal is said of them. Mr. Pipe calls himself The Excelsior Shoemaker, and really does make the finest shoes and boots. Mother and Father buy all of their shoes, even for fashionable wear, from Mr. Pipe."

"They do sound interesting," agreed Alice. Her curiosity piqued, she was more determined than ever to get to know the most private person of Miss Annie Pipe.

The weather continued warm and sunny as Alice resumed her stroll the next day, directing her steps toward the churchyard, where she found Annie Pipe again seated upon the low tomb, engrossed in her book. Annie looked up as she heard Alice's footsteps, but did not turn back to her reading. Instead, she gave Alice a long, appraising look with a derisive half smile upon her face.

"You came back," she stated, with a little toss of her head that seemed to indicate that it didn't matter at all whether Alice had returned or not.

"Why yes," said Alice calmly. "Are you surprised?"

"I didn't even think about it." said Annie airily.

"The Kenyon girls told me something about you and your family, Annie."

"Did they tell you I was a witch?"

"No, indeed. Why would anyone say that?"

"Because people like to talk about anyone who chooses to be a little different," said Annie. Her manner was challenging, with no hint of softening. It seemed to Alice that it would be difficult, if not impossible, to break down the barrier the young woman erected, but there was only one way to find out.

"I'd like us to be friends," said Alice.

"Friends!" said Annie, clearly taken by surprise by this forthright suggestion, and without any change in her own blunt manner, asked flatly, "Why should we be friends?"

Her answer was not one to encourage a better relationship, and Alice could see how Miss Pipe had become a solitary person. But the dark girl attracted her. Alice was sure that, underneath the forbidding front, there was a warm, intelligent and exciting person.

"I think we can be friends because we're alike, Annie," said Alice evenly. "We do have things in common," she insisted. "We both have to work for a living, and neither of us have many friends here." She could see that Annie Pipe was still scornful, and added with a great deal of vigour, "However, if you're determined to shut yourself up and refuse a sincere offer of friendship, that's up to you!" A little shaken by her own boldness, Alice was surprised to hear herself say in no uncertain terms, "MAKE YOUR MIND UP, ANNIE PIPE!"

Outrage warred with Annie's sense of justice as she looked, open mouthed, at her would-be friend. This was the girl she had thought entirely too prissy for her liking. The show of spirit came as a surprise, and the implied rebuke for Annie's rudeness was stinging.

Alice had read the village girl correctly. Annie was desperately lonely, but in her pride had always presented a studied air of indifference to the people of Beccles. She was unhappy in the narrow confines of thought in the village, and despaired of being accepted into its society. Annie was intelligent and ambitious. She longed for a better education, and avidly devoured every book that seemed to offer more than the mincing romances read by other girls of her class in Beccles. She was poles apart from her contemporaries in the village, and wretchedly lonely as a result.

Annie rose to her feet, one hand going out tentatively to the other. "I must ask your pardon," she said painfully. It was the most difficult apology wrung out of the young woman in all of her nineteen years, certainly the only apology given of her own free will; and with the ice of rigid habit thus broken she was able to continue in much warmer tones. "I'm sorry I was rude, and if you still want me to be your friend I'd like to be friends with you."

That said, the two girls, dark eyes sparkling at one another, smiled a little foolishly, and laughed at nothing at all.

CHAPTER FIVE

Beccles, 1891

As spring turned into summer, the early blossoming of friendship between Alice and Annie became secure and firm. For Alice, it was the first friendship with a girl near her own age since Mary Sweeney had lost her heart to a young man.

She had come to dearly love the Kenyon family. Everything about them lived up to the early promise. She enjoyed her work, which was light, and adored the senior Kenyons as she had the Duke and Mrs. Carr at Arundel. She had come to think of the Kenyon children almost as younger brother and sisters; they and Mr. and Mrs. Kenyon encouraging this affection with their own warmth and acceptance of Alice as a family member.

But young Mary Kenyon was not, and could not become, the bosom friend that Alice needed. The disparity in their development was greater than the year or so of difference in their ages. Alice had been away from the shelter of family for more than two years, and the environment of the servants' quarters at Arundel was worldly in comparison to the nursery at Gillingham, from which Mary and Margaret Kenyon were not far removed. As well, in spite of the Kenyons' kindness, there existed a gap in circumstances that precluded intimacy, and the exchange of confidence which Alice discovered in her friendship with Annie Pipe.

She had barely given a thought to the young chap who had shared the Kenyon pew a few months earlier; and it was Annie who brought up his name one afternoon in late August, as the girls met as usual in the churchyard.

"Do you know Joe Atherton?" asked Annie without preamble, as she seated herself on the low tomb.

Alice flicked away some fallen twigs before joining her friend on the hard surface. "No, who is he?"

Annie laughed. "He is that young man that you told me was in the Kenyon pew, and shared his prayerbook with you."

"Oh, him," said Alice, "how do you happen to know his name?"

"Father Ford introduced him to me last evening. I had to go to the rectory to deliver a bill from Papa, and there was your young man."

"He isn't my young man," said Alice, "and how did you know that he was the one in the pew?"

"He told me!" said Annie triumphantly, "And does he have a crush on you!"

"Oh, nonsense, Annie, really!" Alice coloured nonetheless.

"That's not all, there's to be a play put on in the parish, and he's going to direct it!"

"Who is going to be in it?" This was a big event for Beccles.

"The young people!" cried Annie, hugging Alice's arm. Two months earlier, Annie would have raised a sarcastic eyebrow at the idea of an amateur performance, but she could now express her true feelings in Alice's company.

Alice looked at her curiously. "Would you like to be in it?"

"Well, I wouldn't mind helping out," said Annie lamely. A sudden panic, at the thought of exposing her emotions publicly in a play, overcame her first enthusiasm. "Maybe they need prompters or something like that."

"Is there to be a meeting, or a selection of the cast, or anything." Alice's interest was growing. It might be fun, and she couldn't resist Annie's evident interest. It would be good for her friend to meet others, too.

"Father Ford is to announce the play on Sunday, and will call for volunteers."

"Let's do it, Annie!"

"Do you really want to?" Annie wasn't so sure. Did she really want to 'make a fool of herself' in front of everyone in Beccles?

"Yes, of course, we'll have lots of fun," said Alice.

St. Benet's parish hall had served as the temporary place of worship until the new Gothic church had been built. It was undistinguished and plain, but could seat a hundred or so people comfortably and boasted a stage and curtain for the many social events and entertainments that the parish would sponsor. Since its conversion to a church hall, it had already seen a St. Patrick's Day concert and a dance celebrating the end of Lent.

The young people drifted in, in twos and threes, and occupied those chairs facing, and nearest to, the stage. They looked expectantly at the former actor who sat, with apparent indifference to them, while directing his whole and flattering attention to the priest. For the occasion, the young man had dressed in his modish best. The cut of his trousers might have raised the eyebrows of a Bond Street tailor and the lapels of his jacket might have been a little too flamboyant, but he looked most dashing to his rustic audience.

Joe Atherton was not as unaware as he pretended to be. As he played the part of the sophisticate for his audience, he was cocking a watchful eye for the appearance of a particular young lady. Hugh Ford, out of his long experience with young men, was enjoying his companion's pretence, gravely discoursing while chuckling within at Joe's evident desire to impress Miss Heffernon.

True to his promise, Father Ford had found both lodgings and work for the young man who had breakfasted with him in the springtime. He was quite taken with the young fellow, and had readily agreed when Joe proposed the play production. He had followed up discreetly on his protege's reception into the town and found that he fitted in quickly at both lodgings and printshop, and was well liked by his mates at both places. Actually, he found the boy to be straightforward, despite his colourful career, and despite a tendency, which Father Ford found amusing, to show off outrageously in a group.

Joe's nonchalant vigilance was finally rewarded. There she was, the lovely young lady of the pew and, thanks be, with another girl and not a prospective male rival! He gave up the pretence of indifference and smiled warmly at all the young people. Annie Pipe nudged her companion, as Joe looked directly at them and as they found places at the rear of the auditorium.

A few minutes after eight Father Ford rose, his height emphasized by the three cornered biretta he wore on his head and the long soutane that buttoned all the way down to his shoe tops.

"Good evening, everyone!" he said, welcoming the some twenty young people who had gathered in curiosity about the play. "I hope this is the first of many functions that will promote friendship between the young men and young women of this parish and encourage you to meet members of the opposite sex who are of the same faith as yourselves."

This thinly veiled allusion to the function of the parish as a matrimonial bureau was not new to Father Ford's listeners, even if his own approach to the subject was much softer than that of his Church. He continued his speech, "Young ladies and gentlemen of St. Benet's, here is Mr. Joe Atherton who will tell you about the play."

Joe bounded to his feet and came to the edge of the platform. "Hello everybody! The play we have picked has a large cast, so those of you who want to act will be able to do so. We're going to need others for the making of scenery and costumes, and people to work on the sidelines, ticket sales, and things like that." He went on to outline the plot of the play, a comedy, quoting lines from it with great vigour, and relaxing the audience with his own and the play's humour.

"Will those of you who have had any experience, raise your hands." Two or three hands went up uncertainly. "Any kind of acting experience," Joe urged. "Were you in a school play or concert, a church choir?" Several more hands. "Did any of you put on a play for your families when you were a young-un?" His audience laughed, as nearly all hands went up. A relaxed chatter started, and the self-appointed producer and director had to call loudly for attention.

"Will the young ladies who would like to try out for the part of 'Maggie,' please come forward." Three girls came giggling to the stage. "Anyone else?" There being no response, he pointed out another girl on the right side. "You Miss, wouldn't you like to try out for the part?" As he expected, she shrank back, and Joe turned to the left side of the auditorium.

26

"Miss Heffernon, and your friend, won't you try out for the part?" If he could coax her to take a major role he would see more of this peerless creature. Alice ignored the use of her name and looked at Annie.

"You go Annie, you'd be wonderful as Maggie! Go on up," she urged the hesitating Annie Pipe. "I dare you!"

Annie might have been reluctant to parade herself before the young people of Beccles, but was not one to refuse a challenge to her courage. There was a moment's silence as she started up the stairs to the left of the stage, then someone started to clap. The audience quickly picked it up and Annie came on to the stage in consternation, looking down at the smiling faces as they expressed good will with their applause. She smiled at the people in the auditorium, then took her place with the other girls.

There was no contest. Annie was the last to read for the part, and the quality of her speech and expression was so superior that she was the obvious choice. The other girls retired with glum expressions, aware they had been outclassed. Annie returned to Alice's side, flushed and happy.

A tryout for the male lead followed, and the young men who offered themselves just could not satisfy Joe as they read the lines. "No, no, more expression! Like this!" and Joe would declaim, with fervour, the lines of the young hero of the play. His perception of the part and his professional rendition of it were obvious to the audience and eventually someone called out to him, "Why don't you play it yourself?" A murmur of yesses went up from the audience, while Joe protested, somewhat weakly, that he couldn't do justice to both acting and directing. They were able to overcome his reluctance without too much difficulty and he agreed to play the part of 'Horace,' as well as to produce and direct the play, all with a becoming modesty as false as his role on the stage.

Excitement increased as all the parts were tried and assigned. There were a few disappointed people but Joe, by coaxing and joshing, managed to keep the entire group eager to return and participate in one way or another. Although Alice had not tried out for a part, she agreed to return with Annie and accept whatever chore she was given. She was pleasant with Joe and appeared not to notice that he paid more attention to her than to the new leading lady.

Annie didn't mind. Her emergence into the social world was triumphant and delicious. She promised herself that never again would she retreat into a world of loneliness behind a facade of unconcern. How different her life had become with Alice's arrival upon the Beccles scene!

CHAPTER SIX

Beccles, 1891

The practice sessions continued throughout August and September. Within two or three weeks, Joe had the acceptance of the troupe as its acknowledged leader and was on an easy basis with everyone. He harried and bullied and coaxed and wheedled his cast until it began to lose its woodenness and took on the spontaneity that was to ensure the success of the play.

Once over her initial nervousness, Annie was brilliant as 'Maggie.' She enjoyed the new sensation of power evoked by the response of the small audience to her acting. She was good, and she knew it. Her ambition 'to be somebody' had found at least a temporary satisfaction in having a part in the little play at St. Benet's.

Joe felt he was making progress with Alice. She seemed to enjoy his company, and obviously thought he was terrifically funny. Early attempts to charm her in other ways had been fruitless, so he brought out his most extravagant puns and outlandish posturings to get her attention. She responded with hearty and helpless laughter, as Joe mimicked and quoted and clowned before his troupe of players, with a keen ear cocked especially for her reaction.

Thanks to Annie's participation, Alice was present at every rehearsal, and was seated in the wings as prompter. If Joe played to that side of the auditorium more than to the other, the troupe was indulgent, and Alice, pleasantly aware of the director's looks in her direction, didn't mind the attention a bit.

The change in Alice's attitude towards Joe did not go unnoticed by Annie Pipe. Annie had no designs on Joe herself. Her goals were set much higher than on an itinerant printer in Beccles, but twinges of jealously assailed her occasionally, when Alice laughed too heartily at the leading man's jokes. Annie was possessive of her friendship. It was too recently gained to be shared with anyone else.

"Pay attention, 'Maggie.' "

It was towards the end of September and they were rehearsing the final scene between the male and female leads.

"This is the Big Clinch," said Joe. "This is the hardest part for the actors to play. Because you are among friends and are going to be performing in front of your families, you are apt to get all embarrassed and silly about kissing and hugging. I'll tell you this," he said to his cast, "if you do it gingerly and prissily, you'll be laughed off the stage by the audience. But if you kiss your partner with imagination and enthusiasm, you'll bring down the house with applause, and make a smash ending to the play, like this!" and without warning, Joe seized Annie expertly around the waist and shoulder and, bending her back, planted a kiss full on her lips, to the delighted laughter and applause of the troupe.

Annie was started. She pulled her head back and struggled her way out of Joe's embrace. "What do you thing you are doing?" Her cheeks were crimson. This was too great an invasion of her privacy.

"Shall I show you again?" asked Joe, with a devilish glint in his eye.

"Don't you touch me!"

Joe shrugged. "You read the script. What did you expect? A kiss on the cheek with my hands behind my back? I'm supposed to be in love with you!"

"Well, I wasn't ready." Annie was angry and confused. She struck out as only Annie Pipe could. "If you have to practice on someone, why not Alice? You're always making eyes at her!" And with her feelings blurted out in this childish manner, Annie Pipe swung on her heel. "I'm going home. You can have your old play!" she said, and snatched her coat and hat from a chair at the rear of the hall and ran from the building.

Alice, like the others, had been entertained by the exhibition of lovemaking, and amazed at her friend's reaction. Annie's caustic remark was hurtful in the extreme. "Wait, Annie," she cried, and hurried after the fleeing girl, collecting her street wear on the way.

Joe looked after the girls with regret. All the fun had gone out of the evening. "That will be all for tonight," he told the cast, and with many murmurings of disappointment, the group dispersed.

The girl was well on her way, by the time Alice came out of the hall. Alice called to her in vain, as Annie raced away without response. Her friend stood and watched her disappear from view. It was the first time there had been a rift and Alice was desolate and hurt by Annie's attack upon Joe and herself.

Joe was emerging from the auditorium as Alice retraced the few steps she had taken after Annie. "I'm sorry, Alice, I didn't mean any harm. Can I walk you home?"

It was the first time that Alice was to respond affirmatively to one of his many overtures. "Yes, if you don't mind." She was very quiet. Until now, Annie's company had been all that Alice had wanted, and as the young man fell in beside her, she said, "You mustn't be angry at Annie, she has just been getting used to people."

He couldn't help but admire her loyalty. "I know." He shook his head ruefully. He had heard about Annie Pipe's solitude. "I shouldn't have grabbed her like that." His generosity paid off.

"Well, after all, it was part of the play." Alice found herself defending him.

It was a pleasant night and she had thrown her coat across her arm and swung her hat unconsciously as she walked along. The evening breeze fluttered at the loose tendrils of Alice's brown hair in a most fetching way, and Joe's heart pounded a beat higher.

"I wish you were playing the lead, Alice."

"Oh?" she answered in a small voice. Then, struck with alarm that the tiny feeling that plucked at her was a betrayal of her friendship with Annie, she said resolutely, "Well, I'm not, and Annie was doing very well until tonight. What ever are we going to do to bring her back?"

This last was said with such appeal that Joe rallied to assure her. "Don't worry, I'll see her tomorrow. I can grovel or be charming, or whatever else is needed to get her back into the play."

"Thank you!" she said, and as they had reached the driveway gate at Gillingham, she offered her hand instead of the cheek Joe would have wished for. "Goodnight, Joe!"

He squeezed her hand fervently, and was delighted with the tiny pressure in return. She withdrew her hand quickly though, and flashed a smile as she ran to the house. He stood foolishly for a moment or two after the door had closed, then in the bright moonlight he leaped into the air, his long legs flying up after him. One heel kicked to the side and the other heel went out to meet it in a triumphant click, before Joe returned to earth.

Annie's head was in a whirl of emotions as she ran home; anger, embarrassment and resentment crowding her thoughts. Her fierce pride had always been a defence against deep hurt, but it now deserted her. Instead, a niggling sense of justice told her she had reacted meanly to an innocent bit of fun, even so the wound to her feelings was almost more than she could bear.

Although Joe was the cause of her agitation, her resentment, contrary to all reason, turned against her friend. There was a brief flash of Alice laughing with all the others at her discomfiture. How could she! Bitterness overwhelmed Annie once more and drove out any regret for her own part in the evening's depressing ending. There was to be no peace for Annie Pipe that evening. It was late before she fell into an exhausted sleep, and tangled dreams allowed her no easy rest.

She went to the ladies' shop the next morning in something like despair. The brief emergence into the world of friendly society was over. How foolish she was to have presumed that everything could change overnight. Her guard would be up now more than ever. She avoided the churchyard that afternoon and instead, tried to immerse herself in work in the office which fronted her father's shop. It was there that Joe found her as he took a late noonday leave from the printshop.

"Hello Annie." There was no welcome on her face for the visitor. If she could have escaped, she would have done so, but the only place to go was the shop, and her father would have asked questions. Instead she faced Joe defiantly.

"What do you want?" she said ungraciously.

"I want to apologize, Annie. I shouldn't have grabbed you like that last night. I don't blame you for being angry, but I hope it won't make any difference to your being in the play."

"You made me a laughing-stock in front of everybody. And as far as the play, and everybody in it, I don't care if I never see any of you again."

"Ah, don't be that way." Joe thought to appease her with a message from her friend. "Alice feels terrible about the way you ran away last night."

"She laughed like everyone else. A fine friend she is!"

"That's not fair," said Joe with some heat. "Alice is your best friend and she is very upset about all this." He tried again to placate her. "Come on Annie. It was just a little fun. Alice wasn't laughing at you, she was just enjoying the play and the nonsense."

"*Let her!*" said Annie, and her chin went up to indicate that the subject was closed.

The injustice to his darling was more than Joe could bear. "Who the hell do you think you are, Annie Pipe?" Annie's mouth fell open in protest at his language but Joe allowed her no opening. "If you'd stop thinking of yourself for a change, and how badly done by you are, maybe you'd spare a thought about somebody else."

It had been a long time since anyone had stood up to Annie and her sharp tongue, and after Joe's abrupt leavetaking, she sat down slowly and stared unseeing at the papers in front of her. She knew that what Joe had said was basically true. Her self esteem tried to reassert itself in indignation, but the fire was not there. What have you done now with your rotten temper? You've ruined the best friendship a person could ever have, she told herself and felt miserable, as never before in her lifetime.

The September skies were as sunless as Alice's thoughts, as she sat on the low tomb she usually occupied with Annie. Even the birds seemed hushed this afternoon, and the usually brilliant shades of green that emerged in the dappled sunlight were absent on this gloomy day. Alice sighed. She had so much hoped that Annie would be here. Apart from the estrangement from her friend, there were other disturbing thoughts in her mind. It was obvious that Joe Atherton was becoming something more than merely interested in her; and, though this was not the first time that a young man had tried to establish himself with her, her own feelings were somehow different this time. Now she wished she could talk it over with Annie, but Annie had not come this afternoon and possibly might never come back. The thought made Alice desolate. The surroundings here were too closely associated with her friend for her to remain any longer. Unaware of Annie's own approach to the churchyard, or of that young lady's dismal thoughts, she picked up her things to go.

The mood of the girls could not have been more open to reconciliation. As they saw one another, there was less than a moment of hesitation. Alice was the first to call out.

"Oh Annie, you did come!" she cried, and she ran towards the other girl. Annie waited no longer. If Alice was ready to forgive her there would be no more foolishness. Their friendship was too precious to waste in childish hostility.

"Alice!" and Annie's cheeks were wet with tears as she clung to her friend. "I'm so sorry. I've been acting like a baby," she wailed, and felt the comfort of Alice's arms around her. Alice, too, was openly weeping and half laughing with relief as they parted, hands clasped, to gaze upon one another fondly.

Annie's return to the rehearsals was not easy, but with Alice's support she gamely faced the troupe the following evening. She found it hardest of all to confront Joe, but he quickly put her at ease by acting as if nothing had happened.

The rest of the cast was generous, at least in her presence, and the only really awkward time was when the director said with a smile, "Shall we try the Big Clinch again?" Annie's answering smile was tremulous but she said, "Why not?" and that small hurdle was over.

The October presentation of *Make Believe Maggie* was an unqualified success. The auditorium was filled to capacity. It rocked with laughter and applause. Mr. and Mrs. Kenyon brought their older girls and afterward they greeted Alice with chatty compliments for the show. The air was electric with excitement as the cast milled about with members of the audience, and Annie blushed at the warm praises of the Kenyon family.

Joe lingered nearby until Alice called him over. "Mr. and Mrs. Kenyon, may I present our director and leading man, Mr. Joseph Atherton." If the Kenyons eyed him more closely than a casual introduction might warrant, Joe was unaware. Margaret and young Mary looked at Joe's tall frame and easy bearing with approval; both determined to later pester Alice about her young man.

Alice chattered eagerly about the play and its success. "There is to be a party tonight for the cast and all the troupe," she told the family. "Father Ford has invited us to stay, if you don't mind? I won't be late."

"I'll bring Alice home," offered Joe, before the Kenyons could answer. Alice looked to her employers for their consent, and Mrs. Kenyon said impulsively, "Of course, Alice." The family left, not without a longing look, cast at the entertainers by the eldest daughter, who wondered if her mother was ever going to allow her to grow up and be with other young people.

The October evening was cool as Joe walked Alice home after the party, and he was in seventh heaven when she tucked her hand into his arm and pressed close to him. For warmth, she told herself, but didn't pull her hand away when Joe covered it with his own. They were both a little giddy from the excitement of the play and the party, and laughed at everything and nothing in particular.

The walk home was all too short, and after they had traversed the driveway at Gillingham, they faced one another, neither sure of the next move. "Goodnight," said Alice, and tentatively held out her hand.

"Goodnight," said Joe, taking her hand. He eyed her closely, and he hoped, ardently, but got no answering signal. There was only one thing to do. He quickly leaned over to kiss her. Alice did not pull back, but moved her head slightly and received the kiss on her cheek. To the young man's chagrin, she then released her hand from his grasp, and with a brilliant smile, stepped back from him.

"Thanks so much for walking me home. It was a wonderful evening, truly it was, Joe!" She touched him lightly on the arm. "Thank you again," she said, and turned from him to the entrance, giving a small wave as she closed the door.

He was more than a little let down, after the heady excitement of the evening. He stood for a moment staring at the empty doorway, then turned away with a kick at a particularly offensive and malicious little stone in the drive.

"Damn!" he muttered.

CHAPTER SEVEN

Beccles and Yarmouth, 1891-1892

Joe saw Alice infrequently after the play. He wrote a little note once asking if he might see her, but its appearance at Gillingham provoked such a teasing from the children that she hastily wrote him that she was busy with Christmas preparations. In fact, she was not sure of her own feelings and protested laughingly to the children that she had no interest in Joe Atherton, then tried to put him out of her mind.

His mother's letter had arrived shortly after Alice's polite but noncommittal answer.

"Dad and I think you should come home for Christmas," she had written. "With William at college, it is hard enough trying to manage all the young ones, and of course they would like to see you. William tells us there is no doubt he will be accepted into the novitiate, but he has to spend such a time in training. If he had been content to be a secular priest he would have been ordained by now. But that's William, it's the Jesuits or nothing."

She went on to tell him the news of the rest of the family, and ended her letter on a disturbing note. "You'd best give thought to staying home after Christmas. Dad can get you a job in Yarmouth and the pay is good for printers here. Some of your wages coming into the house wouldn't be amiss, and you could sleep with Alf and young Ernie since they've a big enough room."

She closed her letter without any great show of affection. Sarah Atherton was a no-nonsense person; not one to go all soft and maudlin over nothing at all.

Alice's seeming indifference did not faze Joe. He was not ready to give up pursuit. Just seeing Alice at church was enough to keep his ardour strong; and so, on a Sunday in mid-December, he was waiting for her as she emerged with the Kenyons. "May I see you for a moment?"

Mrs. Kenyon smiled benignly on them. "We will wait for you in the carriage, my dear," and moved her offspring along with warning glances that told them to behave.

When they were alone, he said, "I am going home to Yarmouth for Christmas, and I wanted you to have this," and he handed her a small box tied with holiday ribbons and a sprig of holly.

Alice's composure was shattered. She felt the whole world was watching, certainly the occupants of the coach.

"Take it please, Alice. To tell the truth I'm not sure when I'll be coming back to Beccles."

The news was more than a little disturbing. At any rate, she decided suddenly, he was leaving for an indefinite period and deserved better of her.

"Thank you, Joe, that's very nice of you," and she accepted the gift with a smile so warm that his heart leaped with jubilation. He took the hand she offered him and squeezed it.

"May I write to you?"

"Yes, I'd like that," she said incautiously, and pressing his hand in return, said with animation, "Merry Christmas!"

"Merry Christmas, Alice, and many of them!" His heartfelt words followed her as she ran to the waiting carriage. Joe saw her settled and the vehicle start up without any further sign from his beloved, but he was more than content. *Alice, my love, I'll get you yet,* his heart sang as he watched the carriage out of sight.

She was overwhelmed by the barrage of questions that burst on her in the coach.

"What did he give you, Alice?"

"Are you going to give him something, too?"

"Are you engaged?"

"Children!" said Mrs. Kenyon sharply, bringing a halt to their chatter but not decreasing their avid curiosity one bit.

"It's only a Christmas present," said Alice defensively, "and he's going away. That makes it all right, doesn't it, Mrs. Kenyon?"

"Of course," Mrs. Kenyon replied. "Personally, I think it was very nice of the young man," and, at that, directed a glance at her children that told them the matter was closed.

They were not to see one another for six months. Joe went home, to be caught up in the excitement and preparation for Christmas in a house filled with nine children younger than himself and one older sister.

He did not tell his parents of his plans to return to Beccles until after Christmas was over, then met with instant opposition. "How can you talk of marriage when you've hardly been able to support yourself 'til now?" his father asked, without any particular malice. "You've been running around the country like a feather-brained gnat without putting anything aside for your own family, let alone a wife."

It hurt, but Joe had to admit the truth of his father's remarks. Surprisingly, it was the feisty little Sarah who found the solution to her son's disappointment. She squirmed up to her seat at the kitchen table, the one with the cushion that allowed her to get her elbows on the table.

"Give it time, lad. If the girl's worth it, she'll wait for you if it's meant to be." A rare glimpse of compassion flashed momentarily over Sarah's austere features as she saw the disappointment on her son's face. "Tell you what," she said briskly, with a side glance at her husband for support. "Keep in touch with this girl, Alice, and if, in a year's time, you both feel the same, and more's to the point, have put some money aside, then you'll have our blessing. Right, Dad?"

Joseph senior wiped his heavy moustaches on the back of his hand after a last sup of his tea. "Right," he agreed.

"Six months!" said Joe.

"Well we'll see," said his father. Knowing Joe's short-lived enthusiasms, he thought six months would be ample time to test his son's regard for this girl.

He had no trouble getting a job as a printer and, in the bigger city of Yarmouth, Joe drew a much better wage than in Beccles. He worked hard and started to put away some of his wages.

Alice answered his letters openly, and at the beginning of their correspondence he was careful not to frighten her off by being too ardent. Instead, he wooed her with humour and nonsense and basked in the sunshine of her obvious enjoyment. He began to recognize that he was becoming an important factor in her life.

He eagerly shared her letters with his parents and they began to look with favour upon her as a possible daughter-in-law. Maybe Joe was settling down at last.

His twenty-first birthday, in May, was recognized by his parents, not only with a gift of five pounds to add to his growing savings, but also with a little celebration where, for the first time, they shared a drink with one of their children.

In July, he made arrangements to go to Beccles, and wrote Alice that he was coming.

With the coming of spring and summer, Annie and Alice had resumed their meetings in the secluded churchyard glade. This afternoon they made an appealing picture in their light summer frocks, wide straw hats and pretty slippers replacing the high laced boots of a late spring.

"Joe will be here next week."

The remark, without undue emphasis, was edged into the conversation for Annie to pick up in any manner she deemed appropriate. "That's nice," she said, trying to inject a little warmth in her voice. Alice *had* enjoyed Joe's company and was at her gayest when Joe was being his most absurd self. Was it possible this could be the basis for a romance? Not for Annie. She envisaged a man, even more arrogant than herself, who would sweep her off her feet with the sheer power of his personality. But Annie relented. "Why Alice, that's wonderful! You will be so glad to see him!"

Warmed a little by Annie's reception of the news, Alice allowed some of her pleasure to show. "Of course! My goodness, it's been nearly seven months since he left, and Annie, I *have* missed him." This was the first time Alice had admitted any strong feeling for Joe, even to herself.

"You know that he's coming back just to see you, don't you?"

"Yes, I suppose I do."

"What are you going to do if he asks you to marry him?"

This had been the question in Alice's own mind since receiving his latest letter; a question she had resolutely put aside as being silly and unrealistic. Annie's words made the proposal of marriage a distinct possibility. "Oh Annie," she wailed, "I don't know! I like Joe a lot, maybe even love him a little. But marry him?" It was too much to consider. "Maybe he won't ask me!" she said determinedly, as if this would solve the problem.

"Well, I think you'd better have an answer ready. He was head over heels in love with you before he left here, and the number of letters since shows he hasn't cooled off one bit!"

Alice sighed. "I wish we didn't have to grow up and think of marriage and husbands and babies." It was an earlier Alice, right out of Wonderland, who spoke so wistfully.

"Then all you have to do is say 'No' if he pops the question."

"I know, I know!" Alice's indecision was plain. "But I *do* like him an awful lot, and I enjoy being with him, and I've never met anyone before that I would consider for even one moment." She felt somewhat better after this, as if she had not been quite fair to Joe. At any rate, she would put the question out of her mind until it became a reality.

She had really made only one decision by the time Joe made his declaration of love and proposal of marriage. It had been on the first night of his return to Beccles. At Gillingham, Mr. and Mrs. Kenyon made Joe welcome, then prudently left the young people together. Joe had wasted no time in pressing his suit, and Alice's reply was to the effect that she did love him a little and would give him a firm answer before he returned to Yarmouth. She permitted a small embrace and a short-lived kiss, and was alarmed at the depth of her own feelings when this happened. Joe sensed her response, but had wit enough not to press his luck.

The younger Kenyons had hovered as near to the closed door of the drawing room as their mother allowed. They were caught off guard by Joe's early leaving that night, but Alice did not volunteer any explanation. If the older Kenyons did recognize her heightened colour and sparkling eyes, they were discreet enough not to remark on it, and a glare from the father shushed any comment which the younger members of the family might have essayed. In the meantime, Joe was jubilant as he made his way to his temporary lodging in Beccles.

Alice walked down the high street the next afternoon, consciously avoiding a meeting with Annie Pipe. She was in a whirl of conflicting emotions. Above all, she felt a surprising exultation and a tenderness for Joe which she hugged to herself with delight. He had been so sweet! The thought was replaced with some of her other doubts. Did she actually love him enough to spend the rest of her days with him? A little nagging doubt about his suitability as a husband came, without her knowing why. He had a good trade which would seem to promise security, as well as personality and good looks; so why should there be a reservation in her mind? Alice guessed she was just being silly, and in her newfound happiness, she was glad to see Father Ford approaching.

"May I walk with you, Father?" she called out to him, and the priest smiled at the picture she made. Her dark eyes were dancing, and her long hair blew in the slight breeze, retained only by a scarlet ribbon tied behind her ears.

"What man wouldn't want to walk with such a vision of loveliness!" he replied, and, noting her excitement, commented, "Something is making you happy today, my dear." He offered her his arm, which she took, and they resumed their walk.

"I *guess* I am happy," she said with a little laugh.

"Guess?"

"I *am* happy!" she exclaimed, and turned her head to face him as they walked along. "I suppose any girl is happy at her first proposal!"

"Ahah!" said Hugh Ford, "and I'm sure I know who the lucky fellow is. I see Joe is back in town."

"Well that's the point, I haven't given him an answer yet." He saw the indecision on her face, but wisely refrained from comment. "Oh Father, how does a girl know when it's the right man'"

"I'm sure you are not really asking me for an opinion, Alice." He grinned. "After all, what does an unmarried clergyman know of such things? At least I won't tell you piously that you will know him when you see him."

"I'm glad to hear that. I don't have all of those overwhelming feelings of thunderous love I'm supposed to have." Her rueful laugh was echoed in kind by the priest.

"Do you like Joe?"

"Oh, much more than that. I'm sure I really love him; quite a lot!"

"Well, that's a good start anyhow. It's the basic ingredient of all human relationships. 'The greatest of these is love,' " he quoted, but then found himself in alarmingly deep water. Alice was hanging on his words like one of his philosophy students.

Good Lord! he thought, *now I'm a bloomin' marriage counsellor.* He struggled to remember something from his university classes, and was able to declaim, "A similar economic and social background, and unanimity in philosophy." He continued wryly, "Bluntly put, that pedantic nonsense says that you and Joe are of the same class and are both Catholics. At least it cuts down by two the number of causes for argument in a home." He was grateful to see her relax and smile up at him.

"Go on," she said, "I'm listening," and they continued their walk.

He looked at her searchingly after a while. "Of course, money, or the lack of it, can be a destroyer of marriage, Alice. You will have to decide if Joe will be a good provider." He had reservations of his own on this score, but her answer reassured him.

"Joe's put quite a bit by in only six months, Father, and we wouldn't be getting married immediately." Her confidence, and his belief in her good sense, relieved him. Undoubtedly Joe could earn a steady and good income, if he put his mind to it.

"Then there's only one other requirement," he told her lightly, as again he drew out another profundity from his past. "Tastes and interests of a similar nature." He looked at her fondly. "You both have a love of life and laughter, God bless you!" He nodded his head emphatically, as he smiled down at her. "That well may be the most precious thing you will bring to a marriage."

Her doubts seemed to be resolved. She was gleeful as she skipped back to Gillingham, reviewing her conversation with the priest; and his good sense and helpful summation of the half-formed questions in her mind. There was only one tiny shred of indecision about the suitability of a marriage to Joe. The third condition to a happy union was to have "tastes and interests of a similar nature." Well, she and Joe did have lots of interests in common, she told herself. But she knew that Joe's interests and enthusiasms were many and far ranging; whereas her interest would be in having a home, a man to care for, security, and eventually children. Resolutely putting aside the finicky little thoughts, she came up with the most conclusive reflection yet. Joe, as a husband, would never be an uninteresting stick-in-the-mud!

CHAPTER EIGHT

Beccles, 1893

February 7th, 1893 was a significant date for the Catholic community of Beccles, Suffolk. Not that the participants in the event were either distinguished or important, but the date was unique in marking the first wedding performed in the new church of St. Benet's. Of even more historical meaning was the fact that it recorded the first marriage in Beccles performed by a Catholic priest in over three hundred years.

Father Hugh Ford married them and celebrated the nuptial Mass. Samuel Churchward, who was the butler at Gillingham Hall, stood up for Joe, and Annie Pipe almost, but not quite, outshone Alice, as the bridesmaid.

Joe's tiny younger brother, Teddy Atherton, though twelve, looked eight, and had the precocity of a fourteen year old. As the altar boy for the wedding and nuptial Mass he drew indulgent smiles as he stood on tiptoe to hand Father Ford the cruets of wine and water, and alarmed expressions as he moved the heavy missal on its stand from the epistle to the gospel side of the altar. He managed it all with a certain *sang froid* which bespoke familiarity with his duties, but when he bent over double to repeat the Latin words of the Confiteor, he nearly vanished out of sight.

The Kenyons, who had been largely responsible for the building of St. Benet's, were delighted to have someone from their household be the first to marry in the new church. It was just a matter of course for them to hold a reception for Alice afterwards at Gillingham Hall.

Nearly all of Joe's family were present, but none of Alice's. John and Patience Heffernon had been sent invitations, along with a handwritten note from Alice begging them to come to her wedding; but whether they refused to attend a Roman service, or were angry at Alice, they did not acknowledge the invitation. It could well have spoiled the day for the bride, had it not been for the generous good wishes and presents sent by her sisters Jess and Jinny. Her brother Will sent reserved greetings, and Alice could still see the powerful influence of her parents directing his thoughts. Still, he had responded, and she knew how much courage that had taken.

Joe's parents, Joseph and Sarah, were a little awkward in the imposing air of Gillingham Hall, but John and Mary Kenyon's hearty and unpretentious welcome soon put them at their ease. The Hall was gay with white ribbons and paper bells and with a profusion of flowers throughout the house. The staff had polished the bannisters, floors, and panelling until they shone with a brilliance matched only by the glitter of chandelier and silver. Two huge crystal punch bowls were kept full, and sandwiches, cakes, and other delights were served by the Kenyon girls.

Joseph Kenyon, although two years younger than Teddy Atherton, was taller and just as precocious. The two sprats rushed through the house, getting into all sorts of mischief. Sam Churchward twice had to stop them from helping themselves to the punch, and they returned so often to the sandwiches and cakes that Margaret and Mary had to banish them from the drawing and dining rooms until the appetites of the other guests had been satisfied.

The gifts to the bridal couple were displayed and admired by the company, with some private speculation as to the worth of each gift and the affluence of the giver. Few could be faulted. Alice's and Joe's friends were generous and perceptive of the needs of the young couple. They gave linen, chinaware and utensils for the little house that had been rented in the village; for Joe had regained his job at the Beccles printshop.

The Kenyons were lavish in their provision of household needs, and these presents had been put in gaily wrapped bushel baskets ready to be carted down to the cottage the next day.

"To the Bride!" Hugh Ford ended his eloquent toast, and the guests gave a ringing response. Joe looked at his bride before his reply, his thoughts echoing and more, the compliments of the priest. How lovely she was, and how lucky *he* was! His heart swelled with love and noble promise. Nothing would ever happen to spoil the look of happiness on Alice's face if he could help it! Her colour heightened with the excitement of the moment, and a slight moisture of emotion making her dark eyes enormous and brilliant, Alice was indeed a vision of beauty. Her finely chiselled but strong features were caught in the proud lift of her head, the classic bone structure of her face framed within her bridal veil.

"Thank you, Father Ford!" the groom began in commanding tones. An audience always inspired Joe to heights of oratory. Without any degree of insincerity, and with no consciousness that he was emoting, he slipped into a speech that was enthusiastically received by his listeners. If a look of indulgent amusement passed between Father Ford and John Kenyon, it was brief and unnoticed by the other guests.

"Ladies and gentlemen, I thank you for your attendance at our wedding today. It has enhanced this special day for Alice and me more than words can tell. Mr. and Mrs. Kenyon," (directing his attention to his hosts) "your hospitality is beyond belief!" (murmurs of approbation from the guests). "Father Ford, the marriage ceremony was beautiful in both an aesthetic and spiritual sense," Joe allowed a little smile to play upon his face to preface a lighter vein, "and the imported altar boy could be considered a success, if not a *huge* success." (Polite laughter).

"But to be serious," and Joe composed his features into a more earnest expression, "I will let the hero of Shakespeare's immortal story of lovers speak for me," and his voice softened as he quoted,

"O, she doth teach the torches to burn bright!
It seems she hangs upon the cheek of night
As a rich jewel in an Ethiop's ear —
Beauty too rich for use, for earth too dear!
. . . .
Did my heart love till now? Forswear it sight!
For I ne'er saw true beauty till this night."

The words were spoken eloquently and sincerely; briefly, there was no hint of melodrama in Joe's offering to his bride.

Alice listened to the poem in growing delight. She looked up at Joe, her shining eyes revealing the complete surrender of her heart. She faced him with pride and love and devotion as never before, and turned up her face to receive his heartfelt kiss.

Hearty applause, mingled with appreciative laughter, greeted the end of the speech and the embrace. Some of the ladies surreptitiously dabbed handkerchiefs to moist eyes, and all the guests closed around the bride and groom with congratulation and good wishes.

CHAPTER NINE

Beccles, 1893-1894

Their first home was a stone cottage on the remote outskirts of Beccles, unoccupied for some time but basically habitable. In the six months of their engagement, Joe had zealously patched it up, bolstering a sagging door here and repairing loose tiles there, earning the gratitude of his landlord-to-be and a reduction in the rent. As they accumulated a stove and other furniture, the goods were stored in the old place. Then a great deal of floor scrubbing, closet cleaning, and polishing of window glass became necessary before Alice could add the touches of curtains, linens and other ornamentation. At last the cottage, ready and with a cozy fire blazing on its hearth, welcomed them on their wedding night.

The Kenyons' principal gift to the couple had been a large and luxurious Ostermoor down-filled mattress. Somehow, the gift symbolized to Alice all the love and affection that the Kenyon family had poured out on her during the comparatively short time of her employment. The mattress was of such splendid quality of material and workmanship that Joe and Alice could never have afforded it themselves.

The Ostermoor was her marriage bed. It was also to become a reminder of the love and comfort that had been the mainstay of her existence at Arundel and Gillingham, and an anchor and a rock in the new life upon which she was embarking. Its warm softness was to enfold her and Joe in their moments of love, as it was to comfort her in times of trouble and loneliness. Her babies were to be born on it, and sick children brought to its comfort. The Ostermoor was to become to Alice the symbol of Home, wherever that might be.

Their first child was named William, for Alice's only brother and for Joe's older brother. His second name was Joseph, not only for his father and grandfather, but also for the carpenter saint who headed the Holy Family. This was fitting because the baby, William Joseph, was born on New Year's Day, the feast of the Circumcision, in the year of 1894.

Willy was dark complexioned like his mother and gave promise of having her features. His eyes were large and of the dark blue hue which, given time, becomes meltingly brown. His serenity, so much like Alice's, was evident from the beginning: he slept through the night almost from the day of his birth.

It had been a deliciously happy eleven months for Alice. All her doubts and hesitance had evaporated in the joy she found in her husband and home. Their lovemaking had been mutually satisfying, enthusiastic and frequent. Alice's three years in service had taken her away from the overprotectiveness of the Victorian family, and, while retaining her own innocence, she had been prepared for the sexual aspect of marriage by the frankness of conversation in the servants' quarters. Joe had been tender and patient with her, and had found delight in her fast response to his lovemaking.

Joe's initial pride in his son was not of the sort to be described as quiet. He was vociferous on the subject of his child to the point of boredom for his mates at the shop and the pub, and he only learned to keep his peace when a near brawl arose over the statement of one of his friends that, "Ye'd think 'un was only father in't country."

But the novelty of the baby wore off soon enough for him. Apart from the inconvenience the newcomer brought to the little cottage, Joe found himself being pushed to one side, as he thought of it, by Alice's complete absorption in the child. He had known that the baby would take up a great deal of her time but, somehow, after pregnancy had ended and her body regained its attractiveness, he had foreseen a happy return to uninhibited lovemaking. It was foolish he knew, but his nose was somewhat out of joint for all that.

Alice was aware of her husband's feeling of loneliness, and as soon as she was strong enough, made it clear that she wanted his love, and gave herself to him lovingly and completely when he responded.

A short period of perfect connubial bliss followed, then she conceived again, only two months after the birth of her first child. By the end of April, she knew without doubt that she was pregnant. It was not an age of family planning nor was a second child conceived so quickly, considered any sort of social failing. Alice was perfectly happy herself, and since she enjoyed Willy so much, looked forward to the second child with contentment. She broke the news to Joe in bed that night, as she snuggled in his arms.

"Do you know what?" she said, her cheek against the soft flannel of his nightshirt.

He was half asleep. "What?" he mumbled dutifully.

"We're going to have a baby."

Drowsiness had almost overtaken him. His head had nodded to one side and her hair muffled his reply. "We already have a baby," he advised her. Odd that she didn't know.

"Joe," more insistently.

"H-mm?"

"We're going to have *another* baby."

The words struggled through the maze of his consciousness and finally reached home. They jarred him upright to a sitting position, dislodging her head abruptly from his shoulder and startling her out of her serenity. His less than ecstatic reaction floored her. "Aw-w-w hell!" he said miserably.

"Joe!" she cried, sitting up and gathering the bedclothes around her. She had presumed he would have mixed feelings about the coming event, but this was really too much. "Is that any way to talk?" she asked indignantly.

Fully awake, he regretted the blunder. "Jiminy! I didn't mean that Alice, gosh, that's some news, how do you feel about it yourself, Mama?" He had started this endearment even before Willy's arrival.

"Well, I think it's just fine," she said, with her chin in the air. If she had any reservations she certainly wasn't going to express them now.

"I'm really sorry, Alice." His contrition was obvious, but he looked bleak just the same. "It's just that we don't seem to be getting ahead as I hoped. Kids kind of tie us down."

She was not ready to accept either an apology or an explanation. "Just what did you expect? Don't you want children?" It was as if he was bent on destroying the very essence of their marriage and he hastened to clear himself.

"Now Alice! You know I do!" He thought to impress her with his real intentions. "I love young Will, am really proud of him. You know what plans I have for him." Indeed Alice was aware of the pleasure Joe took in his son, and the grand ideas he had for the baby's future.

She was somewhat mollifed and he was successful this time in getting his arms about her. Even so, he voiced the thought that had been in the back of his mind for weeks. "But we're not going to get anywhere in Beccles, Mama, and that's a fact. Sooner or later I've got to go to Yarmouth or Birmingham or someplace where there's more opportunity."

He felt her stiffen in his arms, and, seeing her stricken look, told her hastily, "Now Alice, as far as moving away is concerned, I only mean that we should keep it in mind. You do want us to get ahead, don't you?"

For the first time since their wedding day, the troubling little doubts returned. She tried to put them away by telling herself resolutely that he was a good husband and father, and it was only right that he should be forward looking. Nevertheless, she freed herself of his embrace and faced him with loving concern.

"Of course I want us to get ahead, but be realistic, Joe. We're comfortable here, we are getting by nicely on your wages and our best friends are here." She spoke the thought newest in her mind. "You have to settle down someday." It was a tacit reminder of his colourful career thus far, and she added her own little word of regret. "I had hoped it might be Beccles." Then the rest of her worry came out. "There're the children to think of, too."

He put his arms around her once more and tipped her serious face up. "We'll not neglect them, lass. I'll love them as I do you. We'll get along fine, you'll see!" His heartfelt kiss and hug did not dispel all her qualms. She did not have his confidence and she needed reassuring. She hugged him in return. His ideas of satisfaction and contentment were just not the same as hers, that was all.

There was no doubting the sincerity of Joe's intentions, but the same appetite for change that had driven him before he met Alice, began to reassert itself. It was three years since he had left the touring players, and without any feelings of disloyalty to his marriage, he began to resent the sameness of daily routine in Beccles. He dwelled more often, in his thoughts, on the glamour of his previous life, as much for the excitement of new faces and new towns seen, as for any longing for the stage. He was not ready to exchange the comfort and stability of marriage for the ephemeral delights of an acting career, but surely a more exciting career in printing and journalism could be found in a bigger place than Beccles. He stoutly reminded himself that part of being a good father was to be a good provider. After all, he would have two children by December, before his own twenty-fourth birthday.

This last thought was depressing. His youth was slipping away, while he was tied down with the responsibilities of job and family. He had to do something about it.

By August he began surreptitiously writing letters to large printing establishments in Birmingham, enquiring about employment and citing his abilities and experience. He assured himself there was no disloyalty to Alice in this, he was just testing the job market, a person should know what was going on in his own industry.

Three replies came so swiftly that they caught Joe by surprise, and without any answer for Alice's question of who might be writing him from Birmingham. He had no option but to admit he had been making enquiries, and had to face the disappointment in her eyes that he had not seen fit to confide in her. Even before he opened the letters, he told her elaborately that he hadn't wanted to bother her with what was just curiosity on his part, that he really had no intention of making a move. The urgency with which the three letters were written, and the promising messages they contained, surprised Alice as well as Joe. Each company offered immediate employment. One quoted a wage about half as much again as he was earning in Beccles, and the other two indicated they would like the opportunity to meet him and discuss terms.

"Oh, Joe!" Now Alice didn't know which way to turn. Her disappointment in his secrecy lessened as he read aloud the enthusiastic replies. She was quick to realize that she could not stand his way, but saddened by the sure knowledge that they would be leaving Beccles, and Annie, and the Kenyons, and Father Ford. She determinedly put aside these selfish considerations, and did not wait for Joe's reaction.

"I think you should go to Birmingham right away."

Her suggestion was made with more decisiveness than she felt, and with a rueful recognition of the ending of an idyll. She did not realize that her seemingly forthright approval was the beginning of a course which would usually see her voluntarily submerge her own desires in those of her family.

CHAPTER TEN

Birmingham, 1894

He had forgotten how big and bustling Birmingham was. The city's streets, rivers and canals were alive with traffic, and its sounds and smells smote the senses in continuous waves. The filth in the back streets was unbelievable. Wet and dry mud from the country roads mingled with the rotting vegetables cast from the farm stalls, and at the curbs cats tore at stinking fish. Animal droppings were everywhere, in the streets behind the passing of draught and hack horses, and in the open spaces around the stalls where lambs, rabbits and geese were penned and tethered. To an ear unattuned to the city, its sound came as a bedlam of noise. Huge horses drew lorries, rumbling, creaking and rattling on the cobblestones, harnesses jingling and hooves clattering. Hawkers bawled, animals bleated and crowed and barked. Lorrymen cursed at the traffic. Bargemen shouted to their horses. Farmers called their wares and tinkers sang the songs of their trade.

Even in the more fashionable part of the city, where smartly dressed ladies and gentlemen were catered to, the smells and sounds penetrated, thinned by distance. And everywhere, in outskirts, fashionable suburbs and midcity, there hung over Birmingham a depressing pall of coal smoke, acrid in the nostrils and clinging to the linings of throats and lungs.

Joe loved it.

It had taken little of Alice's urging to convince him that a future awaited in the city, and he had accepted a position with The Midland Printing and Publishing Company on the day of his arrival. It was a big plant, larger than any Joe had ever worked in, but the diversity of his skills, developed in small and medium sized shops, was highly desirable to his new employers. He was fascinated by the advanced state of the plant's machinery, and marvelled at the speed at which the craft of printing was developing, enjoying his involvement in an interesting industry.

Alice had remained in Beccles after Joe's departure to Birmingham. It was understood that she would be better off near friends in her situation: pregnant and with one infant to care for. He missed her, but had other excitements to fill his days and nights. He enjoyed convivial company, and could always find a pal or two in the local after work. He had taken a room in a boarding house not far from his work, and as the rent was modest, he was able to put some money aside, as well as provide for Alice's needs. If he did spend money on a pint after work, it was no more than he had in Beccles, and not begrudged by his wife. He wrote her happily and she replied in kind, not wanting to put the burden of her loneliness upon him.

He came into the cozy atmosphere of The Bullock one evening in September. Its patrons were men, mainly from the plants and mills of the area, though a few women, street characters of the neighbourhood, dotted the crowd. Tobacco smoke rose in the air, creating a blue haze and filling the room with a variety of aromatic scents. A few younger men and most of the women smoked cigarettes, but the pipe was predominant, curved and straight, carved in briar and clay.

Joe peered through the veil of smoke in search of friends, was beckoned to a handily chosen table in a corner near the bar and offered refreshment. Joe's foreman, John Butler, was a heavy-set man in his early fifties, grey templed and moustached. He smiled at this newest and youngest member of his pressroom staff, revealing a large gold tooth through the shaggy moustache that covered his mouth.

"I'll have a Guinness, if you don't mind," said Joe, seating himself. It was flattering to have attention from his boss, and pleasant to meet him socially.

"You've settled in well, then lad," he told Joe briefly after placing the order. "I like your work." It was said with the laconic brevity of the north countryman, and as if reminded by his own manner of speech, he mused, " . . . Atherton," and nodded to himself, "You'll be a Lankie yourself, then, but you can't tell it by your speech."

"Aye, I'm a Lankie," intoned Joe in a suitable Lancashire dialect, "but I've Yorkshire in me as well as Lancashire, so there's no telling what I sound like anymore." He resumed his normal voice. "I've travelled a bit, Mr. Butler, and picked up the language of wherever I've been."

"Ah, so that's it. Never mind, you speak fine, lad." John Butler peered at Joe speculatively over the pipe he was lighting. "Are you enjoying your work here, young Joe?"

"Yes sir!" said the young printer enthusiastically, "The Midland is a nice place to work."

"Aye, it's not so bad," said the foreman cautiously, "but we've had to fight for what we have."

"What do you mean?" asked Joe. "Aren't the owners fair employers?"

"Oh aye, they'll be about as good as you'll get, but even they'd be hard enough to get along with if 'tweren't for the unions."

"But this isn't a union shop," Joe protested, "I'm not a union member."

"More's the pity, young feller," and Butler looked with mild censure at him. "The Midland's an open shop, so it employs union and non-union workers." He leaned over the table earnestly. "Why do you think that you're earning more than other lads in good trades? Because of the union, boy, that's why." He relaxed back into his chair and draped one arm over its back. "You should belong, lad. It's your solemn duty."

Joe was a little disconcerted. "Well, no offense meant, Mr. Butler, but what I've seen of union men, they're a rough lot, with no sense of responsibility."

Butler warmed to his subject. "That's true of some unions, and more particularly it's true of some union *men*. They're bad for unionism; give it a bad name," he wagged his forefinger at Joe, "but that doesn't make the cause any the less important to all of us."

For the next half hour John Butler harangued Joe on the subject of unionism. He explained why the printing trade, above all others, attracted well educated and intelligent craftsmen. He was impressive as he told how the unions had come into being in the various segments of the trade; of the ongoing struggle with plant owners for decent working conditions, for better treatment for less skilled workers, and, above all, the need to abolish the evil of child labour.

"Do you realize that in some shops in Birmingham, not ours, thank God, there're kids of ten and twelve working up to ten hours a day, doing the jobs that don't require the skill of a pressman or a compositor?"

Joe looked at him in disbelief. "But surely the law . . . "

"The law is in the same boat as the owners. It's a tight little society that puts profit above everything else." He spat onto the already littered floor. "The pious bastards have the nerve to say that the children sometimes are the only means of support for a mother with five or more brats at home!"

"My God!" said Joe, "I had no idea." He was entirely honest as he said this, even though the corruption of child labour and the exploitation of the ignorant and poorly trained was common throughout England. His own background, while not providing many luxuries, had always seen enough to eat on the table, and warm clothing and shelter accepted as the norm. Even though his new status as a married man and father had begun to make him more aware of broader problems, he had not considered even dimly that children could be consciously mistreated so callously. He was outraged, and echoed John Butler's words. "The bastards!"

His involvement in the cause of unionism began on that day. With John Butler as his mentor, he eagerly embraced this new interest with customary ardour. He discovered that there were several unions in the printing trade, and he joined the Pressmen's at the first meeting of that union he attended with the foreman. Thereafter he was a committed attender, enjoying the dispute and the debate between the hot tempered younger members and the cautiously conservative old timers. Butler himself, for all of his zeal for the union movement, was one of the latter. He believed in responsible unionism with fairness to employer and worker alike, and knew that it took time to gain rights and benefits. Many of the members wanted instant Utopia and men like Butler had to cool them down from precipitate action at least once a month.

The younger printer's work continued to be absorbing. He was introduced to several sizes and types of presses, and was used for every purpose from the careful production of formal and embossed invitations, to the hammering out of handbills. Business forms, personal cards, labels, letterheads, and every other conceivable kind of printing were handled by The Midland, but its big business was in the production of books of every variety. It was a marvellous opportunity for the young printer to learn more of his trade.

His letters home to Alice revealed how he was enjoying the experience, and although she missed him terribly, she would not spoil his happiness with her own problems. Not that anything untoward was happening to her and to young Willy; but she was often tired and sometimes unhappy. She not only missed the companionship and sharing of difficulties with her husband, but it was the first time in her life she had been entirely alone, and in the quiet house, found herself aware of small noises that induced nervousness and anxiety. She was becoming uncomfortable in her seventh month of pregnancy and it was difficult to lift the chubby Willy, who fortunately was healthy and happy. It was his good company in the daytime that made Alice scold herself for her fears and occasional unkind thought about her husband's absence, with the result that her letters to him were always cheerful and entertaining; making the most of what little social life she enjoyed, and never revealing the woeful feelings she sometimes experienced.

Joe continued to put money aside, and planned towards Alice's joining him by Christmas. He did not realize his dreams of good fortune and early marital reunion were to be shattered by the events of mid-November.

His troubles began after a union meeting, which broke up early after the transaction of its regular business. Joe repaired, with four of his fellows, to The Bullock for a nightcap and learned the reason for the unusual lack of confrontation earlier that evening.

Three of his companions were young chaps from the pressroom, sallow faced youngsters with slick city ways. They had tried some bullying tactics when he had first appeared at The Midland, but the quick manner in which he had reacted had shown that he was not to be browbeaten. He was not completely accepted by the gang, but that was not important to him. He did not actively seek their society, but they were better than no company at all. The acknowledged leader of this pack was a couple of years older than Joe, and four or five years older than the rest. His name was Arthur Weldon, and he was in the forefront of the most radical group in the union. He was a good talker, and in four or five years of union debate he had acquired some skills of verbal persuasion. He had been elected an officer of the union as a result.

Arthur was pensive this evening, but insisted upon buying several rounds. He explained that he had come into a few pounds, and could afford to be generous. As the others became more hilarious with the drink, it could be seen that Arthur was becoming more solemn, and Joe was aware of his calculating gaze upon him again and again.

"What's up, Arthur?" Joe asked the question quietly, but the noisy conversation at the table ceased.

Instead of answering directly, Arthur Weldon leaned back in his seat and asked a question himself. "How much are you committed to the union, Joe?"

"I've come to think a great deal of it," said Joe, even more aware of the silence at the table.

Arthur Weldon leaned forward. "I mean how far would you go in defence of the union? Would you fight for it, actually fight, with your fists if necessary, for it?"

"What are you getting at?" Joe didn't care for the trend of the conversation. "Is this some sort of hypothetical question, or are you planning to beat up somebody?" There was no reply, so he added, "If that's what you're talking about, the answer is no, I wouldn't go out on some damnfool brawl for the union or anyone else!" He slammed down his tankard for emphasis, and eyed Weldon with some truculence.

Arthur Weldon was unperturbed. "What would you do if your own family, your wife and kid, were threatened? Would you fight to defend them?"

"That's a stupid question, and you know it, Arthur," said Joe evenly. "Of course I'd fight to defend them, but that's got nothing to do with a trumped up brawl in the name of the union."

"But I've made my point, haven't I?" smiled Weldon. "You would fight in a cause you felt to be your own, and worthy, now wouldn't you?"

Joe shrugged. "If the cause is big enough, a man'll fight for it."

It was time for Arthur Weldon to test Joe's commitment to the union; Arthur's concept of commitment. "How do you feel about the scab shops that work young kids to death?"

"I don't like them any more than you do."

"Do you agree that they must be stopped, eventually?"

"Of course."

"Well, where do we start?" Weldon allowed Joe some time to consider the question, then continued himself. "The conservatives in the union would have you believe that strength of numbers will eventually force the shops to stop hiring kids; while some of the men at the low end of the scale are fed up with waiting and are demanding violent action." He let his words sink in, before continuing, "I believe there's a middle ground." He was choosing his words carefully to gain Joe's cooperation. "If we continue to wait, and take no action, more kids are going to work for starvation wages, more of 'em will become consumptive, and more of them will be killed while dropping off to sleep over dangerous machines!" It was a shocking statement, but Joe knew its truth.

"What's your alternative?" he asked Weldon.

"A protest picket."

Joe was confused. "A protest picket? Where?"

Weldon named a small plant, notorious for its use of child labour, and detested by the printers for its holdout against the unions.

"There's no strike there," Joe pointed out, "and even if there was, the law only allows action of any kind, strike or picket, to protest wages or working conditions. Furthermore, if the workers themselves in the place won't protest, what's there to support?"

"It won't be a support picket," said Weldon casually, as he pulled out his packet of cigarettes. Joe refused the open pack and brought out his pipe instead.

"You're talking about an illegal action," he said evenly, opening his rubber pouch and releasing its pungent aromas. Weldon watched the blue smoke curl up from Joe's pipe before answering.

"Possibly," he said, with a shrug. "I doubt if there'd be any repercussions from the peelers for a peaceful little picket." But Weldon grew more serious as he leaned across the table. "We've got to stand up and be counted sometime!" and, aware that Joe at last was pondering his words, he pressed on, "For the sake of those kids!" Arthur Weldon's challenge to Joe's manhood, fatherhood, and sense of justice was shrewd and well timed. Whatever his motives, his words were a call to excitement and adventure, missing from the young man's life since his departure from the theatre.

"What are your plans?" he asked, and the five heads drew closer across the table.

CHAPTER ELEVEN

Birmingham, 1894

The November evening was cold and wet; a fine drizzle of rain fell on the shoulders of the dozen or so men gathered by the miserable little printshop, on a deserted back street in Birmingham. Two or three lanterns spread a watery light around; their weak glow revealing the main group of men turned towards the building. In the foreground of the group stood Arthur Weldon's three thugs. They were haranguing the little knot of men, trying to stiffen again the resolution that was fast dissolving in the gloom of the rainy evening. They were mainly young fellows, rallied by Weldon with his fine words of justice and solidarity, words which Joe was finally realizing were hollow. The picketers had come this evening immediately upon the ending of the day shift at The Midland, where most were employed, and had been handed placards, secretly printed by Weldon and his henchmen during a temporary absence of John Butler. Joe couldn't believe the provocative phrases printed on the posters. There was little about the noble causes with which Weldon had recruited his picketers; and plenty of inflammatory cant about the rights of workers and the iniquity of all employers.

For Joe, the sense of adventure that had followed the evening meeting in The Bullock had gradually worn off. A feeling of distrust over the whole affair had persisted, even through Arthur Weldon's oratory. He had been sworn to secrecy about Weldon's plans, so had not been able to discuss the situation with the one man who might have put him right: John Butler. Tonight he realized what was wrong. Weldon himself was the only member of the group who had any credibility. The ragtag lot that surrounded him indicated the extent of his rejection by the left-wingers, as well as by the moderates in the union.

A half smile of enjoyment on Arthur Weldon's face decided Joe to quit the picket line, but as he turned to Arthur, who stood with him at the rear of the group, the door of the printshop opened and a stream of frightened men and children left the building. Their shift had just ended, and, as the miserable line of hollow-eyed boys and ragged men went past, Joe's heart did another turnabout and he resolved to stay with the picketers, come what may.

The two owners of the printshop followed their employees to the doorway, but did not emerge. A burly, red-faced man faced the picketers defiantly, his frightened partner peering over his shoulder, as a chorus of catcalls from the mob greeted them. Red Face hadn't learned how to cow his employees without some experience of opposition. He showed his contempt for the mob now. "Bugger off!" he shouted, with great disdain. "I'll have the police onto the ragged lot of you!"

Weldon's three young cohorts screamed epithets in return, as Red Face spat upon the ground contemptuously, before turning back into the building. He was out again immediately, dressed for the street, and elbowing his way through the knot of men, not at all intimidated by their black looks and muttered curses. As he reached the street, he was pushed violently by one of the three thugs who followed him, and stumbled a few paces. He turned as he regained his footing and directed a malevolent glare at the picketers, including Joe in his baleful survey, then broke into a shambling run along the street.

A wave of derisive laughter followed the owner as he hurried away. The men turned back to the shop, and directed their jeers at the frightened face of the partner in the window. The noisiest of them all were Weldon's goons, who had succeeded in rousing the others to some degree of enthusiasm for the demonstration. Joe was amazed to hear one of the three say vehemently, "Let's burn the bloody building down!"

He turned to Weldon, fully expecting him to put an end to such nonsense. Instead, he saw a look of unholy delight on the picket leader's face. It was obvious that Weldon had no intention of controlling the men. Joe felt sick. The whole affair had taken an ugly turn. He had never shied away from a good standup fight with a worthy opponent, but this was something else. The picket, started as a noble adventure, was turning out to be a confusion of ideas, with the scent of violence strong in the air.

Without thinking of the possible consequences, he left Weldon's side at a run; the leader's hand reaching after him as if to delay the young printer. At the front of the mob, Joe waved his hands and tried to get the attention of the men. "For God's sake, fellows, have a little sense!" he pleaded. "This is supposed to be a peaceful picket!"

His words were lost in the hubbub led by Weldon's firebrands, and worse, Joe found himself pressed back against the building as tempers mounted. A particularly violent shove while he was off balance knocked him off his feet, and he was up in a moment, fighting mad. Automatically his fists shot out, his right finding a nose and his left a mouth; and he became the new target for the aroused men's fury. Joe was no slouch with his fists, and he got in a few telling blows and one knockdown, before he was borne back against the building. A violent assault by his three former cronies pushed him through the window with a tremendous crash. At the same time, someone yelled "Police!" and the picketers took to their heels.

Joe, somewhat dazed, was half in and half out of the broken window when the police arrived, and he was grabbed roughly. The nervous shop partner recovered his courage with the coming of the constables, and shouted imprecations at Joe, the only remaining picketer.

"He's one of them! Broke my window, he did!" His burly partner, who had come back with the police, agreed that Joe was one of the leaders, and had to be restrained from assaulting the printer himself. The Black Maria arrived on the scene with a jangle of ringing bells and a racket of hooves on the pavement. Its rear doors were swung open, and Joe was unceremoniously shoved inside and driven away.

He was unable to return to work until the following afternoon, pale and haggard after a horrible night spent in the cells with thieves and drunks. His court appearance that morning had resulted in a heavy fine, but no jail sentence, thanks to the kindly offices of John Butler. The foreman had been notified the evening before of Joe's arrest, and had gone immediately to the home of the manager of The Midland to plead indulgence for his young friend. Convinced by the words of his senior employee, The Midland's manager not only urged Butler to take off the following morning in Joe's defence, but also penned a note to the court, requesting leniency for the young offender.

John Butler's own appeal to the court, his sturdy strength and respectability, swayed the judge in Joe's favour. Joe had to tell his story, and did so honestly, admitting he had been on the picket line, but without intent of violence. Fortunately, the court had accepted his word and that of John Butler against the owners' of the damaged property. His Lordship privately considered the latter unsavoury characters, having some knowledge of their exploitation of workers and children. Nevertheless Joe was found guilty of illegal picketing, and brawling, and fined accordingly.

Thankful as he was to escape imprisonment, Joe was in despair over the amount of the fine. It had not only taken all of his savings, but a considerable loan from John Butler as well. It would take three months of close living to pay it all back. He was depressed beyond words. Even the pleading of his foreman had not swayed him from his decision to protect the others who were with him on the picket line, and none of them came forward to acknowledge their involvement. Butler had a good idea of the identity of the culprits, but without Joe's confirmation, had nothing to support his suspicions. The foreman seethed as he saw Weldon and his thugs laughing together. That Joe was their gull was obvious, and the foreman vowed private revenge.

In the meantime, the young printer's thoughts were anywhere but on his work. He had not slept the night before, and had had no food for twenty-four hours. His fatigue, the demeaning experience of the jail, and despair at losing all his funds gnawed at his mind, and his thoughts were dangerously scattered. He was working on a hand operated platen press, turning the handle of the heavy machine with his right hand as he removed with his left the just printed sheets from the platen surface. His motions had become automatic, as he agonized over his problems. *What am I to say to Alice? How did I get myself into a mess like this? This is going to hurt her deeply.*

The heavy type bed, sliding smoothly on its oiled arms, swung down toward the platen, as Joe turned the wheel. A new thought overwhelmed him. *I don't even have any cash to send her for rent and food!* In his consternation, his timing slowed for a split second, and his hand remained under the descending type bed too long. With almost malevolent certainty the machine completed its cycle, the jagged edges of the type seized his two middle fingers, and crunched them between the bed and the platen like two steel jaws.

Joe's scream of agony could be heard over the rumbling of the presses of The Midland, stopping the shouted conversation of the workers in a moment of stunned silence. John Butler was the first to react. Without knowing where the cry came from, he automatically reached for the lever which disengaged the main drive belt from the building's steam plant, and the heavy presses shuddered to a halt. For an instant, absolute silence prevailed, then the shouts of the men and the pounding of running feet sounded through the plant. John Butler, inured by experience to bloodshed in plant accidents, dropped to Joe's side before anyone else. Mercifully Joe had fainted, his lack of food and the anxiety of the past twenty-four hours contributing to the shock of seeing his fingers severed.

The foreman pulled out his own polka dot handkerchief and unwrapped his neck cloth, to apply them to the bleeding hand. The two fingers of Joe's left hand were gone forever, two small stumps remaining above the palm. "Poor silly young bugger!" said Butler, a catch in his voice belying any censure his words contained.

CHAPTER TWELVE

Beccles, 1894

Monday's post did not bring Joe's usual letter. When, two days later, the postman did come up her walk, Alice's anxiety turned to relief, then exasperation. Ordinarily he was prompt with his letters and remittances, but she had just about run out of money.

The postman turned away as soon as he had handed her the letter, and did not see the colour leave her face. Instead of Joe's familiar embellished script, the envelope was addressed in a strange hand, and she had to steady herself for a moment against the doorpost before she opened it.

John Butler's bluff words, meant to reassure, tore at her heart with the plainness of his description of the jailing and the accident. Joe was doing as well as could be expected, but would be in hospital and convalescence for at least two weeks. They would be holding his job open for him. It had not occurred to the kindly foreman that her financial situation would be precarious. He just assumed that Alice was well established in Beccles with relatives and friends.

It was the worst thing that had ever happened to her. Her quarrel and parting with her parents two years before had been upsetting, but not devastating. Her first thought, to share the trouble with Annie Pipe or the Kenyons, was suppressed as soon as it was born. How could she tell them of her penniless state, let alone Joe's imprisonment? John Butler's letter had said that the jailing was no fault of Joe's, and she tried to bolster her belief with this. But at this distance, and without the comfort of Joe's own easy reassurance, doubt and fear flooded her mind.

She was in a turmoil over what to do, her concern for Joe now equalled by her fear for Willy and the child to come. Her full term was less than a month away, and panic threatened to overcome her as she remembered tales of premature birth brought on by shock and anxiety.

Willy awoke from his nap and called out to her, so she got a grip on herself. She would go and see Father Ford. He would know what to do and she could face him with this humiliation as she could not Mrs. Kenyon or Annie. It was something to do, and she hurriedly dressed the baby and put him into his pram. He was as happy as ever, not sensing his mother's turmoil.

At the rectory, she tugged on the bell pull, girding herself to face the priest and tell him of Joe's accident and her own situation.

"Yes?"

It was not Hugh Ford who answered the door, but a plain woman unknown to Alice.

"May I see Father?" she asked.

"He's on retreat, Mum, and won't be back until Sunday." The woman didn't have any time to talk, she had cleaning to do, and had only half opened the door.

Now Alice was defeated. She had put so much hope into this visit, and to learn that he would not be back for another three days! "Thank you," she managed to say, and the door closed upon her.

It was a terrible afternoon and evening. She went about her usual routine somehow. Fortunately, there was food in the house, and Willy was not yet threatened. She was nearly despairing when she went to bed, with her mind made up to see Mrs. Kenyon in the morning. She knew that she would find kindness, sympathy and help, but that was not the problem. The shame was her own, and she dreaded sharing it with someone who had already done so much for her. Her sleep, when it did come in the small hours of the morning, was troubled and dreamfilled.

Her help came from an unexpected source.

She answered the knock to her door on the morning of the second day of her misery, as she was about to leave for the Kenyons'. At first, she did not recognize the middle-aged figure in the rusty suit before her, then, "Dad Atherton!" she cried.

Joe's father smiled at her through his drooping moustaches, his round face crinkling warmly at her. " 'Ullo Alice" he said. He couldn't have been more welcome if he had been Joe himself. "There, there," he said in embarrassment, as Alice sobbed on his shoulder. "Don't take on so, lass. Everthing's goin' to be fine now," and he patted her shoulder. He held her off and looked whimsically at her swollen belly. "Looks like I've just coom in time," and she laughed shakily at him, as she dabbed at her eyes with the back of her hand.

She drew him inside, sat him at the kitchen table, and made him a cup of tea. It seemed that he and Sarah had received the news of Joe's accident a little earlier than she, and they had wasted no time. He had come on the first train he could catch from Yarmouth, with instructions from the salty little Sarah to bring back Alice and the baby with him.

In no time, he had settled her affairs in Beccles; directed her to make her farewells to Annie and the Kenyons while he stayed with the easy-going Willy; then took her, bag and baggage, on the train back to Yarmouth. They'd settle on what to do about the furniture later on, he told her.

CHAPTER THIRTEEN

Birmingham, 1897

The two little boys were decidedly unalike.

At three years, the placid good nature that Willy had exhibited as an infant had begun to develop into a calmness and confidence that greatly pleased his mother, who quite adored him. Like his two year old brother, Ernest, he displayed an early sense of humour, but his was as measured as Ernie's was boisterous. This shared sense of fun was an inheritance from their father, but there the resemblance ceased. Willy was all Alice's, in temperament, features and complexion. His eyes were dark brown and liquid, like hers, his nose straight, if a little prominent; certainly not aquiline like his father's. His lips were full and his jaw line firm, even at this early age.

Ernest John, born two years earlier, was as much like Joe as Willy was like Alice; mischievous, impetuous, and at this age, as scatterbrained as the older brother was level headed. Ernie's mouth was wide and generous like his father's, and usually curved in the same impish grin. His hair and complexion were light coloured, and his eyes were blue and wide. He loved to tease his big brother, hiding from him and their mother until he would spring out at them, collapsing in hysterical delight at their pretended distress.

For all their differences, or possibly because of them, the little boys got along exceedingly well and were good company for one another, thereby relieving Alice of the unremitting demands for attention, which a single child might make.

Ernie had not been born in Beccles. His birth was imminent when his mother received belated word of Joe's accident and hospitalization.

Joe had joined her in Yarmouth two weeks before Christmas, and two days after the birth of his second son. He was still weak from his accident in November, and several pounds lighter. His contrition was obvious, and any resentment she might have borne against him melted at the sight of his pale, thin face. Her welcome, from her bed, was unreserved and did more to restore Joe to his usual frame of mind and health than any medicine.

Before he returned to Birmingham after the Christmas holiday, he and Alice had talked out all the things bottled up during their long separation. Their understanding of one another was more complete than at any time since they had first met. Alice's love overrode Joe's unpredictability, and she was sure, at least, of his personal loyalty to her and the family. Joe, on his part, recognized his good fortune in having such a devoted wife, and determined once again that he would never make her unhappy. He applied himself to work assiduously, took on extra assignments to build up his funds, and was able to send for Alice in the spring of 1895.

The two years that had elapsed since Joe's recuperation from his accident and his new start with Alice in Birmingham had been a time of quiet contentment. The printing trade had been good to him, and he and Alice enjoyed a comfortable existence on the wages paid to journeymen printers and compositors. They were free from debt and worry, and had been able to put money aside, in addition to purchasing the modest effects necessary for their rented rooms.

For Alice, the two years had gone quickly and enjoyably. Two young children limited her scope for social activity, but she was busy and contented. She had made no close friends, such as Mary Sweeney at Arundel, or Annie Pipe at Beccles, but she carried on a correspondence with Joe's family and with her sister Jess, and was in weekly contact by post with Annie Pipe.

Joe had resumed his interest in the trade unions. In spite of his devastating experience with the left wing group, he remained committed to what he saw as unionism's legitimate aims, and was in the forefront of discussion and debate at the meetings. Arthur Weldon and his lackeys had long since departed, following the union executive's recognition and rejection of the trouble makers. His good friend John Butler, from The Midland, was still active, he and Joe usually sitting together at meetings. John was still cautious to a degree sometimes nettling to Joe, but his respect for the older man was unlimited.

Joe now worked as a compositor for a large Birmingham newspaper, an infinitely more exciting and gratifying job than the production of handbills, letterheads and formal announcements. He could still, in spite of his two missing fingers, turn his hand to meticulous manual typesetting, but he loved the clatter of the composing machines and the roar of the huge newspaper presses, as they spewed out their daily diet of good and bad news.

Unlike the Americans, who long ago had adapted to the linotype, British newspapers were still using machines like the Hattersley, which required the redistribution of type slugs upon completion of the print operation. It was over this feature that bitterness between the unions and the publishers was forever erupting.

In London, the non-union *Times*, which had adopted composing machines as early as 1872, damaged their forward-looking image, by hiring cheap juvenile labour for the unskilled operation of type redistribution. The *Times'* competitor, *The Daily News*, though having taken to the composing machines in recent years

60

only, was a union shop, and as such opposed to the employment of unskilled and child labour.

It was this situation, of unionism versus child exploitation, that compelled Joe and Alice to move to London.

Joe sniffed the March breezes of Birmingham as he walked home from work. Even the smog laden air of that city couldn't repel the insistent currents bearing the scents of bud and blossom, of earth turned over, and of wet leaf mould. Joe could even detect that most elusive of fragrances in Birmingham; fresh air. He breathed in deeply, his risk of lung damage lessened slightly by the cleaner flow of air from the country. Strong longings and urgent deliberations persisted in his thoughts, even as he savoured the promise of the new season.

By the time Joe reached home, he was determined to put the question to Alice, and he quickly marshalled his thoughts:

Item: There were good work opportunities in London.

Item: He would be twenty-six years old in two months, and if he was ever to reach the goal of his own newspaper, he should be about it.

Item: London would be a good place to raise and educate the children.

Item: The union, he earnestly told himself, needed support in London against the use of young kids in the industry; a practice now largely suppressed in Birmingham.

He mounted the steps to their rooms with resolution, sure he could sway Alice to acceptance of his plans; but before he could open the door to their flat, two sturdy figures hurled themselves upon him from the darkness of the landing. Willy and Ernie had been watching their father's approach, and had run to the head of the stairs to surprise him. Alice, smiling, opened the door and made appropriate noises of alarm at the fierce expressions of the two assailants who clung like leeches to Joe's legs, one child wrapped around each limb as he strode jerkily into the room.

Before he could shake them off, Ernie, in the excitement of the game, sank his teeth into Joe's leg, doing little damage, but evoking a yell of protest from his father. "I'll get you for that, you little devil," Joe yelled, and with Willy still clinging to one leg, he upended Ernie and put him across his knee. A beating followed, accompanied by loud noise from Joe and Ernie, but all in fun, as Joe's flailing palm was descending upon his own open hand.

Willy and Ernie were hysterical with laughter, and Alice was moved to reproach them all. "Stop the racket, all of you, before the neighbours think we're being murdered!" Finally the children were persuaded to leave him alone and he took off his jacket and cap. It seemed a good time to tell Alice of his ideas, so he sat down on the sofa and started to unlace his ankle boots.

"Alice," he said.

"Joe," she started, then added, "Yes?"

"No," he said, "you first." He was surprised to see Alice looking at him anxiously. "Go ahead Mama, I'm listening."

She didn't know quite how to begin. "I got a letter today from Jess."

"Anything wrong?" he put in quickly.

"No, no, everything's fine, but Joe . . . " Her distress was evident.

"For God's sake tell me, Alice, or I'll believe the worst!"

Alice screwed up her courage and blurted out, "Joe, what are we doing in Birmingham?"

Of all the things that she might have said, this caught him entirely off guard. "WHAT?" was all he could manage, and she rushed on with her explanation.

"Well, it's kind of lonely here, we don't have any relatives or close friends, and with Jess and Richard living in London, I've been wondering if maybe you could get work there . . . " her voice trailed off, as she saw his look of astonishment.

"But Alice . . . " he said.

Since Alice had broached the subject without any response, except bewilderment, she was encouraged to push on.

"You've always wanted to have your own newspaper, and you are going to need all the experience you can get." Joe's mouth hung open. "Besides," Alice continued quickly, her arguments evidently rehearsed, "there are good schools in London, and it isn't as if we had to pull the children away from school here." She babbled on. "You know you have always said that you'd like to be with a London union."

Joe finally recovered his aplomb. "All right," he said.

It was her turn to be startled. "What?" she returned, "I mean, I beg your pardon?"

"I said, all right, we'll move to London."

Alice couldn't believe her ears, but delight in his response overcame her astonishment. "Oh Joe, darling, do you really mean it?"

"Certainly," said Joe calmly, relishing the moment, as Alice cast herself onto his bosom. "If you want it, Alice," he said nobly, "I'm ready to make any sacrifice."

She looked at him with suspicion, holding him at arm's length. "You rascal, you really want to go to London yourself, don't you?" and with this happy knowledge of mutual aspiration, hugged him in delight, her happy laughter mingling with his gleeful chuckles.

CHAPTER FOURTEEN

London, 1897

The hansom cab that brought them to Chelsea stood at the curb, while Joe unloaded a small steamer trunk from the boot. He kept an eye on Alice as she rang the bell, aware that the two little boys by her side were being exceptionally solemn under the circumstances, wearing their Sunday best and about to meet new relatives.

There was no need for anyone to be shy. Straightening up after lowering the steamer trunk to the ground, Joe saw the door open and the large figure of his sister-in-law appear in the doorway, her face aglow with anticipation and delight, and uttering wholehearted sounds of welcome. He smiled in appreciation, as she enclosed the three newcomers on her step in one huge embrace. Her use of the name "Polly" seemed strange to Joe, but there was no strangeness or reserve in the sisters' greeting of one another. The little boys too, relaxed as Jess released her hold on them, managing bashful smiles at this large lady who apparently presented no menace and, surprisingly, knew their names and got them in the right order.

He paid off the cabby, and carried the brass bound trunk to the doorway. Setting it down, he doffed his hat and started to offer his hand to his sister-in-law; but she grabbed him with the same warmth she had exhibited to his family, and planted a moist kiss on his lips. "Joe, I'd know tha' anywhere from Polly's description. Tha' is a handsome dog, tha' know," and she looked back archly at her sister. Alice was beaming with pleasure, and Joe grinned his approval at the obvious enjoyment Jess was taking in their arrival.

"Richard, it's Polly and Joe!" Jess called over her shoulder, then turned back to her guests. "What am I thinking about? Come in, come in!" and she herded her guests into the hallway. "Bring that trunk in, Joe. Richard'll show you where to put it in a minute." Again she surveyed them all with great satisfaction, and stooped once more to kiss her sister and the babies.

Jess and Alice had the same features, Joe could see. Possibly the older sister's were a little heavier, but she was decidedly handsome, with dark eyes, patrician nose and high cheekbones. She was bigger than Alice in every way, but had the height to go with her girth. Now thirty-two years old, she had married Richard Kitson some five years earlier. A very impressive lady was Jess Kitson.

Richard Kitson appeared in the hall, a warm smile on his face. He too was tall, but lacked the stately carriage of his wife. Richard was fifty years old, and his pallor and posture revealed the ravages of the illnesses that had plagued him all his life. Even so, his greeting was as welcoming as that of Jess. He kissed Alice and gave Joe his hand, the glow of his smile expressing his pleasure rather more than the listless handshake he was able to offer.

The three Kitson children appeared. William, the oldest at four, was a slim dark lad, not overly robust like his younger cousins, but tall for his age. The little girl, May, was between Willy and Ernie in age, and took after her mother in her stocky build. It was she who took the initiative by leading her new cousins away to explore the house, her brother William seeming content to accept her leadership. The Kitson baby, Ada, toddled in after the others, and was immediately scooped up by Alice to be hugged and petted. She was dark like her brother, with dancing eyes and a happy smile for everyone. She remained in her aunt's arms, as the adults entered the drawing room.

The Kitson furniture was heavy and impressive. The carved chair and mahogany armoire, which Joe had noticed in the entrance hall were, even to his untrained eye, of superb workmanship and material. In the large drawing room they found themselves surrounded by upholstered and carved sofas, chairs, and cabinets of such quality as to have easily graced Gillingham or Arundel. Jess saw Alice and Joe exchange a look of surprise and laughed in delight. "Did tha' not know that Richard and I were wealthy?" she asked.

Richard also laughed, but remonstrated with his wife. "Stop it, lass, you'll have Polly and Joe all mixed up about us." He addressed the others, "Jess has told you, I'm sure, that I was a cabinet maker at the Parliament buildings, before I got too ill to do the work steadily."

"He was the head cabinet maker!" clarified Jess indignantly. "My Richard is the best cabinet maker in all London!"

Richard looked down sheepishly. "I don't know about that, lass," but he added, "At any rate, that's how we came to scrape together this lot." He shrugged in his deprecating Yorkshire way. "Most of it was smashed that bad, it couldn't be sold at auction, and I was told to get rid of it." He smiled at the memory of the fussy little trustees who consigned classical furniture to the scrap heap, but his smile became wry as he added, "This is the only legacy I have for Jess and the children. Maybe it will be of value to them someday," and he looked with affection at his wife.

"Don't talk nonsense!" said Jess briskly. "You don't have to think about legacies and such. You still earn a good wage with the two days a week you work on the Victory." The restoration of Nelson's flagship had been a recent item of interest in

64

the newspapers, and Jess explained proudly. "Richard's the only one the Admiralty will allow to maintain the furnishings on her."

"They must think a good deal of you, Richard," and Joe looked at the older man with the respect of one craftsman for another.

The talk eventually got around to the women's parents and others in the family. Jess rapidly brought Alice up to date. Her mother and father were well, but difficult to deal with. Jess herself managed to keep a fair relationship with them, but only by a great effort on her part. "They still resent you becoming a Catholic," said Jess candidly, and shook her head at the estrangement in her family.

"How do you feel about it, Jess?" Alice asked the question with some restraint. There was enough conflict among the Heffernons without a new confrontation.

"Well lass, I can't say I was thrilled to hear that tha' had become a Roman Catholic." She paused to look at her brother-in-law. "No offence, Joe, but we weren't brought up to have any love for the Romans," Jess smiled. "I guess as we get older, we find that tha' don't have horns after all, unless they're very small ones!" They all laughed, Alice a little shakily. It would seem her religious faith would not cause strife in this household.

"You're a dear, Jess!" she said with real gratitude and fondness.

More family talk followed. The aunts in Brighton were well, "but getting on, tha' know," and interested in Alice's welfare. Nobody had heard anything more about Margaret, their older sister, since her disappearance years before.

"I wonder if poor Margaret ever did become an actress?" said Alice.

They talked of their sister for a while and speculated on whether Joe had ever met her on the stage.

"If you say she looks somewhat like Jess and yourself, I can't say I ever met her. Of course, I didn't meet every actor in England," he grinned loftily, "only the stars!"

"Give over!" said Jess happily, but her sister steered her back to family matters. "What about Will then, Jess?"

Will Heffernon, it appeared, was still shy and dominated by his parents. He lived at home, but did not have his father's trade, and had difficulty in keeping steadily employed. Will lacked the gumption of his sisters and would have been better off away from the criticism and heavy handedness of John and Patience Heffernon. "But I worry more about Jinny than I do about Will," said Jess. "He will break away from mother and father soon enough and get married, I hope. He's got his health and all, and if he meets the right girl, he's got a chance at a happy life." Jess shook her head. "Poor Jinny, though. She's suspected of having consumption, tha' know?" She saw her sister's troubled nod. "Her chest is delicate, and she gets feverish very easily."

"Has she been able to go out to work?" Joe put in.

"Not recently. She does a little simple sewing for mother, but she weakens quickly. I don't know what is to become of her after mother and father go." The thought that Jinny might die before either her mother or father remained unspoken by Jess and Alice, but was depressingly present in their minds.

"How are they, with Jinny?"

"That's the best thing about mother and father," said Jess emphatically. "They are kind and sweet with her. You wouldn't know they're the same people as they are with us." This last was accompanied by a rueful laugh. "It would seem they save all their goodness for Jinny!"

"Thank God for that!" said Alice sincerely.

CHAPTER FIFTEEN

London, 1897

"Jess thinks I should visit mother and father."

They were in the comfortable walkup flat that Jess and Richard Kitson had found for them a week earlier. The place was light and airy, for a London dwelling and Alice thought it might have been an artist's studio at one time, though much too tidy to have accommodated a recent Bohemian tenant. The flat consisted of two bedrooms, a tiny parlour and an enormous kitchen with a skylight, through which the sun shone brightly, this Sunday afternoon.

She sat with Joe at the oilcloth covered kitchen table, he with a ritual cup of tea in his hands, and she poking into her mending basket as the sunbeams picked up highlights in her dark hair. The quiet tones of the boys playing in their bedroom lent an air of welcome peace to the day of rest.

Joe shared her concern about her parents. The quarrel was neither to her liking nor to his; both would have preferred an uneasy truce to this outright alienation. On the two occasion on which Alice had attempted a reconciliation, that following her baptism as a Catholic and again at the time of her marriage, she had been rebuffed. "There's no reason why you shouldn't be able to see your mother and father regularly," he said firmly, "as well as Jinny and Will." He eyed her sympathetically over the pipe he was lighting. *Damn it, she didn't deserve the enmity of her parents.* He blew out the match emphatically. "Look," he said, "what does it matter if they turn you away again? You'd be no worse off than you are now, and maybe this will be the time they'll come around."

She turned to him hopefully. "Do you really think so?"

"Sure I do. If you want, I'll go with you, if you don't think my being there will make them angry." He grinned at the thought, even as he sympathized with Alice's problem.

She looked at him lovingly. He could always restore her confidence, but with resolution of her own she decided, "I think, for all our sakes, we should both go. I am not going to compromise with them. They're going to have to accept our marriage, and you, Joe, as well as me." She gave him an appraising side look. "That is, if you behave yourself. We may have to eat humble pie and I don't want any of your deviltry!"

Joe took his pipe from his mouth and turned pious eyes to heaven. "S'elp me Alice, I'll crawl the floor for them if they want it."

"I can just see you!" snorted Alice, not at all convinced that her husband would respond meekly to provocation from her parents.

"Ah, and to show what a wonderful, thoughtful son-in-law I am," proclaimed Joe, "let me suggest a present for your mother."

"A present?" Alice considered. "That would be nice. What do you have in mind?"

He gestured like a master of ceremonies. "For the seamstress: a sewing machine!"

"A sewing machine! We could never afford it." There were few machines in private use, at the same time, she was turning over the idea in her mind. What an ideal gift, something to be of great use to her mother, and a lavish present bound to impress her father as well!

"Say no more," said Joe, "my mind's made up. We've got some savings, love, and if it helps bring your father and mother around, the money'll be well spent."

It was a tremendous idea and, in their enthusiasm for the thought of reconciliation, the couple were happier than they had been all week. They busily began to discuss details of the visit and where they might purchase their grand present.

The problem with her parents was the only remaining cloud on their horizon, and one that loomed a little larger here in London than it had in Birmingham.

The couple's fond welcome by the Kitsons was only the first of the exciting and rewarding events that marked their move to the capital. Joe had been engaged quickly by the London *Daily News*, which permitted a union shop, and he operated a composing machine at that news sheet's plant. His wages were higher than the average tradesman and, by reason of union scale, he was receiving the same pay as older men. He was well able to afford the decent rooms they occupied. Already he had been welcomed into the London Society of Compositors, and had enthusiastically recited to Alice that union's aims for improved conditions within the industry. Now the last burden to complete happiness was to be overcome.

On the following weekend, with the children left in Jess's care, the couple hired a cab and set out in bright sunshine, with their crated gift on the seat opposite them. Alice was apprehensive about the impending meeting, but Joe had confidence enough for both.

It was not far to her father's shop and lodgings. In the warm summer sun the street looked different than on her last visit, on a wet and dreary Christmas eve, seven years before. Maybe it was a good omen. She had been barely seventeen on that last occasion, and hardly capable of judging the lives of her parents. She recalled with regret the bitter parting with them, and blamed the young girl she had been for her lack of understanding. She also took heart from her husband's easy confidence and resolved that the mature woman she now was would find a path to reconciliation.

Below the faded goldbeater's sign that swung above the shop door, their cab came to a halt. Joe assisted her to alight but, uncertain of their welcome, asked the cabman to wait, leaving the crated sewing machine in the cab, before he accepted Alice's arm to escort her to the door. She drew a deep breath as the remembered silvery bell tinkled to announce their arrival, then blinked in the change from sunshine to the shop's interior as they entered. It took a moment for her eyes to adjust, before they were drawn to the workbench behind the counter where her father worked.

He did not look up immediately, as he was engrossed in his engraving of an exquisite golden goblet. He was older looking than ever, and somewhat stooped as he peered, by the watery light, at the fine piece in his hands. Joe saw that he wore a dundreary moustache, like that of his own father, but with the addition of muttonchop sideburns. When John Heffernon did look up from his work, the stare he threw at the newcomers was not welcoming. Evidently recognition was instantaneous. "So you've come home, then. Patience, come out here." Heffernon's demeanor was blank. His wife came from the quarters in the rear of the shop, and stopped in complete surprise as she recognized Alice.

"Mother, dear." Alice made the first move, impulsively going to her mother, taking her hands and kissing her cheek. Patience made no response, evidently still in shock at the sight of her daughter. Alice turned to her father, but his expression discouraged any attempt at affection. She folded her hands in front of her instead and said quietly, "Hello father."

"Ullo," he mumbled and, ungraciously, "I suppose this is your husband?"

She introduced them all, and Joe, sensing his handshake would be rebuffed, did not offer it. He smiled at his parents-in-law and inclined his head in something not quite a bow. Patience recovered herself, and she at last remembered her manners. "Please come in," she said stiffly. "John," directing her eye to her husband, "will you put the latch on the shop door?" With this, she led Alice into the living quarters.

"If you'll excuse me, I'll let the cab go," said Joe quickly, before John Heffernon could close the door. He went out and with the help of the cabbie, brought in the large crate containing the treadled sewing machine. The women had vanished through the inner door, and Heffernon stood at the entrance, not attempting to conceal his impatience. Joe paid off the cabman, and said lamely in answer to Heffernon's suspicious looks, "A little present for Alice's mother."

"Alice?" asked Heffernon, stressing the name although he well knew the circumstance of his daughter's name change.

"Polly," acceded Joe, keeping the peace. They left the closed crate where it had been set on the floor, and Joe followed his father-in-law into the rear room.

Her parents' stiff greeting, and particularly her father's unyielding attitude were disappointing to Alice, and her earlier optimism and resolution faded. Looking at her mother now, she felt deep regret but little other emotion for the severe and rather drab appearing woman before her. She felt some guilt at her own lack of affection, and was saddened by the new lines on her mother's forehead and the downward creases of dissatisfaction that tugged at Patience's pursed lips.

The silence of the appraisal, for Alice too was under her mother's scrutiny, was broken with the excited entrance of her young sister. Only a little more sedately than seven years earlier, and still with unaffected pleasure glowing in her face, Jinny Heffernon ran to her sister. Her coming brought pleasure and welcome into the strained atmosphere of the parlour. "Polly!" she cried, and threw herself into her sister's arms.

For Alice, the meeting with Jinny was a mixture of joy and dismay. Her arms around the girl's shoulders discovered her frailty, and her hands felt each contour of the slender frame they held. "Dear, dear Jinny!" and she clung to the girl, as if she might impart some of her own strength and warmth to the slender figure. She drew back to look at her, but was devastated by her appearance. The telltale spots of high colour still falsely enhanced the pretty features of the thin young woman. Alice hugged her again. "Oh Jinny!" She sensed the tension under which Jinny existed, and felt the convulsive manner in which Jinny's hands clasped hers.

"Sit down, Polly, sit down, and you too, Mr. Atherton," said Patience formally.

"My name is Joe," said her son-in-law, producing the grin which usually melted those he met, but neither John nor Patience responded with any noticeable relaxation of manner.

Awkwardly, but with some civility, the three women talked about family members, of Alice's children, and of her employment prior to her marriage. Alice was encouraged to think that progress was being made, Jinny's presence the catalyst that encouraged amity between them. The peace was not long lived. John Heffernon, silent until now, suddenly entered the conversation, addressing himself to Joe. "You're a printer."

"Yes, a compositor," said Joe, relieved to see the end of Heffernon's silence.

"A union man, no doubt?" The enquiry, made with deceptively polite interest, led Joe into the trap.

"Oh yes!" he said enthusiastically, unwarily launching into a glowing tribute to unionism, until he was rudely interrupted by the other.

"Unionism is the curse of this century!" cried John Heffernon. His face had turned ruddy with barely controlled rage and his raised voice and clenched fists indicated the extent of his feelings. "The unions don't do a bloody thing but stir up trouble and make ordinary folks disrespect their betters," he raved. "How can an honest tradesman or a manufacturer make a decent living if a bunch of upstart workmen come in and tell him how to run his business!" Righteously, "Let me tell you, young feller, when I was a lad, there wasn't any such nonsense allowed. I was indentured to my guild for eight years and did as I was told, and it didn't do me any harm."

Joe, astonished at the attack but not understanding it, made a fatal mistake. "But you are a guild member. Surely unions and guilds . . . " but he got no further.

Heffernon lost control of himself. In his rage he choked and stumbled over his words. "Don't you dare mention trades, or trade unions in the same breath as GUILDS!" he shouted. "There's no comparison, ab-so-lutely none. D'y hear!" He leaned toward Joe in fury, nearly upsetting his chair.

Out of the corner of his eye, Joe caught his wife's frantic signals to be quiet, but he couldn't resist the argument. He had no reason to fear Heffernon and was not cowed by his threatening manner. Heffernon continued his diatribe. "Look at your own damned trade. If you get your way, some sturdy young lads who are the support of their families will be turned out of the plants and factories. Printers!" he said, almost spitting in disgust.

Joe's dander was up at this slight to his trade, but he kept cool. "Yes," he said mildly, while ignoring his wife's disapproving head shakes, "if we get our way some sickly kids won't have to work anymore." Then he dropped his mild manner and said snappishly, "Their fathers, God willing, will get jobs and be able to support their families, and let the kids go to school where they belong!" He and Heffernon were now glaring at one another with noses almost touching. A thought came to Joe's mind. "Don't demean printers," he said witheringly. "Gutenberg was a goldsmith like yourself before he invented printing!"

"AND DIED PENNILESS!" trumpeted John Heffernon with malicious triumph. "He should have know when he was well off!"

Score one for you, you old devil, thought Joe, enjoying himself. Alice jumped into the breach. "Mother," she said, "we have a present for you. Joe, will you bring it in, please?"

He received no offer of assistance from Heffernon, so he brought the heavy crate into the room and dumped it in the centre of the parlour. He wrenched the lid off and, with an air of triumph, removed the last cloth covering, exposing the sewing machine in its polished black enamel and shining nickel splendour. Patience's reaction was completely unexpected.

"Migawd," said that lady, "Are y'out of your minds? *I'm a seamstress*, not a bloody machine operator!" Her language and lapse into Londonese gave indication of the depth of her outrage. "Y'can tyke that newfangled thing right out o' 'ere!"

Her mother's outburst would have been comical if it had not been for its drastic effect upon Jinny. She was visibly upset and shaking, and dejection settled on Alice as she realized the initial promise of the visit was over.

"All right, mother," she said quietly, and smiled reassuringly at Jinny, who was looking at her in despair. "Our address is written here; please come and see the children when you can." Her invitation was addressed to the room at large, but only Jinny, risking her parent's wrath said anything.

"Oh Polly, of course we'll come!" Her colour was higher than ever, and Alice, in her concern for her sister, was in no mood to add anything to upset their visit further.

"I'll get a cab," said Joe, surprisingly restrained.

As he left the shop, Patience attempted some degree of civility. "Are you expecting again then, Polly?"

"Yes, mother," said Alice, "in October."

"I hope everything goes well," said Patience, still stiff but trying to compensate for her own and her husband's outbursts.

"Thank you, mother," replied Alice, as Joe returned and picked up the sewing machine. It was heavy, but he managed it without assistance from his father-in-law. The waiting cabman helped him load it into the hansom. Restrained goodbyes were said all around, and Alice kissed her mother and Jinny quickly, giving a hug of reassurance to her sister. Nothing was said as they drove away. The Heffernons quickly ushered Jinny into the shop, and closed the door.

Alice's feelings were curiously mixed. Overlying the sadness that their mission had failed, was indignation at the bad manners of her parents. It wasn't so much for herself, she thought, but they could have been nicer to Joe. Embarrassment at having put him in the line of their malice was suddenly cut off by a startling guffaw from her husband. Some crazy whimsey had occurred to him. She was indignant at first but, as he continued to laugh infectiously, she couldn't help but chuckle ruefully along with him as she also began to remember the spiteful nonsense they had listened to. Reluctant to lose entirely her mood of censure for her parents, she asked accusingly of Joe, "What's so funny?"

Between outbursts of mirth, he finally managed to tell her. "Did you see the piece of handicraft your father was working on when we entered the shop?"

Alice thought back, and remembered the beautiful golden goblet that her father's talented hands had obviously just completed. "Yes, I remembered. A chalice, wasn't it?" At least there had been no mention of religion, she thought with relief, though aware this subject was the underlying reason for the Heffernon pique. Now, at the incongruity of her fundamentalist father creating a sacred vessel for the purpose of Catholic worship, she recognized the cause of Joe's mirth, and joined her already gasping husband in gales of laughter.

The cabby shook his head in disapproval as a new burst of merriment from the cab followed Joe's final word on the subject.

"I'll bet he puts a curse on it!"

CHAPTER SIXTEEN

London, 1897-1902

For most of the six years that they spent in London, there was occupational interest, and action aplenty for Joe. Not that he became involved with violent elements of the unions as he had in Birmingham, but between the extremists of the left who were near to being nihilists, and the ultra conservatives of the right, he found plenty of opportunity for acrimonious opposition and gleeful challenge.

Nothing could be more exciting than to be part of a major London newspaper, with its dramatic deadlines and press stopping stories of world events; events that were shaping the end of the nineteenth century and preparing the Empire for the twentieth.

As well, he was enjoying the role of husband and father, proud of his two good looking sons, rough-housing with them and delighting in their courage when he teased them into physical response. When his daughter was born in the fall of 1897, he was nearly as obnoxious as on the occasion of Willy's birth. This time, the newcomer was highly prized, not only because of the change in gender but because, as he saw it, of better timing; it was close to three years since Ernie's birth. Margaret Mary increased the household work extensively, but by this time they could afford a mother's helper, and life moved on much as it had before Margie arrived upon the scene.

Jinny came to visit as often as she could, but not so her parents. Alice's sister took great delight in her nephews and nieces in both families, but grew tired in their clamouring presence and would have to take her leave at an early hour. Alice and Jess were troubled by Jinny's appearance, but there was nothing that could be done for their sister except to love her and make her visits to them as enjoyable as possible. In spite of her lack of stamina, Jinny's trips to her sisters' homes highlighted her existence, and for all three women this short time in which they were together was to be a treasured memory for future years.

Richard Kitson's health failed, and he moved his family to Walthenstowe in Essex. The seaside air was much easier on him than the smoggy atmosphere of

London, and Walthenstowe was the home of his parents. The Kitsons' leavetaking was a cruel blow to Jinny, and it was fortunate that Alice and her family were in London to soften the disappointment. Alice and Joe redoubled their efforts to keep up Jinny's flagging spirits; Alice, by including her sister in as many family functions as possible, and Joe by being his most clownish in diverting her, imitating the pantomime of the Lupino family, or assuming the pomposity of Germany's Kaiser Wilhelm, while attributing a low German accent to that poor man.

In September of 1898, Joe received a letter from his mother. Her pride damaged, and bitter beyond words, she had delayed informing him that his unmarried sister Nellie had given birth to a son two months earlier. She had just brought herself to writing to William and Joe, her two eldest sons, and it was plain to see how the event had demolished this fiercely proud little woman. Sarah's letter revealed that she and Joseph Senior were quite sure that the father was the son of a councillor of their town, who had taken advantage of the artless Nellie. To make things worse, the angry Joseph had confronted the boy's father in front of witnesses and a slander suit against Nellie's father had commenced. Sarah, in her letter, vehemently declared their determination to fight the suit, but Joe had misgivings about the outcome.

By Christmas time, the legal battle had become so acute that Joe's parents wrote that Nellie, with her little son, Johnny, was being sent to Walthenstowe to avoid the unpleasantness. Jess Kitson, always a warm and mothering person, took the unhappy Nellie into her home, where the girl slowly regained her self-respect. Johnny was made welcome by Jess's children; little May particularly taking over as a miniature nursemaid.

It was just after Margie's second birthday in 1899, that the smouldering animosity between the dissident Boer farmers and British settlers in South Africa broke out in several hostile incidents. As Joe explained the background to Alice, the Boers had set up an independent regime, unrecognized by Britain. Troops were sent by the British to the Transvaal border, and President Kruger, of the new republic, demanded that they be withdrawn. When Britain ignored his request, the Boers opened hostilities, overran British Natal, and besieged Ladysmith and Mafeking.

By this time, Willy and Ernie were in school and learned of the war from their schoolmates. "Fighting the Boers" became the fashionable pastime after classes, with the younger children usually forced to become the despicable Boers. Ernie and Willy bore this indignity with stoicism, learning that the faster and more often they dropped dead in writhing agony, the better the big boys liked it.

They were unaware that their mother miscarried at this time. Margie was two years old and a great chatterbox, therefore good company for her mother in convalescence. Although Alice was disappointed when she lost the child, the event was to allow her some respite from infant care. The live-in hired girl had long since departed, and Alice took full charge of her household before her complete recovery from the miscarriage. Joe was sympathetic, if not particularly helpful, being somewhat vague as to what he might do to help. Willy, going on six, was of more assistance to Alice than any of them. Calm and reflective even at this age, he recognized his mother's infirmity, while not understanding its reason.

In November, the British doubled their forces in South Africa to 54,000. Australia and Canada sent volunteer battalions to support the mother country, their patriotic action sending a thrill of pride throughout Britain and encouraging home recruitment. Stirrings for faraway places, rather than the call of duty, prompted Joe to thoughts of enlistment, particularly after he learned from his mother that his brother Reg had received a commission and had gone to South Africa. He was thwarted in his intention by Alice, who took a particularly strong stand, saying she would not be left alone, with the small income of a soldier, and with three small children to care for. Partly because she had put her foot down, and partly because of her recent miscarriage, he gave in and blew off surplus steam thereafter in matters pertaining to his union.

His mother's letter brought other news, as well as that of his brother's enlistment. The law suit against her husband had been won by the plaintiff, and Joseph and Sarah now carried an enormous burden of debt. Nellie and her little son Johnny were back at home, and the bitterness of public censure resumed. It appeared that the older couple would have to dispose of their business to pay their indebtedness, and move away from Yarmouth to make a new life for Nellie and her child. The bright spot of the letter was that William, Joe's older brother, had received his doctorate in philosophy, and was now continuing his progress within the Jesuit order in Wales. This news had come as a needed balm for Sarah's battered pride.

The war dragged on. The Boers were excellent guerrilla fighters and Britain neither conquered them easily nor restored peace quickly. Ladysmith was relieved in February, 1900, and Mafeking shortly thereafter. By June, the stiff resistance of the Boers was overcome to the extent that Paardeberg was taken by the British, and the Boer general Cronje surrendered. Guerrilla warfare continued, but Lord Roberts felt sufficiently confident of the eventual outcome to return to England, leaving Kitchener, the hero of Mafeking, in command.

Queen Victoria died in January, 1901. She had been on the throne for sixty-three years, for all of the lifetimes of Joe and Alice, and even through the earliest memories of their parents. England could not remember when she was not Queen. To Joe, her passing meant the excitement of the news: the extra editions, the reports of the gathering of all the royal families of Europe, the endless pieces about the state funeral arrangements, and the sombre but majestic funeral procession that followed. Alice was the one who was saddened by the Queen's death. It was the end of an era for the young woman. She recalled her own unnoticed entry into the magical world of castles, royalty, and nobility twelve years earlier, and realized that even that remote association had ended forever.

It was not until May of 1902 that the South African war ended. It had taken more than a year to conclude the peace, and waging it had been costly to the British. The British death toll was three to four times that of the Boers. Nevertheless, Kitchener returned triumphant to England and his victory parade in London was witnessed by the three Atherton children and their parents. It was an event never to be forgotten. The first faint sounds in the distance, thin cheers and fragmented martial music; then, still distant but clearer and recognizable, came the martial tunes and the unmistakable pounding of boots and clatter of hooves, increasing in volume by the second. At a louder burst of music, the first brilliant uniforms were seen far down the street; then suddenly the parade was upon them in overwhelming sound and colour. Bandsmen passed by in scarlet and blue tunics, in trousers and kilts, wearing busbies, bearskins, and feather bonnets, their pipes, horns, and drums loud on the ear, followed by marching riflemen, bombardiers, and pioneers, and prancing cavalry with matched horses of grey, dun, or black. Rattling artillery pieces were drawn by spirited teams, and everywhere the sun glinted off musical instruments, chain burnishers, spurs, buttons, rifles, bayonets and harness.

They marched to the cheers of Londoners great and small, with the loudest cheers reserved for Lord Kitchener himself, mounted on a prancing charger and looking as fierce as he had appeared in his lithographed campaign posters of two years earlier.

But the winds of change were sweeping over England and the Empire. A new century had begun, a new monarch was on the throne, and new nations were challenging Britain's supremacy in world affairs and trade.

Her own colonies of Canada, Australia, New Zealand and South Africa were shaking off the protection of the old country, finding world markets for their own agricultural products, and examining the richness of the vast, untapped resources of their lands.

The ending of the war in South Africa brought unemployment and labour strife to Britain, and new strength to the labour union movement. In Joe Atherton's industry, the long sought after association of all printing trades became a reality, as the Printing and Kindred Trades Federation was formed. With it came Abolition, an end to the use of child labour in the publishing industry and, moreover, a huge letdown for the ardent unionist of Chelsea.

"You know, Alice," he said, "it's not going to be the same. Oh, I know it's going to be better for everyone," he added, to her quick look of enquiry. "But . . . well, we'll be merged with a bigger union, and it will all be cut and dried."

She watched him with sympathy. She knew how much he had enjoyed his union association and the club-like atmosphere of the smaller group. Even when the controversy had been at its highest pitch, he had come home from his meetings charged and excited like a little boy describing the conflict in the schoolyard. It definitely was not going to be the same.

From then on, Alice sensed the restlessness in her husband. She was perfectly content herself with their house, the children, a few friendly neighbours, and frequent visits from Jinny and her brother Will, but she was keenly tuned to Joe's moods. Ever since the near destruction of his ego in Birmingham, she had realized his dependence on her under stress, and had quietly determined at that time to sink her own desires beneath his own. It was not an act of martyrdom. Part of her nature now was the ideal of service, not subservience, but prideful service to her family. To Alice, there was nothing demeaning in her role of partner to, and supporter of, her husband's enterprise. Joe was the better family head for her constant support, and never misunderstood her attitude, though occasionally, she thought wryly, he took advantage of it.

Nevertheless, he was restless and it was apparent that his instinct to ramble would soon reach a climax. This came when the posters advertising the opportunities that awaited colonists in Canada and Australia began to appear on the streets of London. Even a few of the new motorized lorries were seen, their sides emblazoned with pictures of vast plains of swaying wheat, imposing mountain scenery, and busy city streets. The lorries, their advertisements, and the crews that accompanied them, were sponsored by the governments of the Dominion and the Commonwealth, and in the case of Canada, were a joint effort with the Canadian Pacific Railway.

Very casually, Joe threw the pile of brochures onto the kitchen table.

"I'm trying to set the table," Alice told him flatly.

"Sorry," was his automatic reply. "Thought you might be interested in these."

"What are they?" It was perfectly obvious to Alice what they were, but she could be as casual as he.

With recollections of his attempt at enlistment a few years earlier, and Alice's firm stand against it, he was determined to approach the new consideration with caution, not to say guile, if necessary. "Just some advertising for the colonies," he said, flipping over a page or two so Alice could see the brilliant colours. "Nice work." Thereby showing his approval as a printer rather than as a possible candidate for their enticements.

"Hm, yes, very nice." Alice's polite reply did nothing to further his cause.

"The print is of good quality, too," he pointed out.

"Is it?" Alice displayed only nominal interest, as she continued to set the table.

"Oh yes!" Joe allowed a little enthusiasm to creep into his voice. "Amazing, considering . . . "

"Considering the primitive conditions of Canada and Australia?" she asked innocently.

"Well yes," he started to say, when he caught the hint of mischief in her eyes. "Dammit, Alice, you know as well as I do that the big cities of both Australia and Canada are just as modern as Birmingham, Leeds or Manchester."

". . . WELL I DON'T CARE!" sang Alice, to complete the line from the current hit.

"Funny, aren't you!" said Joe, but with a grin of rueful appreciation for his wife's catching him in his deceit. "All right," he admitted, "I am kind of interested in the folders. Will you look at them after supper?"

"Why not?" she asked airily.

It was agreed that the question of emigration would be pursued. Alice, while not standing in her husband's way, required the assurance that the idea was practical. Given her tacit approval, he hurled himself into the plan with unreserved enthusiasm, quickly ascertaining from the recruitment officers that boundless opportunities for experienced printers existed in the new lands. Neither of them had a preference for either Canada or Australia. The claims made by the recruiters for the new countries were so extravagant that it became evident they would have to make up their own minds.

"None of my family or relatives are in Canada or Australia. How about yours?"

"I can't think of anyone," said Alice, wondering if any of the Lawrences or Heffernons had emigrated. She fleetingly wondered if her runaway sister, Margaret, was in either country.

"Let's toss a coin," said Joe.

She was scandalized. "Really! If you can't think of a good argument for either country, it would at least be more fitting if you said a little prayer for guidance."

"Let's do both," said Joe jauntily. "Dear Lord, I'm going to toss this coin, heads for Canada, tails for Australia. If You have any preference, please so indicate." With that he tossed the coin in the air and it fell to the carpet.

Alice's eyes were round with amazement at the temerity of her husband. Dissenting households didn't treat the Lord so lightly, and certainly didn't involve Him in a gamble. Joe laughed at her expression. "I mean it with respect, love. Since we have examined all the advantages of both countries without coming to any conclusion, we have to put it in the hands of the good Lord, with maybe a little help from fate." Alice still was not sure that this wasn't sacrilegious, and she kept her eyes averted from the coin on the floor.

"Come on, Alice," he urged her. "Look at the coin!"

Gradually her glance was pulled to the big penny on the floor.

"I can't see it. What is it, Alice?" Joe's rather myopic eyes were squinting to see the coin.

"It's heads . . . for Canada," said Alice faintly.

"Heads for Canada, it is!" confirmed Joe gaily, as Alice stared at him in consternation, as much at the manner of the determination, as for the final decision to leave England.

CHAPTER SEVENTEEN

At Sea, 1903

The steamer *Canada*, of the Dominion line, was nearing the end of her September, 1903, voyage to North America in cool, calm, sunny weather. The passengers were enjoying the change in conditions from those of the crossing when, for thirteen days, the North Atlantic had plunged the ship up and down in choppy seas. Seasickness had overtaken many, and even seasoned travellers had been affected by the rolling motion of the ship. Since the *Canada*'s stop at Boston, two days earlier, the weather had turned easier, the near gale winds had softened to autumn breezes and, in the lee of the Atlantic coast, the ship had sailed northward to and around Cape Breton Island and into the Gulf of St. Lawrence. Soon she would be in the St. Lawrence River and the passengers would disembark at Quebec on the following day.

High in the rigging, Midshipman Willy Atherton, in fancy, swept the horizon with his telescope. "Sail ho, sir!" he cried, with little regard for the inconsistency of mingling steam and sail. Far below him he could see the tiny figures of his brother and sister quietly perusing a book together, not knowing that he had left their side and was now providing vital information to a grateful ship's captain. "Good work, Atherton!" the captain called heartily, clapping him on the shoulder as he slipped easily to the deck, and Willy returned to his deck chair without either Ernie or Margie having been aware of his absence.

What a marvellous adventure it had been. Even the tearful and painful parting between his mother and his Aunt Jess two weeks earlier had only a temporary saddening effect upon Willy. Sensitive as he was to his mother's moods, the appeal of the experience to his nine year old imagination was not to be suppressed for long. He'd had a few anxious hours at the beginning of the voyage, when his mother came down with mal de mer until he realized that the best thing he could do for her was to take his brother and sister out of the way and let her be quiet. Throughout the trip the cabin staff kept an eye on the resting Alice and the nine month old baby, Reggie, and the others had the run of the ship.

There was so much to see and do. Their very own stateroom, for example, familiar now as any home, but so posh! And the banquet salon, scary at first in its stiff formality, now a thrice a day revelation of dining delight. The romance of uniforms, the seamen with their middy collars and wide trousers, the short-jacketed stewards, and the officers in their brass buttoned blues. And the marvellous reliving of every sea romance he had ever read, with Margie and Ernie supporting him in minor roles. It was a heady experience for Willy Atherton, and for his younger brother and sister too.

For some of the time, the children were able to take to the outside passageways, sometimes with the baby Reggie in tow in a little wagon from the ship's toyroom. On the stormiest days they were not allowed on the rainswept and windy decks; instead they roamed the saloons and galleries, poking their noses into forbidden doorways, and learning the ship's geography as well as any member of the crew. They had played hide and seek with a freedom and scope never before realized. Ernie was especially venturesome and, as a result, was yanked by indignant seamen from tarpaulined lifeboats, and chased off the first class decks. He was yelled at by a Chinese cook for invading his galley, and was threatened with irons by a seemingly irate captain when, from the bridge, he was fiddling with a steam valve. For the most part the crew and passengers enjoyed the children, admiring the quiet authority of the eldest, and chuckling at the antics of the irrepressible Ernie.

On the second class deck, propped up in a deck chair and surrounded with cushions and blankets against the cool breeze, passengers were aware of one of their recuperating group, a dark haired and dark eyed woman of thirty. Though still pale from the rough passage, Alice nevertheless presented a striking profile to the others, many of them seeing her for the first time since the voyage began at Southend.

Some of the male passengers and deck officers were conscious of her good looks, unaware that she was the mother of the lively and seemingly unattended three young children and baby who had become familiar to the second class section. The young woman was enjoying the sunshine and the temporary freedom from the care of the family. Still lethargic from her illness, she knew she would be ready on the next day to cope again with the children, see to the handling of their many pieces of luggage, and get in touch with her husband. She was to wire him in Winnipeg upon her arrival in Canada. She was thinking fondly now about Joe. *It will be so good to see him,* she thought. A year was much too long to be away from one's husband and she wasn't going to let him out of her sight again! She hugged a pillow to her, in anticipation of the warmth of his arms.

The intervening months had not been easy, but she was much better off than some wives who had to wait two or more years for their colonist husbands to become established. She put out of her mind the loneliness and fear that threatened to overcome her after Joe's leaving, and thought ahead to his goodnatured presence, his sense of fun and his competence as a lover. Life would never be dull around her husband, she mused, but sighed a little for the placid security she once associated with marriage. There had been times in the past year in which she had bitterly resented her husband's absence.

Reggie had been born in December of the previous year, just two months after Joe's departure for Canada. The little fellow was goodnatured and little trouble for Alice; indeed, he had been a joy to her after the absence of an infant in the house for several years. But the time had been lonely in London, and the intervening weeks since Joe's leaving were filled with the uncertainty of his progress in the far away country. He had not been the best correspondent during this time, and doubts as to the wisdom of their decision had begun to haunt her, and fleeting thoughts of the temptations he might be exposed to created a dark mood which lasted for two weeks after the birth of her baby.

Christmas time had brought not only a huge box of presents from Joe, but good news of employment in Winnipeg. As well as extra cash for Alice, he sent her a warm winter coat from Canada. It was cosier than the light rainwear common to England, and surprisingly fashionable. Alice could feel Joe near when she wore it. For Willy there was a pocket watch which became his pride and joy, for Margie the biggest doll she had ever seen, and for Ernie a set of four boxing gloves. With these last was enclosed a card which was enscribed: "For my son, Ernest, so that he may learn the manly art of self-defence." Ernie was ecstatic, and he and Willy used the gloves often.

Even more welcome to Alice was the letter accompanying the Christmas parcel. Joe's breezy style and nonsensical prose were almost like having him by her side. She read and reread the letter, regaining more of her usual common sense and good humour with each reading. She still missed him dreadfully but was prepared to make the best of the situation under the circumstances.

A visit to Walthenstowe at Easter time reunited the sisters. It had begun joyfully for Jess and Alice and was a happy time for the children, as they became acquainted all over again. Both families had new babies to show off, the young Reggie, and his cousin Doris, born a month or so before him. Fortunately for the Kitson family, Richard had been well paid for the period furniture he had sold upon leaving London, and was able to maintain his family comfortably. Richard still was not robust, but welcomed his wife's relatives with his usual warmth and good manners. He was not one to impose his own health problems on his guests.

In August, the long-awaited letter from Joe had arrived, enthusiastic about a new position with the Winnipeg newspaper that employed him; and best of all, containing a cheque for the family's fare to Canada.

She made one more try at reconciliation with her parents before leaving. It was as unsuccessful as the previous attempts, and her parting from Will and Jinny the more painful therefore. Even poor Will had wept under the circumstances.

After a last weekend with Jess and Richard, she accepted an invitation from the Kenyons to visit them before she went overseas. Leaving all the children with her sister, she travelled to Beccles, where she was greeted with warmth by John and Mary Kenyon, as a friend rather than a former employee. It had been eight years since she had seen them. Only the three youngest children remained at home, Mary and Margaret having entered the Order of the Sisters of the Sacred Heart. The two youngest girls were rather shy with her, but Joseph, now twenty and as exuberant as ever, greeted her with cheeky fun.

Father Ford had been gone for several years. He was presently the venerable abbot of Downside Abbey, a Benedictine establishment in Somerset.

Annie Pipe had done exactly as she had promised. She had married into a distinguished family, the Chichesters, and was long departed from Beccles. It was to be many years before Alice would hear of her again.

The Kenyon family's parting gifts to Alice illustrated how little was known about Canada, even by informed people like the Kenyons. For Joe, they had a revolver; for Alice, a pair of sturdy boots made by Annie Pipe's father, The Excelsior Shoemaker. At the time, Alice saw nothing incongruous in this choice of gifts for a couple travelling to a modern city in western Canada.

In her deck chair with the sun caressing her cheek, Alice came back from her reverie of the last weeks in England and looked ahead to her life in Canada. Probably her life would not be too different from that experienced in English cities after she married Joe. Certainly, life in Canada would be completely different from her girlhood at Arundel, and quite unlike her happy days in Beccles with the Kenyons.

CHAPTER EIGHTEEN

Quebec, 1903

Quebec City was surprisingly small. From the ship's deck, Alice had a quick glimpse of narrow, winding streets leading up to the Plains of Abraham and a few imposing homes. Close to the waterfront, the houses and warehouses were ancient and decrepit, with many chimney pots, and with patches of brick showing through their plastered surfaces. They were a hodgepodge of styles, dating from the earliest French settlements in Canada and all noticeably different from the English architecture she was accustomed to.

The passengers from the *Canada* disembarked at midmorning and were met by English-speaking immigration and customs officials. The passenger list was not overly filled with immigrating families, so Alice had been quickly and courteously processed. Now, with the aid of one of the officials and with a nurse carrying the baby, they left the immigration shed. From the line of horsedrawn cabs at the curb, a vehicle was called for them, all of their luggage was piled into the boot, and their driver directed to the Canadian Pacific depot. "One of our people will meet you and the kids, Mrs. A. They'll be expecting you." The casual informality of the Canadian officers was a diverting change from English officialdom as Alice knew it. Class conscious bureaucrats in the old country were polite only to their betters. She waved and smiled her appreciation of the new land and its people. It was a good beginning.

The waterfront streets were busy with horse drawn traffic; vans, lorries, carriages and carts, with many automobiles interspersed, chugging along at traffic speed. Their cab passed through markets selling produce and fish, the stall tenders bawling their wares in the heavy accents of Gascogne and Bretagne. The Atherton children hung out of the cab windows, noting those unfamiliar things which marked Canada's individuality to them; the caleches, the motorized vehicles, and the dress variations seen in the uniforms of police and others. It was a new and entertaining world.

The rail depot was crowded, with hardly a foot of space uncovered. Every seat in the building was taken, and luggage spilled out into the aisles. If the *Canada* had not carried many immigrants, many other ships from Britain, the Balkans and the Ukraine had dumped their human cargo on Canada's doorstep. A roughly dressed man with a luxuriant moustache and fiercely drawn eyebrows caught Alice's eye and glared threateningly at her. Surprisingly, he jumped to his feet, his expression lightening in a wide, gap-toothed smile. What he said was unintelligible to her, but his meaning was clear. He swept off his hat and gestured in a grand manner towards his seat. He was rewarded with a smile and grateful acceptance of the proffered space. Meanwhile an immigration official, with the assistance of a French-speaking porter, headed to the baggage room with the larger pieces of luggage.

Alice established her little stronghold. The hand luggage needed on the train was spread around her feet, and the children were sent out to locate washrooms and food outlets. The noise of conversation in the depot was deafening, as it bounced and re-echoed off the cavernous roof. It was a Tower of Babel, the volume of sound increasing with the variety of tongues spoken, and the loudness of those who shouted to make themselves understood.

"Here're your tickets and baggage claim checks, Ma'am," said the returning immigration official, "but I hate to tell you that your train departure is delayed by twelve hours." He looked rueful. "Sorry, if there's anything we can do in the meantime, you can get us at the booth." It was 11:00 a.m. Instead of the two hour wait anticipated, Alice realized it would be midnight or later before she could leave the overcrowded station. If most of these travellers were westbound, it was to be an uncomfortable twelve hours with only one seat among the whole family. It was a dismaying thought, but there appeared to be no help for it.

"May I ask you to send this telegram for me?" she asked. "I'm afraid the baby . . . "

"Certainly!" interrupted the official, glad he could do something for the young woman. He took the telegram she had composed the night before and corrected the arrival time. It read:

J.J. Atherton, Esq.,
Farnham Hotel,
Winnipeg.
Arrived Quebec City this morn arrival time in Winnipeg noon Sept 24 everyone well love

Alice

Sending the telegram seemed to Alice to be her first direct link with Joe for nearly a year. The train delay was merely an inconvenience now, and she dwelled on Joe's surprise and delight as he received her message.

The children returned with their report on facilities. Alice dispatched the boys for sandwiches for the noonday meal, and milk for the baby's bottle. Some of the wait was taken up by this activity, but the day continued, dragging slowly for Alice. Occasionally she would give her seat to Willy, and pass the baby for him to hold, as she stood and eased her aching muscles. The others occasionally found a seat nearby, as the immigrant children in the depot played a kind of musical chairs. The adults, men in tieless shirts and women with shawls upon their heads, jealously guarded their temporary homesites.

The boys and Margie did not mind the delay, at first. They roamed the huge depot looking at the notice boards and restaurants, held sign language discussion with other children, and checked out the magazine and candy counters. Willy was the spokesman for them when they returned from one expedition. "Mama," he said, "can we each have a nickel for a sweet?"

"What's a nickel, Willy?"

"Five cents, Mama."

"Let me see, five cents is . . . tuppence ha'penny." She stopped to gather this in, then said with indignation, "Tuppence ha'penny! Why you'll never have tuppence ha'penny to spend all by yourself, Willy!" But she relented after a while, and brought out the required sum to allow them to share a nickel candy bar.

At intervals during the day, she took Margie and the baby with her to the washroom, leaving the boys to guard her precious seat. She would not allow Margie to go near the washroom by herself, and the boys had strict instructions to stay together always. Again, at suppertime she ordered food for herself and the children, but was appalled at the high prices. They were at least three times what she would have had to pay in London.

By nine o'clock, the din of the station had died to a murmur. Even Margie and the boys showed their weariness, as they, in turn, lounged against Alice, propped themselves up against pillars, or seated themselves on the floor among the heaps of baggage. One by one, they were given seats by compassionate fellow travellers, and quickly fell asleep, despite their uncomfortable postures on the benches. Alice was completely worn out. She had risen early that morning on the ship in order to pack, and was still weak from her seasickness. Occasionally, in the station, some woman had relieved her of the baby, but she had borne his not inconsiderable weight in her arms for most of the day and evening. Her head was beginning to nod, when a messenger boy in uniform appeared at the far end of the depot. She was unaware of him until his persistent voice penetrated her sleepy mind as he called, "Message for Mrs. Atherton, telegram for Mrs. Atherton."

She called to him, and he delivered his message and got her signature in his receipt book in return. He waited momentarily for a tip, but seeing her preoccupation and frantic opening of the envelope, he shrugged and went about his business. Alice, in the meantime, was looking at the form with growing confusion and alarm:

Mrs. Alice Atherton,
C.P.R. Depot
Quebec, Quebec.

Mr. Atherton no longer at this address
checked out two weeks ago no fwdg address.

Farnham Hotel
Winnipeg

Two weeks ago! That was just around the time she was leaving for Canada. She read and reread the telegram for some clue to this crazy turn of events. Had he just moved to a better or cheaper dwelling? But no forwarding address. Was he running away from something? She shook this aside as unworthy, but fear for his safety came instead. At least he must have been all right when he checked out of the hotel, or they would surely have advised her. Panic started to build, and she drew a long and shaky breath to regain her calm. The immigration people! They'd know what to do, and just the thought of sharing the burden made her feel better.

Leaving the sleeping Reggie with a woman who had earlier given her assistance, she went to the immigration desk. New staff occupied the booth. There were no other travellers there and the pair of officers, a middle aged man and a youngish woman, gave Alice their attention. The two exchanged only one glance after reading the telegram, and then became briskly reassuring. "Ah yes, we've had experiences like this before, Ma'am," said the male officer with great certainty.

"Communication problem, usually," added the woman vaguely.

"Don't you worry, Mrs. Atherton, you husband will turn up," said the officer.

The woman was more reassuring. "Don't change your plans, Ma'am. Go on to Winnipeg, and we'll have our people meet you there. In the meantime, we'll set the wheels in motion to find your husband. Most likely he'll be there at the Winnipeg station, as well!"

Of course! He had just moved to another address. She was not entirely convinced but she had to put her trust in someone. She readily agreed with their suggestion to continue on to Winnipeg, telling herself that news of Joe must surely await her there.

"I'll see if we can't board your family a little sooner," said the older official, and he was as good as his word. By ten o'clock, he and his partner came to get Alice and her family, assisting with the sleepy children and baggage, to get them through the great station hall to the tracks, where they boarded the westbound train. In the colony car to which they were assigned they were allowed a choice of seats, an appreciated luxury after the crowding of the day. Three seats, two of them facing one another, and near the big coal stove at the rear of the coach, were selected with the help of the officers.

"Will you be all right, Ma'am?" It was obvious that they were concerned for her, and their manner did not add to Alice's peace of mind. She would get little sleep this night.

"Yes, we're quite comfortable, thank you," she told them, "and the children seem to be settled for the night." She looked ruefully down at them. Even Willy was asleep. There was no one to share her vigil on this, her first night in Canada.

CHAPTER NINETEEN

Winnipeg, 1903

They were four days going to Winnipeg. Their train of colony cars pulled into one dreary siding after another, as the opulent expresses roared past in disdain. It was a decided comedown after the relative luxury of their shipboard cabin.

The colony cars, designed specifically by the Canadian Pacific Railway for the transport of colonists or immigrants were comfortable enough, but stripped of the plush, the panelling and the gilt of the coaches provided for the more affluent. The cars were well-maintained, and at the start of the journey were clean and fresh, with scrubbed floors and fresh varnish everywhere. The seating consisted of slatted benches on either side of the centre aisle, constructed of wood and wrought iron and with no upholstery whatever. The seats and backs were curved to the contours of the human body, and were not uncomfortable for daytime travel. At night, with the family's luggage stored under the seats, Alice and the children could manage with coats and railway blankets to cover them. Willy and Ernie, with boots off, would grumble themselves to sleep on one benchlike seat, while Margie and the baby appeared to be content on the second. Alice, with legs tucked under her long skirt, endured the rigid boards of the third, but was reluctant to compose herself until drowsiness began to overwhelm her.

Apart from the worry about Joe, never far from her mind, she enjoyed the daytimes. The distances were a revelation to her, as mile after mile of brush and forest rolled past the window. In Quebec and Ontario, the passengers were treated to the first onset of autumn. Sudden patches of brilliant colour, such as she had never seen in England, would make Alice's throat catch with the beauty of the scene. In the celebration of colour, the leaves were putting their last burst of energy into the painting of the forest before they were to wither and die. She shivered, and put this concept out of her mind.

The evenings were cool enough for them to appreciate their proximity to the big stove. As well as providing welcome comfort, it also heated Reggie's bottles, and cooked the food of all the families in the car. It became the community centre for the women, as they prepared their meals. Sometimes the ladies would combine their culinary supplies and talents, to produce a huge stew to feed everyone in the car.

She learned the reason for the frequent stops. They were lengthy enough to allow the passengers to hastily get to the stations, where supplies were available. Occasionally, a store was close to the station, and would do a brisk business until the conductor hallooed them back aboard.

The passenger list was about equally divided between British and other European immigrants. Although conversation, even among the passengers from different parts of Britain, was hampered by language and dialect, still the people managed to communicate by one means or another. Good will and good humour marked the first two days of travel, but inevitable boredom plus the problem of limited bathing facilities began to make communal living less pleasurable. The stench from some unwashed bodies in the car became intolerable, and certain sections were best avoided. Alice made the children change their stockings every second day, and she sponged herself and Margie in the washroom. Others were not so considerate; the English began to eye the Irish with suspicion, and the Irish the Central Europeans. The latter looked at all the English-speaking people with barely hidden disgust so, by the last day of travel, the once amiable passengers were ready to part company.

She had put out of her mind, as far as she was able, the mystery of Joe's whereabouts, and looked forward with hope to his being in Winnipeg to greet her. Early on the last day, she packed all their belongings and cleaned up the children, in anticipation of seeing their father. Her own costume was thankfully changed from that which she had been wearing for four days.

The train rolled through beautiful forest country dotted with emerald green lakes, through small resort towns, and into a small range of low hills with outcropping rock. They were passing through the dividing point between forest and prairie. Once through the rocky hills, the prairie emerged quickly. For most of the travellers it was like no other landscape seen. Alice had read about the Great Plains, but was unprepared for the vast sweep of prairie that unfolded. It stretched from horizon to horizon, with the bluest of skies touching down to earth in every direction like a faultless vaulted dome. A few trees here and there marked the site of a distant farm, but in every direction the land was flat and monotonous. No, not monotonous, she decided. The earth was patched like a quilt. Great squares of gold with waving heads of grain, green squares of prairie grass, brown plowed earth, and yellow fields of mustard. Its beauty was lost on her. She found herself feeling depressed at the wide scope of the plain; it had no comforting quality. *Farms should be cozy,* she thought, *set in rolling hills, and with vision limited to one's own locale.*

Within two hours of emerging from the forestland, the train arrived at the outskirts of Winnipeg. Alice recalled the dingy edges of Brighton as seen from the train, on that remembered, but so different, train journey. She felt again the thrill of anticipation, which she had experienced on the other occasion, but this time it was mixed with feelings of dread and despair for what might be in store.

The children excitedly watched out the window as the train entered the depot, searching the faces of the people on the platform. "There he is!" called Margie, and spirits lifted until it proved to be someone not like Joe at all. The train rolled to a stop, without them having seen their father.

She stoically began to get their packed things together, and made sure that the children had their outer clothing. Before she could leave her seat, the conductor appeared with a man in the, by this time, well known uniform of Canada Immigration. As the conductor pointed out the Atherton family to him, Alice felt hollow inside. "Mrs. Atherton?" he enquired, taking off his peaked cap.

"Yes?" she answered. She couldn't hide the fear in her eyes.

"Well now," he said easily, "we haven't located your husband yet, but don't worry, we will." His smile was meant to be reassuring, but the news was difficult to bear. The children were intensely disappointed and the official could see the desolation in their mother's eyes. "Come now, Ma'am, no news is good news," he said heartily. He was wondering what sort of a husband and father could neglect or desert such a fine family, but his manner was confident. "We're going to look after you and the children. You come with me to the shed." Forlornly, the little group gathered up its things and followed the immigration man. He stepped down from the train, lifted off Margie and the baby, and gave a hand to Alice as she stepped down, managing her long skirt with difficulty on the high step.

In the immigration building, a room had been reserved for them. It was not large, but had been made as comfortable as possible with three cots and a couple of plain chairs and a table. There was no facility for cooking, but the immigration people assured Alice that they would provide meals from the depot restaurant. Weary and disappointed, Alice thanked the people for their help and was left alone with her family and her thoughts.

During the past few days of travel, she had bolstered her morale with the hope that he had merely changed his abode, that he would be at the train station to meet her.

His failure to appear was the last straw, and the culmination of all the doubts and fears that had plagued her during the past year. He had been unpredictable on many occasions, but there had to be more than just a mistake this time. What did she really know about what he had been doing in all the months of his absence, months of difficulty for her; her pregnancy, coping with a young family, and bearing a child without the support of his presence.

It was not Alice's nature to feel pity for herself, but fear and anger became a bitterness like bile in her mouth. She had made excuses aplenty for him, and God only knew what capers he had been up to!

The night was an unhappy one for her.

The children went quickly to sleep on two of the cots, and she had made Reggie comfortable on two chairs lined with pillows. She herself stretched out on the other cot, covered herself with a blanket, but did not sleep until exhaustion eventually overcame the darting images in her mind; then her rest was broken by bad dreams and unaccustomed sounds from the depot.

In the morning she awoke from a deep sleep, to a tap on the door. The sun was shining through the grimy window, and the children were beginning to stir. She answered the door, peering around it to the cheerful face of a new immigration clerk, a woman, gaining hope that they had some word of Joe. "Good news, my dear!" beamed the middle aged employee. "Your husband has been found, in Medicine Hat!"

"Medicine Hat?" said Alice, apprehensive and still not properly awake. "What is a medicine hat?"

"It's not a 'what,'" the woman laughed, "it's a town in the Territory, and your husband has gone there to work."

She was still stunned, relief not an immediate reaction. She pulled on a robe, and followed the woman to the table where the children gathered to listen. They were gleeful with the news, knowing nothing of their mother's despair of the night before. As the woman recounted the story, they laughed and made light of his disappearance. Alice listened too, her emotions mixed and unsatisfied by the unfolding story.

It seemed that Joe had left his employment with the Winnipeg *Tribune* three weeks earlier. A little detective work at his hotel, followed by discussions with former fellow employees on the *Tribune*, revealed that he had spoken of going further west, maybe to Lethbridge or Calgary. Telegrams to those cities, as well as to other major centres, located him at the Medicine Hat *Weekly News*.

She finally drew a shaky sigh of relief. At least he had come to no harm and was working, but there was still a lot to be explained. "You tell him I'm coming, and not to move another step!" she cried, indignation warring with relief in her voice.

"We've already done that," said the pleased woman. She and her colleagues were happy for the young mother, and relieved to have solved the problem. She continued, "Your train leaves this afternoon, and you will be in Medicine Hat tomorrow."

The children whooped with glee at this good news. They, as well as Alice, were tired of travelling, and were looking forward to seeing their amusing and entertaining father. Alice belatedly thought to thank the immigration employee, as well as to breathe a short and silent prayer for the deliverance of her husband. At least she still had a spouse, and her children, a father.

That afternoon, the family boarded the train with four Department employees to see them off. They presented Alice with a large basket of fruit tied with a red satin ribbon, for all the world as if she had been a favoured guest. They had been so good to her that Alice finally broke down, all the suppressed tears and fears of the last week coming to the surface. She was comforted by the motherly clerk, and the train pulled out with goodbyes and good wishes called between them.

The trip to Medicine Hat was uneventful. Alice had enough time to consider her situation with Joe. She still didn't understand why he would leave Winnipeg without notifying her. She was both dreading and looking forward to seeing him, but for the children's sake put a bright face on things. There was no point in burdening them with her uncertainty.

After a long day and night, the train arrived at Medicine Hat, and to the delight of the children, they spied their father alongside the train waving his hat and smiling his absurd smile. Alice saw him with love, relief and exasperation, but all emotions changed to outrage as he helped her down from the train.

"Why did you come, mother?" he asked in a perfectly reasonable voice.

CHAPTER TWENTY

Medicine Hat, 1903

The late afternoon sun shone through the windows of Father Jeanotte's little kitchen, its rays laying golden stripes across the wooden floor. The priest sat contentedly in the rocking chair beside the stove, puffing at his pipe and admiring the skill of his temporary housekeeper, as she thumped and pulled at the bread dough on the kitchen table. Alice's face was flushed from the heat of the oven and her exertions, and a fine dew of moisture lined her upper lip. A fine looking woman, Father Jeanotte thought to himself; Joe was a lucky man. But it was high time for any remaining coolness between the couple to be done with.

The family had been with him for close to two weeks. Alice cooked the meals and gradually got the priest's cluttered cottage into a semblance of order. Father Jeanotte was delighted with the arrangement, and made Alice feel that she was the benefactor instead of the other way around.

She had become devoted to this big, round, warm man. She learned that his vocation to the priesthood was a late one. He had been a miner in Flemish Belgium and, although he had always felt the pull towards the Church, had the responsibility for the care of elderly parents until his own middle age. After they died, his restlessness brought him to Canada where he had applied in Calgary for entry to the seminary. He had been ordained only two years before, and following a brief indoctrination as a curate, he had been given the parish of Medicine Hat to administer.

The children, as well as Alice, warmed to the man. He had wasted no time in becoming close to them, giving both Margie and Reggie, whom he called "my boy Raitchie," rides on his back, as he crawled on all fours, his soutane taking a great mauling from this exercise. He obligingly threw a ball back and forth with the two boys, and taught them and Margie how to play Snap and Old Maid. In these games he roared protests and threw down his cards in pretended anger, to the delight of his young adversaries.

She expertly slashed the top of each loaf with a knife and dusted her handiwork with a twirl of the flour sifter handle, then consigned the loaves to the oven.

"There!" she said triumphantly, and transferred the remaining flour on her hands to her apron, pushing a damp tendril of hair into place with the back of her hand. "Are you ready for a cup of tea, Father?"

"Please," and he introduced his subject with care. "It has not been easy for you, Alice."

She looked up warily at him. "Oh, it's been fine, just fine!" she exclaimed," And you've been so kind, Father," But she busied herself with the tea things.

"All d'same," he said, "D'shock of coming to a strange new country and not finding your husband . . . " he nodded wisely. "You are brave, my dear."

"I guess it has been the same for other wives coming to Canada," she protested, while cheered by his sympathy.

"Are you still angry at Joe?" he asked.

The question, coming from anyone else, would have been resented, but she recognized his gentle concern. Still, she was not ready to completely forgive Joe for his careless treatment of her and the family.

When he had first come to the priest with the news that his family was unexpectedly on the way from Winnipeg, Father Jeanotte had warmly offered to share his limited quarters. He had the tiniest of rectories, which consisted of a kitchen and a bed-sitting room. The family was welcome to the run of the house, while he would content himself with a cot in the kitchen. Joe, though, would have to continue living at the boarding house until a rented house became available.

After his outrageous question to Alice at the train, her husband had embraced the children and attempted to kiss Alice, but she turned a cold cheek to him. She was seething with anger, but because of the curious stares of loungers on the station platform, she remained outwardly civil, though distant, while their luggage was gathered and put into a wagon. He handed her up to the seat beside the driver, then piled into the box with the children. He was acutely mindful that Alice was angry, but discreetly held his peace. If there was to be a confrontation, it would be according to their rule: Not In Front Of The Children. In his confidence that all would be straightened out satisfactorily, he settled down to enjoy his reunion with his sons and daughter, and to become acquainted with Reggie, the newest member of the family. His apparent lack of concern increased Alice's outrage so that, by the time the hired wagon discharged them at Father Jeanotte's, she was literally boiling over with pent-up wrath.

The man who was to become her close friend came out of his rectory to meet them. A big man, dressed in a black soutane buttoned to his ankles, and with a four-cornered biretta perched on his head, Father Jeanotte was quite unlike the polished clergymen she had been used to in England. His garment was wrinkled and threadbare, and positively grimy in spots. His kindly smile was almost hidden by an enormous and shaggy drooping moustache. He was broad shouldered and carried himself erect, and his humour-filled eyes, behind steel rimmed spectacles, welcomed an unhappy Alice to her first home in Canada. Joe's extra hearty introductions and Alice's reserve did not go unnoticed by the priest. Very sensibly, he ushered Joe and Alice into the house and called the children to come and see his garden and the church. Willy, with a worried glance at his mother and father, went with the others.

It was the first time in a year that they had been alone together. Joe, in the kitchen of the tiny house, tried to take her in his arms with a mollifying, "Now what's eating you, Alice?"

As if his outrageous behaviour hadn't been enough, now he had the nerve to patronize her! "Don't touch me!" She wrenched away, and stood facing him with furious eyes and a grim mouth. "Will you kindly tell me," she said in icy tones, "what you have been up to for the last month?"

He was nonplussed. Whatever else was wrong between them, this was not expected. Discomposure made him hesitate, until a quick mental review of recent activities told him he really hadn't been up to anything. He was highly indignant. "What are you getting at? I've been working my head off trying to get a place for you and the children!" Who could understand women? "Why did you come when you knew there was no house available?" He folded his arms in exasperation.

It threw Alice off stride for a moment. "How was I supposed to know that?" she exploded. "Your letter told me to come, and you sent me the money!" Her anger flared all over again, and she threw her hands in the air.

Now Joe's face fell and his confidence vanished. "My God, didn't you get my letter, my other letter?"

"Other letter!" said Alice witheringly. She had turned away, but now looked at him with something like loathing. "You know you aren't the best correspondent in the world."

He was both embarrassed and placating. "I wrote you from Winnipeg not to come, until I could get a place for you here."

Alice was in complete confusion at this point. She was not mollified, but his last remark made no sense. "Why in the name of everything holy would you want to come to this godforsaken place when you had a good job in Winnipeg?" As an afterthought, she added, "No, I didn't get any letter from you telling me not to come. We made our travel arrangements as soon as we got the passage money, then I went to stay with Jess for a while after disposing of the furniture in London."

"Oh, so that's it," said Joe largely. He was ready to forgive and forget. "My letter didn't arrive in time. Never mind, we'll make the best of it."

She was not as prone to quick reconciliation as her easygoing husband. "Did you ever hear of the . . . the cable!" she cried. "And do you have any idea of what I have been going through since I landed in Canada?" As she told him of her fright and anxiety in Quebec and her despair in Winnipeg, she burst into tears; all the pent-up emotions released by her arrival at Medicine Hat coming to the surface. Relief at seeing Joe, wrath at his casual and reproachful greeting, and frustration and indignation at his easy expectation of her understanding, reduced her now to a sobbing and woebegone being not at all like her ordinarily resourceful and cheerful self.

But part of her, even now, was assessing the situation with practicality. Joe was safe, thank God. She and the children had a place to live, and the terrible suspense of the past two weeks was ended. Her sobs subsided, as she realized she was in Joe's arms and he was telling her sincerely, "I'm sorry, Alice, truly I am. I didn't realize what you've been going through."

She blew her nose, wiped her eyes, and regained her composure, as he told her of the breakdown of his job at Winnipeg because of continuing animosity of other workers towards the English. He waxed enthusiastic as he held her hands and told of his present position, obtained through an advertisement in the Winnipeg *Tribune*. Her breath was still catching in little sobs, and he squeezed her hands the tighter. "Alice, I'm assistant editor here as well as compositor, which means I have a chance to report the news and write some editorials. I'm very busy, but enjoying every minute of it, and I'm making twenty-five dollars a week. That's almost five pounds, which is more than I was getting in Winnipeg!"

Most of her anger had melted and her emotions were more or less under control. "What about a hou . . . house?"

"This town is so busy, there hasn't been anything available for months, hotel or house," he told her. "But a house is coming vacant in two weeks that I've taken. In the meantime, you'll stay with Father Jeanotte." He eyed her wistfully as he added," and I'll continue on in the boarding house." His meaningful look indicated how much he was going to miss the comfort of her bed.

She didn't respond to his ardent gaze. Alice was drained, and content to avoid his ardour for a while. The longing for him, which she had felt since his departure from England, was dissipated in the emotional storm that had wrung her, and there was still one more thing to be said. "All right. I'm glad you have work that you like. We'll get along; we always have." She looked at him with new resolution. "I love you. I'll always go along with your plans." In spite of herself she was becoming indignant all over again. "But if you ever let me down again, we're through Joe, do you understand!"

He knew when to hold his peace. Sufficiently wise not to declare his innocence, or protest her manner of speaking to him, he merely nodded gravely, accepting the ultimatum as a just condition to the ongoing health of their marriage.

"Angry?" Alice responded to Father Jeanotte's question, "I think I was more hurt than angry," she decided. "He is such a good husband in so many ways but he is so unpredictable at times." She felt a twinge of conscience at this disloyalty, but it was good to get her thoughts into the open.

The priest regarded her with a little smile, his head tipped to one side. "Most husbands haf one fault or anudder Alice. I've heard most of dem in Confession."

"I'm sure that's true." Impulsively, she touched his hand in appreciation of his perception.

"You know Joe is very highly regarded around dis town?"

"Well, I haven't had any opportunity to meet people yet."

"It's d'truth, my dear," he insisted. "Your husband may be, unpredictable, did you say? But dere has been no breath of scandal touch im since he arrived in Medicine Hat," and he looked directly at Alice, to make sure his meaning was understood. "Dey like him at d'newspaper office too, and he has made many friends already in d'town." Father Jeanotte was going to pursue the subject until Alice surrendered.

She had to laugh. Here was dear Father Jeanotte trying to sell her on the merits of her own husband. Her last resentments against Joe disappeared. It would be sinful and selfish to nurture hard feelings against him in the face of the priest's pleading. "All right," she said. "I am no longer angry, or hurt, or disappointed, or anything!" She looked at the priest with pursed lips, but merry eyes. "That isn't to say I won't get mad at him the next time he does something outrageous!" Somewhat wistfully, but with an odd sense of pride, she knew for certain that Joe was bound to be unpredictable again and again.

Fortunately, her first sight of the house Joe had rented came after her coolness to him had melted. He had told her the house needed some work, but that did not prepare her for what she was to find. It was barely larger than the little rectory, but with two stories. Its paint was peeling, and its windows, sashes and porches were thickly coated with dust from the road. Any indication of a garden was lost in a welter of unkempt weeds and shaggy bushes.

The inside was even more dreary than the exterior. A single room, containing a battered and rusty stove and a deal table and chairs, occupied all of the first floor. A few dilapidated cupboards, and a sink without taps, marked the kitchen area. A shabby staircase led to the second floor, which contained two bedrooms with two bare iron bedsteads. There was no running water in the house, that commodity being delivered twice weekly at twenty-five cents the barrel, and of course there was no bathroom. There was, surprisingly, electricity, a ceiling fixture in each room, from which dangled a bare and flyspotted bulb at the end of a cord. Another surprise was a light fixture on the front porch which was perpetually alight, Medicine Hat's common-sense approach to street lighting.

A series of transient tenants had left their marks on the house. The young Englishwoman's tendency to make the best of things was strained, but she rallied and began to plan how to make a home of it. Before moving in, she embarked on a cleaning, disinfecting and scrubbing project, enlisting her husband's and the boys' aid. They shopped for a new wood and coal stove and a heater, and a mattress for the boys' room. They bought some white lace curtain material, which Mrs. Wheatley, their next-door neighbour, volunteered to sew up when she realized what the younger woman was trying to do with the old house. Mrs. Wheatley also, firmly and over the weak protests of Alice, loaned them a cot for Margie and a crib for Reggie.

The blankets, sheets and pillows were brought from their steamer trunk, along with the few cherished ornaments and pictures. In the larger bedroom, which Joe and Alice were to share with Margie and the baby, she washed and disinfected the white cast iron bedstead and carefully covered the rusty spring with newspaper before placing her treasured Ostermoor upon it. Fresh bedclothes adorned the ancient bedsteads, and Alice began to feel that she was at home. The final touch was a table cloth for the scratched kitchen table, and a couple of runners, improving a pair of upended orange crates.

On the day they were to move in, it was uppermost in both their minds that they would be sleeping together for the first time in a year. There was a diffidence between them all day, under which they hid from themselves and each other their mixed feelings. While they longed for the comfort of each other's arms, they were aware of the recent quarrel, and there was some awkwardness and apprehension in each of them.

The children went to bed and to sleep. Thee was no reason to further delay their own retiring, and Joe and Alice undressed in the dark because of their still uncurtained windows. The old bed creaked as they crept in and reached for each other with restraint; but the old familiar Ostermoor worked its magic and Alice and Joe were as one again.

CHAPTER TWENTY-ONE

Medicine Hat, 1903-1904

Medicine Hat, as it turned out, was to be a stopover. Not that Joe didn't enjoy the town and his work at the *News*. This was his element; a place small enough to get to know people, and become known. A newspaper business in which he could use his skills at compositing, printing and writing, and where, most of all, he could enjoy the freedom to range about, exchanging ideas about sports, politics, the local economy, and life in general. He attended meetings of the town council, and joined the board of trade. He became an ardent town supporter, and sat on every conceivable committee from entertainment to farmers' union, and from church activity to town improvement. He met, and was accepted as an equal by, the leaders of the community; the doctors and lawyers, the magistrate, the school principal, and the clergymen. And an almost imperceptible change began in him.

Father Hugh Ford, back in Beccles, had first noted a chameleon-like quality about the ex-actor, an adaptability of speech and an acceptance of local custom that came of his stage career. As Joe savoured the salty essence of the Canadian west, not only did his accent become more like that of his fellow westerners, but unconsciously he adopted the flowery writing style affected by newsmen of the frontier. A person's name became his "monicker." Things were never given, but "bestowed" or even "rendered." A journalist's writings were described as being "from his versatile pen," or "inspired by the Muse."

This propensity to adapt helped him to overcome the western prejudice against the English. The British were considered to be lazy and haughty, and not employable; in fact, many help wanted notices carried the rider "No Englishmen need apply." But it helped too, that Medicine Hat was kinder to immigrant Englishmen than most communities. The town's economy, based on cattle and horse ranching, was more open to the English remittance men who came to Canada after the Boer war. These sons of wealthy families were usually accomplished horsemen, and many of them settled down to become successful ranchers. Others, having dissipated whatever funds they had been allowed, were hired as cowboys. Joe had no such gentlemanly aptitude to offer, but he overcame the usual unfavourable reaction to English accents and mannerisms by his good humour, his refusal to take offense at jibes, and by managing to turn the tables on would-be tormentors, all in such a way as to retain the goodwill of even the hard core anti-British.

The weather turned very cold within two months of the family's arrival, and they had their first taste of the Canadian winter. Medicine Hat could get cold enough, even though the weather was not as severe as in other North West Territory cities. The Chinook wind, that phenomenon of the southern border cities of the Territory and of Montana, eased an otherwise rigorous climate; but when the Chinooks were absent and the temperature slid to zero and lower, Alice felt the bite as never before. She was glad to have the warm coat Joe had sent to England from Winnipeg, and in the first cold spell saw to it that the rest of the family was warmly equipped for the weather.

The young housewife understood now why the house had become vacant so conveniently. It was draughty and cold beyond belief. It had no basement, and cold winds circulated beneath the house, and blew through the boards on the floor. Daylight could be seen through cracks in door and window frames, and cold winds seeped in at front and rear doors, strong enough to lift the mats Alice had placed inside the sills. With newspaper and felt stripping bought at the general store, she stuffed the cracks around the windows and tested the result with her hand for incoming air. In November, the first storm dropped a foot of snow on the town. Acting on the advice of their neighbours, the Wheatleys, the family banked a wall of snow around the house, cutting off the inflow of cold air under the building. They were amazed at the comfort this added to the floors, but when a Chinook melted the snow, they were in the same plight as before. Joe ordered three wagon loads of earth, and he and the boys shovelled a permanent embankment around the house.

When the severe cold came in December, the frigid air drifted through the uninsulated house, like an inexorable deathly presence. The heater and stove had to be stoked with coal, by day and by night, for them to exist in even a basic degree of comfort. The children went to bed with bricks warmed on the stove and wrapped in towels, to aid them into their icy sheets. In the morning, Joe would leap out of bed in his long underwear (his nightshirt discarded for the winter), and throw more coal on the fires, opening draughts to increase the heat, then leap back into bed, to Alice's protests about his cold feet.

She would always remember the first sub-zero morning, when the water barrel on the back porch was frozen solid. For several weeks before this, it had been necessary to break the thin ice topping the barrel, to obtain water for washing faces and heating the kettle. This morning, her attempts to chip enough ice were fruitless, and it became necessary to melt snow for her water needs. Everyone was out of sorts and late for school and work that day; and the barrel was moved, thereafter, into the kitchen to prevent its freezing over again. The adjustment to this kind of living was made a little easier by the fact that others were in a similar position. By January there were no Chinooks, and life became largely a fight for survival against the winter. Machinery, fuelled engines, and wagon wheels would all freeze solid overnight. Power would go off and lights fail. Until noontime of the day following a particularly bad night, the town would be digging itself out, or trying to defrost stubborn mechanisms. Fortunately, intense cold rarely came together with heavy snow, so the people of Medicine Hat usually had only one or the other problem to contend with.

If the citizens of the town were uncomfortable, it was nothing like the distress suffered in the Cree settlement outside of Medicine Hat. Some of the tribe still lived in teepees, although the majority were in rough wooden shacks that made Alice's house seem like a palace. This January an epidemic of highly infectious impetigo swept through the Indian village, probably the result of malnutrition and lack of sanitation. Food supplies had dwindled to nothing, and the Crees who came into town to beg for food and warm clothing were turned away by the townspeople because of the ugly pustules of impetigo on their hands and faces. Father Jeanotte appealed to his congregation for help, but little was forthcoming, though groups of Indians appeared at his door every day. Alice overcame her fear of the natives to help the priest, ladling out soup to those who came to the door of the rectory.

A much greater problem were those natives who were too ill or too weak to come into the city, or afraid of the townsmen who had told them to "stay the hell out of here." The editor of the *News*, pressed by Joe, wrote an editorial and open letter to the Indian Department. It shamed the townspeople into action, and a petition was circulated, hundreds of citizens signing a request for quick aid to the settlement. Better still, many members of the community ransacked their cupboards for food and clothing and brought them to the *News* office. The paper hired a wagon, the snow at the time not being heavy, and loaded it with the goods. It took a jubilant Joe and Father Jeanotte to the village in time to prevent further suffering. The sight they found was pitiful in the extreme. The old people were shrunk to skin and bones, and the children covered with sores. Many of them were clothed in rags that did not protect them from the winter's cold bite. The evidence of head lice was apparent in caked patches scratched by frantic little fingers. The wagon was received with little show of emotion, but with great gratitude by the Indians. Back in Medicine Hat, the dishes used to feed the natives at the rectory were boiled for hours by Alice to prevent the infection from spreading; and Joe and Father Jeanotte were ordered into steaming tin tub baths upon their return with the empty wagon. At Alice's command, they scrubbed themselves with disinfectant soap and gave her their discarded clothing for washing. Three weeks later, the Indian Department brought additional relief supplies to the settlement, including medicines to fight the disease and the mites.

Winter gradually drew to a close. March was comparatively mild, after the intense cold of January and February. The ground was still frozen and banks of snow unmelted, but the sun was bright and welcome as it shone upon Joe, sitting in the *Weekly News* office, struggling with the paper's typewriter. He was absurdly pleased with this new and intriguing piece of equipment; one he was determined to master this afternoon, in the absence of his employer, whose pride, joy, and jealous possession it was. This machine was particularly appealing, as it did not demand the full complement of fingers he usually had to compensate for. He could stab at this one with his two forefingers, his speed picking up, as his familiarity with the keys increased.

Whether a shadow fell across his machine, or a small sound interrupted his preoccupation, he was suddenly aware that he was not alone. He started and looked around to see three Indian men, silently watching, and waiting for him to acknowledge their presence. Startled, he jumped to his feet, nearly knocking over his chair. He hadn't heard them come in, and how they managed to do this without bringing the cold air from the outside, he couldn't conceive. "Ah, er, gentlemen," he said lamely.

He relaxed as he recognized one of them, Joseph Little Deer, and was happy to note they all seemed healthy and warmly dressed. In fact, they were wearing, under their mackinaws, their carefully saved native costumes of fringed deerskins. This was evidently a ceremonial visit, and he became suitably solemn as Joseph Little Deer spoke for them.

"We want thank you for helping Indians." There was no accompanying smile and he had to accept this as part of their natural solemnity.

"You're welcome," he replied with a dignified bow.

"We want you come with Missus tomorrow--sundown."

"What for?" Wariness brought this out before he could catch himself. "Excuse me, for what purpose?" he asked with more courtesy.

"Make you chief," said Joseph Little Deer.

Their answer astounded him. He swallowed with an audible gulp, then tried to recover and do justice to the occasion. He bowed low again to the delegation and said, "I will be honoured, Gentlemen," much as if he were accepting an appointment to the Supreme Court. Indeed, it was quite prestigious. The Indians did not give chieftanships away lightly, and though many Canadians despised the natives, there wasn't one of the prominent citizens of Medicine Hat who would not have given a month's salary for such recognition.

He ran most of the way home to tell Alice the good news, and found her serving tea to Mrs. Wheatley, that lady having just sewn together a ten dollar bill ripped apart by the baby. Alice was less than elated by his announcement. To the Englishwoman, the natives, with their unsmiling faces and glittering black eyes, appeared to be full of menace. She did not fancy an entire evening spent alone in their company. Mrs. Wheatley was the one to convince her. "Take Father Jeanotte along with you if it'll make you feel safer," she advised. "I'll keep the children while you're at the ceremony. Besides," she added extravagantly, "it isn't every day I get to look after the kids of a real live Indian chief!"

Billy, no longer Willy since his first week at school in Medicine Hat, was finishing a lunchtime sandwich at the front window on the following day, a Saturday. The noonday sun was bright over Medicine Hat, and cast only a short shadow of the vehicle he was idly watching. He was surprised when it stopped at his door.

"It's the mayor!" he yelled in startled recognition, and indeed it was no less a personage than His Worship the mayor of Medicine Hat, who was calling upon them. All the family had gathered at the open front door before he could knock, and he called greetings to them from the steps.

"Do come in!" said the pleased Alice.

"Haven't time, thank you," said His Worship. "Just wanted to tell you that I've been invited to the powwow too, and I'll be glad to call for you this evening." Their response was grateful and flattering. "No trouble at all," he assured them. "I have room for Father Jeanotte also." He raised his hat to Alice, smiled at the children and took his leave.

Alice, somewhat self-consciously, called after him, "What sort of dress is usual for this kind of occasion, Mr. Mayor?"

His Worship paused and looked back over his shoulder at them. "The very best, Madam," he said solemnly, "the ve-ry best!"

They were ready when the mayor came to pick them up. Alice wore the same costume worn on her first Sunday in Medicine Hat, a dark, wide and full length skirt, a white blouse buttoned to the throat and with leg-o-mutton shoulders, and a black felt hat with a feather on her high piled hair. Joe sported a standup collar with an ascot under his only three piece suit, which was sponged and pressed to make the most of it, and the wide brimmed light coloured hat he had bought in London some two years earlier. They looked highly fashionable to Mrs. Wheatley and the children, as they were seen to the door.

The evening was cool. Alice was glad to have her heavy coat, as well as the buffalo robe that Father Jeanotte threw over her lap. The huge fur was tucked under her feet, and her hands were snug in an astrakhan muff. She was going to enjoy this journey abroad much more than her previous walking forays, when her head was hunched into her coat collar against biting and breathtaking winds. As Joe greeted Father Jeanotte, he belatedly wondered why the priest was not being honoured for his part in the Indian rescue mission.

Father Jeanotte shrugged. "I am a chief already," and he added airily, "because I am so good-looking," and refused to tell them anything else.

Arrived at the Cree village, they were met by the full populace, who escorted the wagon at a slow pace to a clearing, with a roaring fire in the centre. Beside the wagon, the younger people shook rattles and bells, and in their progress towards the fire, performed a shuffling, bobbing kind of dance step, in time to the music of these instruments and the drums. Joe by this time, had doffed his stetson and holding it to his heart, nobly nodded to the Indians lining the way. Alice was struck by the garb of nearly every person, young and old, along the route. Instead of the ragged castoff white man's clothing she had seen on them before, most of the natives were wearing traditional costumes, of a pattern she had only seen pictured in London periodicals. "Don't they look beautiful!" she exclaimed impulsively, and the priest beside her nodded his happy agreement.

"Dere must have been many times when dey wanted to put dem on for warmth, or maybe even sell dem," He shook his head. "Dey are a proud people!"

The ceremony of induction was not long. The solemn faced elders, distinguished by their war bonnets, gathered around Joe, and a crooning chant ensued in their native tongue. Following this, the Cree chief, impressive with gray braids and stony features, placed an elaborate bonnet of eagle feathers on Joe's head. Alice's husband was half a foot taller and the chief had to stand on tip toe to put the head dress in place. "You helped Cree in time of trouble, my friend," he said sincerely to Joe. "Now you Chief Meyototam of Cree," and he added, "means 'Good Friend.' Wherever you go, you be accepted in lodges of our nation."

This surprisingly articulate speech in English for a moment left the usually garrulous Joe without words. "Well, now . . . " he said, then rallied. "Mighty Chief," he said, in the style of James Fenimore Cooper's noblest Mohican, "unworthy though I am, I accept this great distinction you bestow upon me this day. I promise to conduct myself as a Cree with pride and honour."

As a rather nice bit, he thought to add, "So help me God."

His speech was incomprehensible to most of the tribe, but taking their cue from the elders, they roared their approval. They circled around the visitors and began moving in one direction, with great shakings of rattles, ringing of harness bells and beating of drums. Chairs had been provided for the guests in the centre of the ring near the fire, which also was enclosed by the moving mass of dancers. The tempo of the drums picked up, as did the rhythm of the dancers. The crooning cry had a *hai-ya*, *hai-ya* sound, employing no more than four notes of the musical scale, and keeping time to the beat of the drum as it increased in volume. The din, as it sounded to Alice's untuned ear, was deafening and more than disquieting. She kept Joe's hand clasped tightly in hers, and was glad when the music and song stopped as abruptly as it had started.

A feast followed, for which she had little appetite. Joe, having learned to cope with tripe, bloaters, pig's trotters and other delicacies in London, did not question the contents of the simmering cauldron that was placed near him. He accepted a heaping bowl and followed the example of his brother Crees, as he dipped his fingers into the plateful to convey the stew directly to his mouth. He appeared to enjoy it hugely, and Alice picked at hers in an effort to be courteous to her hosts. The mayor and Father Jeanotte were manifestly enjoying themselves, chatting with the elders, and applauding the dancers at certain and specific times, for no reason that she could determine. The evening finally drew to a close with expressions of good will all around. As they climbed back into the buggy, the chief deftly retrieved the beautiful head dress from Joe. "We keep for you," he said firmly, and someone handed Joe his hat. The exchange was so neatly accomplished that Joe didn't have a chance to protest until they were out of hearing.

"Hey," he said, "don't I get to keep that?"

Father Jeanotte chuckled. "Dey tell me dat d'war bonnet is part of deir sacred ceremonial dress, which must not be profaned by an outsider. Besides, Joe," he added philosophically, "Dey really can't afford one right now."

CHAPTER TWENTY-TWO

Medicine Hat, 1904

Weekly newspapers abounded in Western Canada. Some of them, like lower forms of life, lasted for only one season. Those that did survive changed hands with monotonous regularity. Many famous publishers, like Colonel Lowery and Bob Edwards, had six or eight newspapers in different locations and on separate occasions.

Each community of five hundred people or more had its weekly paper, the sole source of news to the average townsman or farmer. Local merchants relied upon the local press as the only medium for advertising their goods and services, and as a source for other needs: stationery, invoices, handbills, and business cards. News from the outside world was meagre, and published only if of major interest; readers were far more avid for local news of sports, social events, court appearances, and the comings and goings of familiar individuals. The townspeople, too, availed themselves of the printing facilities for fancy wedding and birth announcements, for invitations, and for black bordered notices of death.

The reporting, by the Medicine Hat *Weekly News*, of the induction of one of the staff members into the Cree tribe received front page prominence. The article had been written by Joe Atherton himself, and in the third person to avoid any undue concession to modesty. It had a fateful effect.

The circulation of the *Weekly News* was wide. Its editor, like others, extended the courtesy of a free subscription to those he esteemed. The *News* was circulated to other communities, and crossed provincial borders to east and west. In lieu of wire services, the *News*, like its counterparts in other towns, was scanned by editors of weekly papers throughout the west, as well as in major cities in the east.

One issue of the *News* arrived in the post office in the mining town of Ferguson, British Columbia; population 1,000. It was subsequently picked up personally with other mail, chiefly newsprint, by Parm Pettipiece, publisher and editor of the Ferguson *Eagle*. Back at his dusty, cluttered desk at the *Eagle*, Mr. Pettipiece propped up his feet and began to go through the news sheets received

105

that morning. He had a special interest, other than news, today. He was looking for an employee; a particular kind of person, one who could double as a reporter and printer, one who might be open to direction, and one upon whom the mantle of editor and publisher might eventually fall.

When he unfolded the Medicine Hat *News*, the article about the Indian ceremony caught his attention. He read it through with interest, but was riveted by the words "compositor and assistant editor" in relation to the hero of the piece. The article also revealed Joe's marital status, his English origin, and his comparatively short residence in Canada. The description of J. J. Atherton did seem to fit the kind of person Mr. Pettipiece was looking for. He rightly guessed that the young immigrant might be open to a proposition. Parm's feet came off the desk, and with loving care he began to employ the skills of his profession in the composition of a letter.

> J.J. Atherton, Esq.,
> c/o Medicine Hat *Weekly News*,
> Medicine Hat, North West Territory   *PERSONAL*
>
> Dear Sir,
>
> I read, sir, with admiring interest the account of the ceremony, at which you were honoured by the Redmen of your community.
>
> The *News* with the aforementioned article arrived in our bustling little community this morning, at a time when I am desperately situated, requiring the services of a journalist like yourself to assist me in the production of our newspaper.   The Ferguson *Eagle* has the largest circulation in North Kootenay. This phenomenon is due not only to the hearty acclaim and support of our readers and advertisers, but to an economic factor: the prosperous gold mines of the Lardeau which continue to draw hundreds of new citizens to our fair land every month.
>
> I would suggest, sir, that if you are interested in making a fortune in this new land of your adoption, an excellent opportunity awaits you in Ferguson, in beautiful, prosperous British Columbia.
>
> I would be honoured if you will get in touch with me at the earliest.
>
> With esteem for your heroic example of good will and good works to our native brethren, I remain,
>
> > Obed'ly yours,
> >
> > R. Parmiter Pettipiece, pub.

Parm Pettipiece could be forgiven for some of his exaggerations on the basis of community pride, and the balance on journalistic embroidery. It was true that he required an assistant, his pressman, Al Pelkey, having quit the uncertainties of small town newspaper publishing to become the chef at the Black Warrior mine. While Ferguson might have been termed bustling by some of its supporters, it had already entered the decline of those communities which relied entirely upon gold production for their existence.

The discovery of gold forty years before, at Wild Horse Creek in East Kootenay, had lured ten thousand people into an area that was formerly wilderness. But now, along the Lardeau River and Trout Lake (Lardeau Country, as it was called) the mines were petering out, and frantic efforts by land developers were just as unrewarding. Furthermore, Parm's boast of the *Eagle* having the largest circulation in the North Kootenay was questionable. Only one other paper remained, of the dozen or so that had existed within a thirty mile radius of Ferguson. The Trout Lake *Topic* in the town of Trout Lake, seven miles distant, was the only rival of the *Eagle*. Its proprietor, J. L. Langstaff, one of the colourful editors of B.C.'s interior, was known to have printed his first issue of the *Topic* in earlier and palmier days, on silk. Currently the *Topic* was faring no better than the *Eagle*.

To do him justice, Pettipiece had a dream that he could turn the *Eagle* into a mining review, thereby increasing its circulation with its usefulness to the mining community, as well as to the general citizenry. He hoped that the Englishman in Medicine Hat might be the answer.

The first thaws of spring in Medicine Hat did not hold much promise. Rivulets of dirty water coasted down muddy and ice-rutted roads. Mud was tramped into stores, schools, and public buildings with high disregard for the steel scrapers situated at each entrance. Children on their way home from school were still wearing winter clothing, each garment looking its most dismal after a difficult winter and two weeks of the current thaw. Mothers would greet the sight of their children with shaking heads and with shouted instructions to "take-off-your-dirty-boots-before-coming-on-to-my-clean-floor."

Alice looked out her window to see if the children were coming, and observed the scene with distaste. She could see where the snow had melted unevenly, making dirty shadows and exposing patches of lifeless grass around the tree trunks. On the Wheatley house next door, the roof was half uncovered as the snow melted and dripped from the eaves in a monotonous symphony of sounds. The drops hit the puddles and the various discards of the winter now uncovered by the thaw, so that an upturned pail gave a deep bass note, and a Prince Albert tobacco can, an off-key treble.

Alice's porch was dirty in spite of constant shovelling of snow and sweeping of mud and dirt. *It needs a scrubbing again,* she thought with irritation, knowing that another six weeks of the same conditions could be expected. Her mood, like that of every other person in Medicine Hat, was one of discontent with the season. She felt an uneasy longing, and she thought of other Marches, and remembered the green fields and the blossoms of Arundel and Beccles in the advanced springs of England.

Joe was affected by the weather and the outlook as well. It had been ten days since his evening of excitement at the Indian village. The congratulations of the citizens of Medicine Hat had all been received and enjoyed in the first few days, but the succeeding days were flat and monotonous. Parm Pettipiece's letter could not have been delivered at a more propitious moment. Joe's editor had given the envelope to his employee with a look of suspicion, and the younger man thought it wise to put the envelope in his pocket for later perusal. He remembered the letter as he took off his overcoat at suppertime. "Here Mama," he said, handing her the envelope as he hung up his coat.

"What is it?" she asked, studying the envelope.

"Let's have a look." Taking the envelope from his wife, he deftly slit it with his thumb and began reading aloud Parm Pettipiece's missive. The offer of employment came as a complete surprise, and his own and Alice's interest grew as they read the letter, then reread the paragraph offering a position on the *Eagle*. Such is the influence of minor things that, had the letter come two months later, during the Territory's overwhelming rush of true springtime, it might not have rated a second inspection; but in the dreariness of their first early prairie spring, they both felt quickening interest in the prospect of change. In conscience, she had to put the obvious objections to him, but was more than half ready to have him overcome her arguments.

"It isn't any kind of promotion," she reminded him. "The position is no more than you have now."

"That's true enough, but Pettipiece seems very confident about the opportunities along the road."

"It would mean pulling up stakes again before we're decently established here."

"Maybe that's a good thing, Mama. We don't have any roots here," and he added grimly, "God knows this house isn't anything to write home about!"

"What about the children? They are getting along so nicely at school."

"There're just another two, three months at the most before the summer holidays. This change needn't happen overnight, you know." The discussion went back and forth between them, both ready to convince and be convinced that the move just might be desirable. They finally agreed that it wouldn't do any harm to answer the letter and indicate an interest, if the move would mean a substantial increase in salary.

That night in bed, as rain drummed on the roof, they discussed the letter, and the possibility of moving to a kinder climate and a better house, with growing excitement.

Their fifth child was conceived in the dingy bedroom of the ramshackle house in Medicine Hat on that miserable March night of 1904.

CHAPTER TWENTY-THREE

Ferguson, 1904

Parm Pettipiece's shot in the dark had found its mark. Correspondence with Joe ensued, and an agreement was reached for the printer to come to Ferguson as soon as he could part company from the *News*. He was to receive thirty dollars a week, plus expenses, if he travelled on newspaper business. The twenty percent increase over his Medicine Hat salary was the deciding factor for the couple, and the editor of the *News* accepted a week's notice.

Joe's eye was on the distant horizon from that day on, and he was eager to meet the new challenge. Alice did not look forward to the separation, and she put up with the delay with an underlying impatience to shake the soil of Medicine Hat from her own feet.

In the middle of April, Joe left Medicine Hat for his new position. His wife had agreed that he should have ample time to find a decent house, before the family's arrival in Ferguson at the end of the school term. They saw him off at the C.P.R. station, Father Jeanotte accompanying Alice and assuring Joe he would look out for the family. Alice's misgivings were the less for his sturdy support.

Joe's letters home came with a greater frequency than on their last separation. He remembered his previous shortsightedness with some shame, and he made up for it with cheerful and enthusiastic reports of his new job, and with endless descriptions of the beauties of British Columbia. He experienced a feeling for, and kinship to, the natural beauty of B.C. and the Lardeau, that he had never felt for any land. Like most Englishmen "in a foreign strand," he'd been nostalgic for the soft, rolling, and well-tended English countryside. Now something in his restless nature responded to the wilderness. He exulted in the vastness of the forests and the majestic beauty of the mountains.

His first letter home (with a conscious attempt at literary style at its beginning) spoke with enthusiasm about the new land's beauty and appeal.

> You would not believe the amazing sight of the Rocky Mountains, through which we passed as we left the Territory. You see them first as distant blue

hills, exciting enough after the flatness of the prairies. As the train gets nearer, the blueness of the hills becomes the green of wooded mountains, with the snow capped Rockies looming up behind them. Before you know it, the bare and craggy heights are not only in front of you, but on either side, and *behind* you. You are in the heart of these towering peaks, their tops covered in snow or completely hidden in cloud. Unbelievable!

Your eyes stretch up and up, as far as the windows of the train will allow, but you can't see the crests. It is as I always imagined Switzerland to be.

At Banff, the train stopped for nearly half an hour and everyone got off to crane their necks at the mountains. They completely surround the town. Each peak is named. Well-named, so as to describe its appearance, each one different and with a personality of its own.

At Lake Louise and the Columbia Ice Fields, the train again stopped, long enough this time for us to see the Chalet and the lake, which is the most incredible shade of turquoise. At least, it was the day we were there. I am told it takes on different hues according to sun and season.

I am staying at a handsome new hotel, the City, in Ferguson, owned and run by an Englishwoman named Alice Jowatt, who is a salty old duck. Actually, she's only about ten or fifteen years older than us, but her face is craggy due to exposure to the weather. She not only runs the hotel, but has an interest in several small gold mines which she visits on horseback, taking grub stakes to her partners.

Parm Pettipiece is a good newspaperman. He has introduced me around and people are extremely pleasant. The plant and office are small and the press kind of old, being a relic of the defunct Kaslo *Prospector*.

I haven't had a chance to look at houses yet, but will start this week. Am told that there are several nice ones available, some with furniture.

Alice, you will love this country. Ferguson is about a thousand feet in elevation above Trout Lake, the town at which the steamer docks. There are mountains all around us, heavily forested, and wild flowers are beginning to show up between the patches of melting snow. There are creeks everywhere, rushing at this time of year and filled to the brim with the clearest, coldest water you ever saw.

Unlike Medicine Hat, the snow that remains is still white and clean, and the soil is sandy, SO THERE IS NO MUD!

Joe's subsequent letters home spoke of his part time employment, setting type and making up the pages of the *Eagle*. He told Alice of the handsome insignia at the top of the front page of the newspaper, probably filched from some long dead American journal, a majestic bald eagle, talons clutching a beribboned banner, and fierce eyes fixed upon the reader. It obviously symbolized the keen watchfulness and fearless stance of its publisher, Parm Pettipiece.

He also regaled her with an account of his first assignment to make mine reports. He described whimsically how he had mounted a horse for the first time in his life, and travelled on this first occasion a distance of some ten miles on a circuit of mines. He dwelt more on his aching seat and chafed thighs than on his assignment, but as he became accustomed to riding, his letters told her more of his job and the people he met.

> I visit small mines and large mines. The big ones are staffed by fifteen to thirty men, and are equipped with great machinery which had to be hauled piece by piece up the mountains by packhorse. A man named Andy Daney, who I have got to know and like, is the main packer around here. He has at least twenty horses which he packs with provisions at Trout Lake, and carries up the mountain to Ferguson and the mines. The ore from the mines is "raw-hided" down the mountains by the same horses. Heavy horse and cow hides are anchored by ropes to the horse and he eases a load of ore down, enclosed in the hides, sliding and scratching over the rough road and propelled by gravity. The horse's job is to see that the load doesn't get away from him!

> Andy Daney is married to Eveline Jowatt, the daughter of my hotel keeper. You will get to meet them when you come.

> The small mines are my main responsibility. I pick up ore from them and mark it carefully. When I get back to Ferguson, I take the samples to the assay office, and the results of the assays are published in the *Eagle*. We are hoping that our subscriptions will increase with this service.

> My travels are considerably farther than that first ten miles I told you about. I can ride twenty miles a day now without difficulty, and am gone from Ferguson for as long as a week. I stay with the miners when I'm on the circuit and you wouldn't believe how most of them live! In the small operations, say of two men, a tiny plank shack or badly built log cabin is the usual abode. Some of the newer operations, sprung up since the winter, are still in canvas tents. Without exception, they are *all* filthy.

> I carry my own blankets, and when the weather allows, I sleep out in the open. If it is cold or raining, I have to put up with the smell of unwashed men and stale cooking until I drop off to sleep. This doesn't take long as I am dog tired after a day in the saddle.

> The bunkhouses of the larger operations aren't much better, although the grub is superior. At the Nettie L. mine, one of the biggest, they have a cook

named Mattie Gunterman, who is a caution. She came to the Lardeau on foot from the United States six or eight years ago with her husband, Bill, and her son, Henry. She's not afraid of man or beast. Can hunt and shoot as well or better than any man around here and does the damndest things. The first time I was at the Nettie L., Mattie and her assistants, Anne and Rose Williams got up to some deviltry and before anyone knew it, Mattie climbed up astride the big barrel stove with its four legs, and she hung on to the stovepipe as if it was a horse's neck, for all the world as if she was riding a bronco. In the meantime, the other girls pulled on her legs on either side in a most unladylike way. The mine crew nearly died laughing.

The best part of it is, Mattie Gunterman is one of the best photographers I have ever known. She had loaded her camera with a new glass plate that night, and had someone aim it while she and the girls did their crazy stunt. I saw the finished photograph on my last visit to the Nettie L., and it is as professional and natural as anything I have ever seen in London.

Another, and most welcome, letter from Joe toward the end of May reported to a delighted Alice that he had found a house for rent, far superior to the one in Medicine Hat and, "wait 'til you hear this," nearly completely furnished, with an upholstered sofa and chair set in the sitting room.

Now she need wait only until the children were out of school at the end of June.

Her move came even more unexpectedly. By the beginning of June, the school principal advised that the children were doing well enough that they might leave school two weeks before the start of summer vacation. A frenzy of last minute preparations began. Now she was faced with the task of disposing of their furniture, cleaning up the house, packing, and dealing with other details of moving, all within two weeks.

She swept the mud from the front porch for the last time on the morning of June fifteenth. It was her final task, and she was ready when Father Jeanotte and Mrs. Wheatley came to accompany her to the depot. Her only regret, now that she had time to think, was the loss of these two friends. Father Jeanotte, especially, had become almost a member of the family, having his Sunday suppers with them and dropping in to see the children often. She was somewhat quiet as a result, so the others covered her silence with their own busy chatter. They were also losing a friend.

Her later recollections of Medicine Hat would include the sight of her neighbour and the priest seen through the train window, waving and smiling as the train pulled out. And, as on another occasion years ago in Brighton, she couldn't help but think regretfully, *I never appreciated them until now.*

The journey to their new home was exciting and full of interest for the children, and Alice soon caught their mood of adventure. Like Joe, the family was overcome with awe at its first sight of the grandeur of the Rockies, and when they departed the train at Revelstoke, they had some idea of the type of country in which they were to reside for several years. They were in a deep valley, surrounded by tree shrouded mountain slopes. Huge spruce, fir and cedar trees stood, as green in June as they had been in December. Tiny clearings on the hillsides around appeared, like minute cloth patches on a green garment, marking the sites where loggers had helped themselves to the seemingly unending bounty of the forest. Homes in the city of Revelstoke had a more permanent and glossier look than those of the mining communities, which the Athertons were to know. The railway families were secure and prosperous, their neat homes and gardens reflecting their position in the community.

Alice and the children stayed at the Revelstoke Hotel overnight, enjoying the luxury of pleasant rooms and service in the dining room. They were to continue their journey by stagecoach the next morning.

"You won't like it," the hotel proprietor told them. "There's just a narrow road cut through the forest. The trees are so tall they block out the sky, not to say the view. If you don't want choking dust and complete boredom for a whole day, Ma'am, I suggest that you go by rail and steamer."

The advice was good, and Joe was notified of the change by telegraph. The next morning they boarded the train of the Arrowhead and Kootenay Railway. Both the rail cars and the C.P.R. steamer, to which they transferred at Girard, had been in service for less than two years and were spanking clean and comfortable.

On the steamer, the older children ran about as they had when crossing the Atlantic, nine months earlier. The huge stern paddle wheel which propelled the ship was new to them, towering fifteen feet above the waterline, and churning seething water, as the steamer backed away from the Girard dock. In midstream, the engines reversed, with even more frantic thrashings at the stern, then the ship began its voyage down Trout Lake.

At the town of Trout Lake, the passengers lined the rail to get a glimpse of friends ashore. On the low deck, Alice could see Joe's tall frame, with an even taller and slimmer man beside him. "Wave at your father," she told the children, and when they spotted him they shouted and waved frantically. Even Reggie, caught up in the excitement, called out a whole string of words in his own unintelligible language. As the boat docked, Joe strode up the gangplank to take the baby in one arm, while he embraced Alice with his other.

"Lord, it's good to see you all," he said fervently. He kissed them all soundly, and received their hugs in return. "How have you been, Mama?" he asked, his eyes scanning her still slim figure.

"I'm just fine," she laughed. "Everything's just fine, and it's so good to see you!" She gave Joe another hug, in her pleasure at being with him again. On the dock he introduced her to the tall stranger.

"This is my friend, Andy Daney, Alice. Andy, my wife Alice."

Andy Daney was a typical frontiersman, bronzed by his work in the open, and muscled from the heavy loads he swung onto his wagons and packhorses. He was not a talkative person, but gave Alice a shy smile and told her, "We're pleased to have you with us, Ma'am." She was attracted to him immediately, liking his direct blue eyes and the sense of trustworthiness he imparted. She gave him a warm handshake.

"Andy is going to take us up to Ferguson tomorrow, but tonight we stay at the hotel, here in Trout Lake.

Alice could see that Joe was bursting with some as yet undisclosed news. Good humouredly, she allowed him the pleasure of breaking it in his own time, and fondly watched him assemble their bags, with the help of Andy Daney and her sons. Managing their hand luggage, the group left the wharf on foot and headed for an opening between dockside warehouses.

Trout Lake's main street was dusty, and the buildings that faced it were, for the most part, faded, though an occasional brightly painted store front relieved the town's dreary aspect. A wooden sidewalk ran on either side of the street, barely wide enough for two persons to pass.

Their destination was the Windsor Hotel, one of the more pretentious buildings in the town. A handsome, three storey, frame structure, it had a broad roofed verandah across the entire facade of the building. Intricately carved, the porch served the second floor as well as the street level. No more than five or six years old at this time, the hotel was maintained in style and dignity. Its proprietor, Mr. McLennan, welcomed Alice with a warm "Glad to have you with us, Mrs. Atherton," while Joe wrote in the register, "Mr. and Mrs. Atherton and family, of Medicine Hat." They were then shown to their rooms.

Andy Daney brought up the bags Alice indicated they would need for the overnight stay, and bade them goodbye until the morning. "I'll pick you up at nine," he said. "I hope you rest well." He started to leave, but turned to add, "Don't wear your best clothes, it's a dusty ride."

As usual, the children wanted to explore, and their father gave them money for a soda drink. They left, leading Reggie, unsteady on his fat little legs. Joe took Alice's hands and burst out with his news. "Mama, you are looking at the new editor, proprietor and publisher of the Ferguson *Eagle*!" He released her hands and struck a pose, hooking one thumb into the armhole of his vest.

"Joe!" she burst out, "how in the world . . . how can that be possible in just two months?" But it was obvious that he was not teasing.

He laughed and grabbed her briefly in his arms before he said, "Come, sit down and I'll tell you. First, though, this calls for a celebration" He produced a bottle and glasses and poured some whiskey for each of them. He drank his own quickly and replenished his glass as Alice sipped hers slowly.

"It only happened five days ago," he said.

"Parm Pettipiece has wanted out for some time," he explained. "He hoped, by bringing me here and adding the mine review feature, that circulation would increase enough to allow the hiring of another printer, and I could gradually take over the writing of the paper." He took another swallow as he said reflectively, "It hasn't worked out that way. Parm can't even afford my salary with the present circulation, and advertising the way it is. And with me away half the time, he had to do a great deal of the work himself. He says he's too old to work like a slave any more."

"But if the paper's failing . . . " Alice began, but Joe interrupted and over-whelmed her with his enthusiasm.

"The paper's not failing," he cried eagerly, "It just needs some talent and some hard work to make it a winner. Look," he explained, "Parm has been paying me, and Al Pelkey before me, a wage for something he could have done himself. I can make a living just by writing as well as printing the paper." As an afterthought he added, "Bill and Ernie can help by turning the press, folding the paper, and so on."

Wanting his wife's support, he held her hands between his and, pressing them for emphasis, said, "Alice, if I can make a wage just putting out a readable paper, think what I can do as circulation and advertising increase!"

His enthusiasm was so contagious that Alice had to put aside any misgivings to say, "It sounds wonderful! The children can help, and so will I!"

The Athertons were used to the city sound of horse-drawn traffic, but were unprepared for the noise that smote the comparative silence of Trout Lake the following morning. The street outside the hotel suddenly erupted in a London-like racket of clattering hooves and jangling harness. A new sight met Alice's eyes as she looked out the hotel window; the children and Joe crowding her side to see. Coming to a stop was an immense open wagon, drawn by a six-horse team. The rangy animals were not like the great draught horses teamed to pull the drays and lorries of England, but tall and wiry like their master sitting upon the spring seat behind them.

"Good morning, Mr. Daney!" the children called and waved enthusiastically, while Joe and Alice called a friendly greeting down to the street. Andy Daney took his hat off and waved to them. "I'll be right up to get your baggage."

"Are we really going to travel in that rig?" Alice was amused and interested at the same time.

"Certainly," said Joe, "you'll find out why shortly."

In the street, their bags were put into the wagon, already loaded with a variety of goods; boxes of food stuff, liquor, hardware, a bag or two of mail, sacks of cornmeal and flour, and some wood stoves, crated so that their shiny black lacquer and nickeled surfaces could be seen through the slats. "You come up here with me, for now," said Andy, offering his hand, as Joe placed a box to aid Alice in stepping up to the high seat. "You kids jump in the back with your dad." They did so with great glee, and the wagon moved noisily out of town to the sound of Mr. Daney's shouted directions to his team.

At the outskirts of town, the wagon started to climb a grade, which Alice could see became steeper and more rutted as it curved out of sight. Andy stopped the team at this point and said, "Now that we've observed the niceties, I'll have to ask you to ride in the wagon, Ma'am."

Alice looked at her husband, to find him grinning broadly. "It's too rough to ride up on the seat. Andy's prepared a soft place for you back here."

She was glad she moved. After the wagon started, the hill slanted upward sharply and the rutted and stony road became even more bumpy. The wagon lurched around impossible turns and leaned over brinks that made everyone gasp. Andy slid and bucked all over the seat. He needed all of it, as well as his feet firmly planted in two stirrup-like rings on the floor, to remain in the wagon; and it required all the combined strength of the six horses to maintain their progress up the hill. The passengers were thrown around violently. Alice was glad of the warning to wear old clothes, and grateful for the sacks of straw which softened the movements of the wagon box.

The jolting and tossing ended, just as they were beginning to adjust to the motion of the wagon. They left the last hairpin turn at the brow of the hill, and Alice had time to draw a breath and smooth her skirt as she looked back and down, along the way they had come. Her breath caught at the height they had attained, and at the magnificence of the view, at the top of the hill. The lake stretched long and curving to the northeast, its waters sparkling in the June sunshine. The forest stretched out interminably, the myriad hues of its bright hills and sombre valleys vying with the intense blues of the lake and sky.

Margie spoke for all of them. "Well I guess that rough ride was worth it."

Prior to starting his descent into the little valley enclosing the town of Ferguson, Andy Daney again observed the niceties, and allowed Alice to return to the dignity of the high wagon seat, before rolling into town.

Ferguson lay on the other side of the brow, which they had just surmounted. Alice could see that it was even smaller than Trout Lake, if a little newer. It lacked a look of permanence, no one building being as pretentious as the Windsor or the Lakeview in the other town.

Bill and Ernie were not inclined to be critical of their new home. The mountains gave promise of places to roam and run free, to play games of Robert the Bruce and Rob Roy MacGregor. The far-off mine entrances spoke of great fortunes to be discovered, panning gold and discovering the mother lode in the best tradition of the *Boy's Own Paper*; and Margie was content to sit with her parents, her father's arms warm around her in long-missed comfort.

Joe pointed out some of the buildings before they arrived. "That one," he indicated, pointing out a fairly new miniature of the hotel they had vacated that morning, "is called the City Hotel. Mrs. Jowatt owns it." He swung his arm around. "Across from it is the Lardeau Hotel, run by Sandy Laughton. Beyond the Lardeau is McKinnon and Sutherland's general store, and the O.K. Barber Shop." The large mines, Nettie L., Triune, Silver Cup and Surprise, he noted, all had offices in the Mining Building at the end of the street. "That's the school over there." He indicated a small one room structure at the near end of the street they were approaching, and the children craned their necks to see.

"Do the miners live in Ferguson?" asked Alice.

"A few mine officials and office staff do, but, for the most part, those employed by the big mines live in bunkhouses on the mine site. In darned dirty conditions, too. There is a big turnover of men," he continued. "Mostly they come from the mining country in Idaho and Washington, with a sprinkling from other states."

"What about people with small claims?" asked Alice.

"Same thing," he said. "As I told you in my letters, the fellows who do the actual mining live at their mines. They stick closely, afraid of claim jumpers." He shook his head. "I don't envy them. It's bad enough, at this time of year. When the winter comes, most of them will stick it out, but every spring a few more mines are found abandoned." He changed the subject. "That's the telephone office we're passing now."

"The telephone office?" Bill burst out. "Do they really have telephones here, ·Papa?"

"Yessiree," said Joe with pride, "that's the office of the Revelstoke, Trout Lake and Big Bend Telephone Company. They have lines to Arrowhead, Complix, Thomson and Cambourne," he said, "oh, and of course Trout Lake."

"Will we have a telephone, Papa?" asked Margie. They had never had a telephone before.

"Sure," said Joe grandly. "I have one in the newspaper office now".

Andy Daney rolled right through town, the noise of his passing bringing someone to nearly every door along the street. The people stared with interest at the good looking young woman in city clothing seated high beside Andy, and waved, as much for Alice's benefit as for the teamster's. One or two children ran after the wagon, and would have climbed in for their usual ride to the Daney Livery and Storehouses, but fell back when they saw the wagon already occupied. Margie smiled smugly at her brothers.

The team turned at the next corner toward the mountain slope. Tucked in at the end of the street, with the forest behind, was a neat two storey house quite by itself, with a whole mountain for a back yard. "Here's your home, Mama," said Joe, watching for her reaction.

He need not have worried. The house was as attractive as its setting, and vacant only because of the present low ebb of the mine companies' fortunes. The children charged into the yard, and around the house twice to find its treasures. A wood house at the back, along with a decent privy, were quickly investigated.

Alice's inspection brought her delighted approval of the house's furnishings and appointments. A cheery kitchen window looked out upon the mountain slope, over a sink with a pump. She was to be freed from the tyranny of the detested water barrel! "Isn't it nice, Mama?" Bill asked eagerly, aware of her pleasure and glad for her.

"It's just beautiful, Billy," answered Alice.

There was a sitting room with upholstered furniture, a dining room with an oak table and chairs, and three bedrooms on the second floor.

"This one's just for you, Margie." The little girl's eyes grew big as her father pointed out the smallest of the three rooms to her.

"Just for me, alone?" asked Margie unbelievingly, and she twirled around three times in the empty room. "Just for me?" she repeated joyously. "Oh boy!"

She's not a little English girl anymore, Alice thought. But the occasion, for the child, was too rapturous for silly regrets. Margie ran downstairs, for her small bag and favourite doll. She had to establish ownership of her Very Own Room.

The other two bedrooms were furnished, each with a double bed and dresser, but lacked mattresses. Alice chose the front room, over the sitting room, for her own and Joe's use, and told the boys to rearrange the bed and the dresser in the other room as they wanted.

The initial upstairs inspections had only taken five minutes, and Alice and Joe hurried down the stairs to say goodbye to Andy Daney. He had brought in all their bags, and had primed the pump to get it working; gushing streams of fresh cold water. "Thank you, Andy," she said, "for everything," and she added, "Especially for making us feel so welcome in Ferguson!" Andy, with a pink and pleased face, left the family alone.

CHAPTER TWENTY-FOUR

Ferguson, 1904

Ferguson's City Hotel tried to outdo the Windsor, in Trout Lake, in splendour, notwithstanding its smaller dimensions. Mrs. Jowatt's newer establishment, like its counterpart in the other town, boasted a two storey verandah on its street side, with a pillared canopy and gingerbread railing, and a false front at the top to hide a pitched roof. Rattan mats ran from the verandah edge to its twin doors, one leading to the lobby on the left, the other to the saloon on the right. All the woodwork was newly painted, and the rattan matting freshly renewed since the winter.

In the shade of the canopied verandah and against the hotel wall, chairs were set for the benefit of the hotel's patrons. Today, only a couple were occupied. Mrs. Jowatt had warned the usual loungers not to "loll around like hicks," because a lady was coming, and only two men were brave enough to stay.

It was a momentous day for Alice Jowatt. It was not just that a new family was to be welcomed to the community, but an *English* family. The hotel proprietress looked forward to having another Englishwoman to talk to, after all these years. In honour of the occasion, she told her girls that morning to clean the silver immediately, rather than wait for the usual cleaning day. She passed a last critical look over her gleaming white table linen, freshly cleaned carpets, and just-brushed drapes of plush, then went to the lobby entrance to watch for her guests.

Mrs. Jowatt had come as a bride to Vancouver, some twelve years earlier. Her husband had died at an early age, and she was forced to work in order to support her family. The young woman had started a bakery on Cordova Street near the waterfront in downtown Vancouver, and it prospered. She took in boarders, and when the mining boom brought her to the Kootenays, she was only a step away from being in the hotel business. Her first venture in Ferguson was a modest but profitable lodging house, and she was able to build the City Hotel with the proceeds from the first investment. The City was the pride of Ferguson.

Her guests were arriving. The characters on the porch gravely raised their hats to the lady, and refrained from using the cuspider until the procession had passed them. Joe Atherton carried a baby on one arm while his wife's hand engaged the other. Behind the couple came three obviously English children walking sedately, but the hotel keeper's attention was all on the young wife and mother. Alice Jowatt approved. The new arrival was in her early thirties, Mrs. Jowatt estimated, only a little roundness showing in her trim figure. Good features and dark complexion were noted, but most of all, a confidence and serenity in her carriage that satisfied Mrs. Jowatt that this was a real lady. She hadn't made a mistake in going all out for her.

Going to her own threshold, the hotel keeper greeted the young wife and mother. "You're Alice, and so am I. Pleased to meet you I'm sure!" said Mrs. Jowatt briskly as she pumped the newcomer's hand. "Joe, you sonofagun, why didn't you tell me that your wife was a looker?" Without waiting for a reply she turned to the children and said, "Hello kids, what're your names?"

"I'm Bill, Mrs. Jowatt."

"I'm Ernie, Mrs. Jowatt."

"I'm Margie, Mrs. Jowatt."

"Would you listen to that!" roared Alice Jowatt, slapping her thigh. "If that ain't a sound for sore ears."

Mrs. Jowatt had no idea that her own language sounded incongruous to her newly arrived countrymen. Alice could detect the Liverpool accent, still remaining in the hotel keeper's speech, and she was accustomed by now to Canadian accents. However, Mrs. Jowatt's combination of North Country dialect and North American slang opened a whole new dimension of English to the astonished newcomer's ears. She liked what she saw in her hostess. Obviously kind behind the rough exterior, Alice Jowatt was a sturdy middle aged figure with the craggy face Joe had described. Her blue eyes could blaze at a recalcitrant guest, Alice was sure, but now they were filled with good humour and hospitality.

The newcomer's friendly smile was enough for Mrs. Jowatt. She ushered Joe and the children towards the dining room, but held Alice's arm as she gave the younger woman a conspiratorial look, and asked in a hoarse whisper, "D'you want to freshen up, or anything?"

"No, I'm fine," Alice whispered back.

Luncheon for this day had been arranged several days earlier by the former publisher of the Ferguson *Eagle*. As the family moved into the dining room, two gentlemen at a large table near a window rose to their feet.

Mrs. Jowatt led the family to the table, establishing her position as hostess with an "Eat hearty, folks," before departing for the kitchen.

Joe introduced Parm Pettipiece, and the other gentlemen, to his wife, saying, "Alice, may I present Mr. J.J. Langstaff, the former publisher of the Trout Lake *Topic*." Alice acknowledged the introductions, and the gentlemen bowed as she took her seat.

She was curious about Mr. Pettipiece, the man who had sold his newspaper to her husband. He appeared to be an easy mannered person in his fifties, a little flamboyant in his style of dress, but pleasant and polite to meet. He spoke with an accent which would seem to place his origin as the United States, below the Mason-Dixon line. "Mrs. Atherton. Delighted to meet you," said Mr. Pettipiece with a welcoming smile.

Mr. Langstaff was more typical of the western editors. His black suit was a little rusty and his shirt front, though clean, looked as if it had not been ironed. He, like Parm Pettipiece, put Alice at ease with a smile, and a brief "Ma'am." The children were introduced, the gentlemen gravely shaking hands with Bill and Ernie and bowing to a highly impressed Margie, then they all sat down.

The excellent noonday meal was served by a waitress on her best behaviour, Mrs. Jowatt's unseen presence being sensed by all of the diners. Conversation ranged from questions about the children's reaction to their new home, to enquiries about Alice's trip from Medicine Hat. At the end of the meal, cigars were lit by the men as they pushed back their chairs for comfort. Mrs. Jowatt appeared again, to take the children on a tour of inspection of the hotel and Parm Pettipiece harrumphed nervously once or twice, to indicate he had something to say.

"Mrs. Atherton," he began, "and Joe, I, er . . . um feel responsible for bringing you to Ferguson." He added quickly, "And I'm sure you are going to be very happy here." It was evident that he was not comfortable with what he had to say. "The fact is," he began more forcefully, "I believe I may have misled you people with my invitation to join me here, out of my enthusiasm, or rather hope, for a strong future for this community.

"I'm sure Joe has told you, Mrs. Atherton, that I have been wanting to dispose of the paper for some time. In Joe, I have found a person who has the energy and the skills to carry on the *Eagle*, if anyone can." He paused to gather his thoughts. "There is a possibility," he continued, "that despite Joe's efforts, the state of the economy may be such that the *Eagle* will not survive."

Alice's growing disquiet at the direction of Pettipiece's conversation found culmination in his last statement. It had been too good to be true, she thought, and felt great disappointment. Joe listened to Mr. Pettipiece with bewilderment, but there was no despondency in his mind. He started to protest that he could manage very well, thank you, when J.J. Langstaff spoke for the first time since the cigars were lit. "Parm and I have discussed the situation, Mr. and Mrs. Atherton," he said in his quiet voice, gaining their whole attention.

"We have been fortunate in our businesses since we began publishing our respective newspapers. We came here when both Ferguson and Trout Lake were booming, and fortune has been kind to us." Turning to Joe he said, "You are aware that I retired several months ago, and put my business in the hands of Jim Murray." He paused for effect, and said, "What my friend Parm has said of Ferguson and the *Eagle*, applies equally to Trout Lake and the *Topic*."

Joe wondered where the conversation was going, but held his peace. Langstaff leaned forward to make his point. "Mr. Pettipiece told you, as I earlier told Jim

Murray, that he would accept a note, payable in six and twelve months, for the tangible and intangible assets of his newspaper. Is that right?" and Joe nodded. It was the first time Alice had heard of the buy-out arrangement. Langstaff continued. "Mr. Pettipiece and I have decided to go a step further to assist you, and my successor." He took a deep drag on his cigar and watched Joe through the exhaled smoke.

"If you and Murray find that it is impossible to continue to operate both papers at a profit, we will cancel our individual agreements and draw up a new contract among the four of us, an agreement that will allow you and Murray to continue in business with just one joint newspaper for both communities."

Joe and Alice were thunderstruck. Until these disclosures, both of them were confident that Joe's efforts would result in success for the *Eagle*. While the offer of the two newsmen appeared to be generous and practical for Joe and Jim Murray in the event of failure, the former didn't plan on that eventuality. "Well, personally, I intend to make the *Eagle* a success, gentlemen," said Joe, "but I thank you for your offer." He thought for a moment. "Have you discussed this with Jim Murray?" Parm Pettipiece spoke up, but didn't answer his question directly.

"The offer still stands, Joe. I like your writing, and you are a highly competent printer. I hope the *Eagle* and you are successful." Then, answering the question, he said, "No, we haven't told Jim. We wanted to tell you first."

The former owner of the Trout Lake paper spoke up again. "You understand, Mr. Atherton, should either you or Jim Murray be successful on your own, there will be no question of salvaging the other paper, or the other publisher. He will have to make good his original contract with Mr. Pettipiece or myself." He smiled as he added, "This should ensure that you and Mr. Murray do your damndest — pardon me, ma'am — to keep your own newspapers going."

Alice spoke for the first time. "I'm afraid I know nothing of business, gentlemen, but it seems fair to me. Thank you for your frankness."

Parm Pettipiece slapped the table with his hand. "Done, then!" he said, obvious relief showing on his face after his embarrassed revelations. Joe Atherton certainly had confidence and ability, his wife was a reasonable and supportive lady, and maybe, just maybe, they'd make a go of it.

CHAPTER TWENTY-FIVE

Ferguson, 1904

The two stalwart figures in Lincoln green trudged through the thicket, broadswords sheathed but good yew bows carried at the ready, as their fierce eyes peered into the forest deep for signs of the sheriff's men. Behind them the damosel, none other than Maid Marion, had difficulty in keeping up with them. "Wait for me, Billy," she wailed, bringing the others back to the twentieth century.

"Why did she have to come?" said Ernie, lately Will Scarlett.

"Come on Margie, we'll go a little slower," said Bill patiently. "We're almost there, kid."

The summer was continuing as a new and glorious holiday for the three children. Their memories, apart from the brief winter in Medicine Hat, were largely of city life in England, with occasional short visits to country relatives. The limitless forest, the dozens of hilly trails, and the unexpected sight of an abandoned mine or rude shack provided all sorts of new enchantments for their imaginations.

There were very few other children in Ferguson. None of them lived close by, and the English children were content to range and discover the woods by themselves. Their mother's misgivings gave way, as the weeks went by, and she became used to them disappearing for a whole morning or afternoon. Frequently she packed a lunch for them, and on these occasions they were invariably home by one or two o'clock in the afternoon.

Alice was also enjoying the summer. She suffered no discomfort from the expected child, and the mountain climate in July and August was warm, but never exceedingly hot or close. Reggie was now nineteen months old, and active. He was into everything, and Alice kept doors closed and her best things out of reach. He could be distracted easily when surrounded by pots and pans in dull weather, or by a sand pile in the back yard on a fair day.

The small community she had moved to was much more socially inclined than Medicine Hat. For whatever original reason, boredom, curiosity, or plain sociability, the ladies of Ferguson had called upon Alice, and she had struck up friendships with several. Mrs. Jowatt dropped in frequently, bringing her married daughter, Eveline Daney. The teamster's wife was like Andy, quiet and pleasant. She had an amused admiration for her mother's free and easy style, and was usually an appreciative spectator in her mother's presence. The hotel keeper would regale Alice with stories about the characters who were attracted to the mining communities: the newsmen, who attempted to outdo each other in extravagant nonsense in their papers, and who, when they met together, would try to drink one another under the table; the professional men, doctors and lawyers who restlessly moved from one small town to the next, seeking something they could not find in the cities, and failed to find anywhere else; the clergymen of all faiths, who generally were missioners, appointed by their superiors to attend to the spiritual needs of as many as twenty or thirty mission congregations. These last were dedicated men, quite unlike city clerics, much more ecumenical in their association with one another, and far more forgiving of the sins of their flocks.

Alice Jowatt told Alice and the other shocked but attentive ladies who might be gathered together, of the red curtain districts of Ferguson and Trout Lake, and the shameful antics of the prostitutes and their patrons (the latter being largely unattached miners, she was quick to assure them). Some of the fallen women were known by sight and by name to the respectable citizens of Ferguson, because they boldly came into MacKinnon and Sutherland's to shop for groceries, and for dress materials. These they would inspect for much longer periods than the uncomfortable proprietors would wish. It was Sophia, the madam of the largest establishment in Ferguson, who became acquainted with Alice by accident. It was all Will Scarlett's doing.

Ernie had run ahead of the other children, as they approached the entrance to the abandoned mine that was their favourite play place. In his eagerness to beat the others, he carelessly ran across the rotting boards, which they usually avoided, and Bill and Margie heard his startled cry, accompanied by the sound of cracking timbers and the thud of his fall.

The children didn't notice the approach of the lady who was taking a different route today, on one of her frequent walks along the mountain. She heard the same cry and cracking sounds that galvanized the children into action. She increased her own speed and hurried after them into the mine entrance, and was reassured to see Ernie standing on his feet, eight or nine feet below them, just inside the entrance to the mine. The board platform over the dugout was intact except for that portion which, weakened and rotted by dripping water, had collapsed under the boy's weight.

Margie began to cry and Bill, seeing Ernie appeared to be all right, comforted her. They both turned at the sound of the newcomer's entrance; Margie feeling immediate relief at the presence of an adult, and Bill amazed to see a well dressed lady with a parasol, of all things, in this out of the way spot.

Addressing Margie, the lady matter-of-factly told her, "There, dear, don't worry. We'll get him out," and Margie's crying subsided to a few sniffs and sobs.

"Lend a hand, young man," the lady told Bill, reaching her parasol, handle foremost, to the woebegone Ernie. As he grasped it, the lady gave a sharp tug upward, and Bill was able to reach his brother's upstretched hand. Between them, he and the woman easily pulled Ernie up to the platform edge, and helped him climb to his feet. "You kids come on out of here," admonished the lady, now that the rescue was accomplished.

In the sunlight she surveyed the soiled Ernie, moss and wet earth clinging to his anatomy where it had come in contact with dirty boards and damp ground. "Are you hurt?" she asked.

Ernie, still with traces of his English accent, told her, "No I'm quite all right, thank you."

The lady smiled at the speech, realizing who these children were. Gossip wasn't limited to the respectable homes of Ferguson. "Are you all right, honey?" she asked the now quiet Margie. The little girl was quite dazzled by the efficiency and style of their benefactress.

"Yes, thank you," she said, with a shy smile.

"Well, you had better dust yourself off before you go home, young fellow," she told Ernie, "and keep away from these old diggings, they're dangerous." With a smile at them all she turned to continue her walk.

"Please, I'd like to tell my mother your name," called Bill after her.

Their new friend turned and looked at the children with a quizzical expression. There was both defiance and regret in her manner as she tossed her head and said, "Tell your Mama that it was Sophia that helped you, just Sophia," and, turning on her heel, she left them.

The story came out at suppertime, under Joe's prodding. They had changed their minds and decided to keep quiet about their adventure, fearful of the loss of their freedom, but their father wanted to know all about that day's adventures. Their hesitance made him probe until the whole story came out. They couldn't understand why he nearly choked on his dinner, or why their mother said sharply, "Joe, behave yourself!"

Alice's first reaction to the near accident was anxiety, then annoyance at herself for having exposed the children to the dangers of the mountain. Sensibly, she realized that Ernie's fall might have been a good lesson for them all, and she imposed no strictures upon them. Her second thoughts were of the woman who had rescued them. As a creature of her time and environment, Alice felt about prostitution and shady ladies much as did everyone else in Ferguson. This was the first time the Englishwoman had to regard one of them as a sister being, capable of decent motivation. Gratitude prompted Alice Atherton to precipitate action, astonishing in one of her background and training.

The next day, the town buzzed with the news that Mrs. Atherton had gone calling upon the foremost madam of the largest House in Ferguson. The gossips would have loved to have known what took place between the two women, and would have been disappointed, had they found out. The Englishwoman was asked into the parlor by the children's benefactress, but it was obvious that Sophia wished to make the visit brief. She acknowledged Alice's thanks, but told her that her house was no place "for a nice lady like yourself." Alice had been ready to proffer her friendship, but Sophia did not intend to accept it. She had set her course many years before and, while appreciating Alice's good will, was not about to change her lifestyle one iota for a representative of those she regarded as "the prissy-faced do-gooders" of the town. It was not likely that any sort of relationship could have developed between the two women. Even so, the encounter left both Alice and Sophia a little richer for its being.

Discomfort from the new child was not unbearable for Alice in September, but with an active baby still in the house, she was happy to see the beginning of the school year. Not that the three others were particularly troublesome, but for six hours a day she would know where they were. Best of all, when she put Reggie down, she was able to have an afternoon nap herself.

The Atherton family's entry into the school increased its enrollment from nine children to twelve. Since it was much smaller than their previous school, they were received with friendly curiosity, and soon made new friends. Bill, nearing his eleventh birthday, was assigned to the most senior class the little school had to offer.

In the meantime, Joe had never worked so hard in his life.

Hand-setting the type for a four page weekly paper took a considerable part of his time. As well, he had the full responsibility of searching out news, attending meetings, soliciting and discussing advertising proposals, and writing the articles that were to appear in the paper on publication day, every Thursday.

He didn't feel sorry for himself. This was what he had always wanted; his very own newspaper! And though he laboured far into each night, he groomed the *Eagle* with care, deleting tiny errors and turning out faultless copy. He spent much time and thought on content, his mind busy upon rising and retiring, while he was typesetting, and at mealtimes, preoccupied as he composed the rich phrases and whimsical prose he put into his stories.

The *Eagle* ran on credit. Advertisers paid after publication, subscribers after delivery of their copies of the newspaper. Out of necessity, Joe was also his own credit manager, telephoning the merchants who were overdue in their payments, and walking to the homes of careless subscribers for the purpose of collection. Cash seemed to be becoming a scarce commodity in Ferguson.

In spite of all his efforts, circulation began to dwindle in September, and continued downward in October. Fewer copies were printed each week, yet unsold papers were destroyed each Monday morning. He redoubled his efforts, using his sons more and more in the print shop, after school and on Saturdays. He talked to the merchants, arguing that they should increase their advertising if business was slow. He wrote to large concerns in Revelstoke, soliciting their advertising in the

Eagle, and he courted the drummers he met at the hotels for print notices of their schedules.

By late October it was evident that the approach of winter, temporary or permanent mine closings, departing subscribers, and pessimistic merchants, all spelled the doom of the *Eagle* as an independent newspaper, after four months of dedication and hard physical effort by its publisher.

On the third Friday of the month, the day after the *Eagle*'s smallest circulation ever, Joe swallowed his pride and telephoned J. C. Murray at Trout Lake, and arranged a late afternoon meeting with him. At lunchtime, he told Bill to come into the print shop as soon as school was dismissed to take in any cash or advertising material that might be proffered. He caught a ride with a drummer who was going down to the other town, and got to the office of the Trout Lake *Topic* by four o'clock.

The two editors had met once or twice but, knowing the terms of their former owners, had maintained friendly rivalry and frankly competitive relations. Jim Murray was known as a bon vivant and an entertaining character. Like most of his profession in the small western towns, he had a great sense of humour and a mischievous turn of mind. He loved the company of other good fellows and enjoyed nothing better than an evening of banter and tricks in one of the hotel bars. In other words, he and Joe had much in common, but there the resemblance ended. Jim Murray was short, where Joe was tall. His complexion was that of the black Irish and his hair a shock of unruly dark curls.

Murray greeted his fellow newsman heartily. It didn't need much guesswork on his part to divine the reason for Joe's visit to Trout Lake. Murray himself was going through the same problems as the Ferguson newspaperman, and he felt nothing but relief at the prospect of sharing the load with someone else. "Com in, young feller-me-lad," he called from his desk, then sprang up to shake Joe's hand warmly.

The two editors grinned at one another. Their faces reflected their relief, their awareness of the subject they were about to discuss, and the hope of a mutually beneficial outcome. Of course, they had first to observe and uphold the tradition of all devil-may-care journalists. Joe returned Jim Murray's greeting and handshake, and said, "I've decided to put you out of your misery, Murray, and make a newspaper out of this yellow rag you've inflicted upon the poor people of the Kootenays."

Jim Murray, delighted with this approach, pretended scorn. "How could a benighted Limey like yourself know anything about the great profession of journalism. I understand the London *Times* is still being scratched on a clay tablet."

"My boy," said Joe loftily, "Britain has brought enlightenment by means of its press, to all corners of the Empire, including the savage reaches of Canada." He helped himself to the editorial chair.

"I'll thank you to move to a lower place," said Murray and, as Joe grinned and obliged, the editor of the *Topic* regained his seat. "In spite of your uncanny lack of discernment, Mr. Atherton," he said, "not to say your grotesque mouthings, I am reminded of my manners. Join me in a drink." The amenities thus observed, Murray pulled a full bottle of whiskey and two grimy glasses from his desk. He gave them a quick polish with a piece of clean newsprint, and poured two generous drinks.

"To the confusion of the Kaiser," he said.

"And to the dismay of all banking men," said Joe, and they both emptied their glasses.

Gradually, the men got to the business at hand. They were both more than ready to end the struggle of the past months, and engage in the publication of a single newspaper to serve their two communities. They would have to discuss their plans with Pettipiece and Langstaff, but they already had the prior assurance of those gentlemen that a partnership would be acceptable to the note holders.

They replenished their glasses frequently, as they discussed their plans. Joe agreed to handle most of the printing, while Murray would do the bulk of the writing. Joe was to stay in Ferguson for a month or two, to maintain the continuity of reporting Ferguson news, and to retain Ferguson advertisers and subscribers for the new venture. They would use neither "Ferguson" nor "Trout Lake" in the paper's new title. They would instead refer to the locality as "The Lardeau," hoping this might result in an even wider distribution of their product. To promote Parm Pettipiece's notion of making the newspaper more useful to the mining community, they would call it by the title which he had used. Thus, the newspaper was named. It was a nice ring to it; "*The Lardeau Mining Review.*"

These decisions took longer in discussion than in the telling, and they had to seek inspiration frequently from Murray's bottle of whiskey. In fact, half of a second bottle had disappeared, when Joe looked at his watch to see that it was eight o'clock. "My God, I've got to get home somehow," he said, "Alice will kill me."

As the two men stood, the full effect of the liquor they had consumed hit them. "Don' you worry, m'friend," said Jim Murray. "I'll see that y'get ho . . . home. We're par'ners arn' we?" He nudged Joe. "Arn' we?"

Joe examined him owlishly. This heretofore rival was now not only his esteemed associate in a respectable business enterprise, but a boon companion as well. "Cer'ny we're par'ners . . . an' here's my han' on it, Jim Murray!" They shook hands, and clapped each other's shoulders to emphasize their new relationship.

"Gotta lock th' door," said Jim thickly as they went outside, both being very deliberate in order to present a sober appearance. This was difficult, as they were both nearly falling-down drunk.

By the providence which protects inebriates and fools, the two were able to get home without incident. Jim Murray borrowed a rig, drove Joe home, and got back safely to Trout Lake that night. He slept during the last stage of the journey, as the horse knew the way home.

CHAPTER TWENTY-SIX

Ferguson, 1904

Two miracles occurred before Christmas. They were to ease, for Joe and Alice, any disappointment suffered in the demise of their first venture into independence.

For demise it was. Never again did the *Eagle* soar over Ferguson. The issue, which Joe had distributed just before his decisive trip to Trout Lake, proved to be the *Eagle*'s last gasp of life. Thursday, October 14, 1904, was the final publication date.

It seemed pointless to waste any more money on a final sentimental farewell issue, no matter how tempting that prospect appeared. Instead, a letter to subscribers and advertisers, printed in the form of a dodger, was issued on Monday afternoon, and by Wednesday evening, a copy had been delivered to every house and business in Ferguson by Bill, Ernie and Margie. Copies were mailed to *Eagle* clients and readers at a distance, with the assurance of the editor that a bigger and better newspaper was on the way. All commitments were to be honoured by the new enterprise. Joe followed this up with as many personal visits as he had time for, and his customers, for the most part, were cooperative and supportive of the new venture.

Legal arrangements, and the making of the lead slug for the *Lardeau Mining Review* flag, delayed the printing of the joint effort for almost a month, then on November eleventh, the fledgling paper appeared under its new title.

The *Lardeau Mining Review* was an instant success. No subscribers were lost in Trout Lake or Ferguson, and new advertising clients appeared, to test the worth of the new publication. Production and distribution costs were cut in half, with only one paper to circulate, and the expertise of the partners was revealed in the attractive format of the new paper. It was light and breezy in style, and the readers chuckled over many a paragraph, like the one that appeared in the December ninth issue:

> A strange female of no uncertain age, who visited town on Tuesday
> evening, made herself a general nuisance. She entered the abode of our Joe,

129

whilst that worthy was shaking off the too pressing caresses of La Grippe. The female, who was an utter stranger to our Ferguson representative, was very scantily attired. She behaved in a most indecorous manner, making the night hideous by her piercing screams for a drink, which disturbed the whole neighbourhood. Mrs. Atherton appeared to expect the visitor, who weighs about eight pounds and has a featherless thatch. When she's big enough (and has quit the drink habit) we shall find her a job in the *Review* office. Born on Tuesday, 6th instant, to the wife of J.J. Atherton, a daughter, Winifred.

Hence the first miracle. The new infant, replacing Reggie as the baby of the family, was Joe's and Alice's first little Canadian. She was small and dainty, with blond curling hair, even at this early stage, and she had no difficulty in assuming a firm place in the growing family. Margie was delighted to have a baby sister to play with, while the boys accepted her with casual interest. Reggie was inclined to resentment at first, but was too good natured to hold a grudge. When he found that he was not ignored by the rest of the family, he graciously consented to share his mother's attention with the newcomer.

Alice always did love tiny babies. Even Reggie, now a sturdy two year old, couldn't satisfy his mother's strong maternal response to any minute and helpless infant. Joe passed around cigars, and accepted the good natured raillery of his friends, enjoying the limelight. It was a busy and happy time, and Winifred was not the only early Christmas present for the family.

On the Friday afternoon a week after her birth, the infant had just finished nursing and had been put to bed, when a knock came at the door. Presuming it was one of the ladies of Ferguson arriving with more food or gifts for the baby, Alice opened the door to the second miracle, there on her own doorstep.

Father Jeanotte stood there, shapeless black felt hat in hand, and a rusty black overcoat covering his clerical garb. "Hello, my dear Alice," he said, his eyes crinkling as he smiled at her. He was enjoying her consternation, the young mother's open mouth and wide eyes making his surprise a complete success.

She recovered, to give a delighted cry of "Father! Dear Father Jeanotte!" and, taking his hands, drew him inside. She was tempted to hug him, but one did not hug a priest. Instead, she showed her intense pleasure by her beaming face, and by linking his arm in hers, as she brought him into her front room. "What on earth are you doing here?" she asked, but continued, "Oh, it doesn't matter, I'm so glad to see you!" She took the priest's coat and hat, settled him in the most comfortable chair, and sat on the edge of the sofa near him.

He leaned back and smiled at her, pleased with what he could see. Alice appeared well and happy, and in much more pleasant surroundings than when he had last been a guest in her home. "You are looking very well, my dear," he said.

"Oh, so are you!" she told him happily, "But how . . . what . . . ?"

He laughed again. "What am I doing here? Well, my dear Alice, I haf good news." He savoured his words. "Who do you t'ink is your new pastor?"

"Father!" she said again, unbelieving, "are you telling me that you are going to be situated here, in Ferguson?"

"Not quite," chuckled the old Belgian, "but d' Bishop, he has given me d' missions of Trout Lake and Ferguson for my pastorate." He let this sink in before he added drily, "along with t'irty t'ree others!"

"Oh that's perfectly wonderful! But what about Medicine Hat?"

"'Dey have a new young priest dere," he told her, and peered whimsically at her over the top of his steel-rimmed glasses. "I'm not sure if it's a pasture or a pastorate dey're putting me into." He didn't tell her that the bishop had selected him carefully for the mining towns along the Kootenays, and for the rough mining men of his own calling.

"I'm so happy!" she said. "How often will we see you?"

"Every four or five weeks," he assured her, "and I will be living in Sandon." The town he named was the most notorious of the mining towns of the Kootenays. If any place needed spiritual guidance, it was Sandon.

A thought struck Alice. "You've come at the right time to welcome your newest parishioner into the Church!" With this, she took him upstairs and, with a cautionary finger at her lips, led him past a sleeping Reggie, now in Margie's room, to her own bedroom, where the new baby lay in a much beribboned and lacy bassinette. "This is our Winifred, little Winnie," she told him in a whisper. "Will you baptise her on Sunday?"

A cry from the other room took Alice to Reggie, as the priest called softly after her, "Of course." He followed her to the little boy's room. As Alice picked him up, Father Jeanotte said with emotion, "My little Raitchie," and held out his arms. Reggie gave a startled look at his mother, then a big smile of recognition came across his face, and he leaned over to accept the embrace of his old friend.

Father Jeanotte was quite overcome by the child's reception of him, and for a little while he couldn't talk. He and Reggie beamed at one another in obvious fellowship.

The children came home shortly, and it being Friday, Joe also arrived home early. They all expressed their pleasure at seeing the priest again, by crowding around him, and insisting that he stay to dinner. "Do you know who d' Catholics are in d' towns?" he asked Joe.

"There're the Maddens and Levesques. They're partners in the Lakeview Hotel," Joe explained. "Oh yes, the O'Connors, here in Ferguson."

"The McDonnells," remembered Alice.

"The Groffmans and the Cummins," added Bill, "and Mr. Parisian who plays the violin." Among them, they named a dozen households. Joe and the children volunteered to round the families up for Sunday Mass, and their children for religious instruction on Saturday.

It was like old times having dinner with the priest, and laughing at his droll wit. He wanted to know all about Joe's progress, and showed alternate consternation and elation as he learned of Joe's purchase of the *Eagle*, the decline of the paper, and his subsequent successful partnership in the *Mining Review*. He congratulated them on their nice house, and Alice had to tell him, "I'm afraid it's only temporary, Father. Joe has to move to Trout Lake next month, and we still have to find a house there." She looked around wistfully at her cozy home. "There're not as many nice houses vacant, as here in Ferguson."

The weekend, in Father Jeanotte's good company, went very quickly. The news of his appointment got around rapidly, and he had good attendance at his catechism class and at Mass on Sunday. Mrs. Levesque had a much larger house than Alice, so Mass was said in her big living room, with sliding doors to the dining room thrown open, to accommodate the crowd of about thirty people.

Trout Lake and Ferguson fell in love with Father Jeanotte. His devotion, as he spoke the Latin of the Mass, was apparent to his new congregation; and he delighted the children, and drew indulgent smiles from their parents, in his homily, which he delivered with little humorous asides, and with amusement at his own desecration of the King's English.

For Alice, the Mass was the culmination of her happiest week since leaving England. The arrival of another dainty little girl in a houseful of sturdy boys was reason enough. Gladness and relief, at the initial success of Joe's new venture, was topped off by the unexpected pleasure of Father Jeanotte's arrival in town.

She had been starved spiritually, as well. With no Cahtolic church in Ferguson or Trout Lake, she had missed dreadfully the solace of the sacraments. Joe, like many who are born Catholic, took his religion for granted. Alice, as a convert, had a deeper perception of the Church and its meaning. With Father Jeanotte's appearance, her whole being had responded, not only with warm affection for him as a person, but with a joyous recognition of her spiritual adviser and priest.

The family had all gone to Confession on Saturday evening, and to Holy Communion this Sunday morning. They all experienced the cleansing and healing effects of the sacraments, after their long absence from them. On Sunday afternoon, the priest solemnly baptised the latest addition to the Atherton family, in the presence of her family and many members of the congregation. True to form, Father Jeanotte had his usual difficulty with English. He entered the baby's name in the formal documents to be sent to the capitol in Victoria, not as Winifred, or even the Germanic Winifreid, but as Winefried. In later years, whenever Ernie wanted to plague his baby sister, that's what he called her: "WINE-FRIED."

CHAPTER TWENTY-SEVEN

Trout Lake, 1904-1905

Christmas mail from England added to the pleasure of the family's second celebration of the Nativity, in Canada. It brought the news of Joe's brother Teddy's imminent arrival in Canada, the first of many of his relatives to join them in the new land.

Although Father Jeanotte had celebrated his Christmas Mass in his home parish of Sandon, the memory of his December visit to Ferguson was warm and reinforcing, and Christmas Day the better for it.

Moving, however, was on the family's minds. The distance to Trout Lake was too great for daily commuting, and the start of the new term in the New Year was a good time for the children to switch schools. As well, young Teddy was coming to live with them, and they would need a bigger house.

"Jim, you've got to help me," said Joe. "You know this town better than I do."

Jim Murray eyed this partner airily, as he tilted his green eye shade up on his brow. "Aha! The Fort Steele detachment finally caught up with you, did they now?" He was trying to coax a little heat from the cold barrel stove, the print shop having been unoccupied over the holidays.

"Don't be a damn fool," said Joe sourly. "This is no time for kidding. I've got to get a house in Trout Lake for the start of the school term." Christmas had come and gone, and the printer's crankiness was not entirely due to concern for his children. Scottish Ferguson had celebrated the New Year last night and the partners, with other Sassenachs, had joined the authentic celebrants of hogmanay at the Lardeau Hotel. Neither was at his best this morning, but delicate stomachs and sensitive craniums notwithstanding, a new business and school year was commencing, and the fun and games of the past few weeks were not to be pursued with the same enthusiasm.

Murray looked up from his efforts with the poker and pondered. "Joe, d'you remember The Park? It's just been closed for lack of business. It's between Trout Lake and Ferguson, but too far from either to attract the drummers or saloon trade."

His partner looked at him with disgust. "I don't want a hotel! I want a house. Be serious, man!" The cold room was not adding to his well-being nor improving his disposition.

"Don't be so hasty," Murray soothed. "it's really not a bad idea." He considered the possibilities. "It's not a very big place, so it wouldn't cost a fortune to heat. You could close off rooms that aren't needed, and it's completely furnished." The more he thought of it the more he approved of the suitability of the hotel. "There're not many places that are furnished," he coaxed. He could see that Joe was beginning to waver. "Take a look at it anyway," he urged. "I've got the keys. Why don't you and Alice trot over there, and I'll see what sort of deal I can make." He turned back to the heater. Finally, a little warmth was coming from the coals.

"A hotel?" Even as she put on her coat, and drew a scarf about her head and around her throat, Alice was sceptical of the proposal. The joy of the Christmas season was overshadowed today by the problem of housing, and by one other matter. She could forgive Joe for getting a little tiddly at home as he had on Christmas day, but his arrival at home early this morning was not funny. She had no intention of becoming a shrewish wife, but she had been frightened when he had not come home; then reacted to his eventual arrival with more than a little asperity. He knew her anger was justified and, in spite of his general debility this morning, he was more than anxious to resume good relations. He now hurried to explain that the hotel was Jim Murray's idea, not his.

"It really isn't bad looking, is it?" In spite of herself, Alice was impressed with the exterior of The Park. The ride in the rented cutter, down the steep Ferguson hill, had been exhilarating, and had dispelled most of her annoyance with her husband. He was quick to note her change of mood, and allowed himself to consider the possibilities of the hotel for the first time. By far the smallest of the hotels in either town, The Park was of the same architectural style as Mrs. Jowatt's City, and as new. Its distance from the two towns, which had been its downfall, added to its attractiveness for the young wife and mother. *Why, it's like a private chalet!* she suddenly realized, *but much more convenient. Only a couple of miles from Trout Lake, and within easy walking distance for Joe and the children.* The Park put on its best face, that morning. The sun shone on its icicle-laden eaves, and poured warmth and colour on the heaps of snow banked against its walls. A scenic backdrop of forest and mountain was claimed exclusively by the hotel, as no other buildings marred the landscape. A curl of smoke rose reassuringly from its chimney, as if to take away any aspect of isolation. Most of Alice's resistance melted, in The Park's appeal.

The children, who had ridden in the back of the cutter, were even quicker to acclaim the hotel as a possible home. They jumped out, as Joe handed down their mother, and preceded their parents to the entrance, where Jim Murray awaited them.

"Have a look, but don't make up your mind until you've seen all of it, Alice," he told her earnestly. Like Joe, Murray was somewhat apprehensive of wives this morning, and he was so unlike his usual ebullient self that Alice forgave him immediately. "I've got the heat on," he added, happy to see her smiling upon him, and he turned the key over to them, with the request that they lock up when they had seen the place.

Joe ushered his wife onto the wooden verandah and through the entrance, with its small-paned door and shining brass hardware. The children crowded in with their father, as he carried the baby, Reggie toddling along after the others, and they all stood looking about them, charmed by their first view of The Park's interior. "Wipe your feet," said Alice absently. She was taking in the fireplace against the side wall, not large but welcoming, with its round stone facing and marble mantle. From the centre of the ceiling, a crystal chandelier spilled its light down on the comfortably upholstered pieces grouped around the fireplace, and upon the red patterned carpet on which they stood. A small reception desk in a corner opposite the doorway was not obtrusive, but it caught the eyes of the children as a source of future play and games.

"What do you think of it, Mama?" Joe was careful not to show too much enthusiasm.

"Why, it's very nice," admitted Alice. They followed her to the door behind the desk, which led to a small private sitting room, and beyond to the kitchen. Compared to her last two homes in Canada, the kitchen was immense, and filled to overflowing with the gleaming black and nickel of appliances and the polished copper of pots, pans, ladles, and spoons that marked the professional establishment. It reminded her immediately of that gathering place for servants at Arundel, and she felt deliciously at home. "Oh Joe, let's take it!" she exclaimed.

"Hooray!" shouted Ernie, and the others jumped and yelled their approval.

"Don't you want to see the rest of it?" The hotel had appealed to Joe's sense of the ridiculous the moment he had seen it, and it was now apparent that the notion of having a whole hotel to herself piqued Alice's fanciful turn of mind as well.

"Well, of course!" She tried to make up in brusqueness for the impracticality of her sudden decision. She led the way again, through the small sitting room, which she had already decided would do for a family dining room. "We can close off the big dining room during the winter," she explained.

"Isn't it nice and warm, Mama?" Billy was enjoying his mother's reaction to The Park.

"Of course!" said Joe in recognition. "We have central heat!" Nowhere in England had Alice or Joe enjoyed this luxury; even in Canada their experience with the comfort of central heating had been restricted to public buildings. Jim Murray had laid more than one fire that morning, and The Park, in its welcoming warmth, was slowly but surely capturing the hearts of these latest guests.

Upstairs, each family member could have a separate bedroom. Joe decided that the large one with the fireplace would do well for himself and Alice, and the older children were allowed to choose their own, at the same end of the building. The boys and Margie raced from room to room, changing their minds with each one they found. Margie finally decided on a tiny one that seemed cosiest to her, while the older boys each chose a large and grand room; these were later abandoned for the security of one room and one bed. Until the baby Winnie was able to sleep through the night, her bassinette would remain in Joe's and Alice's bedroom. After that, she would join Reggie in the room next to theirs.

Each room had a comfortable bed and dresser, and its own commode, holding a chamber pot within its small cupboard, and a flowered water pitcher and wash bowl on its top. Toilet facilities were at the end of the long hall, and had to be tried out by each of the children in turn.

Andy Daney moved their personal belongings that very afternoon, using one of his small rigs, and Alice put the older children to work unpacking and settling into their new home. Joe escaped, on the plea of urgent business at the printshop, but he returned at suppertime to find an indefinable change in The Park. The fireplace in the lobby glowed in welcome, and his wife's loving touch had changed the impersonality of the room into a home.

That diminutive altar boy of the wedding in Beccles, twelve years before, arrived in Canada early in the year.

Joe's younger brother, Teddy, now twenty-two years old, was not a great deal taller than when he was ten. He was a good eight inches shorter than his brother, who was one of the few in his family who attained any height, but what he lacked in that direction, he made up in personality. An engaging, friendly sprite, he had a ready laugh and a puckish humour.

But for all his good nature, Teddy was a peppery little fellow, and could speak up quickly in the face of what he felt to be injustice, or behaviour that did not meet his standards. This was the difference in the brothers; where Joe was easygoing to a fault, Teddy was a shade too inflexible.

The young Englishman was engaged to be married, and he had preceded his fiancée, Maude Harold, to Canada, to find employment and make a home for his intended. His advent into Trout Lake society was recorded in the *Review*:

> Theo. C. Atherton has arrived from England, and is staying with the Joe Atherton family. He is looking for a job, and doesn't mind what it is, unless it's wet-nursing; or running a newspaper.

It was a wonderful winter for Joe and Jim Murray. They worked well together, enjoying one another's company in the newspaper office and plant, with each trying to outdo the other in nonsense and tricks. Jim Murray's sense of humour was as stimulating as Joe's, so their days were enriched, as was the quality of their writing for the newspaper.

The partners' lifestyles had improved tremendously with the amalgamation of their two newspapers. They had more money and more time, and if other businesses were suffering reverses, it had no apparent effect upon theirs. If some subscribers and advertisers were a little slow in paying their accounts, it was all to the good, just like money in the bank, with plenty more coming in to cover the pair's salaries and expenses.

There was more than a little resemblance to the story of the Grasshopper and the Ant, in the heedlessness of Atherton and Murray in that first winter of their partnership, and the rousing atmosphere of the mining towns was only a spur to their folly. Teddy Atherton, in the meantime, had neither the means nor the inclination to join his brother in the revelries, and was not present at the affair of the con man in February.

The Payroll Centre saloon, so named for its generosity in cashing miners' pay cheques, was filled that weeknight with a good number of local patrons and a sprinkling of mine employees. The din, as usual, was deafening.

The two newsmen sat, with one of their regular cronies, Ed Bell, in a corner as far away as possible from the noisy bar, but observing the colourful characters it attracted. A group of patrons were clustered around a smallish, vociferous miner, so identified by his rough and dusty clothing and heavy boots. A growth of whiskers, and bushy eyebrows under an ancient, broad-brimmed hat, gave him the look of the typical backcountryman.

"He's a phoney," pronounced Jim Murray.

To Joe's astonishment, Ed Bell nodded his agreement. "Take a look at the people around him, they're on to him."

Sure enough, the men nearest the little miner were straight faced and apparently impressed, as he waved his hands in accompaniment to his urgent speech. Others on the fringe were nudging and winking to attract other listeners to the centre of attraction. Bob Madden, taking a busman's holiday from his own tavern, broke away from the group to join the trio in the corner. "It's an old con game," he told them. "The boys are on to him, but he's buying drinks like mad, so nobody's letting on." Joe looked over at the solemn appearing group around the bar, amazed at their insight.

"He's discovered the mother lode in the diggings he's worked on all winter," continued Bob Madden sarcastically. "Wouldn't you know that the poor fellow now has to go back to Idaho, because his dear mother's dying. Of course, he has to sell the mine for a pittance, the poor dear man!" The Irish hotel keeper shook his head in deep sympathy.

"It's the oldest game in the mining country," said Jim Murray. "I'm amazed that he'd try it."

Another local resident left the group at the bar, to join Joe and his friends in the corner. E.C. Benson, of the Five Mile mine, was laughing as he told of the latest development. "Our friend is really getting carried away now," he said. "He really believes he has fooled the boys, and he's getting careless. For one thing he's drinking too much, and his claims are getting wilder by the minute."

"I wonder if we might just give him a little encouragement?" Jim Murray had a wicked glint in his eye, and the heads of the men in the corner drew closer together across the table, as the editor spoke in low tones. An occasional smothered laugh or delighted slap on the table indicated their ready acceptance of his plan.

Ed Bell and Joe Atherton slipped into the lobby where they enlisted the aid of the proprietor and the desk clerk in their scheme. Madden, Murray and Benson, in the meantime, joined the fringe of the ever growing crowd at the bar. Warnings not to give the game away were whispered, as they gradually worked their way to places on either side of the little miner. He was quick to recognize new victims.

"Hullo my friends!" he cried to the newcomers. "Come and join in my good fortune, and my sorrow." The little man dropped his head briefly, in deference to his mother's condition, then tossed off the remainder of his drink before calling, "Bartender, another round for my friends!"

On the bar in front of him were some exceptionally good samples of high grade ore, sparkling with the evidence of gold, silver and nickel deposits. Benson turned over one or two with evident respect, then he was addressed by Murray. "E.C., I wonder if we were to make an offer for his property, would this gentleman possibly consider . . . ?"

A gleam came to the eye of the little man at the counter. "May I introduce myself," he said. "M'name . . . my name," he said more distinctly, realizing that his tongue was thickening with the drink, "my name is Travers Wilcox. You have ev'nently heard of my situation. Of course, I will not dispose of my c'mplete holding, but since I am not able," he shook his head in regret, "to d'velop the mine m'self, I am willing to dispose of half of it to some party or parties who are know . . . knowledgeable," — a discreet cough here — "and who have the resources with which to, shall we say, enter into a lucrative par'nership."

At this point, the entrance, from the lobby, of the other two plotters caused a little stir, which drew eyes away from the drama at the bar. Ed Bell, selected for his imposing appearance and expensive city tailoring, was accompanied by Joe Atherton who had borrowed a frock coat from the hotel owner. An enormous diamond stickpin in his cravat, and the desk clerk's new and glossy plug hat, gave him an unwonted air of affluence.

For a wonder, the tavern did not erupt in laughter. Guffaws were smothered and faces kept straight, as Joe and Ed Bell made their way determinedly to the centre of action. "Damn!" said Jim Murray, in a chagrined voice, as they watched the approach of the impressive looking newcomers. "It's J.J. and Mr. Bell," he continued. "They must have got wind of, that is, they must have heard of your good fortune."

The group around the bar respectfully made way for Bell and Joe. "Let me come right to the point my friend," said Ed Bell as soon as introductions were over. He leaned on the bar, and hooked his thumb in his vest, carelessly exposing a sheaf of Imperial Bank cheques in his inner pocket. Their presence did not go unnoticed by

Mr. Travers Wilcox. "Mr. Wilcox, I would not think of investing in your mine until I have seen it; but I am willing to give you a substantial deposit, in good faith, of five hundred dollars for an option to purchase." To Joe, he added, "That all right with you, J.J.?" Mr. Wilcox managed to keep his elation hidden.

J.J. considered the proposition very briefly. "Mr. Bell," he said unctuously, "you are the engineer, I am merely a businessman. If you believe that the quality of the ore is such that an investment is indicated, I am with you."

"Hold on!" cried Jim Murray, before the miner could reply. "Shall we have another drink?" he asked the small gentleman, and the con man obligingly nodded to the bartender. "Just a minute," continued Murray. "E.C. and I were talking to this gentleman before you muscled in!" In a conspiratorial tone he said, "Mr. Wilcox, Mr. Benson and I are willing to make a deposit of *one thousand dollars* in earnest of *our* good intentions."

Travers Wilcox's injudicious consumption of liquor was surely his undoing that evening. "Whaddaya say to that, gen'emen?" he asked of Bell and J.J., the drink slurring his words, as he though to close in for the kill.

"Two thousand!" said Bell, as Joe nodded.

"Twenty-five hundred," said Murray desperately, "and that's my final offer!"

"Three thousand," topped Bell. "Done, Mr. Wilcox?"

Travers Wilcox looked at the dejected Benson and Murray. It was evident that they were not in the same class as the others. "Done," he said precisely, shaking hands with his new associates. "I'll see you t'mo . . . tomorrow afternoon, and we'll discuss the perms . . . terms of the purchase."

"Write out a cheque, J.J.," said Bell grandly. "I believe we have made a shrewd investment."

For a moment, Travers Wilcox's eyes narrowed in suspicion, as the "business-man" began to write a cheque for three thousand dollars, drawn on the account of Bell and Atherton, Lardeau Financiers. He was reassured by the obvious esteem in which Bell and Atherton were held, and put the cheque quickly into his pocket.

"Bartender, m'account, please!" and, as he reached for his money to pay the bar bill, it was clear that he was experiencing more and more trouble in preserving a sober front. "Until t'morra, gen'men," he said with difficulty, as he headed for the door.

Joe was close behind him, holding his fingers to his lips for the benefit of the bar patrons. He saw the conned con man clear of the building before turning to the expectant crowd.

"He's gone," he said, but held up his hand to forestall the expected burst of laughter. "Can I interest anyone in shares of a gold mine?" he asked, then the saloon rocked with the pent up glee of Trout Lake's Payroll Centre.

The Imperial Bank manager was told of the incident before the night was over, and was prepared to tell the first customer the next morning, Travers Wilcox, that no account existed for the cheque he tendered. The banker refused to return the cheque to Wilcox, who beat a hasty retreat, more than willing to get out of town without preferring charges against his tormentors.

The facts of the incident were duly reported in the *Review*, and subsequently copied with relish in other journals of the Kootenays. It had the effect of adding to the growing reputation of the two newspapermen as Real Cards, and unfortunately encouraging them to greater efforts of mischief and fellowship, which tended to interfere with more gainful pursuits.

Business in the community had a seasonal improvement with the coming of spring, and the outlook for the mines seemed favourable, with a start being made on the "Big Tunnel Proposition" through the Nettie L. Mountain, by the Reward Mining Company. Atherton and Murray, through the pages of their newspaper, spoke glowingly about the future of the Lardeau, but after two months Uncle Ted, as the children knew Teddy Atherton, still did not have steady employment, and Joe placed another notice for him in the Review:

> T.C. Atherton is a competent plumber and decorator and he is prepared to paint a palace, fix a cesspool or mend a teapot on the shortest notice.

For all the light-hearted optimisim expressed by the newspaper, the inability of a good tradesman like Teddy Atherton to find steady employment should have been an indication of the mining community's continuing decline.

After eight weeks of unemployment, Teddy began losing his good humour, and he became increasingly testy. His unhappiness was understandable; he missed Maude terribly and was no nearer to sending for her. He was good to Alice and found little fault with the children, but took out his ill humour on Joe, criticizing the town, the employment situation, and Joe's casual assumption that the future of the mines and the prosperity of the community were a certainty.

"I shouldn't have come here!" said the little Englishman, bitterly. "I'm no better off than I was in England." They were alone in the printshop at the close of one afternoon in June.

"Now, Teddy, just be patient. There'll be lots of work when the tunnel is driven through." Joe uncorked a bottle from his desk and brought out two glasses which he proceeded to fill, as his brother burst out with the repressed frustration of two months.

"No, you be patient!" he retorted. "You never could see your nose before your face, Joe!" Teddy had gone too far to turn back. "And while I'm about it, you might as well know that I think you're drinking too much!"

"That's none of your goddam business!" The printer was furious at this criticism from a much younger brother.

Teddy stiffened. He had never heard the easygoing Joe react so violently. "Well, it's the truth, and it's time someone told you!" He picked up the jacket he had tossed over a chair. "Anyway, I'm leaving, and if you had any sense you'd get your family out of this town, before you go broke yourself!"

He flung off into the street as Joe leapt after him. "You can go to hell," Joe shouted, "if that's all the thanks I get for trying to help you!" He glared after the retreating back of his younger brother, as an elderly lady passed by the printshop door. A horrified and scandalized expression was her response to the bad language, so with Teddy out of range, Joe had a new target for his displeasure. With a terrible grimace, he stuck his tongue out at her, thrust his thumbs in his ears and waggled his fingers in a juvenile display of temper.

"Well, I never!" she said in outrage, and hurried in the same direction as the retreating Teddy. His action had been unforgivable, and he got little satisfaction from it. He grew more morose as he returned to the shop, and consumed the drinks he had poured for his brother and himself.

CHAPTER TWENTY-EIGHT

Trout Lake, 1905-1906

"You've overreached yourselves, gentlemen!" J. J. Langstaff's tone was as soft as ever, but the words were curt and uncompromising. "When Mr. Pettipiece and I agreed to back you in your joint venture, we certainly expected you to use sober judgement and sound business methods in the operation of the *Review*." The censure raining down upon the partners was long overdue. Only good luck and good times had delayed it, and now their excesses of the winter and spring, combined with an unseasonable decline in business, had brought him to their office.

Langstaff leaned back in the only swivel chair the office boasted, and produced a stogie from an inside pocket without taking his eyes off the partners. Jim Murray had occupied the other chair, and Joe had to stand like a guilty school boy. He didn't like it. While Murray's face wore a look of embarrassment, Joe's wore one of defiance.

"See here, Mr. Langstaff," as his chin jutted out. "We have a business arrangement with you. You are not our employer, and I resent your words and attitude, sir!" It could have been a line from one of his plays, Righteous Indignation being the direction.

Teddy had been gone for a month, and his relations with Alice were cool as a result. He had not accepted her criticisms any more than he had Teddy's, and he wasn't going to accept interference by Langstaff now, by God!

"Take it easy, Joe." Murray looked at the others uneasily; Joe bristling with resentment, and Langstaff calmly, even contemptuously regarding him.

"No Jim, our friend is quite right," he said softly. "I am not your employer, nor your mentor, and you both have the right to go to hell in any way that you care to." His tone lost its mildness and the words became biting and specific. "I hold a note, I would remind you, as does Mr. Pettipiece, against the assets of the *Review*. The first payment on the notes was due in May and you may recollect it is now July. If you are prepared to make the payments in full, and instantly, I will apologize most humbly for my remarks." The retired editor calmly tilted the chair as far back as it would go, dragging deeply on his cigar. He fixed his eye upon a spot on the ceiling, and directed a succession of perfect smoke rings at it. His calm was infuriating.

Joe choked on a tart reply, the import of what Langstaff was saying suddenly very clear. Murray's mouth had dropped open and a look of alarm appeared on his face. "We can collect some of our advertising accounts and past-due subscriptions in a few days," he proffered, but the note holder only looked pained.

"Really, Jim. I have been running papers for years. Since when can one collect a decent proportion of overdue accounts?"

"Perhaps the bank," Joe ventured with less confidence.

"With what collateral?" asked Langstaff in guileless enquiry, and Joe was silent. The other continued. "I take it that neither of you has the wherewithal to pay off your indebtedness." It was a statement rather than a question and the next words were shockingly abrupt. "Mr. Pettipiece and I are as one in this matter. As of now we are taking over the assets of *The Lardeau Mining Review*."

Jim Murray gaped unbelievingly at their creditor, while a turmoil of thoughts went through Joe Atherton's head. This had to be some sort of joke. Why, the paper was his, his and Jim's, in every sense of the word. They wrote it, they produced it. Nobody, during the whole nine months, except themselves, had contributed a nickel's worth of time to it. It was theirs. But, even as he justified his own and Jim's proprietorship, he realized he hadn't a leg to stand on. A nagging conscience also told him that J. J. Langstaff's moral position was unassailable, and that the paper was being lost through carelessness. He felt hollow inside, and wondered dully how the hell he could break this to Alice.

"We have another proposition for you," Langstaff's words interrupted the bleak thoughts of the two newspapermen, and they looked up with a little hope. "But before I tell you what we have in mind, let me point out, gentlemen, just what Mr. Pettipiece and I deplore in your business methods," and the older man proceeded to lash the partners. He blasted them for their careless assumption of prosperity, for their poor handling of accounts, and for their squandering of profits. He castigated them for inattention to business, while frolicking with their saloon playmates, and he threw in some words about their lack of responsibility to their families.

"In justice to you," he told them, "you have produced a newspaper of superior quality, both in its writing style and its composition, and that is the reason why Mr. Pettipiece and I are willing to go a step further with you." He paused briefly as his words gave them heart, but his expression hardened again and they listened meekly.

"You are not children, and I will not mince words. I am well aware of the reputation that newspapermen feel they must uphold, that of the hardest drinking, most cussing, devil-may-care rascals in the country." His glare wiped out their weak grins. "I put it to you that you have been neglecting your business for other, and much too convivial, pursuits. You have also allowed ne'er-do-wells to run up bills against your establishment; and lastly you have rapidly gained the reputation of being a couple of rips!"

His next remark followed immediately and was for Joe alone, causing him to colour with embarrassment. "You, Mr. Atherton, had the bad taste recently to insult a senior member of our community, and a lady at that!" Oh Lord! Any bluster remaining in Joe was successfully dampened by the older man's stinging revelation that his indiscretion was public knowledge. How much did his family know about this?

"What is your proposition, J. J.?" Jim Murray asked of Langstaff, in the silence that followed the scourging.

Surprisingly, Langstaff smiled broadly at them as if his harsh words had never been uttered. "Just this," he said, "I'll take over the management of the paper. You fellows will continue to write and produce it, and do the bullwork of course, soliciting advertsing, collecting accounts, etc., *but under my direction.* I'll pay you each a living wage, until the paper gets on its feet, then if you are still of a mind to own a newspaper, we'll negotiate the terms again!"

He sat back triumphantly in his chair with an expression of delight for their dumfounded expressions, relishing his new role of benefactor. Neither Joe Atherton nor Jim Murray demurred. Sheepishly, they thanked him and agreed to his terms; generous ones, since Langstaff would have to run the business at a loss for some weeks. In his turnabout, the former publisher seemed as anxious to please Murray and Atherton as he had been earlier to flay them.

By August, the names of Murray and Atherton had disappeared from the editorial masthead, as Pettipiece and Langstaff took over the ownership of the *Review.* Publication was uninterrupted, but Joe and Jim Murray, having accepted Langstaff's ultimatum, abandoned the free and easy style of their lives, and of their writing.

During September, indications of a recession were seen, some mines closed down and the *Review* urged optimism; beseeching in a headline, "Stay with your Town!" Throughout September and October, the lighthearted reports of Atherton and Murray-related events were completely missing from the paper, as the much chastened former partners worked as they were directed. On November second, however, with better management turning a profit for the paper, the sun began to shine again upon the two, as their employers relented and allowed them a modicum of leeway. An editorial in that date's issue of the *Review* remarked upon the first anniversary of the newspaper, and a full year of operation, by frontier standards a tremendous achievement. Regardless of ownership, the editorial stated:

Jas. C. Murray still attends to the windy end of the business, while Jno. J. Atherton pursues the various duties of a "devil." We are still withstanding attacks from the sheriff.

This little whimsy was the first indication that the new publisher might permit Murray and Atherton some expression, at least in the matter of content, but his firm grip on managerial and fiscal affairs was not to be eased until the spring.

Alice's home at the foot of the Nettie L. Mountain was not The Briars or The Brambles or The Meadows, like the genteel country cottages of the old land, but The Park. The former hotel, now converted to a dwelling for her family, was never referred to otherwise. As some people affectionately allude to their homes by street number, "One Double O Five" or "Fourteen Ten", or as others refer to their summer places as the Cottage or the Cabin, Alice always called her home The Park. She and her family went home to The Park. Papa was late getting home to The Park. She invited her friends to The Park. She had loved it from the beginning, and sitting on the wide verandah to enjoy the Lardeau spring was just one more delight the home afforded her. Now everything was so marvellously alive!

Their two winters in the Kootenays had been so unlike the one in Medicine Hat. Outside, it had been as cold, but inside, cozy fireplaces and a big coal furnace had given winter comfort. It had been scary, too. The hotel was remote from the town, and all sound had ceased after the snow descended on the forest and streams trickled to a stop. The silence had awakened her at night, the very stillness having a frightening quality; a menace that had made her move close to her sleeping husband, listening for sounds that never came.

But if the mountain slopes behind the hotel had been silent in recent months, now they were exploding with sound as the snows and ice and frozen cataracts were released from the grip of winter. A month ago, a warming sun had sent the first drops of icy water swelling together, until they became a myriad of tiny streamlets seeking their way to the lower levels of the mountain. Encountering one another on the forested slopes, the streams had swollen in size and clamour, hurling themselves down the mountainside, until now, at lake level, their first faint murmurings had become a deafening torrent of sound.

The noise would lessen as the seasons progressed, but, for the moment, she embraced it; enjoying the tumult as a welcome change from the winter's white silence. By now, she was accustomed to the thunder of the streams, her sleep undisturbed, and in her waking moments, the sound was only a pleasant accompaniment to the harmony of her days.

The month that had seen the angry leave-taking of young Teddy, had not been so tranquil. Joe had felt the weight of her displeasure, a condition to which he was not accustomed. Not until Teddy wrote from Calgary, happily and without constraint, to tell them he had found employment in his trade with the C.P.R., did Alice relax her stiffness toward Joe. The episode of his insult to the old lady had, fortunately, not come to her attention, and with Langstaff riding herd on the two mavericks, Joe had shown more prudence in his social habits. He really was a good man, she told herself fondly, just a little too carefree at times.

From inside the hotel, over the sound of the rushing streams, she heard whoops of delighted laughter coming from her two youngest children, and wondered briefly what they were up to. She was not really concerned. Reggie, still too young to go to school himself, was getting big enough to keep an eye on his year and a half old sister, Winnie.

Soon, the other children would be home from school. The spring sun was warm, buds were bursting everywhere, and pine and cedar scents from the forest hung in the air. Most of the birds had returned from their winter vacations in the south, and their mating songs were heard above the sounds of the creeks.

Life was good, and after two years in the Lardeau, Alice knew she would be content to stay here forever.

She could see him running down the road like one of his own children, waving his hat in exuberance, and shouting something that was lost in the racket from the creek. She stood up, as he ran on to the low verandah, and was immediately yanked off her feet in a bearhug embrace, while he twirled her around three times. "Put me down!" she gasped, but noted with pleasure that his big infectious grin was back, as if to stay. It had been replaced in recent months by a sober expression, befitting a serious business man, and she couldn't help but feel that the old look was more becoming. She hugged him back. Peace, harmony and security were all very well she decided, but the Joe of the past few months was not the man she had married. "Well?" she asked, as she straightened her skirt, "What have you been up to?"

"We-have-the-newspaper-back, Trala!" he sang, to the music of *The Mikado*, and he capered accordingly on the porch.

"Oh Joe, how wonderful, how . . . when did it happen?" This was indeed great news, and Alice's own eyes glowed as she shared her husband's delight.

"We're going to cel-e-brate, Trala!" he chorused and did an impromptu do-si-do the length of the verandah, until she grabbed him and pulled him into one of the porch chairs.

"That's enough of your nonsense," she said firmly, "Now tell me what this is all about." He relaxed, leaned back in the chair, and let out a long pleased sigh.

"Well," he explained with satisfaction, "Mr. Langstaff came to see us this afternoon, and told us he was ready to sign another contract with us, if we wanted."

"And you both accepted!"

"Like a shot! Jim is just as happy as I am, and we're determined to continue to run the *Review* at a profit." He was sober for a split second. "We've learned a lot from old Langstaff." Excitedly, he revealed all the details of the arrangement, very much like the first, and with the former partners once more in complete control.

"Mr. Langstaff was pretty complimentary, and pleased too!" he said jubilantly. "So much so, that he is taking off for the States this week; feels he doesn't have to worry about us."

"I'll bet the Murrays are pleased."

"They sure are, which reminds me, the celebration! The four of us are going to a party next week." He was tickled with her glad response. "It's the At Home next Friday at the Oddfellows Hall. The Anglican Church Ladies Guild is sponsoring it. There'll be dancing and other entertainment. Jim and I have been asked to do a turn."

"How nice!" Then she asked, with some apprehension, "What will you do?"

"Haven't decided yet," he said carelessly. "We'll think of something."

The celebration was hardly on a par with some of the town's more intemperate revels, in which Murray and Atherton might have indulged; but in the new spirit of righteousness which they had assumed, as family men and examples to the community, they did allow themselves a little Good Clean Fun.

Alice felt as if she had not danced for years. She laughed until she was weak at the extravagant nonsense exchanged by her husband and Jim Murray. While she danced with the latter, he confided that he had always been passionately in love with her. "I suggest that we elope this very night," he told her, with no effort to lower his voice. "We won't take the rig," he explained, "just two of Andy Daney's great beasts. That way, there'll be more room for the children." He explained how they would all ride astride, he and Alice and the baby on one steed, and the rest of the Atherton children on the other. "Each child can carry a nosebag, for himself or for the horse, whichever he chooses."

"What about your own children?" she asked.

"Hmm, that's right! Forgot about 'em for a moment. Well, if you don't mind waiting until they're grown up . . . ?"

"Certainly not!" she assured him sweetly. "I'll wait forever!" and she batted her eyes at him.

Later that evening Professors Notrehta and Yarrum gave an exhibition of legerdemain and mystery. The pseudonyms did not fool any of their audience, any more than did their turbans and darkened faces, or their absurd mind-reading performance.

It just whet Joe's appetite for applause, and at the end of the month, he was quick to respond to a request that he appear in another evening of entertainment. This was for the Victoria Day concert, in which he sang a duet with a young lady named Miss Hoe, did a solo number of "John Peel", and performed a shadow display of animals behind a sheet hung on the stage. If that were not enough, he took part in a one act farce entitled *A Precarious Predicament,* and wound up the evening singing "Larboard Watch" in a duet with his oldest son. It was an embarrassment of riches for Alice. She said nothing though, knowing that her husband needed a constant outlet for his enormous vitality. Much better, she thought, than having the gaming table, or a roving female eye, competing for his attention. Besides, he *was* entertaining.

On Dominion Day, it was the turn of the Catholic ladies of the Altar Society to produce a concert. In additon to the expected patriotic songs and recitations, an

148

ambitious farce entitled *Betsy Blue* was presented, to a full house at the I.O.O.F. hall. Alice, for once, was not a spectator; the cast of characters included her name:

Marmaduke Mouser (in love with his wife)	J .J. Atherton
Mr. Crummy (Mouser's partner, with a plot)	P. E. Groffman
Betsy Baker (in the plot with Crummy)	Miss Susy Cummins
Mrs. Mouser	Mrs. Atherton
Robert	Master Billy Atherton

The *Review* said later of Alice, that as Mrs. Mouser she had well sustained the part. Damned with faint praise, thought Alice philosophically, not aspiring to stardom on the stage or elsewhere. Nevertheless, people crowded around her, at the dinner and dance that followed the performance. Margie was the chief among her fans, bringing up her friends, and basking in the light of her mother's reflected glory. Mrs. Jowat came by with Eveline and Andy Daney to congratulate her.

"Alice, you looked purtier than a roast beef dinner on a Friday!" She roared with laughter at her own humour and commented, "Ain't that a corker for an Altar Society party?"

Andy looked shyly at Alice, and told her, "We didn't know there was another performer in the family, Alice. You're the best of the bunch!" Having said this, he left hurriedly, his face red with embarrassment at his boldness.

Eveline didn't mind. "Andy's a big goose," she laughed, "but he thinks that you are very special, and so do I." With which, Eveline Daney smiled broadly at Alice, and followed her husband and mother through the crowd.

CHAPTER TWENTY-NINE

Trout Lake, 1906

Mr. Shannon was Trout Lake's lone educator. He ruled the lives of some twenty children, aged from five to thirteen, and in classes from the First to the Fifth. He taught with a polish and skill that was admired by the parents and respected by the students, but, as good a teacher as Mr. Shannon was, the Fifth class was the highest the little British Columbian town could afford, and the graduates of 1906 were far from possessing a secondary education.

Billy's early start in English schools had given him a year's advantage over his classmates. At twelve, the boy was still the source of his mother's greatest pride. He was wiry, like his father, but the man to come could be detected, an even sturdier and taller version of Joe. In temperament he was like her, reflective and observing, rather than precipitate and headstrong like his father, and his sensitivity was purely Alice's.

Billy's final report card lay on the dining table, under the light of the tulip shaped lamp fixture. "Isn't it marvellous!" Joe crowed, as the couple pored over it. "Look at some of the comments, 'better than average grasp of subject matter,' 'competence in analytical reasoning,' and look at this, 'well adjusted, shows leadership capability!' Hey, mother, we have a genius on our hands!" There was no hiding his glee; but Alice's own pride was restrained by another emotion. She pointed out the last entry.

He adjusted his glasses, the better to scan the paragraph; with a little twisting and turning the words came into focus. "If it is possible for Billy to continue his education, I would strongly recommend it. He has the capacity for study, and I believe, the interest." Mr. Shannon's crisp initials punctuated the remarks.

Joe did not notice his wife's expression. "Isn't that great, mama? By gosh, we'll have another educated person in our family. Maybe we can even get him into a Jesuit school like his Uncle William, or St. Mary's High School in Calgary..."

"Joe," Her soft interruption went unheeded, as he continued to dream.

"...or the Christian Brothers' School in Vancouver!"

150

"Joe!" she said, a little more loudly, and finally got his attention. "There's the matter of tuition and board," she reminded him. "You're not thinking of applying for needy scholars' assistance, are you?"

"I hadn't even thought of *that!* Why, we'll get the tuition together." He brushed the impediment aside, as always. Practicality was his wife's long suit, not his.

She did not relish the role of spoiler; her dreams for Billy were as great as his own. She looked at her husband with affection. Joe would have blithely chosen one school or another, and worried about the consequences later. She, however, knew that their income just would not stretch to cover board and tuition for one privileged child, out of five.

"Maybe conditions will improve next year, Joe," she said hopefully, and then, as a thought struck her, "In the meantime, what about the printshop?" With this, she brought him back to reality.

"Well, of course, it's an education in itself, mama," he told Alice. "School subjects like grammar and spelling are needed in our trade; yes, dictation and composition as well." Joe grew enthusiastic. "Matter of fact, the printing business can develop skills quicker than anything else." On reflection, Joe was just as keen to apprentice Billy as he had been earlier, to pack him off to school. "Journalism is a great profession too," he continued. "If he can write *and* print he'll never go hungry."

His tone of conviction did much to restore her own equanimity. If Billy was to be deprived of his opportunity for a higher education, temporarily or otherwise, then training in his father's calling seemed to be a reasonable alternative. "Let him have the summer though, Joe." Wistfully, she reflected, "We're making a man of a child, one who hasn't yet had his chance at boyhood."

So Billy had his summer.

And what a wonderful, golden summer it was! The boy led his brother, Ernie, and young Carson Murray, as he roamed the slopes and the glens of the Nettie L. Mountain, playing the roles of Henty's and Scott's magnificent heroes. His speech, throughout the summer, was laced with *prithees*, and *by my halidoms*, and *methinks*.

When he tired of the mountain, the lake always beckoned. He and his companions built a raft, and poled it along the reedy shores. They went swimming in the secluded pools, out of sight of the town, and lay in the tall grasses after, speculating on the adventures they would enjoy one day, in the vast world beyond the mountains.

He captained their raft out to the pile driving barges, and his crew begged great wedges of apple pie and cheese from the indulgent Chinese cooks of these craft. The boys were always on hand when the steamer docked on its semi-weekly visits.

On the second Saturday of August, they were at the dockside when the familiar cry, "Here she comes," went up, and the C.P.R. vessel poked its bow around the bend in the lake. As it came fully into view, thick smoke poured out of its single stack, and a frothy veil of water churned in the wake of the slowly turning paddle wheel at the stern. Father Jeanotte was due today, and the youth of Trout Lake would vie for the honour of bearing his luggage. In the year and a half that the big Belgian priest had been visiting his missions in the Kootenays, his popularity had grown with townsmen and miners alike, with all ages, and people of every religious persuasion.

As the steamer headed toward the dock, he could be seen at the railing, his black suit and commanding figure standing out against the light summer clothing of the other passengers. When the gang plank was put into place, the boys, at least ten of them, rushed forward in the usual competition to reach the clergyman first. Billy and Carson were among the largest and fleetest of the youths, and each possessed himself of a piece of luggage. Ernie, slighter in build, was knocked into the side of the gang plank, where he sustained a gash on the side of his knee from a rusty bolt. He aimed a kick at the offending bit of metal, managing to get a sore toe in the bargain.

The parade of clergyman and boys went up the street toward the hotels, greeting friends along the way. Miners, enjoying a Saturday afternoon off, called out hellos from the doorways of the taverns, and waved from the bench outside the barber shop, where they waited their turn for a bath or a haircut.

Father Jeanotte favoured the lodgings run by Levesque and Madden, so he paid off his luggage bearers there, with the token fee permitted by the boys' parents, and went up to his room, to brush away the dust of Trout Lake's main street.

At The Park, preparations for Sunday were under way. As well as all the sponging and pressing and starching and ironing of the family's best outfits, for the morning service, seven baths had to be taken before nightfall.

Bill and Ernie arrived home just as Margie had finished hers, and were next in line. They were allowed one tub full of clean water between them and to save time they bathed together, there being plenty of grime to be removed, after a blissful but grubby week on the mountain and at the wharves. Ernie was still cranky as he towelled himself, telling his brother to be careful of his sore leg.

Alice was tired after the day's activity, and not looking forward to the card party she had arranged in honour of Father Jeanotte. She felt better after bathing and dressing, and with guests arriving shortly after, she had no time for weariness. The priest came with Madden, the hotel keeper, and his wife, while Doctor and Mrs. Robinson brought with them Miss Hoe, to make up the second table of whist.

Alice's busy day caught up with her in the form of drowsiness at the card table and, fight it as she might, she fell fast asleep midway through the evening.

The other players gradually fell silent, as they watched her with embarrassment, and with even greater fascination. Her sudden awakening, in a churchlike silence, and with a clergyman present, brought a perfectly natural response from her; she piously made the sign of the Cross.

Joe led the friendly laughter, his, a hoot of delight and the others more forbearing. Her apologies and the guests' gentle teasing were both silenced abruptly by the scream of pure anguish that rang down the stairs. It was followed by boyish voices raised in altercation, and Alice excused herself and hastily mounted the stairs.

Her initial panic subsided. Ernie and Billy, in their nightshirts, were confronting one another; Ernie hopping on one foot and nursing his sore leg. "I told you to be careful!" he accused, half crying with pain.

"I tell you I didn't mean to touch it." Contrite and anxious, Billy would have avoided involving his mother. As the oldest, he felt it was up to him to keep peace in the family.

The sore leg was news to Alice. "What's this all about?" she said severely. "What's the matter with your leg, Ernie?" The gash was quite deep and had broken open again when, in his sleep, Billy's thrashing foot had banged against the sore knee. It was angry and swollen around the lip of the wound. "Why didn't you tell me?" she scolded, and she called down the stairs for Doctor Robinson.

The physician was intent as he probed and cleansed, causing young Ernie to cry out in pain. "Sorry, young fellow," he said, "we don't want blood poisoning, do we?"

He finished with iodine and a dressing, and gave the boy a dose of laudanum to help him sleep. Then, with a reassuring word to Alice, he joined the other guests downstairs in an early departure. Billy was all the more conscience-stricken at the evident concern of the adults.

There was no Mass for Ernie the next morning. He was ill and irritable and Alice kept him in bed, poulticing his wound throughout the day. On Sunday evening, his skin was dry and his breathing laboured; the treatment had clearly not confined the infection to the wound. By midnight, he became delirious with fever, awakening most of the family. He had been put in a bed by himself, but his wild cries and tossing about brought Joe and Alice on the run.

They took turns sitting with him throughout the night, applying cold cloths until the fever broke at dawn, drenching the boy with sweat as he dropped off into a deathly still sleep.

Billy felt terribly alone during the three days of his brother's illness. He couldn't avoid his own part in this. After all, he was older, he should have reported the accident, and it was he who had kicked open the wound. Worst of all, the finely tuned accord with his mother was missing.

Mercifully, he was unaware that his mother's exhaustion and anxiety were triggering another ordeal for her.

It was Tuesday afternoon, before Ernie could be considered out of danger, when Doctor Robinson lanced the festering sore and removed the worst of the poison which had gathered there. It was only after the doctor had left them, that Alice gave in to the first of her sick headaches, or "megrims," as Doctor Robinson was to call them. With the letdown, she felt an unusual depression; her vision became blurred and vertigo assailed her. Then, as she closed her eyes, a spot of light grew in her vision until it exploded in a flash of brilliant colour. The pain began.

"Get the doctor back, Billy," she managed.

As she staggered, Billy saw the colour drain from his mother's face, and her features become drawn with suffering. He was near panic, but reacted instinctively to her command. As he pounded down the road, he got a grip on himself, even as the weight of responsibility increased.

The doctor had not quite reached home when Billy overtook him, and they returned on the run. Alice had managed to get to her bed, and lay as quietly as she could, each movement seeming to be a hammer blow to her aching head. Doctor Robinson satisfied himself that she was not experiencing some kind of cardiac attack, and quickly diagnosed the seizure for what it was. The only treatment that he could prescribe was the taking of aspirins in massive doses, and the constant application of cold cloths by Billy, to his mother's forehead. His reassuring and parting words to the youth went unnoticed, as Billy began his vigil.

The pain of the migraine began to withdraw after two hours had passed. It happened after Alice became violently and suddenly ill, vomiting into the cold cloth basin beside the bed. As the boy watched, his mother's face became more peaceful. Most of the anxiety and guilt lifted from him, as she smiled with her old intimacy. Then she fell into a deep sleep.

He tiptoed out of the room to meet his father, who had just come home. Doctor Robinson had been unable to find Joe at the printshop, as the newsman had gone with his friends for a before-supper drink, which had extended to two hours of conviviality. Joe was not tipsy, and any pleasant effect of the liquor which remained, vanished as Billy told of his mother's illness.

The week had been one of growing up for the boy. The dread that he had felt at the onset of his mother's pain, coupled with the anxious hours of waiting beside her, brought him to the mature realization that his mother was not invulnerable. He also, for the first time, recognized in his father a strain of irresponsibility, and came to the understanding that he, Billy, would have to compensate for some of his father's shortcomings. He felt no resentment, and would continue to respect and love his father for his obvious good traits, but from that moment on he accepted a degree of accountability usually associated only with adulthood.

Billy's golden summer was over.

CHAPTER THIRTY

Trout Lake, 1906

The oldest son's future was one of several factors in considering the resources of another town in the Kootenays.

Only forty miles away from Trout Lake and Ferguson, but with a whole mountain range and a day's travel by rail separating it, was the mining community of Sandon, British Columbia. It had been founded early in the final decade of the nineteenth century, and had no rival for its reputation as the wildest of the towns along the Kootenays. Staid towns like Ferguson and Trout Lake had their taverns and red curtain districts, but only as a narrow fringe of wickedness skirting the areas occupied by the upright and God-fearing. Sandon's carousing ways, on the other hand, had been encouraged by twenty-three saloons in the heart of town, and over one hundred ladies of the evening. By the late summer of 1906 these figures could be halved, but since the place boasted only one house of worship, Sandon's forces of evil still offered an almost unobstructed road to perdition.

As many as ten thousand people had crowded the banks of Carpenter Creek and what was to beccme Sandon, in the wake of the initial discoveries of silver, lead and zinc. Nowadays, its population was less than three thousand, and steadily declining, due not only to a decrease in mine productivity, but also to the series of disasters that struck the town.

On several occasions, it was nearly washed away by a rampaging Carpenter Creek, and with annual regularity, avalanches, landslides and forest fires took lives. Only six years previously, Sandon's business district of fifty buildings had been completely destroyed by fire, said to have started in the dressing room of the town's opera house. The play that night, aptly enough, was named *The Bitter Atonement*.

Despite the town's shortcomings and catastrophes, one inhabitant of Sandon, like the biblical patriarch Abraham, continued to believe in his wayward community. Johnny Harris, a man with a tiny frame and the vitality of a giant, was the town's founder. A Virginian by birth, he had come from the mines of Idaho early in the Nineties, following the lure of gold and silver strikes in the north. At age twenty-eight, Harris had travelled by rail to Nelson, thence thirty-five miles by canoe to New Denver, from where he hiked along the Sandon River to its tributary, Carpenter Creek. Within days of his arrival, he uncovered a richly promising vein of silver, and Johnny's love affair with the area began.

Unlike most prospectors, Johnny Harris developed into an astute businessman. Instead of squandering the limited wealth of his claim, he used it to buy into other rich mines and to invest in the businesses that quickly sprang up, as the big syndicates began to develop the mines of the area. Before the end of the century, Sandon had two schools, a three-storey city hall, a brewing company, a cigar factory, two newspapers, and two railroad companies vying for the right to transport the ore produced by the mines. Johnny built the luxurious Reco Hotel, named after the largest producing mine in the area, also owned in part by him, and operated the Harris Power and Light Company to his own advantage, and to the benefit of townspeople and the mines.

If the town was presently suffering some reverses, its short, sturdy founder, at the age of forty-two, was as sprightly as on the day he hiked into the site of the future Sandon. His love of the town had never diminished, in spite of the number of times it had betrayed him. He continued to boost Sandon for all his worth, even as the principal means for this was lost to him. The *Sandon Miner* and its rival, *The Paystreak*, had both fallen victim to the town's recession and now *The Standard*, their successor, was closed, and the press dismantled and taken away.

A lesser man might have admitted defeat, but Johnny Harris was determined to get himself a publisher who would, once again, produce a journal to advertise the sterling qualities of his town, and to become the symbol of respectability he desired for Sandon. It was this pressing need that had brought him to Trout Lake, where he had heard, there were not one, but two, qualified printers and journalists.

"Alice, may I present Mr. Johnny Harris."

The sound of the outer door opening had brought her to the lobby of The Park from the kitchen, wiping floury hands on her apron. She held one out in greeting, to the elf of a man standing in the lobby with Joe. "How do you do, Mr. Harris?" Her welcoming smile and handshake were warmly returned by the visitor. They appraised one another briefly. He saw an attractive woman, face rosy from her baking activity, but not perturbed by the entrance of an unexpected guest. "Do sit down, Mr. Harris," she said. "I'm afraid that you've caught me unaware." Her smiling composure refuted the polite protest, and as she saw that the visitor was still standing, she sank into an upholstered chair, and motioned Joe and Mr. Harris to the settee facing her. The visitor's feet did not quite reach the floor.

"Your home is most charming, ma'am," he told her, in a surprisingly deep voice. He was a person one could be at ease with, thought Alice. Kind, smiling blue eyes in a round, dark complexioned face, a noticeably short figure still well muscled, and scrubbed hands, knotted from the work they had once been used to.

"Thank you." She appreciated the comment, since visitors to The Park usually remarked upon the novelty of turning a hotel into a home, and only belatedly complimented her on its pleasant atmosphere. "We are very happy here," she told him.

The two men exchanged a look at this remark. "I would hope that you could be persuaded to leave it, ma'am," Harris said, and Joe, seeing her startled look, plunged in with an explanation.

"Mr. Harris is a resident of Sandon, and a businessman with wide interests. To put it briefly, Alice, he has offered me an opportunity to start a newspaper there!" He looked at her eagerly.

The words were plain enough, but she couldn't quite believe their significance. "Start a newspaper?" she said. "In Sandon? Do you mean to get one going, put it on its feet . . . ?" But that wouldn't require her to give up The Park, and she realized with consternation that Joe was talking about a brand new venture; another move, with all its uncertainties, a new home, a new school, and new people to become accustomed to.

"The idea takes getting used to, Mrs. Atherton." Johnny Harris's words were sympathetic and his tone gentle, but considerate though he was of her dismay, he recognized in the young woman a strength of character which he possessed himself; a strength that had pried him away from home and family, so that he might progress and build a better life. He had no scruples about giving these people the opportunity of making their own fortune.

"It's a good offer, mama!" said Joe eagerly. "Mr. Harris is willing to provide the plant and premises on a buy-back basis, and we'd be on our own again, but this time in a much bigger community!"

"But why us?" Her thoughts were still in a turmoil, and there was much to be explained.

"Maybe I can tell you," Harris said. He had walked into the printing office that morning, when only the Englishman had been present. He had no preconceived opinion of either Atherton or Murray, and had simply put his proposal to the one available, after a quick appraisal of the man. The suggestion that his prospect's wife be included in the conversation arose out of his own interests. A family man, well and truly supported by a good wife, was the best bet for the kind of investment he intended. He had not been disappointed in what he found. "You and Mr. Atherton have not been established in Trout Lake as long as the Murrays," he told her with a smile, "and you may be a little easier to persuade to move," He paused briefly, and added with honesty, "I must admit too, that Mr. Atherton is the only one of the partners I've talked to."

"Then surely you will talk to Mr. Murray also?" she said, with a little sense of reprieve.

"Not if you and your husband accept my proposal," he told her firmly. He had already made up his mind. Joe Atherton was the younger of the partners, keen and likeable, and capable as a printer, by reputation. Meeting Alice confirmed his decision. "Let me tell you of some of the advantages we can offer in Sandon," and he proceeded to tell her about Sandon's Miners' Union Hospital, the only medical facility in the Kootenays; about the town's businessmen and professional men, all of whom could be expected to support a newspaper; Sandon's fine school, and most of all he stressed that her husband would be on his own, and in a much larger community than Trout Lake.

"Doesn't Sandon have a disreputable image, Mr. Harris?" The selling points had been well made, but she was far from convinced. Johnny Harris was only momentarily confused by this direct question.

"Yes, it has, Mrs. Atherton." He didn't duck the question. "Yes, there is a poor element in Sandon, as in every mining camp. I guess we even deserve the reputation of being the worst of the towns around here in that regard." Johnny's pride and faith in his town always made him look on the bright side. "At the same time, ma'am, the only way we are going to improve is by bringing in good families like your own. Eventually, you'll drive out the gamblers and, er, other shady characters." He was so earnest and zealous for his pride and joy, that she had to smile.

"I doubt that it's the best place to bring up children," she demurred.

"Ma'am," he told her admiringly, "I'll bet you'll bring up a good family in any climate or condition. Takes more than a good town to make fine folks."

She and Joe continued to talk through the rest of the day and evening, after Johnny Harris had gone back to his hotel. Some of the arguments for moving were valid, but she wondered how much of Joe's eagerness to accept the offer was due to his inborn restlessness, and how much to the acknowledged good opportunity for advancement. She was torn between her concern for the children in such a move, and what her refusal might mean to her husband. She thought, as well, of the friends she would have to leave, and The Park, but dismissed these sentiments as selfish and unworthy. There was a new factor too; one which she had not yet discussed with Joe. It seemed certain now that she was to have another child the following spring. If the family did move, they would be established in the new town, which had a hospital, before the baby came. Not that she would go to the hospital for the delivery — all her babies had been born at home — but hospitals were a tremendous comfort in times of emergency, and she remembered Ernie's illness from blood poisoning, that summer, with a little shudder. She counted the moves they had already made, since their marriage thirteen years ago. *Six! We are a lot of gypsies,* she told herself wryly. Yet the good times had outweighed the bad, and they had made satisfactory progress, even if it seemed at times like two steps forward and one step back.

The eternal optimist in Alice won out.

Billy! If he were to have the opportunity to learn the printing trade, he could do no better than in his father's own shop. He would be a great help to Joe as well. In establishing a new business, there would be lots of work, even for a novice. Maybe some day he would even own a newspaper himself.

Father Jeanotte, she suddenly remembered, made his headquarters in Sandon. They would see him more often, and the children would get to know him better. Joe himself would be happier and, maybe, do better on his own. He and Jim Murray might even prosper a little more quickly outside the sphere of one another's influence.

CHAPTER THIRTY-ONE

Sandon, 1906-1907

There were no second thoughts for Joe. Having his wife's blessing, he left for Sandon within days of Johnny Harris's visit to Trout Lake, taking young Billy with him.

His parting with Jim Murray had been amicable enough, Jim agreeing that the split would improve their individual situations. They made many protestations of friendship and vows to keep in touch, but neither was unhappy to see the end of the brief association. There was too much similarity in their natures for a successful business arrangement. J. J. Langstaff also, returning from his vacation in the U.S.A., had declared himself content if Murray was satisfied, and the good wishes of the *Review* owners were cordially expressed in the news item that told of Joe's departure for Sandon.

He and Billy stayed at Harris's Reco Hotel, with the understanding that a suite of rooms above an office building would be available for the family, when the others arrived in a couple of weeks' time. In the meantime, Joe and Johnny Harris negotiated with Bob Edwards, the Calgary publisher, for a printing press and several cases of type. While they waited for this equipment to arrive, the pair swept and washed out the old *Standard* printshop and patched up the few pieces of furniture that it contained. The printing equipment arrived within a week, as did stocks of newsprint, ink and good paper bond for finer work. The *Sandon Standard* was reborn.

The type was fairly new, but the press was heavy, ancient, and impressive in appearance. A relic of the boom towns of the California gold rush of '49, it had a heavily embossed iron head piece, which proclaimed that its manufacturers were "Palmer and Rey, Press Dealers and Founders, S.F., Calif." In circles below the raised letters were likenesses of Franklin and Gutenberg in bas relief. The sculpture served to illustrate a lesson in the history of printing, as Bill began his apprenticeship.

The action of the press was ponderous, but its turning wheel was well balanced and Bill could handle it without too much trouble. He learned the knack of using

159

its momentum to best advantage, switching from one hand to the other, as his arm tired. Eventually, he and his father would divert the water of Carpenter Creek into a small mill which would rotate the press through a form of hydro power; in the meantime, turning the wheel of the big press was his first and most onerous occupation.

Joe was a good teacher, and the boy began to learn his trade. At first, he was allowed only to feed and turn the press, until his movements were sure, safe, and in perfect rhythm with the machine. For the first time, he realized why two fingers were missing from his father's left hand. Joe demonstrated, as Bill grew pale, how, in his youth, he had let his fingers slip into the press through carelessness. It was a grisly but worthwhile object lesson. The boy learned how to handle the heavy paper stock, and how and when to fold the still wet newsprint. Growing proficient as the printer's devil, he watched his father's nimble fingers, as they unerringly flew from the divided cases, where the type was stored, to the make-up frame. As Bill watched, each line grew, with individual letters flicked into the composing stick at lightning speed. Blank spacer bars slid in, as if by magic, to justify, or evenly space, the line with its neighbours. Each column grew, line by line, until completed; Joe working from hand-written copy he had prepared. He rarely looked at either the storage cases or the composing stick, working by a sense of touch that had become instinctive. The printer showed Bill how the reverse type was easiest to read when held upside down. Joe, himself, could rapidly scan a column of type for error with as much ease as reading the finished product.

Printer's pie was an unsavoury dish for the young apprentice to swallow. His very first galley of type, a column of perhaps five lines, which had taken him two hours to assemble, was jarred out of his hand by a malicious door frame as he passed through to seek his father's approval. Joe showed no sympathy whatsoever. "Teach you to be more careful," he said without rancour, "Lucky for you it wasn't a whole form."

It unnerved Bill to think of having a redo a pageful of "pie." In fact, he was to find that the job he most disliked in the printshop was the deliberate demolition of the form, after it had served its purpose. It was a job reluctantly started every Friday morning, after the printing of the previous day's paper. In succession, the four pages of type were overturned on a table, and the sorting of slugs, piece by piece, into their individual boxes, began. Not only was it monotonous, but also, it seemed to the young printer, the wanton destruction of a piece of art. Gradually the son, with practice, attained some of his father's dexterity in both assembling and dismantling the make-up, but it would be years before he could duplicate Joe's deft speed.

There was a new camaraderie in this father and son relationship. Joe delighted in it, confirming as it did, his decision to continue his son's education by this means, and justifying his own break from Trout Lake.

Back in that town, Alice had moving preparations to make, but no furnishings to worry about; just a repacking of the steamer trunks, which they had brought from England. School would start before their departure, but there was no point in the children attending for a few days only. Word of the family's move spread quickly, and there were many visitors to The Park. In fact, the ladies of Ferguson and Trout Lake gave her a surprise tea party there, and she realized then just how much she had become a part of the community in two years.

Early on the day Alice was to leave, Alice Jowatt, who had been at her elegant best at the going-away party, stopped by The Park on horseback. She was leading a packhorse loaded with goods, and the picture she made was bizarre, to say the least. She was wearing a baggy pair of men's pants, rolled up several times at the cuffs, and tied at the waist in overlapping folds. A disgraceful looking jacket was tied to the saddle, so that her gray flannel work shirt, sans collar, was exposed to view. Her hair was tucked into a broad brimmed Stetson of the same vintage as the jacket. She looked anything but elegant on this occasion, yet waved gaily at her namesake, quite unaware of anything unusual in her appearance.

Alice got up from the porch chair, where she had been mending a pair of Ernie's trousers for the journey that afternoon, and went out hastily to say goodbye to her friend. "I'm on my way up to my claim," boomed Mrs. Jowatt, explaining her appearance without self-consciousness. "Got to stir up those lazy rascals once in a while!"

"Alice Jowatt, how nice of you to come!" She reached up her hands and they were enveloped in the large and capable grasp of the hotel keeper. A wave of affection for this unusual but hospitable lady, swept over the younger woman, robbing her of speech and moistening her eyes.

"You take good care of little Winnie now," said Mrs. Jowatt. "I've got a stake in her even if y'didn't call her after me!" Before Alice could answer, Mrs. Jowatt added, "Tell that crazy husband of yours goodbye for me, and that ye're both welcome at the City Hotel any time you come back to the Lardeau." Alice Jowatt turned the horses around and, with a wave of her hand, trotted away to her claims, leaving Alice a little more despondent at the prospect of beginning all over again.

Going to join Joe in Sandon, Alice and the children had to travel south to Kaslo, then take the K. and S. Railway across the mountain pass to Slocan Lake and Sandon. It was a long and tedious day's journey, to a town lacking the charm of either Ferguson or Trout Lake.

The scenic outlook at Sandon was discouraging. The town had been rebuilt, after its fire, on both sides of Carpenter Creek, which ran along the bottom of a narrow gulch. There was no room for side streets, the buildings being hung precariously on the sloping sides of the canyon, and stilted to keep them free of the rushing waters of the creek. Between the downtown buildings, for a quarter mile of its length, Carpenter Creek was bridged by a wooden structure that was both road and sidewalk, over which the foot and horse driven traffic of Sandon made its way, oblivious to the stream below. There was no dust from the wooden road, but ample clouds of it from the mines that lowered over the town. Head frames jutted out like so many gallows trees, to support the cables and buckets which fed the noisy and dirty mills below. At intervals along the gulch, bright red fire hydrants, with nozzles at right angles, stook on their stacks some five feet above grade level, so as to be accessible above deep wintertime drifts.

The Pink Building, in which their new suite was located, was only a few years old, and had originally been designed for offices over the store below. As the lawyers and real estate people had vacated in the post-boom years, the owner had created two suites upstairs, one of which he kept for himself. The rooms were new and clean enough, but lacked imagination, and the few basic pieces of furniture that Joe bought did little to enhance them. After her lovely Park, Alice was less than impressed.

Her pregnancy had been confirmed, before Joe had left Trout Lake. She was in good health, as she always was during child-bearing, but as she looked at the dingy prospect outside the small windows, and at the bare unattractive rooms of the suite in the Pink Building, she did not relish the tedious discomfort to come in this ugly little town.

With a month gone since their arrival, and any novelty of moving now departed, Margie found that she didn't think much of Sandon, either. After the plushed and fringed luxury of The Park, the upstairs apartment that was her family's new home, was dull and small by comparison. Her father assured them all that the suite was an inconvenience to be put up with only temporarily, but after a month in residence, it seemed to be becoming a permanent accommodation for the Athertons.

Margie's house and school were in the Upper Gulch, looking down at the stores, hotels and saloons along the boardwalk. The gulch was wider up here, and an ordinary dirt road wound its way up the mountain. The Upper Gulch, which, in its natural state, would have been more attractive than the lower part of town, was still undergoing a reconstruction after its fire. The only redeeming feature of the section was the rebuilt and imposing Miners' Union Hospital. Everything else had a temporary, drab and utilitarian look, with nothing in it for a little girl's spirit.

Margie did not miss her friends too much. It was always enough for her to have brothers and sister around, even if Reggie was getting to be a nuisance, in his fourth year. Winnie was nearly two, and still cuddly, and Ernie would include Margie in his excursions, lacking new friends as yet. It was Bill whose style had changed, and who was becoming a different person. Of course, he was tired after each full day of work, but Margie would find him more often in discussion with his parents than with her and the other children. He was always kind and patient with the smallest children, but showed a surprising inclination to criticize Ernie and herself, if they didn't measure up to high standards of behaviour.

Restriction of freedom was another grievance for Margie in Sandon. Where before, she had been allowed to roam at will on the mountains and along the lake, she was not confined to her own yard much of the time. Possibly, Bill's absence during the day was responsible for the tighter regulations. The red curtain area of town was definitely out of bounds, and she was able to go to the exciting boardwalk district only when accompanied by her parents.

On Friday evenings and on Saturdays, when she had previously been allowed extra freedom, she had to stay in her back yard because the miners were in town. Mabel Toomey was allowed to come over on these occasions, and the two nine-year-olds would watch for the miners (a somehow deliciously wicked word), as the men hurried past their corner. The miners were rough looking, dirty, and a little menacing, but after a bath and a clean shirt they looked fairly ordinary, as they strolled around the town seeking a change from the hard drudgery of the week. Most of them spent the whole weekend in the saloons or in the red curtain houses. The few socially minded fellows who tried to become acquainted with townsfolk were generally rebuffed, because of the bad reputation of the majority.

Mabel Toomey, on one occasion, accepted a dollar for a kiss from one of them, but Margie, forewarned and also a little too close to home, refused two dollars for the same favour. Still, on her birthday in October, with the permission of her mother, she was allowed to accept a bolt of blue satin for hair ribbon, a box of apples, and a hand-drawn picture of a garden, with this verse:

I know a little garden,
With flowers fair to see,
And the fairest flower of them all,
Is little MAR-JOR-EE.

Alice's first impressions had not changed after two months in Sandon. The town's only advantage, so far as she could see, was the opportunity to see Father Jeanotte more often than once every six weeks. Joe was doing well, but life for the rest of the family was restricted, their rooms confining, and social activity almost non-existent. The church became their social outlet and Father Jeanotte was a frequent dinner guest, when he was at home. He was in his parish in October for the feast of All Saints, as well as for All Souls day, and the little cottage, which had been put at his disposal by the Catholic community of Sandon, was the target for the oldest and most malodorous of Hallow'een pranks. His privy was overturned.

At Mass on the following day, the priest confronted his congregation with mock sorrow, when it was time to deliver his homily. "Last night," he said, peering solemnly over his steel-rimmed spectacles and shaking his head, as his flock waited delightedly, "someone pushed over d'little backhouse of poor old Fadder Jeanotte!"

The word had got around, of course, and at this confirmation, the congregation broke into prolonged laughter. Pretending anger and sorrow, his shaggy moustache wagging woefully, Father Jeanotte held up his hand to stop them. "It is not to laugh," he said reproachfully, and explained, "Everyone has got to go, you know." While this was sinking in he expanded, "Old Father Jeanotte has got to go.

D'premier of d'province has got to go. Mr. Laurier has got to go. Even the Pope, he's got to go!" As anticipated, he brought down the house.

In spite of such joviality, Alice was worried about the priest. He looked tired and worn, and had obviously lost weight. At dinner that night, he pooh-poohed her concern, telling her he was "joost a little tired," but she was not reassured. His heavy schedule was telling on him.

If there was dissent in his family, Joe had no qualms about Sandon. As well as getting the *Standard* operating again, he found enjoyment in the company of the town's merchants and professional men, who were quick to give him welcome and support. The *Standard* was off to a fine start, and its editor was in his element.

"What do you think of these, man?" The speaker was Doctor Gomme, one of the town's more interesting citizens. He thumped several pieces of rock on Joe's counter, and absently wiped his hands on an already dust-laden suit.

"They look all right to me," admitted Joe cautiously. The good doctor's reputation as a mining buff was well known in the community.

"All right?" The doctor's tousled head wagged in contempt. "All right? They're more than all right! If you don't know more than that about ore, you're not fit to be the editor of a mining town news rag!"

Joe grinned at him. "I've got enough on my plate right now."

"Nonsense, man!" Doctor Gomme pulled a handkerchief from his pocket, and with it a cloud of dust deposited there by his diggings. "It's just a matter of priorities. You have to learn to divide your activities equally," and he paused to blow noisily into his kerchief. "In my case," he stated, "I spend half of my time on my two claims, the *Goo-goo* and the *Ga-ga;* one half given over to my family; and the other half devoted to my patients and practice." He chucked as Joe's eyebrows rose quizzically. "Ah, if this seems inconsistent, sir, then it must be seen that I am a very busy man, and occasionally my interests overlap!"

"And the *Goo-goo* and the *Ga-ga* are named . . . ?" Joe was beginning to enjoy this irrepressible physician.

"For my twin baby daughters, sir!" cried Doctor Gomme triumphantly. "The only words they know are . . . "

"I know," said Joe, "Goo-goo and Ga-ga."

It was Gomme's insistence that he learn more about ore and mining that aroused the mining fever in the editor. Soon, like Alice Jowatt in Ferguson, Joe found himself a partner to grubstake. Jim Foley, a nondescript hanger-on in the bars, boasted of the wealth to be found one day in his claim, and convinced the new man in town to take a flier. "All I want is for you to keep me fed, and I'll stay in the diggings all winter," he vowed. "You'll be a rich man in the spring, and just for a few measly sacks of flour, sugar, and so on." He eyed Joe speculatively. "What do you say?"

What was there to lose? As Bill became more proficient, his father would hurriedly set up the paper on Tuesday and Wednesday, and as soon as the *Standard* was published on Thursday morning, he would leave the chore of distribution to Billy, with the promise of Ernie's help after school. Ostensibly to get mine reports and social notes, if any, from the camps, the editor began taking supplies by horseback to the prospectors in the small diggings, giving them modest grubstakes in the promise of rich rewards to come. Foley was his principal recipient, as he always had fine samples to show his partner and progress reports that showed him getting closer to the mother lode.

In mid-January, Father Jeanotte was admitted to the Miners' Union Hospital, in a complete state of exhaustion. Alice went to see him, and almost cried when she saw how he had failed. He looked old beyond his sixty years, his cheeks sunken and hands visibly trembling on the coverlet. His eyes brightened as he saw her. "My dear Alice," he whispered, "did you come to see silly old Fadder Jeanotte?"

"You're not silly at all," said Alice staunchly, her voice threatening to break as she scolded, "but you must take better care of yourself." She made up her mind. "If you don't write to the bishop for help, I will! There's just too much work for you; it's time you were relieved."

Within two weeks, the Catholics of Sandon were advised that Bishop Dontenwill of New Westminster would be coming to see his ailing friend, and would take the opportunity to confer the sacrament of Confirmation on the older children of the parish. Hasty preparations for his visit began, and a shaky Father Jeanotte was able to instruct the class of some ten or twelve Confirmation candidates, including Bill, who had recently turned thirteen.

The bishop came, and the Confirmation candidates were all received into the adult body of the Church. After the ceremony, Father Jeanotte returned to the hospital where he had been staying since his illness. He was very tired and did not accept Alice's invitation to dinner. Compassionately, Bishop Dontenwill had officially relieved him of most of the arduous mission circuit that day. His Grace, however, did accept the dinner invitation as did Doctor and Mrs. Gomme, the doctor being suitably dressed and groomed for the occasion. They had an early meal, and afterward, Joe and Alice walked to the station with their guests.

True to an earlier promise to get the bishop back to New Denver, Doctor Gomme commandeered a handcar for the nine mile trip. The last sight Joe and Alice had of the distinguished churchman, was of his flying coattails, as he faced Doctor Gomme on the platform of the little railcar. The bishop and the doctor had attained a good speed by the time they disappeared around the bend, both of them bending and straining as they pumped their way to New Denver.

The winter was mild, and Joe continued to visit the mines. Foley particularly fascinated him, and week after week, he took supplies to the Irishman, who excitedly pointed out the signs of wealth buried in his claim. Joe had no first-hand knowledge of mining or of ore deposits, and like most speculators, wanted to hear that riches beyond imagination would soon be his.

In the spring, Foley was gone, along with his promises of untold wealth. There was no illegality in his arrangement with Joe, the latter being just one of the dozens of businessmen of Sandon who grubstaked prospectors, in the hope of large returns. About once a year, a backer might benefit from such an arrangement, and that was enough to keep the system going.

Alice's latest baby, her sixth, was born on April 14th. He was as dark as Winnie had been fair; his eyes brown, like his mother's. He was named after two of Joe's brothers, there being plenty of names to choose from in that family. Edmund Theodore was the name given to the infant, but he was to be known as Teddy, like his peppery little uncle in Calgary. Doctor Gomme attended at his birth, having been summoned from his work at the *Goo-goo*. The event was always remembered, because of the enthusiasm with which the doctor threw his latest ore samples on Alice's coverlet for approval, before rinsing his hands for the task to come.

CHAPTER THIRTY-TWO

Sandon, 1907

England and Europe seemed very far away to the immigrants, by their fourth year in Canada. The actuality of their homeland became increasingly unreal, as though it existed only in their imaginations.

Joe, by nature and by experience the more adaptable of the couple, assimilated rapidly into the customs and culture of the mining towns of British Columbia. It was somewhat different for Alice. So much had happened; the experiences were like none other in her past life. Her values had undergone two or three astonishing changes, as complacency with the British way of life came under constant challenge. The Victorian class system had always been accepted by her, without question. In Canada, she was astounded at the endless variety of people encountered on the frontier; none fitting into familiar molds. She had come to realize that it was necessary to assess people, without the reassuring guidelines of a class system and, to her credit, if snobbery had actuated her in the past, it was not of her own making or nature. Certainly, her adaptation to Canada and Canadians, though not as rapid as that of her husband, proved her innate regard for the person, rather than the rank.

Environment was another factor that conspired with time and distance to push England into a haze of unreality, in the minds of Alice and her family. The B.C. mountains were as vastly different from the Canadian prairies, as were the plains dissimilar to England's soft and rolling landscapes. There was no antiquity, no great households, and very little permanence to anything. The children, she realized, were becoming more Canadian than English. Less and less, were they teased about their accents and mannerisms. Their clothing now conformed to Canadian style and drew no comment; but one thing bothered her.

It seemed to her, in this new and rough country, that common courtesies were often overlooked. People were kind and generous in their own fashion, but often failed to observe the little politenesses which help to smooth the way of human communication. Not, she thought, that good manners and consideration for others were traits exclusive to the British, but in this pioneer land, there was a tendency to regard good manners as a sign of softness, or an affectation. Affectation or not, Alice resolved that her children were going to be mannerly to all, respectful to their elders, and considerate of the feelings of others; and her children did become distinctive in this way, developing a courtesy and ease of manner that was acceptable to their fellows.

If England seemed remote, Alice and Joe retained some contact with the world outside Sandon, by means of subscriptions to Toronto and Vancouver newspapers. The papers were a requirement of Joe's profession, but they also served to keep the family in touch with world events.

In 1907, strange things were happening in Europe. King Edward had been on the throne of England since the death of his mother, Queen Victoria, six years earlier, and his nephew, Wilhelm II, was the Emperor of Germany. The Kaiser's jealousy of his royal uncle knew no bounds. Willy, as the British royal family knew him, vacillated between great admiration for British ways, and astounding attacks upon his relatives and the British Parliament. Edward, attempting to establish himself, not only in England, but also on the continent, after his mother's long reign, found his nephew increasingly exasperating, in view of his own diplomatic efforts to maintain calm in an uneasy Europe.

The Kaiser's paranoia at the opening of the century was not to be matched by any other for several more decades. He pettishly told Theodore Roosevelt that he was ignored by the other monarchs of Europe, and threatened that "Soon, with my great navy to enforce my words, they will be more respectful!" He had sought unsuccessfully, for many years, to be invited to Paris, and was never to realize that dream. The Gallic snub was all the more bitter because his English uncle not only visited that city officially, and won diplomatic entente with the French, but left Paris with the cries of the populace ringing in his ears, "Vive *notre* roi!"

Joe and Alice, as good royalists, followed the reports of monarchial didoes with close interest and enjoyment. Joe reacted with amusement, and Alice with indignation, to the report of a banquet for three hundred guests in Berlin. On this occasion, the Kaiser indiscreetly and childishly said of his uncle, the King of England, "He is a Satan; you cannot imagine what a Satan he is!"

Rumours of war had been circulating for years, so these latest outbursts of the German emperor, while adding to the score against him, did not precipitate any hostile action. Nevertheless, many people in England, and other parts of the Empire, felt that war with Germany was inevitable.

With Germany and her Kaiser so much in the news, it was no wonder that Johnny Harris's excited announcement made the town buzz in July. A real live German prince was to visit Sandon within two weeks. A few of the lads at the Reco Hotel were sure he was coming to spy upon the mining operations, and were ready to participate in a lynching party. Johnny Harris told them not to be ridiculous, and explained that the young visitor was not coming in any official capacity, indeed was travelling incognito. The prince, he advised, recently graduated from university in Berlin, was on a grand tour of America, and as a guest of one of the mine owners in the East, had expressed an interest in seeing some mining operations in Canada. Speculation in the Atherton household dwelled upon his origins, but even Alice, with her knowledge of the complicated relationships of European royalty, was not quite sure where the prince fitted in. The dozens of duchies, kingdoms and principalities, which had come together thirty years earlier to constitute the German nation, still maintained their royal houses, and she wasn't sure if he was of Hanover or Hohenzollern; or of the former kingdoms of Bavaria, Saxony or Wurttemburg. Even so, the young visitor was indeed a prince of royal blood, and long before his actual appearance he created a stir not only in the rooms above the Pink Building, but throughout the whole town of Sandon.

It was too great an opportunity for Johnny Harris to miss. A grand ball would be held on the night of the prince's visit to Sandon, one week hence, that would show all the world that the community was a centre of culture and sophistication. The town was agog with anticipation of the event. Anyone who was anyone had been invited. The prince was to be housed at the Reco Hotel, and Johnny Harris outdid himself in lavish preparation. His best linen and silver were brought out and admired by the ladies of Sandon, who were assisting the hotel staff in setting up tables and decorating the hall with bunting. German flags, as well as Union Jacks, were hurriedly sent for, to drape the wall behind the long head table. A volunteer orchestra was mustered to begin practising the fox trots and waltzes for dancing, as well as the national anthems of Canada and Germany.

Joe and Alice were as excited as any in the town. They received their invitations early, and Joe was ready to respond to his wife's anticipated reaction.

"What will I wear?" she wailed, thinking not only of her scant wardrobe, but also of the limited resources of the little mining town.

"I've thought of that already," said her husband. "We'll send to Vancouver for them." With a flourish, he produced a copy of an advertisement from a Vancouver firm, which declared the availability of formal attire "for all occasions for discriminating ladies and gentlemen."

"Oh Joe, we can't do that!" She looked over her shoulder as if in fear he would be overheard. It was scandalous to think of rented clothing.

"Why not? Who's to know?" said Joe practically, and with her desire to attend the dance overwhelming her scruples, he was able to overcome her concern.

Shortly, and in ample time before the ball, a large parcel arrived from the coast, containing a dress suit of tails for Joe and a beautiful gray satin evening gown for his ecstatic wife.

The children were served a hurried supper on the night of the ball, but did not object. They were aware that tonight was to be the climax of the town's excitement. They were also looking forward to seeing their parents "all dolled up," as Ernie put it; but most of all they were intrigued by their parents going out to meet a real live prince, a prince who, it was rumoured, personally represented the Kaiser and all the vaguely wicked things for which he stood. Perhaps he was a spy, some of the children had been saying, but certainly he was a romantic and thrilling personage. Ernie thought that the prince might wear a beautiful uniform, with skin tight white trousers and thigh high black boots.

"And a plumed hat, too," suggested Margie.

When Alice and Joe put in their appearance for the children's approval, the gasps of admiration were abundant proof of the success of the rented finery. Joe's tall and wiry frame showed off the formal evening wear to perfection. His collar was high and winged under the white bow tie, and the bosom of his shirt was snowy, and starched to the cracking point. His white vest boasted a fob, though no watch, and contrasted showily with the black broadcloth of his jacket and the satin of his lapels. His long legs were elegant in the narrow black trousers, the single satin stripe along their seams accentuating the slim cut.

Joe subscribed to the theory that the evening attire of a gentleman was designed by the weaker, and therefore, of necessity, the more scheming sex. This theory held that women encouraged the wearing of a uniform mode of dress for the male, to serve two purposes. First, to allow him the conceit that he conformed to a high degree of male magnificence. Second, to make of him, when in the company of other males similarly clad, a perfect background for the ladies' own coiffed, bejewelled and dazzling splendour. Even though Joe was aware of this feminine deceit, he was quite willing to be upstaged and outshone by his wife this evening. He looked at her with genuine admiration.

"Lord, you're beautiful, Alice!"

His wife's figure was still trim, in spite of bearing six children. The physical work of caring for a large family, with a minimum of household appliances and with no maid to help her, ensured that she was still as slim this evening as on the day she married. Her dress was smashing on her, Billy thought, admiring and happy for her. Alice's narrow waist was accentuated by the stylishly close fit of the bodice, and by a hint of a bustle at the back. Her neckline made Margie gasp, the décolletage revealing an alarming portion of her mother's bosom. If the dress's bodice was revealing, the skirt more than amply made up for it in modesty. The silver gray material was full cut, and gathered, flounced and looped to successfully hide any indication of a shape below.

The dress was exquisite and in the mode; Alice's head was held high, her hair shining and piled in soft waves, to effectively frame her classical features. Her mirror told her that she looked exactly right, and the compliments of her husband and family confirmed her own quiet satisfaction with her appearance.

The large dining room of the Reco had never seen such splendour. The orchestra, on a dais, was sawing out a Strauss waltz when Joe and Alice appeared, late enough to satisfy social protocol, but early enough to be present for the prince's entrance. Johnny Harris greeted them, delighted with the success of his grand ball, as well he might be. The crystal of his chandeliers would have done justice to the court of Versailles. The gleam of silver against snowy napery adorned the tables that took up half the room, and the other end, cleared for dancing, was bright with wall bracketed lamps illuminated by Johnny's own electric company. The lights shone on the festooned bunting, and Johnny had cunningly contrived a spot light to centre on the crossed Union Jack and the eagle of Imperial Germany.

The room was full of swaying and colourful figures. Almost without exception, Alice could see, the townspeople had availed themselves of the same temporary clothier as she and Joe. Never mind, they looked magnificent, and could well have been plucked out of a setting in Mayfair, or from the ballroom fo the Hapsberg Palace. Sandon being what it was, it is not surprising that many of the elite from the shadier realm of Sandon's society were among the guests at the Prince's Ball that night. Alice was aware of faces, which were new to her; their owners at ease and extremely voluble, as they circulated among their own, quite apart from the merchants and other townspeople she recognized. She could not help noticing that the regular townsfolk suffered in comparison, if style and good looks were the criteria to go by. Joe nodded in a friendly manner to two or three of the men in this group, but made no attempt to introduce them to his wife. He had played cards with some of them on occasion.

Exactly at 8:30, Johnny assembled his guests in two long lines on either side of the ballroom, and awaited the prince's descent from his suite. "Here he comes!" the stocky proprietor warned, as the desk clerk signalled to him from the lobby.

This was the moment everyone in the room had looked forward to, and had planned for. Bows and curtsies had been practiced, the orchestra was tuned to a fine edge of perfection, and Johnny Harris certainly could not have done more to set the stage for the prince's dramatic entrance.

And dramatic it was.

A young man, tall and fair haired, as handsome as any romantic prince should be, appeared in the doorway. He was smiling and confident as he entered, but his jaw dropped when he saw the elaborate scene before him. The townsfolk responded with as much consternation. Handsome and patrician as he was, the prince's garb was that of a working miner, rough trousers, heavy boots, and an open necked plaid shirt.

Johnny's signal to the orchestra had just been sent, but the conductor, having caught a glimpse of the guest of honour, hesitated halfway through his downstroke, with the result that the German anthem began with a ragged discord, which petered out with a dismal squawk of the cornet. The leader quickly rallied, and quite splendidly the orchestra played the anthem through while the prince, red-faced, stood at attention. The false start and the unusual regalia of the royal visitor had a numbing effect on Johnny Harris and his guests. Like some stage cast given the wrong cue, they reacted uncertainly. The ladies did not curtsy in concert, and found themselves bumping into one another. More than one masculine head knocked another, as bows were started and hurriedly reversed.

The prince was the first to recover his aplomb. He advanced, smiling, to the mine manager and Johnny Harris, and offered his hand. In turn, they introduced him to their ladies, and band leader had the presence of mind to begin a waltz. Gradually, couples took to the floor, and everyone tried to pretend that nothing out of the way had occurred; but for a little while, the people in the Reco Hotel that evening, from the prince to Johnny Harris and his guests, felt somewhat silly, caught at pretending to be something they were not.

The evening was still a success. The prince was introduced to most of the guests, and danced most graciously with several of the ladies. He was a very pleasant young man and when he escorted Alice back to Joe's side, he agreed to meet with the newsman on the following day. He was firm, though, on the matter of his privacy.

"But no interview, please, Mr. Atherton," he said. "I am here as a visitor to your country, not as a representative of my own."

Joe's meeting with the royal visitor the next afternoon was casual. The prince was without ceremony, and wearing clothing more in keeping with his life style; a Norfolk jacket over a high necked sweater, and summer weight trousers covering his long legs. He ushered the newsman into his suite with a warm smile, and asked him what he would like to drink.

"Skey . . . Whiskey, that is, please."

The prince smiled. "I'm familiar with the abbreviation. Saves time, I understand."

Joe relaxed in his host's easy presence and grinned back at him. "You are very adaptable, Your Highness."

The prince indicated a chair for Joe, and gave him his drink. "I adapted a little too quickly last night," he said, with a wry smile. "I hope I was not too big a disappointment?"

"Not at all, not at all!" Joe assured him. "You were very impressive." It was his turn to be rueful. "And as for the rest of us, we all had a dandy time once we stopped being stuffy!" They were in tune as they laughed and nodded over their glasses and drank to the recollection of last night's little charade.

The conversation was desultory for a while, but the newsman was frankly curious about the other. The prince was not the heel-clicking, sabre-scarred Prussian his own prejudice had told him to expect. He had to get to the core of this man, and he abruptly changed the direction of the conversation.

"What are Germany's aims, Your Highness?" he asked bluntly, and settled himself in his chair.

"Please," said the young man, "call me Otto, Mr. Atherton." His smile was still winning.

"All right, Otto, and I'm Joe," he said, and put his question in a different way. "Look, this is not for publication, but I'm curious. Your emperor seems bound to argue with every country in Europe. What is he looking for?"

"What everyone needs, Joe; recognition, respect, a place in the sun," said the young man reasonably. He leaned forward, elbows on knees. "Do you realize how Germany has grown in the past fifty years? Industrially, politically and culturally, we are bursting at the seams!"

"Do you mean that you need more land, more countries to rule?"

"Possibly," said the young man, taking no offence, "that might be our destiny. It could be a legitimate aim for the Fatherland."

"Couldn't that be a little rough on the smaller countries around you?" The newsman eyed the royal visitor quizzically, over the rim of his glass.

"They would be far better off under German rule. Belgium for example, a nation of poor peasants, would become rich with industry and trade, if it was part of Germany."

"Will Germany impose her might on smaller countries, to obtain her ends?"

The prince stiffened at the blunt question. Still, he wanted this Canadian to understand the extent of Germany's feelings, and the justice of its aims. "Joe, have you ever felt hedged in, and wanted to burst out?"

Joe grinned. "Constantly," he said.

"Then you understand!" said the prince, happily. "You too have been a victim of *einkreisung*: encirclement!" He grew stern as he told Joe, "Your King Edward has made treaties with France and with Russia that are a military threat to Germany. That is why we have to be prepared. We have a phrase in the Fatherland: Blood and Iron. That is Germany's destiny, the mailed fist and shining armour; preparedness, Mr. Atherton, for *any* eventuality!" His eyes blazed and his voice rang with emotion, as he ended his short outburst.

It was obvious that he regretted his words almost as soon as they were said, realizing this was neither the time nor the place to exhibit strong feelings. He leaned forward. "Forgive me," he said sincerely, laying his hand on Joe's. "I am not acting like a good guest in your country. I'm afraid I reacted strongly to your questions."

"No harm done," said Joe; but the prince's remarks confirmed what the papers had been saying about public feeling in Germany. At least in the highest circles, the Kaiser had support for his aspirations.

Joe took his leave of the prince shortly after. He had warmed to the man's personality, but his own national feelings were at least as strong as those of his host. The times did not allow an examination of public conscience in the matter of prejudice, so his own bias was increased by the words of the young German patriot. With similar national sentiments expressed by other Ottos and other Joes, throughout Europe and the Empire, the world rushed inexorably toward eventual conflict, and to a sad end to such events as Johnny Harris's Prince's Ball.

Prejudice of another kind was at work at Yarmouth, in England. Johnny Atherton, illegitimate son of Joe's sister Nellie, was nine years old that summer of

1907, and of an age when the scandal surrounding his birth, and the bitter controversy of the paternity suit were beginning to affect his life.

Joe's mother and father, nearing sixty, still had the responsibility of Nellie and the boy, and there were two other unmarried daughters at home, as well. Their decision for Canada came that year, when young Teddy sent for his bride to be, Maude Harold. Maude, in turn, asked her fiancée's sister, Margaret, to accompany her to Canada, and the remaining members of the family, still living at home, quickly made up their minds. It would be a new start for everyone. The two girls left Yarmouth, to be followed within a month by John and Sarah Atherton, Nellie, now twenty-nine, and the twenty-three-year old Bessie. They joined Teddy and Maude in Calgary.

CHAPTER THIRTY-THREE

Sandon, 1907

September marked the first anniversary of the family's move to Sandon. Although one or two events, like the Prince's Ball, were later to be recalled with pleasure, it must be said that Alice's regard for the town, rather than improving with time, declined with every passing month. Apart from the dusty dreariness of the place, there was the matter of the character of Sandon itself. Billy was to turn fourteen in three months, and Ernie was going on thirteen. Alice felt that the licentious little town was no place to raise the boys, and their growing brothers and sisters.

Joe, too, was a bit of a worry. Not that he was neglecting his family or his business; indeed, they were prospering as never before. Nevertheless, the environment of the roaring little town was a challenge to the adventurer in him. She did not then, nor ever would, suspect her husband of unfaithfulness, but he loved the company of good fellows and had added the stimulation of gambling to his taste for strong drink. She hated to think of herself as a shrew, a discontented wife who would allow her husband no freedom. She told herself that, like many of the businessmen of Sandon, he only played cards once or twice a week, so she refused to reproach him. Yet Alice worried.

He came home, prepared to do a selling job. Calling a greeting to his wife, he removed his hat and jacket and walked into the kitchen. "Alice," he said, "you've heard me speak of the colonel; you know, Colonel Lowery, the grandaddy of all the newsmen of the Kootenays?"

"Yes, I remember." She was preoccupied with the ingredients of her stew. She sampled a spoonful and decided it could do with a touch of pepper. "What about him?" she asked dutifully.

"Well," he said, "the colonel's in Greenwood now; publishes his *Ledge* there."

"Wasn't the *Ledge* a New Denver newspaper once?" she enquired absently; her mind not really caught by his leading remarks.

"Yes, and he published it in Kaslo and Fernie too," said Joe. "Colonel Lowery moved around quite a bit. Came here to the Kootenays just after the discoveries of gold and silver in '91, and has been in one place or the other ever since." He paused to organize the approach to his subject and leaned against the warming closet of the stove. "He spent most of this time in New Denver, ten years in all, and he never really has liked any other place as well."

She was beginning to wonder where all of this was leading. "Then why doesn't he go back there?" She started to set the table for supper.

"Well, he has been in Greenwood for four years now, and he's getting no younger, so he thinks he'll wind up his days there."

She glanced up at him then. "How do you happen to know that?"

"Oh, didn't I tell you?" He was elaborately casual. "I saw Colonel Lowery today." He flipped his fingers into the stew for a quick taste, to indicate how unimportant the whole conversation was.

"Indeed now, did you?" said his perceptive wife. "And what is he doing in Sandon?" She nudged him away from the stew, and put the lid on the pot.

"Well, to tell the truth, he would like me to move our operation to New Denver." Joe was relieved, now that the matter was in the open. He looked directly at his wife, awaiting her response to this disclosure.

She was puzzled. "I don't understand what it is to him, whether you stay here or move somewhere else." Her supper preparations were abandoned altogether now. She folded her arms and gave him her full attention.

"I'm not sure either," said Joe. He straddled a chair as he thought about it. "You know, it's funny, he's got the damnedest feeling for New Denver. He believes it has a future better than any of the towns around here. Doesn't think much of Sandon," he continued, chuckling, "Lowery says that the town's only advantage is that there are two distinct ways of getting out of it!"

Alice's laugh was an unladylike snort; her sentiments and the colonel's agreed on this point, at least. But she sobered. The notion of a change to the bigger and more attractive town on the lake some nine miles away was enticing; at the same time, she didn't seem any closer to getting her roots down and Joe settled in employment. "But darling!" she felt compelled to protest, "you haven't really given this a chance yet. A business isn't built overnight."

"Alice, if you're happy here, and want me to stay, I will." He was evidently sincere, and caught her by surprise.

"What do you want yourself, Joe?" she asked.

He was thoughtful for a moment. "There're things to be said for both towns," he said carefully. "We are doing pretty well here, even if we never get to be millionaires." He voiced her own thought. "I'm not sure that Sandon's the proper town to raise kids in," and he continued on this theme. "New Denver has a lot more to offer to all of us, socially. It's more settled, not as wild, and it's more diversified — fruit growing and logging as well as mining; better for business."

Alice was all but convinced. It was not a great change, after all. More like moving from one house to another, she told herself. The nine miles of distance were far less formidable in Canada, than they would have been in England. "Does New Denver have a good school?" she asked, and Joe knew she was ready to be persuaded.

"Oh, much bigger than Sandon's," he said, "at least forty children." That Alice did not see anything incongruous in this statement, showed how far the couple had come from London, in attitude, as much as in distance.

"What about housing?" she asked, and Joe played his trump card.

"The colonel tells me there's a nice, furnished, four bedroom house down by the lake, that'll be available in a month."

"Oh Joe, really?" exclaimed Alice.

"Yes, really," grinned her husband. "A nice house with a view of the lake and mountains!"

Alice thought of the bleak outlook grudgingly offered by Sandon's narrow gulch, and looked about her at the unattractive rooms of the Pink Building. She made up her mind. "I can be ready in a week," she said.

CHAPTER THIRTY-FOUR

New Denver, 1907

If she had doubts about the wisdom of yet another move, her misgivings vanished as the train carrying Alice and the children left the narrow and dust-laden ravine, and the town built over Carpenter Creek. Almost immediately the horizon expanded, as the train emerged on an open mountainside; clean, forested and sparkling under a sun free of the pall of the mines. It was only a short ride to New Denver and, for Alice, after Sandon's smothering confines, it was like the surfacing of a drowning person.

The first sight of the glorious landscape cradling the new town, was startling in its beauty. Set on the shore of Lake Slocan, New Denver clung to a curving bay, the mountains of the Selkirk range rising all around, snow capped and glistening. A thaw had melted the first winter snows on the lower hills, and little streams could be seen everywhere, sparkling and bubbling as they hurried down the slopes to the lake. Facing the town across the water, the New Denver Glacier sloped down the mountainside, dominating the scene in perpetual white splendour.

Joe had preceded his family to the new town, almost as soon as Alice had made up her mind. He had told Johnny Harris his reasons for leaving Sandon, and pointed out that he could continue to print Sandon news if a local correspondent could be found. Johnny had been disappointed, but could not fault his reasoning. New Denver was bigger and more progressive, and the chances of the newspaper's survival were greater in the more diversified community. He made no protest, and released Joe from his rental arrangement. Further, he was generous in agreeing on a suitable settlement for the *Standard*'s print equipment.

The new paper was to be named the *Slocan Mining Review*, and was to cater to subscribers in the towns of Nakusp and Silverton, as well as New Denver and Sandon. Joe threw himself into the new venture with all his heart and energy. He was bursting with ideas before he arrived in the new area, and the sight of the lake, glacier and mountains once more moved and inspired him, as when he first came to British Columbia.

He quickly set up shop, and started to get acquainted with the merchants, bankers, mine managers, and professional men of the community. He was invited to a special meeting of the newly formed Board of Trade, and his friend, the editor from Greenwood, R. T. Lowery, came over especially to introduce Joe to his favourite town, New Denver.

Colonel Robert Tecumseh Lowery, named after the famous Shawnee chief, was from Ontario. He had come to the Kootenays soon after the discoveries of gold and silver, to start up the series of newspapers he was to publish throughout this land. His appearance absolutely belied his resounding name and title. Small, almost insignificant in stature, and with a mild manner calculated to lull adversaries into a false sense of security, he could lash out with a wit caustic enough to shrivel the most puffed-up politician, or easily defeat his antagonist editors in the wordy duel in which they perpetually engaged. "Colonel" R. T. Lowery had no connection with the military; the soubriquet had been hung upon him in whimsy.

Puffing at his cigar, he rose to introduce Joe and surveyed his audience for all the world like a miniature Mark Twain. The board members grinned appreciatively. "It is a measure of how badly this town needs a newspaper," he said, "that I have no other option but to offer you today, with CONSIDERABLE misgiving, the person of my colleague, J. J. Atherton, as your new editor.

"J. J.," he said, "has been known to me more by reputation than by association; frankly these latter occasions are ones I would rather forget."

Occasionally the editors of the Kootenays convened, and the tales of their shenanigans went the rounds. The audience laughed knowingly.

"Mr. Atherton," he continued, "is a family man. He had a wonderful wife and six children, for which he can thank his good fortune, rather than any good judgement on his part. Fortunately, his fourteen year old son is in business with him, so the *Review* may have some reasonable expectation of survival."

After a few more sallies of a similar nature, the colonel ended his introduction on a more serious note. "You do need a newspaper in New Denver. I'd be the last person in the world to criticize a man who is publishing his fourth newspaper in five years. God knows I've started a good many myself, and I know from experience how dedicated a person can be, and yet fail to cope with the uncertainties of life in these changing mining communities.

"New Denver, though," he said, with a growing ring to his voice, "has a promise far beyond those other communities near us, that rely entirely upon what the rocks may yield, or the mountains disgorge." He let this accolade to his town sink in before ending, "I ask your support for your new editor, J. J. Atherton, so that he may help you promote the resources, the beauty, and the spirit of the Slocan." He sat down and lit his second cigar, as the crowd acknowledged his appeal with appreciative applause.

Alice arrived within a week of Joe, on the day the house by the lake became vacant. It was twilight before they were able to take possession, and they walked to their new home in the dusk of late October. The house itself was charming in its lakeside setting; a composite of the original structure and two added wings. The entire building was clad in white clapboard, which drew the sections into a pleasing whole.

It was quite the largest house, other than The Park, that the couple had occupied in fourteen years of marriage and, to add to its attraction, there came to them, from the adjoining orchard, the lilting notes of a songbird, rising strongly in the air of an unusually mild autumn evening. Wonderment was on all their faces, as the trilling notes were repeated.

"Are there nightingales in Canada?" Alice asked Joe.

"You've got me, Alice. I wouldn't have thought so. But you're right. If that isn't a nightingale, I'll eat my hat."

It was too dark to determine the whereabouts of the little songster, though he continued to warble his sweet welcome to the family, as they entered the house. Alice regretfully closed the door on his song. "I hope he'll be all right, it's bound to turn colder," she worried.

The episode was a happy introduction to their new home, and seemed a good omen for their life in the new town. The house lived up to the promise of its exterior, and in the following morning's sunshine, the glorious view of the lakeshore and the glacier added to their certainty that they had made the right decision.

Bill had stayed with his mother in Sandon when Joe went ahead to organize the printshop, but now he joined his father at work. More and more, the similarity of the youth to his mother could be recognized in both appearance and disposition. Calm and serene, where his father was volatile and energetic to a distracting degree, Bill was a good foil for the newsman's enthusiasms, so the two worked well together.

The new business was a success from the start, and the boy's skills in the printshop were indispensable to his father at this time.

The family, as a whole, fit into New Denver society with more ease than it had in Sandon. Alice relaxed in the new environment, and once more the children enjoyed normal freedom. Ernie and Margie were still benefitting from the head start of one year, gained in English schools, so their late entry into the fall term at New Denver was not a handicap. Reggie was in the first class. For him, the move was of no consequence academically, and he adjusted socially without any problem.

Ernie was in the senior class now, the highest level New Denver could provide, with graduation a prospect for the following spring. He was quickly at ease with his new classmates; big enough to resist bullying, and without the disposition to dominate anyone else. Unlike his older brother, he related well only to those of his own age, being of the belief that adults were in league against him and his kind.

A measure of the family's assimilation into the new community was seen in November. Mr. Circassian, Ernie's teacher and school principal, announced the production of a musical play as part of the school Christmas entertainment. He had written the script and composed the songs himself. The musical had the unlikely name of *Glucoff and the Four Leaf Clover.*

The play with little relevance to its title, had to do with the rescue of a damosel, by a knight in shining armour. Bill, out of school, but known to possess a good singing voice, was asked to take the part of the knight in hot pursuit of the lady Hinda. This unfortunate creature was known to have gone to a neighbouring kingdom with another gentleman. It was obscure whether or not she went willingly, but she did have time to listen while Bill sang a song to her. The words were "Hinda, we hate to see you leaving."

It was an intriguing return for Bill to the boyhood from which he had been plucked a year before. He rehearsed his part in the play with zest, and created an authentic and beautiful suit of armour out of cardboard and tinfoil. It was a labour of love, which took many of his evenings after each day of work at the printshop, but the finished product was a joy to behold and gave the boy more satisfaction than anything else he had accomplished since leaving school.

His brothers and sisters, of course, were under strict instruction not to go near the completed armour.

For Ernie, the order was like a red flag to a bull. Every afternoon after school, the armour drew him like a magnet to the bedroom he shared with his brother. Inevitably he did touch it, and inexorably he was drawn to try it on. He looked magnificent, and this realization drove all other thoughts out of his mind, as he postured before the mirror. So engrossed was he with his dashing reflection, that he dallied too long. The afternoon sped on, and Bill came home from work.

Brought back to reality by his brother's voice downstairs, Ernie panicked. There was no way he could rid himself of the elaborate pieces of armour before Bill arrived upstairs, so he flung up the window sash with a bang, and started to clamber out. The noise of the window opening was heard downstairs. Bill, full of suspicion, raced up to the second floor in time to see his brother, and his shiny suit of armour, disappearing out of the window and down the rainspout. He ran to the window, and let out a scream of anguish, as he saw his beloved armour coming apart and shredding in his brother's wild descent down the pipe. He did not stop to think; he tore after Ernie by the same route.

Fortunately for her second son, Alice, upon hearing Ernie's descent on the outside wall, went to the door in time to see Bill completing his downward climb. Taking in the situation, she grabbed Bill before he could go after his brother. The terrified youth, by this time, was rounding the corner, bits and pieces of the armour streaming out behind him.

"Let me go, mama. I'll kill him," yelled Bill and, annoyed as she was with Ernie, Alice really believed that Bill might do just that. She wisely hung on to her eldest, and tried to calm him.

For the first time in years, she saw tears in Bill's eyes, tears of pure frustration, as he continued to beseech his mother to let him "only get at that . . . that rotter!" In his sputtering rage, Bill lapsed into the language of his *Chums* and *Boys' Own Annual*. He couldn't express contempt for human behaviour in much stronger terms.

It was many months before the incident could be discussed with humour in front of Bill. In the meantime, he rebuilt the costume better and stronger than ever, so no permanent harm was done. The Christmas entertainment and the play were staged, and enthusiastically received by all of New Denver.

The other family member taking part in the concert was Margie. With five other little girls in kimonos, all with slanted eye makeup, she sang:

> We are happy little girls from New Denver School
> And sweet little girls are we.
> And many many things we have learned at school
> Since we started our A B C.
>
> We have lately learned about Japan,
> A country o'er the sea,
> Where everybody has a fan
> And waves it grace-full-ee.
>
> (Chorus) La, la, la, la, the Japanese fan
> La, la, la, la, the Japanese fan
> La, la, la, la, the Japanese fan
> (Waving the fan) We sing of the Japanese fan!

The little girl never forgot that first Christmas in New Denver. Whether because of *Glucoff and the Four Leaf Clover,* or the rendition of "The Japanese Fan," the entertainers were widely acclaimed, and invited to give a second performance in Silverton.

Those performances, and the exciting travel by the troupe in a large open sleigh filled with straw, remained vivid in Margie's memory forever. And, as well as participating in the concert, she had a solo part in the Christmas Eve service that followed hard upon the closing of the school concerts.

The family's old friend, Father Jeanotte, was to celebrate his Midnight Mass in New Denver, before returning to Sandon for a morning service. Margie recalled, in later years, the crisp whiteness and silence of that late evening, as the family walked to church. Her hand was warm in the grasp of her father, and enclosed in the pocket of his overcoat, and her nose was tingling where it escaped the scarf wrapped around her face. The excitment of staying up late, and the knowledge that she was to sing one verse of the recessional hymn by herself, were heady recollections for the years to come. She retained the sharp picture of the choir loft, her father's hands, with missing fingers, upon the organ keyboard, yet playing with competence the familiar carols and hymns of Christmas.

At the end of Mass, Margie sang the opening verse of the closing hymn, "The Snow Lay All Around," and was entirely satisfied with her performance. She left the church in the crush of the moving congregation, with her parents' greetings to their friends and the warm sound of Merry Christmases ringing in her ears.

Bill and Ernie, though, were silent. No one had mentioned her singing. Had she been something less than a smash hit?

Bill, usually considerate of his little sister, finally broke his silence. "That was awful," he said.

Ernie added, "It was rotten!"

Alice and Joe hastened to tell Margie that she had done very well, while they glared at the two boys. She was much more ready to believe her parents than her tasteless brothers.

CHAPTER THIRTY-FIVE

New Denver, 1908

With his family settled and his paper established, Joe had time to nourish his grand concept.

The more he thought about it, the more enthusiastic he became. His excitement about this town and its area had grown by leaps and bounds, since he had first seen New Denver's beautiful vista and had met the solid citizens who represented its industry and commerce. What his vivid imagination could now foresee, was a special edition of the *Slocan Mining Review* to publicize New Denver and the district; an edition printed on slick paper, with printing of a high quality enhanced by artistic titles and stylistic capital letters to begin each article *and*, moreover, an edition to be jammed with photographs!

He was not intimidated by the lack of proper equipment. After all, had not J. J. Langstaff printed his first issue of the *Trout Lake Topic* on *silk*, instead of ordinary newsprint? Ordinarily, photographs and stylized print were beyond the capabilities of any frontier newspaper; but Joe had a plan to accomplish a feat of quality printing, on a one-time basis, that would be the talk of the Kootenays.

He took his idea to the members of New Denver's Board of Trade, in late February. He was listened to with good will; his earlier introduction by Colonel Lowery, together with his steady production of the weekly paper for several months, having lent him some status in the community.

The members began to catch some of Joe's enthusiasm, as he disclosed his plan for a promotional issue of the *Review* to be published on Victoria Day. They listened with growing interest, as he told them how he proposed to gather information about all of New Denver and district's facilities, industries and settlement advantages. He told, in glowing terms, how the paper would be printed on expensive paper, and contain dozens of photographs, not only of the scenic beauty and industry of the area, but more important to his audience, portraits of themselves; the leaders of the community. Joe spoke from the heart, his fervour lending authority and conviction to his words. He was loudly applauded, the men at the tables turning to one another with affirmative nods to indicate their approval and acceptance of his proposal.

Johnny Harris, down from Sandon for the occasion, rose and asked for the audience's support of the plan. He told them that they would be the major beneficiaries of the promotion, but warned them that their advertising support and hearty purchase and circulation of the issue would be essential. Johnny ended his speech with a ringing "DON'T LET OUR EDITOR DOWN!" Then he shook Joe's hand before seating himself. Joe could not have had a more influential supporter. The success of the special edition seemed assured.

As with all his new enterprises, the newsman anticipated unlimited success for the souvenir edition as soon as the idea was conceived. There was no room for doubt in Joe's mind that the newspaper would be not only an instant hit, but also the catalyst in the Slocan's coming prosperity. In his confidence, he wrote to his cousin, Jack Atherton, in England and urged that worthy to join him, telling in splendid terms about the Canadian West, particularly British Columbia, and about the great opportunities for a newspaperman in the new country. Like Joe, Jack was a printer by trade, and a good one.

Jack Atherton and his wife Carrie were a few years younger than Joe and Alice. Joe's cousin, though a typically cautious Lancastrian, admired him a great deal. As a young lad apprenticed to the trade, he had worked with Joe on more than one occasion, and had basked in the popularity of the actor-runner-printer. Now as an adult, and quite aware of Joe's mercurial career, he still liked and trusted his cousin, and expected him to come out ahead someday. Things in Britain were still slow after the war in South Africa, and the Canadian Pacific Railway and Canadian government were still actively recruiting tradesmen and settlers for the West. Carrie, who looked forward to the prospect of seeing Alice and her family again, helped her husband to make up his mind. The couple, with their fourteen month old daughter Florrie, sailed in March for Canada.

"Uncle" Jack and "Aunt" Carrie, as the children called their second cousins, were met at the New Denver railway station by Joe, Alice, and the older boys. Margie had stayed at home, in charge of the three younger children, very important in this, her first job of baby minding.

From the platform, the boys caught sight of their Uncle Jack and Aunt Carrie. Jack's rather mournful face, enhanced by his drooping moustache, came into view as he assisted his wife, who was carrying the baby, to alight. His usual lugubrious expression changed to a beaming smile, as he recognized the Canadian family converging upon him. Carrie's round and placid face broke into a smile, as she caught sight of Joe and Alice. She, like most of Joe's relatives, was highly partial to Alice, and was happy to see the smile and the welcome in the eyes of her cousin by marriage.

"Ul-lo, Joe-oe!" called the beaming Uncle Jack, adding extra syllables, in the sing-song accent of Lancashire.

"Hullo yourselves, Jack and Carrie. It's so good to see you!" said Joe, warmly embracing his cousin's wife, and pumping Jack's hand. Alice and Carrie put their arms around one another and, for no reason that Bill or Ernie could see, wept a little. With many pats and "how are yous," the adults finally got around to the boys.

To the children, Uncle Jack and Aunt Carrie seemed terribly English. Indeed, their broad north country tones seemed strange to Joe and Alice. To the newcomers, their cousins seemed completely Americanized and they could not get over the changes in appearance, speech, and manner of the boys, whom they had last seen as rather precise young Londoners. They were nearly five years older, of course, but the great change was in their freedom of expression and lack of formality, evident in the way they shook their uncle's hand and embraced their aunt without embarrassment.

Even this early in the spring, the boys were tanned and healthy-looking, and mature beyond what the English couple had expected. Florrie was admired by Joe and Alice and acknowledged, without undue enthusiasm, by the boys, who felt they were up to their ears in babies anyway. The greeting of the Jack Atherton family was a great success for all concerned, the adults being glad of one another's company and the children enjoying that special warmth that comes from belonging to a family.

With a little shifting about, the four bedroom house by the lake accommodated the new family in comfort, and Jack and Carrie settled down to a life vastly different from that which they had known in England.

Jack Atherton was allowed no time to relax, after his long journey. The second day in New Denver found him early at the printshop, with Joe and Bill. He was given a general idea of the souvenir issue planned by his cousin, and more cautious and practical than Joe, was aghast as what he felt to be the foolhardy and overambitious scope of the journal, which his cousin presumed to produce. "Lord, Joe," he said, "how the devil d'you propose to produce a paper like that in only two months, with the junk you have here?" He looked at the printing press in disdain, and his next words expressed his feelings about the other antiquated equipment of the shop. "You don't have any means of making plates for all those photographs you've been accumulating, not within a thousand miles of here, and you haven't even ordered that special paper stock you talked about."

"Now Jack, don't get upset," said Joe easily. "There's lots of time, and I know what I'm doing. I've already written several articles so you and I can begin the composition of the edition." As Jack began another protest, Joe silenced him with, "Look, I'll order the paper today from *Saturday Night* in Toronto. Now, here's the way I see the souvenir edition."

While Bill busied himself with the regular weekly issue, Joe and Jack leaned over the standup desk, as the editor began to explain his plans. "We'll do the layout here, Jack," he said. "You set up the columns of type and leave room for the photographs and the fancy capital letters. We'll print the edition here on the slick paper using our own type, then send all the printed stock back east. *Saturday Night* will develop the photo plates in the meantime, and when the stock gets there, they'll just put in the photos and caps where we've told them to. Then they'll send the finished product back to us."

"All this in two months!" protested Jack. "Is your shipping service that good in Canada? Three thousand miles, isn't it?"

"Give or take a thousand," Joe shrugged. "What the hell, Jack, stop worrying. It'll come out all right."

And come out all right it did, after some heart stopping delays. Jack's expert care with the setup not only resulted in characters sharp, clear, and in the highest tradition of the printer's art, but became, as well, a learning experience for young Bill. His Uncle Jack edited the boy's work with a critical eye and a sarcastic tongue. Little imperfections, of no concern in the process of printing the small weekly newspaper, were drawn to Bill's attention with indignation, by his uncle.

"Call that printing, d'you Willy?" Bill gritted his teeth at the name. "You'll never get a job in a decent city with that kind of muck!" Bill was crestfallen, but received no comfort from his father when he protested his uncle's fastidiousness. He soon learned to refine the galley proofs before submitting them to Uncle Jack, so the special edition proceeded with speed and skill.

The four weeks that elapsed while the preprinted paper stock was in the east, were the occasion for much apprehension by Joe and his cousin. For all his confidence, Joe had a deadline, May twenty-fourth, to meet and by May twentieth there was still no sign of the finished product from Toronto.

The advertisers, in spite of their hearty acclaim for the idea of a special edition to boost the Slocan, had not responded as yet to the extent that Joe had anticipated. Even so, those merchants who had placed ads were beginning to demand a look at the souvenir edition. Every day, the three Athertons met the train, but it was not until the day before their deadline that the wooden cases containing the sheets of print arrived at the New Denver station. Shouting with jubilation, the three helped to push the express wagon loaded with cases into the baggage shed, where Joe borrowed a crowbar from the station master. Jack and Bill held their breath, as Joe pried off the wooden cover and folded back the oiled paper that protected the slick pages inside.

Uppermost, was the big centre section of the special edition, its fine printing, so scrupulously overseen by Jack, now enhanced by clear and professional photographs of their fellow townsmen, and by a great photographic scene of Lake Slocan in the middle.

The station master and a few loiterers cast curious looks at the three, as they whooped and shook hands and pounded one anothers' backs in glee. Joe quickly replaced the cover, and arranged for the haulage of the crates to the printing office. At the shop, they promptly opened all the cases, exposing the three double sheets, printed on both sides, that made up the twelve pages of the special edition. The second double sheet was as perfect as the first.

Last to be unpacked was that portion of the paper which, folded, became pages one, two, eleven and twelve. Again perfect. With the exception of page one.

"Damn!" groaned Joe, forgetting Bill's presence. "How the hell could they have overlooked that!" The top ten inches of page one, which were to have carried the paper's identity, were bare of any print, except for two small reproductions of lake scenery done by a local artist. These little black and white pictures looked most forlorn, one at the left and the other at the right of the huge blank space; the space that was supposed to have proclaimed this as the special edition of the *SLOCAN MINING REVIEW.*

Uncle Jack narrowed his eyes at Joe. "Did you remember to tell *Saturday Night* to print the flag?" he asked suspiciously.

"Well certainly!" said Joe with conviction, and with only the tiniest of hesitations. His delay would have gone unnoticed by anyone other than his cousin Jack.

"Joe, you silly bugger," he pronounced without rancour, "you know bloody well that you forgot to tell 'em." Jack commonly used "silly bugger" much as another Englishman might have said "silly ass."

"Nonsense, Jack," said Joe stoutly. "I'm positive I included the instruction."

"Well whoever's to blame, there's no flag, and what d'you intend to do about it, with tomorrow being publication day?"

Joe did not appreciate his cousin's smug censure. "Don't worry, I'll publish on time!" he snapped.

"Make a wood block," said Jack, after a moment's reflection.

"A wood block?" mused Joe, then, as his confidence returned, "By golly Jack, I think that's the answer!"

A clean piece of newsprint was spread on the surface of the standup desk. Joe roughly printed the words *Slocan Mining Review.* His letters were spidery and fancy and, at Jack's suggestion, he embellished the S and the R with fruit blossoms. Several sketches were made, until Jack grumblingly admitted that the result was "about as good as we can do." The drawing was traced onto a block of soft cedar that they obtained from the lumber yard, and Joe started to painstakingly carve out the lettering much as, centuries earlier, Gutenberg must have constructed his first pieces of type.

It was not until three o'clock in the morning of May 24th that the carving, and cutting of the wood block to size, was completed. It was clamped into place on a form, inked, and printed onto the blank space of page one of the special edition. Bill had long since been sent home. Carefully, the two men removed the form to reveal the printed product. The sudden expelling of their breaths indicated a measure of success, as the wood block's impression appeared, clear and sharp, even while it reproduced every cut of the printer's knife. Joe was jubilant but Jack shook his head gloomily at the result. Frankly, he did not think it came up to the standard of the rest of the souvenir edition.

CHAPTER THIRTY-SIX

New Denver, 1908

Apart from its amateurish flag, the edition was an excellent work. The printing was of superb quality, and the photographs appropriate and distinct. Joe's editorial revealed the birth pangs he suffered with the emergence of his precious edition.

> This production has taxed our resources and ingenuity, to say nothing of the financial end, but we entered upon our task cheerfully believing that our words will not altogether fall upon barren soil, and that if we have succeeded in inducing a few homeseekers to locate in the glorious district we serve, then we have accomplished something.

Colonel Lowery, the editor responsible for Joe's move to New Denver, contributed a piece titled "The Early Days." His affection for New Denver could be seen in his rueful article.

> For ten years I ran "the leading excitement" in New Denver, and then moved on to prospect in other fields. It was a mistake probably, but each man's life assays high in mistakes.

The edition contained feature articles on the industries, tales of pioneers, and a total of forty-two photographs scattered throughout its twelve pages. Johnny Harris wrote a story about his exploration of the New Denver Glacier the previous summer, in the company of two other citizens of the town. The trio had been the first to climb to the summit, and it had taken them one and a half days to accomplish the feat.

Joe poured out his heart in a poetic salute to the beauty and promise of his new home. In romantic words, he titled it "Hail Bounteous Slocan."

> I only hear the gently murmuring rill
> Softly singing through the valley clear;
> I only feel the silent, mighty thrill
> That floods the eye without a single tear.

Artistically, the souvenir edition could not be faulted. Financially, it was a fiasco.

Bill and Ernie were on the street with the special edition as early as nine on the morning of the twenty-fourth. It was a public holiday, and they made their best sales at the fair grounds, where a sports program was being held in the afternoon. Even with the holiday mood, sales were sparse. The price of fifty cents for the souvenir edition restricted its circulation to the very affluent or most supportive, but the cost of the production had been high, and the asking price was not out of keeping with the quality of the finished product.

If street sales were disappointing, sales to merchants and regular subscribers were even less rewarding. As the days following the twenty-fourth went by, it was obvious that some attempt at promoting the edition, among merchants and readers, should have taken place long before this. In his preoccupation with the artistic production of the edition, Joe had overlooked the business aspects, the sale of advertising, the presale of copies, and commitment by the business community to participate. Realizing his mistake, he tried, in subsequent issues of the *Review*, to appeal to his readers to send the special edition to friends, prospective settlers, and industrial interests; but after the initial interest in the newspaper, public attention died quickly and the frantic cries of the editor for assistance did little to diminish the pile of papers which remained unsold after Victoria Day. Financial support by way of purchase of copies, like the advertising income from the edition, was spotty at best. Compliments, Joe had aplenty. Cash returns did not allow him to break even financially, and the publisher's disappointment was keen and lasting. He continued to publish the weekly issues, but the thrill had gone and his creative juices dried up.

By the middle of June, it was evident that the special edition was a complete failure as a financial venture; the piles of unsold copies in the *Review* office still unreduced. From May twenty-fourth onward, sales had dwindled rapidly and now, three weeks after publication date, no business or individual was requesting even single copies.

"What the devil is the matter with everyone?" Joe asked of no one in particular. He was sitting with Jack and Bill, as they gulped tea and sandwiches at noontime. "We hardly sold more than our regular weekly circulation, and I was sure we'd sell at least one thousand more, and hoping for two thousand extra sales." With one thousand sales over the regular circulation he would have broken even, and the two thousand he had hoped for would have provided a five hundred dollar profit. "If the damn merchants around here had advertised as they should have, we could have come out ahead by a thousand dollars," he said. "The cheap bas . . . blighters would have stumbled over one another to buy up copies, if they had run ads." Joe slanted a look at his son to see if the boy had noticed his slip, but Bill appeared to be unaware. The editor could not conceal the disappointment and bitterness he felt at the rude ending to his dream.

"You should've got their promises early when they were all steamed up," Jack said wisely, if after the event. "There's nothing to stir up interest like having an investment in a venture."

The publisher was in no mood to accept any blame himself for the financial failure of the special edition. "I didn't hear you telling me that when it might've done some good," said Joe accusingly, and as an afterthought, "let alone soliciting any advertising."

Uncle Jack shrugged. "It's not my bloody paper!" he said.

Jack was not as unsympathetic as his words implied. Like Joe, he felt great disappointment at the paper's lack of success, and was also venting his spleen. The remark stood, however, and pride prevented him from withdrawing it.

"So that's how you feel about it!" Joe now had a tangible adversary. "You're damn right, it isn't your paper, and don't be so ready to tell me what I should or shouldn't do." In high dudgeon, the editor slammed out of the office and was away, before Bill or his uncle could say a word in reply.

Jack was only momentarily nonplussed. "Silly bugger," he commented mildly.

"I'm sorry, Uncle Jack," offered Bill. "He doesn't really mean what he says."

He was concerned for the *causes* of the argument, the blow to his father's pride, and the not inconsiderable financial loss sustained. Five hundred dollars was close to four months' income to the printer. The special edition had taken all of his savings, and some of its expenses were yet to be met. As if disappointment and humiliation were not enough, thought Bill, worry about the debt added to his father's burden.

Still seething from his quarrel with Jack, the editor strode along the street to the Newmarket Hotel, and giving a curt nod to the friendly greeting of the clerk, he entered the bar.

Doctor Brouse was there, taking a noontime break from his busy schedule. The doctor's table was the most crowded in the room, indicating the esteem in which he was held. Brouse was one of the town's earliest settlers, and probably its greatest benefactor, with his establishment of a complete hospital a few years earlier. He caught Joe's eye, and called out, "Come on over, J. J."

The newsman joined the others at the doctor's table, greeting in turn the men seated there.

"Hello J. J.," said the short man sitting to the right of the doctor.

"H'lo Joe," was the greeting from the man on the doctor's left.

The first was Billy Tomlinson, the perky, attractive manager of Bourne Brothers General Store. He and Charlie Nelson, the druggist, on the doctor's other side, had been the companions of Johnny Harris in his exploration of the New Denver Glacier, as reported in Joe's special edition. Ed Agrignon, the ex-blacksmith turned barber, also greeted Joe with warmth, and the printer was introduced to the two strangers at the table. They were youthful drummers who had been calling that morning upon Billy Tomlinson, and had joined him for lunch at the Newmarket.

"You need a drink, man," said Billy, "you look like a thundercloud." The waiter took Joe's order for a whiskey.

"Yup, I guess I do," said Joe, relaxing a little in the company of his friends. "The damn shop has been getting me down." He took a long pull at the drink the waiter put before him, and settled back with a sigh.

"I would have thought that you would be very happy with your successful special issue," said Doctor Brouse, with all the good intent in the world. "My congratulations," he continued. "Your newspaper was worthy of a much larger city than New Denver, and we are all proud to be advertised in such a flattering manner."

"I'm glad you think so," said Joe grumpily.

"Do I detect a discordant note in your voice?" enquired Billy Tomlinson. "Are you less than happy with the special issue?"

"Nothing wrong with the paper," snapped Joe ungraciously, and he signalled for another drink.

"What's bothering you, J. J.?" asked Charlie Nelson, coming right to the point. "You're acting like a goddamned spoilt kid!"

Billy Tomlinson jumped in quickly, before Joe could retort to Charlie's direct approach. "Hey, Joe, we're your friends here. What's wrong?"

"I'll tell you what's wrong!" said Joe acidly, all of his resentment coming to a boil. He downed half the contents of the glass before he let it all out. "This whole damn cheap town is what's wrong!" The shocked expressions on his friends' faces goaded him to further excess. "You're great friends, all right. Oh yes, you all cheered and were going to support me when I talked to you at the Board of Trade." He took another long drink and narrowed his eyes at the group. He had gone too far to turn back. "But where the hell were you when it came to advertising, and what have you done about circulating the paper? Nothing!"

Billy Tomlinson was the first to recover from Joe's attack. The goodnatured merchant was the last person who should have been vilified by the newsman. He had placed a good-sized advertisement in the *Review's* special edition, and bought a generous supply of copies for distribution. Now he was quick to recognize the cause of Joe's ill temper and to overlook his exceedingly bad manners.

"Hold on, old son," Billy said, more softly than Joe deserved, "you're barking up the wrong tree." The others sat stiffly, ready to carry the fight to the publisher if he uttered another word.

Joe had the sense to remain silent after Tomlinson's intervention, and Billy continued. "Why pick on us?" he asked mildly.

He looked at the other merchants, who nodded. These men had all supported the souvenir issue more than adequately, and Joe had no reason to quarrel with those present.

Doctor Brouse asked the question for all of them. "I take it that your special undertaking was unsuccessful financially?" Joe nodded miserably. Doctor Brouse continued, "Nevertheless, I think you owe these gentlemen an apology, Mr. Atherton." The formal manner of address was a sting to Joe's pride; still, he was grateful for the mildness in the doctor's tone. He made up his mind quickly.

"You're quite right, Doctor." He could have kicked himself for losing his temper. He had to gulp down his resentment, even as his animosity towards the town still festered. "I'm sorry," he stated with regret, "I shouldn't have taken it out on you fellows. It's my hard luck, not yours, that I didn't get all the support I needed to make a success of the paper." He tried to make up for his previous outbreak. "Come on, let's have a drink."

Doctor Brouse refused, but cordially, and took his leave. Charlie Nelson's manner was constrained for a little while but he remained. Gradually, with Billy Tomlinson's wit and charm lending a good example, the group did relax, and several drinks were consumed before Tomlinson, Nelson and Ed Agrignon returned to their businesses.

Joe had no taste for the printing and publishing trade that afternoon, and the young drummers, more than willing to have a drinking companion, stayed on with him in the tavern. In the late afternoon, augmented by two more townsmen, the group proceeded to play stud poker, and it was midnight before Joe went home. He was more than a little drunk, but had won twenty dollars from the inexperienced young travelling men.

The summer day was perfect and Alice's contentment was great. Carrie, who had long since moved into her own home, had come over, and the two were having a cup of tea on the porch facing the lake. The blossoms on the fruit trees were long gone, and the trees were now laden with the small and bitter apples and pears, which would ripen at the end of summer. On the faint breeze from the lake was borne the rich scent of grass, fresh mown under duress by Ernie, before he hastily decamped with his chums.

Joe had received a good scolding for his late arrival home a few nights earlier, but his wife was not disposed to brooding over past arguments. Joe was Joe. She loved him dearly and, as long as he did not depart too far from the behaviour to be expected of a good husband and father, she accepted his failings as even payment for his usual generosity and good humour. Not that his mood had been particularly buoyant recently. He was inclined to silent spells, and Alice knew he still stewed over the newpaper's failure. She and Carrie and Jack had all told him that he had reason to be proud of his May twenty-fourth issue of the *Review* but the editor had depended so much upon the paper's financial success that its artistic triumph was not enough.

In spite of this brief cloud over her thoughts, Alice was happy. Joe's disappointments did not last for long, and the *Slocan Mining Review* was still publishing successfully. Fianncial problems did not last forever, and in the meantime, they all had their health, Joe had a good business, and she had her lovely home by Lake Slocan. It was into this blissful state that Joe dropped his bombshell that afternoon.

As he rounded the corner of the porch, Alice and Carrie could see the old gleam of excitement in Joe's eyes, but their pleased reaction was only temporary. Out of the blue, and to their complete astonishment, he declared, "We're all going to Creston!"

Alice showed her confusion at this astounding revelation. "For a holiday?" she asked, only half believing this was what he meant.

"What d'you mean; all of us?" asked Carrie, suspiciously.

"No, not a holiday, and yes, all of us," laughed Joe, all of his mischief and high spirits returning with the news he bore. "We are going to move to Creston to publish a newspaper there." He turned to Carrie, "You and Jack are coming too. The town's bigger than New Denver and the paper will support all of us."

Alice still couldn't believe him. Her calm contentment of the afternoon was destroyed by her husband's announcement.

"You're not serious! Have you made some crazy arrangement without consulting me?" In spite of her husband's propensity for change, this was the first time that Joe appeared to have made plans without conferring with her. Alice's indignation grew. Not since she confronted him in Medicine Hat, had she been so put out with Joe.

"Take it easy, Alice," Joe attempted to placate his wife. "It all came up very suddenly." His face darkened again as he added, with a bitterness Alice had not seen in him before, "I'm not going to stay in this damn town a minute longer than I have to, so we're going to Creston."

Alice looked at her husband in disbelief. Never before had he let anything affect him as had the special edition failure. Further, he seemed bound to blame the town and its merchants for his problem, rather than any shortcoming of his own. She could see there was to be no reasoning with him.

Carrie showed her own consternation at her cousin's high-handedness. "Did you not think to consult Jack, either?" she asked incredulously.

Joe had not expected any questioning of his decision. So bound up was he, in his determination to quit New Denver, that he had quite overlooked the possibility that his wife might not agree. Carrie's questioning of his plans only made him more adamant in his resolution.

"Well, *I'm* going," he stated flatly, "and I don't give a damn what the rest of you do," and he stalked into the house.

It was so unlike him, that Alice's first reaction was concern that he might be ill; but she soon realized that his pique over the newspaper was affecting his whole outlook. His behaviour could not be excused. The women looked at one another briefly before Alice said, "Please stay here, Carrie."

Joe had gone to their room, sulking like one of his younger children, and Alice found him there.

"You had better tell me what plans you've made," she told her husband, her voice deceptively mild as she sat down on the bed.

Joe tried to recapture his enthusiasm as he told her. "I had a visit today from A. T. Pemberton of Creston, over in the East Kootenays. It's a big town now and growing, with land reclamation plans that'll make it the biggest city in the interior." Alice reserved the thought that each new town was to be bigger and better, and Joe continued.

"Pemberton is a businessman looking for an investment. He saw a copy of our souvenir edition, and he's very impressed," Joe paused before he appealed to her. "Look, mama, I'm not going to be happy here, and this is a fine opportunity, for all of us."

She measured Joe and their relationship before she replied. In some ways he was still like another child to her. Until now she had gone along with his whims and, though the family had not suffered to any degree, she seemed always to be teetering on an edge of uncertainty. She remembered too, the pattern of their existence, shifting from one extreme of affluence to another. From near-slum housing in Medicine Hat to the luxury of the Park Hotel, and from the drab flat in Sandon to the comfort of her present home. In a low voice, she told him her decision.

"If you must go, you must; but I'll not expose the children or myself to another move that comes because of a sudden fancy or because of your own selfish reasons."

She had spoken quite calmly and without undue emphasis, and Joe stared at her, unwilling to believe that this was his Alice talking to him. "You can't mean it!" he said.

"I do mean it," she replied, "and if you are set upon leaving everything you've built up here, you leave us here too."

By mid-July he was gone.

The rift between the couple had widened from the day he came home with his announcement. Their only communication was in the presence of Jack and Carrie, or of the children, and then with only the barest of exchanges. It was agreed that Jack and Bill would continue to publish the *Slocan Mining Review,* but no discussion took place, of a later move by the family to Creston. Alice was heartsick at the strained and silent separation from her husband. She longed to write to Joe; even thought of asking his forgiveness for her stubbornness, but realized that their marriage had been one-sided for too long. Pride asserted itself and she became determined to hold out regardless of the final outcome.

To the town, and to the children, Joe's absence was for the purpose of establishing a second newspaper in Creston. Only Jack and Carrie knew of the conflict between the couple, and they held their peace. Both were sympathetic to Alice, but they felt a family loyalty to Joe, and wished their cousins could find a basis of settlement for their differences.

Another problem added to Alice's difficulties, in Joe's absence. Ernie, high spirited and mischievous always, had never been a bad boy, but now, just short of his fourteenth birthday, he became a handful without his father's usual supervision and swift justice. It was mostly a matter of coming home too late, and being too vague about his companions, but Alice had enough to cope with and wished all the more for Joe's comforting presence within the family.

A solution to the Ernie problem came from Bessie Hinde. Joe's sister Bessie had married, and moved to a farm on the outskirts of Calgary. Her husband, Bill Hinde, had a whole section of land in grain, and kept pigs, chickens and some cattle for family use. Bessie wrote that they could use the services of one of the older boys, if he could be spared, to continue his studies but help with the farm work. Ernie was a most unlikely farmer, Alice had to admit, but the boy agreed to go, with the idea that he was to become a cowboy on the Alberta range. Even Alice was unsure what was expected of her son, but this seemed an opportunity sent by providence, and it was always possible that Ernie would carve out a career in prairie farming. She had no fear that her son might fall among worse companions in the country. Uncle Bill Hinde was said to be a heavy-handed disciplinarian.

CHAPTER THIRTY-SEVEN

Creston, 1908

The town of Creston was situated in the valley of the Kootenay River, and surrounded by the Purcell and the Selkirk ranges. The wealth of the community lay in the delta of the river, its earth rich with soil and humus washed downstream over the centuries, and deposited by floods far from the river bed. Even before the turn of the century, agriculturists had visualized the area as the centre for the fruit orchards and market gardens to come. As they had foreseen, trees and gardens were being planted, as quickly as the land reclamation projects pushed the brush ever further back from the stream. In a better frame of mind, Joe would have delighted in Creston's natural beauty, and enthused over the town's obvious prosperity and permanence.

The black mood which had accompanied him from New Denver did not immediately dissipate, as he plunged into his new venture. He was determined to show a vague "them" that he was an astute businessman; one who knew what he was about, and who would brook interference from no one. He missed Alice terribly, but would not admit this, even to himself. In the loneliness he felt most keenly in the evenings, he frequented the bars and backroom gambling tables, meeting the hotel proprietors and other convivial townsmen, as well as those transient salesmen who were looking for something to fill out their long evenings.

His days were much better. He had a loose business arrangement with A. T. Pemberton, the man who had encouraged his move to Creston. Pemberton offered him property, ideal to the printer's purpose. It was close to the centre of things, and consisted of two lots with a modest bungalow set right in their middle. There was plenty of room for a printshop on the site, and with a momentary flash of his ordinary good humour, he renamed the little back street on which his establishment was to be built Fleet Street.

He struck a deal with the firm of Richards and Morritt, said to be the town's leading contractors. The builders agreed to erect a two-room frame print office for

198

Joe, in return for future advertising in the newspaper. This left the publisher's meagre store of funds free for the purchase of printing equipment and supplies.

For his press and cases of type, Joe went to R. W. Northey of Keremeos, like Colonel Lowery, a pioneer printing man, but now retired. Northey was a likeable and easygoing newsman, like others Joe had met in the West. His last venture had been in Rossland, and it was the rusting equipment of this defunct newspaper that Northey now offered to Joe at a good price, on easy terms.

He wrote a guarded letter home telling of his progress. Although unhappy at being at odds with Alice, his tone was stiff, reflecting the stand that he was the injured party. Presuming the letter would bring Alice to her senses, his spirits rose considerably, and he gave all his attention to the paper.

Number one, volume one, of Joe's new paper was offered to the citizens of Creston on Thursday, August twentieth, 1908. As promised to his subscribers, one thousand copies of *The Creston Review*'s first offering were run off, initial circulation being somewhat less than that figure. The merchants were enthusiastic and supportive, their advertising spilling over onto the front page.

The up-and-coming nearby town of Moyie was represented by an advertisement placed by the Moyie Brewery, "Manufacturers of the Celebrated Lake Shore Export." C. O. (Chas) Rodgers of Creston had a dignified ad for his sawmill and building supply business. Brock Moran and his partner Mead boasted of their Creston Hotel, "The Leading Hotel of the Fruit Belt. Our rooms are well furnished, in a manner up-to-date, and the Bar is stocked second to none in the Province." S. A. Speers announced that his was "The Quality Store" and that he was sole agent for Ridgways Teas, Schram's Sealers, Campbell's Clothing and Aylmer Canned Goods. He also purveyed gents' furnishings, hardware and Five Roses flour, in that order. Speers's opposition, The Creston Mercantile, had all of the above merchandise, though not the same brand names, and indicated as well a readiness to supply boots and shoes, feed and harness.

From the presale of advertising space, it was evident that the publisher had become less confident of receiving his town's support without effort on his part. Some innocence had died in the ashes of the unsold copies of the *Slocan Mining Review*'s special edition, and the opening lines of his masthead copy were significant.

> We are here primarily to make a million, and incidentally to advertise the resources of the town and district.

The townspeople took this to be a humorous sally, but at the time Joe's priorities were being stated bluntly, with a determination quite different from the earlier easygoing approach, deplored by his cousin Jack. In this new "get-tough" policy he declared:

> Subscriptions, $1.00 a year, strictly in advance. No pay, no paper.
> No standoff for legal advertising.

Quack ads introduced to the waste paper basket: same with unsigned contributions.

In the first and subsequent issues of *The Creston Review*, Joe was to promote the town and its advantages; and he also had the grace to give the merchants credit for their support.

> We were met by the business community of Creston in a manner that is unprecedented in the annals of newspaperdom. We venture to assert that no town in Western Canada hitherto held at the onset such an enthusiastic and enterprising aggregation of businessmen.

So *The Creston Review* was off to a good start, with the townspeople adding to the paper's income with orders for business stationery and forms, personal cards and invitations, handbills and notices. Joe was never busier and The Creston Publishing Company began to turn a profit soon after its launching.

With the success of the business seemingly assured, Joe had time for the furbishing of the cottage on his property. The house was in fair condition, but needed decorating, to make it attractive for Alice and the family; it being his foregone conclusion that his wife's arrival depended only upon the readiness of her new home.

Once again, Richards and Morritt came to the rescue, and papered and painted the house to make it quite appealing. He tidied up the property, and got a local lad to mow down the overgrown grass and weed that covered the two lots. Thereafter, throughout the summer, a weekly mowing would keep the whole place pleasing, in keeping with the new paper's prosperity. Joe had to admit that the word "compact" would be a kind one for the house, particularly in comparing it to the family's generously proportioned home by Lake Slocan. It was, however, orderly and clean, and a place for the family to be together again. The cottage's two bedrooms would have to be supplemented by cots in the living room for the boys, but it wouldn't be the first time that a certain amount of doubling up would be accepted as the norm by the large family. He was quite philosophical about it.

He had been so busy establishing the newspaper and getting the house in order, that Alice's belated reply to his letter, when it did come, was shocking in the extreme. It revealed, not an apologetic and submissive wife, but an Alice of resolve and spirit. She faithfully reported the affairs of the family and the New Denver business under the direction of Jack and Bill, but if his letter had been guarded, hers was distant and gave no indication that she was inclined to change her situation. He could take little comfort from the dutiful ending, "Love, Alice," as the tone of the rest of the letter reflected the hurt which she still felt, and her determination not to let Joe put the family in jeopardy through caprice on his part.

"I'll be damned!" Joe exploded, when he read the last line. "After all the trouble I've gone to just for her!" He looked about the neat little cottage, building up righteous wrath, at the enormity of Alice's rebellion. "Can you beat that?" he asked the empty room in disgust, as he got out the bottle of whiskey from the top shelf in the kitchen, and poured himself a stiff drink. Again he read the letter, exclaiming over each cool sentence until he came to the ending once more. "Ah, to hell with her," he muttered, and crumpled the letter before hurling it at the far wall. He stalked out of the house, and went downtown to seek solace in the Creston Hotel.

Time dragged slowly and dully for Alice in New Denver. In spite of the tone of her letter, she missed Joe dreadfully; a real ache existed like a cancer inside her. Unlike the occasion of their previous long separation, this time she had the bitter taste of their quarrel remaining, to spoil the sweetness of eventual reunion. The future seemed uncertain and dark to the young wife, even as her immediate security seemed assured. The *Slocan Mining Review*, under the guidance of Jack Atherton and Bill, was publishing regularly and providing an income for the two families. How long this would last was uncertain, as the paper lacked the former editor's whimsical style, and advertising patronage was less than overwhelming.

Letters from Ernie came as frequently as his aunt chided him into writing. His letters home, Alice thought, could have been more discreet, considering the possibility that they might be censored by his aunt and uncle. His state of mind was revealed by his lurid descriptions of his chores on the farm, and his detestation of his present lot was apparent. His mother presumed he was less outspoken in the presence of his aunt and uncle and hoped that his writing allowed him to work off some of his resentment. If Ernie's letters could be believed, he spent his entire life among pigs and chickens, supplying them with copious quantities of foul-smelling swill and feed, which the ungrateful creatures discharged immediately and indiscriminately, in even more malodorous forms. If that wasn't enough, the cycle continued distastefully and hopelessly for the youth, as he acted as chambermaid to the offensive animals. Gritting his teeth, he scraped their filth from chicken coops and pig pens, and deposited it on manure heaps, from whence it would inexorably go to support the growth of even more produce and animal food. With despair, Ernie realized that the cycle would never end. There would never be enough food to satisfy the voracious appetites of his squawking, clucking, crowing and grunting charges.

Meanwhile, in Creston, Ernie's father was deliberately setting out to show his wife that he was his own man, as he plunged into a reckless round of dissipation. Had Joe been in Sandon, rather than Creston, in the succeeding weeks, the wild little mining town would have swallowed him up in its iniquitous depths. Fortunately, Creston's wild life was more limited and, although he drank too much and tried to lure others to late night card games, his best companions were responsible men who vanished at midnight, leaving him to drink morosely alone.

He tried the company of the Bank Boys, who worked at the Bank of Commerce, and lived in the bachelor quarters above it. The young men were not supposed to spend their lives in riotous living but, like Joe, were homesick and in need of company, and took to the taverns as often as discretion and their limited incomes would allow. They were all good fellows, but much too young for the thirty-six year old Joe. Moreover, their interests inclined more toward the young ladies of their own age in the town. Indeed, the Bank Boys were much sought after socially, and were generally approved of by the fathers, matrons, and ministers who arbitrated the social structure of Creston. Joe, on the other hand, was an anomaly, an unattached man in his maturity, and therefore to be regarded with some suspicion. With no wife or family to give him respectability, Joe Atherton was not truly acceptable to Creston society, as much as some husbands regarded him as a good fellow.

The lonelier he became, the more he drank, and often by himself. A climax was overdue and, on a cold night in October, the inevitable happened; he passed out cold on the kitchen floor of his little cottage. There was no one to witness his disgrace, or to throw a blanket over him. He awoke in the morning, shivering with the cold and automatically reaching for the comforting presence of the bottle. It was empty, and he got up from the floor aching in every bone and still shaking as if he had the ague. The repulsiveness of the taste in his mouth and the aching of his head were only exceeded by the wave of nausea that took him as he drew erect. He had to hurtle himself at the sink to disgorge the contents of his stomach. He vomited four times and gagged thrice, deep shuddering convulsions that alarmed him with their intensity. He looked fearfully at the sink, quite certain he had dislodged some vital organ into it.

He looked up and into the small shaving mirror he had hung above the sink. The reflection he saw repelled him almost as much as the thought of more whiskey. His ever-prominent eyes were now crisscrossed with tiny red lines, and pouched from lack of proper rest. His face was blotched, except for around his nostrils, that area being pinched and white.

"My God, you look awful!" he told the loathsome figure confronting him, and disgust, humiliation, and remorse in turn possessed him. He knew now what he had to do.

CHAPTER THIRTY-EIGHT

New Denver and Creston, 1908

Before his mother's eyes, Bill was slimming and lengthening out, as he left boyhood behind. He would be fifteen in January. She worried as the tan that he had gained in the early summer faded, and his cheeks lost their youthful roundness, but she reacted with pride to his quiet acceptance of responsibility, and delighted in what she thought of as his manliness.

In his father's absence, Bill took up himself the role of provider and, to a degree, disciplinarian of the younger children. Oddly, the others did not resent him. He was not obnoxious, as an older brother or sister can be, but he exercised a quiet influence when their exuberance reached untenable limits. It helped that, with Ernie away, the age spread between himself and the others was more pronounced, and gave credence to the adult role he adopted toward the youngsters.

"Is the work at the shop terribly hard, Billy?" his mother asked one evening, her anxiety reflected in the glance she shot at him. Even though their ordinary closeness was the more cherished in this situation, the forced reliance upon her son was hard for Alice to bear. She longed for the days of repose and happiness that preceded her husband's departure, and mourned her son's lost boyhood.

Bill looked up from his book with a reassuring smile. "Not a bit," he said matter-of-factly. "You know," he said in reflection, "Uncle Jack is a tougher boss than Papa in a lot of ways. More strict somehow, but I sure learn a lot from him. Papa was more fun to work with though," and they both fell quiet at this recollection.

"What will you do, Mama?"

Bill was aware of the rift, but until this moment it had been a subject unmentioned between him and his mother. Now, as a result of his sudden question, Alice was forced to face her position squarely. In reflection, she knew

203

she had acted wisely in refusing to accompany Joe to Creston. If the couple's relationship was to survive, it would have to be even-sided for both. Joe was getting no younger, and must realize that it was not possible for him to act upon whim, or without consideration for the effect upon his growing family. Especially, must he never again make important decisions, such as the one that drove him from New Denver, without first getting agreement from his wife. Even as she stiffened her resolve, the pain increased. The four month separation from her husband had been harder in some ways than the twelve months she spent alone in England. At least, on that other occasion she and Joe had not quarreled, and her future had always appeared to be certain.

The first resentment and high resolve she felt upon Joe's departure for Creston, four months earlier, had settled into a dull ache. She was disappointed at the loss of the secure life she had been living; worried for her family; and, as she now faced it realistically, miserable living without Joe nearby.

Bill's question was still unanswered, and she perceived in that instant that she would never be the one responsible for a permanent rift in the family. "Of course, we'll join your father in Creston, Billy, when the business gets on its feet," she said briskly. Bill was quick to note the "when," and was overjoyed to hear the decisive note in his mother's voice, as she continued, "He'll be home for Christmas, and we'll know more then." The new life in her voice did not go unnoticed by Bill, and their smiles at one another showed, more than any words, the closeness of their thoughts and their mutual happiness in Alice's resolution.

Joe's babbling letter of contrition arrived after Alice had made up her mind. It was so abject that she wondered briefly what he had been about, but she was not of a mind to pursue that thought. It was enough that Joe loved and needed her, and the family would be united again. She wrote warmly and lovingly in response to his appeal. Yes, she would come, now that the business was well established, and the new home ready. They were all well, but the business in New Denver was going slowly. Would the *Review* support Jack and Carrie as well, if they decided to come to Creston? She was expecting Joe home for Christmas, and final plans for the move could be made then. The family was looking forward to seeing him. She sent her fondest love, and sprinked the bottom of the page with naughts and crosses.

His reaction to the letter was pure ecstasy. He walked on air for two days after, and at least three of his friends remarked on the silly grin on his face. He celebrated the event with a half-column poem in the *Review* dedicated to "The Missus," and everyone knew that Joe's family would be coming to town after Christmas.

At the Board of Trade meeting in December, it was evident that his status in the community was on a higher plateau. One could detect a warmer acceptance of the printer, by his fellow townsmen. No doubt, the ladies of Creston had discussed Joe Atherton with their husbands, and, while he had been, up to now, a bit of an unknown quantity, it appeared that a small thaw was breaking the ice for him, even before the arrival of the wife and children who would qualify him as a Family Man.

Mr. Mallandaine, the imposing lawyer and coroner who was the new president of the Board of Trade, mentioned the news in his address to the club, and wished Joe a happy Christmas with his family in New Denver, "but hurry back, you hear, Joe? We need you in Creston."

Fred Burton, who had been the first president at the Board of Trade's founding earlier that year, offered the printer a cigar after dinner, and told him he was looking forward to meeting Mrs. Atherton and the family.

The well-to-do and handsomely tailored Chas Rodgers, of the sawmill, broke off his conversation with S. A. Speers to beckon Joe over. He had the reputation of being reserved, if not stiff, but he and Speers were particularly cordial to Joe.

"Mrs. Rodgers asked me to be sure to tell you she wants you and Mrs. Atherton to call upon us, when your wife comes to town," Rodgers told Joe. "We are looking forward to meeting her." As an afterthought, he added, "Understand you have a boy the same age as our lad . . . away at Gonzaga right now . . . high school you know . . . boys can get together in the summer."

After making the rounds, and receiving the congratulations of the others on his coming family reunion, Joe joined his special pals, Brock Moran and Joe Carver. He received a forceful nudge in the ribs from the big Irish hotel keeper, and a sarcastic "Well, I don't suppose you'll have any time for us commoners now?" and from the saddlery proprietor, a reference to the printer's hobnobbing with the senior club members.

"Go to the devil," grinned Joe. No amount of joshing could spoil these days, before his departure for New Denver and, in spite of his friends' remarks, it was good to be recognized and know that Alice would be made to feel at home, when she arrived in Creston.

Christmas time, at home in New Denver, was notable for its blend of gaiety, sadness, and decision. Rapture for Joe and Alice, in their reunion and reconciliation, and melancholy for poor Father Jeanotte in this second leavetaking of his friends. Apart from her joy at seeing Joe again, the period contained a variety of emotions for Alice: excitement at the coming move, regret at leaving the house she dearly loved, enjoyment of the Christmas season, (modified by some apprehension for the future), dread for the almost inevitable departure of Bill from the bosom of his family, and a happy resolution to bring Ernie home as soon as possible.

Joe's appearance, while not significantly changed in the eyes of the less observant, was shocking to Alice. Leaner than ever, through the combination of hasty meals, hard labour, late hours, and indiscretion in his drinking habits, it could be seen that he needed her to regulate his time, and modify his conduct. The always sharp and prominent planes of his face were now emphasized by his thinness, and worse, a tiny network of lines had begun creasing Joe's forehead and the corners of his eyes. His big grin had carved deep creases in his cheeks and, to the concerned Alice, this familiar expression had become almost a grimace. Fattening him up became her prime objective during the Christmas season, and Joe, more content than he had been for many months, relaxed and enjoyed the attention and love, which she lavished on him.

Christmas Day was the gayest in Alice's memory. The three men in her life, Joe, Bill, and Father Jeanotte, were all present for Christmas dinner, and other dinner guests filled the house to overflowing. Two English boys, William and Robert Beames, had come, laden with presents for the younger children. For Winnie, they brought an imported wicker doll carriage for the nine dolls that the young lady had accumulated that morning, and for Reggie, in his fourth year, a fine, red, wooden express wagon. Shyly, the Beames presented to Alice an enormous bouquet of roses, an unheard-of luxury in the limited resources of New Denver, brought in specially by train from Vancouver for the occasion.

Jack and Carrie Atherton, with their baby Florrie, came in time for dinner and were introduced to the guest of honour, no less a person than His Excellency, Augustine, Bishop Dontenwill of New Westminster Diocese. The bishop had come to the Kootenays to spend Christmas with his old friend Father Jeanotte, and had graciously accepted the Athertons' invitation to share the Christmas meal. The Reverend Mr. Baynes, too, had come from Sandon to spend Christmas with his English friends, but was being very quiet, for him, somewhat in awe of the episcopal presence at the party.

Father Jeanotte seemed lost in his own thoughts at first but, under the prodding of his superior, he became his old whimsical self, pretending to be bewildered by the outrageous joshing of the bishop, but managing to give back as good as he got; always "begging Your Excellency's pardon," of course. The bishop laughed uproariously at every sally, and enjoyed every minute of his short visit. Mr. Baynes eventually lost his reserve and got in a few dry remarks, but it was Joe who jumped in with both feet from the beginning. How he loved it, Alice saw. His eyes sparkled and his mind raced, to meet the challenge of wit that bounced about the table. It was good to see him happy, and in his element.

The Beames brothers basked in the warmth of Alice's hospitality, and laughed at the good natured raillery exchanged by the clerics and their host. It was a welcome change from the ribald humour of the mines, and a release from the drudgery and discomfort of their ordinary existence.

The bishop excused himself after dinner, in order to keep another engagement, but gave the guests and the house his blessing before his departure. Father Jeanotte, showing his weariness, made his quiet adieus to Alice and Joe shortly thereafter. It was on all their minds that this was was probably a final parting between friends, but no one cared to voice the thought.

"I don't come to Creston," was the oblique reference made by the priest.

Had they known him for only five years? With all the changes in her life since he had become her first friend in Canada, it seemed much longer to Alice. Tenderly, she recalled his quiet support in Medicine Hat, and the delightful surprise of seeing his beaming face in her doorway in Ferguson. With less reserve than she had shown on that second occasion, she put her arms around the old priest in sudden affection. With her head close to his musty frock-coated shoulder, she could smell the aroma that was particularly his, a scent made up of aromatic pipe tobacco, incense absorbed into his clothing, and a hint of the fruity flavour of sacramental wine. She loved him so much, and now she was not to see him again. But she would not cry. Her resolution nearly melted when he looked into her eyes with tears in his own, and said once again, "My dear Alice."

Joe, too heartily and too loudly, said, "We will be seeing one another soon. Take care of yourself Father!" and wrung the priest's hand.

"I'll walk you to the hotel, Father."

The priest turned gratefully to the boy, his voice rough as he said, "I vill be glad of your company, Billy," and he turned without another look, but with a wave over his shoulder, for the couple on the porch.

"Goodbye!" they chorused, and Joe's arm went around his wife's shoulder, as the old man and the young man trudged away together.

The priest recovered his composure, as they walked along in the calm winter night. He drew his scarf closer against the cold stillness, and matched his steps with his young friend along the planked sidewalk. Bill waited respectfully for the older man to open the conversation. "I understand you are going avay from home, Billy," he said.

"Not right away, Father," said Bill. "I'm going to Creston for a few months with the family, before I go to Michel to work in the printshop there. You see," he continued, "with Uncle Jack there, Papa won't need me, and the printer at Michel has wanted an assistant for a long time." He added earnestly, "It'll be good experience for me too, don't you think?"

Father Jeanotte sighed to himself, at the youthfulness of his companion, quite forgetting his own early introduction to the working world, and the responsibility of parents to provide for. He did not express misgivings though, and hastened to agree with the boy. "Yes, it vill be a fine experience, and you are a goot boy Billy. Ve don't haf to vorry about you!"

"Thanks Father, I'll try to live up to your good opinion," said Bill self-consciously, and he added diffidently, "I guess, I can use some prayers," and he looked straight ahead as they walked along.

Father Jeanotte glanced at his companion with affection. "I vill alvays pray for you Billy," was his simple remark. He was well aware of the effort it had taken to break the youthful taboo on religious discussion, and loved his young friend the more for it. He was not going to labour the point, but he hearkened back to Bill's confirmation instruction. "Remember vot is said to you den?" The boy nodded.

"You are going out into d'world, and since you are only human, 'dere vill be many temptations for you, Billy." He was aware of the lad's embarrassment, but continued steadily, "But God is goot and forgiffing. Just remember to ask for blessing and forgiffness every night before you go to sleep, and wheneffer you are in dan-cher." He peered at Billy over the top of his glasses. "Remember how it goes, 'Oh my God, I am heartily sorry for having offended thee' . . . "

"I remember, Father."

"Goot!" said Father Jeanotte happily. "Dat's all you've got to 'tink about," and, having reached the hotel, the two shook hands warmly. The old fellow watched with pride, as the tall youth walked away, then turned into the hotel with the loneliness of the priest as his companion.

CHAPTER THIRTY-NINE

Creston, 1909

Colonel Lowery, the newspaperman of neighbouring Greenwood, writing in his *Ledge*, summarized the arrival of the Athertons into Creston with the words: "The editor of *The Creston Review* has moved his family from New Denver to that town. This event has made a noticeable increase in the population."

Indeed it had. Including their English cousins, and the child conceived by the couple in the happiness of Christmas week, Joe and Alice would be accountable for ten additional citizens for the town, before the year 1909 was ended. The Colonel's witticism was truer than he realized.

But much was to happen in the year, which had just begun. Joe's rash departure from New Denver, after his quarrel with that town, and his subsequent estrangement from, then reconciliation with, his wife, had set in motion a chain of events which would irrevocably change the course of their lives. The happiness of the couple's present accord would be put to severe tests.

No such brooding thoughts crossed Alice's mind, as she adapted to the new town. Her happiness was too recent to admit bothersome doubts and fears. Despite her initial shock at the smallness of the cottage awaiting her, she rallied to sort out the problem of accommodating family and effects, while another cottage nearby was taken by Carrie and Jack. All in all, Alice was content; she had Joe by her side and, for the time being, Bill. He was to leave in April, when Ernie would return.

As if to make up for their former neglect of her husband, several women called upon her. A few were stiffly formal in style; most were genuinely interested and thoughtful in bringing small gifts for the house. She took an immediate liking to Mrs. Rodgers, the wife of the sawmill owner. Chas Rodgers might have been reserved, as Joe had told her. His wife was anything but. She was open and friendly, and Alice found herself laughing and at ease with a new friend, one without a shred of pretence in her makeup.

Only one episode marred the enjoyment of her introduction to Creston. On the first Sunday after their arrival, Alice and Joe hurried to get the children ready for

209

Mass. Their boxes and cases were still in disarray, and finding the children's Sunday clothing took longer than usual. The service had been in progress for five minutes, when they arrived at the church door, and Father Wagner had begun his reading of the Gospel.

A family of seven can make a spectacular entrance into a church, particularly when three of them are younger than seven years. Reggie's new boots had been chosen to last for as long as possible, so were currently in the Too-Big category. The clatter of his feet mingled with a comment or two by the not quite two year old Teddy; intrigued by this new experience, though not awed by it. The little boy's voice was clearly heard above that of Father Wagner, despite the shushing of his elders.

The family was well aware of the unwritten etiquette on late-coming to church. If the priest had not begun to read the Epistle and Gospel, and was still turned towards the altar, one might slip into a seat without drawing undue attention. Conversely, if the priest was now facing the congregation, it was considered good manners to wait at the back of the church until he resumed the service of the Mass, with his back turned to the congregation. Unfortunately, Father Wagner was not going to allow the noisy interruption of his reading to go unnoticed. "There are plenty of seats down here," he said loudly and disapprovingly.

Winnie held tight to Bill's hand, and was aware that people were turning to see the cause of Father's remarks. She was almost as embarrassed as her brother who, red-faced, followed his mother and father to the only seat big enough to accommodate the family; one a few rows from the front. The priest did not resume his reading during their progress down the aisle, and he waited, his eyes upon the latecomers, until the last, Joe, was seated in the pew. His expression made it evident that this entrance, after the start of Mass, was bad-mannered, if not positively sinful. The other members of the congregation felt embarrassed, righteous, or gleeful according to their bent.

It was not the first time that Joe had been to Mass in Creston. In fact, he had called on Father James Wagner upon his first entry into town; full of confidence for a hearty welcome by his new pastor. Something had gone wrong. The two men were of the same age, but dissimilar in every other way. Father Wagner, for a comparatively young man, was as sombre as Joe was ebullient. Each recognized the other's origin in his speech; Joe's still retaining the accent of his native England, and Father Wagner's revealing his Germanic birth and upbringing. Both were too recently come from their homelands, where animosity festered, not to view the other as a potential adversary.

The seating of the family being completed, Father Wagner could not resist a reference to the necessity of regular, and *prompt* attendance at Mass, before he commenced his regular sermon.

It was not unusual for a pastor to indulge in a little sarcasm or pointed reproof to impolite latecomers, or to shufflefooted youngsters, but Joe smarted under the obvious disparaging reference to his family. He related this to Father Wagner's Germanic origin and unworthy thoughts of *prussian!*, and *hun!* came to his mind, as he compressed his lips and stared down at his boots. Meanwhile the priest continued his sermon, unaware of the hostility churning only a few feet away.

Alice was distressed for Joe, and mortified at the family's singling out by the priest. She was not of a nature to feel lasting resentment, but the morning augured poorly for a rich relationship between the pastor and the newest members of his flock.

The incident didn't bother Joe for long, either. In his newfound bliss, there was no room for petty animosities, and his contentment and good spirits were reflected in the columns of the *Review*. He laughed secretly at the pomposity of the Board of Trade in January, telling solemnly how Messrs. Dow, Compton and Bevan had "disrupted the meeting with complaints that the meeting was not representative." He wryly apologized for an accident which delayed publication of the *Review* for one day, and reported, with taunting quotation marks, that "Brock Moran of the Creston Hotel will shortly take 'a well-deserved holiday.'" He had privately accused the hotel keeper of being perpetually on vacation.

A brief news item stated that his other pal, Joe Carver, ". . . moved his saddlery business and store to a lot near the Munro Hotel. The building was moved Saturday." This moving of a whole frame building was watched with fascination by Joe and Bill and every other kid in town, and was to burn itself into the printer's memory for later reclamation.

Between Joe's newfound acceptability as a safely married man, and the natural result of his own gregariousness, the family found itself caught up in Creston's social whirl. They were just in time to become charter members of the Acme Quadrille Club, established for the purpose of promoting social fellowship in the rapidly growing town. As the name implied, the original intent of the club was to introduce the galloping square dances imported from across the border, but with so many Britishers about, it was inevitable that the dances of the old country would still be enjoyed. As well as the "do-si-dos" and "allthemenlefts" of the American dance, the members learned the intricate measures of the Scottish reels, and danced the courtly *Roger de Coverley* and the exuberant *Lancers*.

The Acme Quadrille Club was fun and Alice, only in her second month of pregnancy, was able to participate in the lessons of the dances new to her, and be a much sought after partner in the English dances she remembered with nostalgic pleasure. Joe's breath would catch in his throat as, unaware of his scrutiny, she swung by in the arms of another partner, her head thrown back, eyes sparkling, and flushed face laughing. Young Bill too, as a working and adult member of the community, attended the dances. Like Joe, he watched Alice with pride, realizing with some surprise, *why, mama is the most beautiful person here!*

It was easy to form a local dramatic society as an offshoot of the Acme Quadrille Club. Although Joe Atherton chaired the inaugural meeting, Captain A. S.

It was easy to form a local dramatic society as an offshoot of the Acme Quadrille Club. Although Joe Atherton chaired the inaugural meeting, Captain A. S. FitzGerald was unanimously elected president, and Joe had to be content with the appointment to acting-manager. Captain FitzGerald was one of the many ex-British Army officers to be found in the towns of British Columbia. The gallant captain and his wife, Cathy, were highly placed on Creston's social ladder, and were considered a great catch and asset to the new dramatic club. Without delay, the club selected *Arabian Nights* as their first vehicle, and Joe was given the task of finding a sponsor. At the Board of Trade, the editor received approval for their sponsorship of a performance of *Arabian Nights*. Its laudable purpose was the raising of funds for a new fire brigade hose.

Even before *Arabian Nights* could be performed, the dramatic club was offering its services to the ladies of the Catholic church for a St. Patrick's Day concert.

As Alice might have guessed, this performance was dominated by her husband. The March 11th issue of the *Review*, advertised the featured turns as being:

(a) an Octette, "The Wearing of the Green," sung by four ladies and four gentlemen.
(including J. J., of course)
(b) a Recitation, "Shamus O'Brien," by J. J. Atherton
(*Really!* thought Alice)
(c) a One-act Farce, "Box and Cox," with,
Mrs. Bounce . . . . Miss B. Moore.
Box . . . . J. J. Atherton.
Cox . . . . Captain FitzGerald

As a result of this mid-Lent performance, and a substantial collection amounting to $69.95, the remaining debt of the church was paid off, and a new bell purchased for Holy Cross parish.

The concert should have been an occasion for warmer relations between the new family and the pastor. Sadly, it was not.

CHAPTER FORTY

Creston, 1909

Jack Atherton moved smoothly into the new operation. At Christmas time, he and Joe had patched up their silly quarrel, and the two now worked together in good humour and mutual interest. Joe attended to the writing chores, for the most part, and to the advertising and other business concerns of the paper. Advertising still rolled in almost without solicitation, and in Creston's economic good times, few problems of account collection were experienced. Uncle Jack did much of the typesetting himself, and the pages of the paper reflected his careful and tidy composition. *The Creston Review* presented an appearance as professional as any big city paper, and with fewer errors.

Bill was fifteen. He had been a wage earner and a provider for two and a half years. Tall and slim, he still had to grow and flesh out the bone structure of the man-to-be. His features, at this age, were handsome but hawklike in cast, with a nose yet a little too big for him. The brown eyes were serene like his mother's, and very direct. He had the quiet assurance of one who knows his own worth, a trait which would eventually win acceptance, by others, of his leadership.

For all his maturity, he found it difficult to be objective about the new closeness and contentment of his parents, since their reunion at Christmas. His mother had been so reliant upon him in New Denver! He tried to ignore a feeling of being shut out, but Uncle Jack's easy assumption of the boy's duties added to his hollow feeling of being a third wheel.

He was too intelligent to dwell on these thoughts with resentment for the others, and stoutly told himself that the new job was good both for him and the family. The *Review* would run smoothly under Papa's and Uncle Jack's direction and he would gain experience, and a better wage than he could expect at home.

His parents were more aware of him than he knew.

"Poor Billy," his mother sighed. Her oldest son had retired to his living room cot, and had fallen asleep as soon as his head hit the pillow. As was their habit, she and Joe were in the kitchen at this time of night, sipping a last cup of cocoa before turning in themselves. "He's not very happy, you know," she added, looking to her husband for some kind of comfort or solution.

"I know," he nodded sympathetically. He thought of his own many partings from his parents, as a youth in England; his recollection being that he always went blithely, without too much consideration for their feelings. Bill was different, more sensitive. "He's going to miss you, as you will miss him," he offered. The close bond between his wife and their eldest son had never been a matter of resentment for Joe; if he lacked discernment in some things, he had the wit to recognize a special boon and blessing when he saw one.

"The play!" he said suddenly, jumping to his feet.

"I thought we were talking about Billy," said Alice in reproof.

"We were. I am," he said. "There's a part in it for him. Don't you see, it'll be good for him, take his mind off his going away for a while!"

Joe's inspired idea was gladly embraced by his son. With only a few weeks remaining before his departure, Bill became a member of the cast of *Arabian Nights*. He was to play Dobson, the butler, while his father had the leading part of Arthur Heminstock.

His participation did relieve some of the gloom of his leavetaking for everyone, but the play, and one other incident which occurred before his departure, had the effect of alienating Bill from his pastor, and opening a permanent rift for the boy, from his Church.

Until St. Patrick's Day, Bill, as a working person, properly contributed to the weekly collections at church, through an envelope system. Upon the announcement that the St. Patrick's Day entertainment had paid off the remaining church debt, and with his own need to save money for his departure, Bill stopped his contributions to the collection plate. Other folk, for various reasons, stopped or reduced their offerings at the same time, and Father Wagner noted the lack, in his accounting.

The Sunday after the decline in revenue, the priest reproached those who were remiss, and in no uncertain terms. His scathing remarks burned into some of his congregation, so that they hurriedly renewed their commitments. Bill was among the few who, for one reason or another, did not feel that Father Wagner's remarks applied to them. At this time, he was spending no money for clothing or entertainment, and felt no qualms of conscience at the priest's remarks.

The pastor's vindictiveness came as a crashing surprise on the third Sunday after St. Patrick's Day. If those unruly members of his flock who refused to make an offering, had gone to him in the meantime, and explained their reasons for withholding funds, he would have been appeased. Instead, as the week drew on, he became incensed with what he took to be defiance, on the part of three of his gainfully employed parishioners, and he resolved to shame them.

Unaware of what was to come, the family sat in a pew near the front of the church. They had come early, mindful of the ill-timed entrance of that first visit to the Church of The Holy Cross. It was at the beginning of April; Palm Sunday, one week before Easter. The day was sunny and warm, and signs of spring had been evident as the family walked to Mass. Now the windows were open and fresh warm air, bearing the scents of the season, brought the promise of the Easter awakening to come. Alice's thoughts were tranquil as she followed the sonorous phrases of the Latin in her prayer book.

Unknown to her, Father Wagner whipped up his wrath against the delinquents, with his recitation of the Introit. "Judica me, Deus, et discerne causam meam de gente non sancta." "Do me justice, O God, and fight my cause against a faithless people; from the deceitful and impious man deliver me." He completed his reading of the Epistle and Gospel, and closed the large missal with a snap.

"It gives me," intoned Father Wagner, with a little more relish than the words would indicate," great pain to advise you of a continuing opposition in this parish, to my appeals for support and obedience to the will of God." His flock rapidly awakened from any somnolence that remained after the lulling Latin phrases of the Mass. It was evident that Father was about to drop a bomb on his congregation.

Oh no, he wouldn't! thought Joe, realizing the direction of the priest's opening remarks. He glanced at Bill, who hadn't gathered the import of the words from the altar.

"It is unfair to the members of the congregation who faithfully fulfil all their obligations to Holy Mother Church," the priest continued. "It is unfair, I say, that you have to be penalized for the ungrateful and miserly attitudes of the few."

The message was becoming clearer now, and the congregation shifted uncomfortably as the weight of words sank in. Bill still did not associate the priest's words with himself. Glancing at his father, he saw Joe's jaw harden, as he awaited the next words from the altar, and finally felt a sense of foreboding of what he might hear next. He didn't have to wait long.

"There are three persons in this congregation," Father Wagner stated clearly and slowly," who, for reasons of their own, refuse to make their just and honourable contributions to the weekly collection plate." He paused to savour the effect upon the people before him, then said, "They are William Atherton, and . . . " He named the others.

Bill didn't hear the other names, in the shock of this denunciation, before the whole parish. Initial shame was replaced by resentment and consternation. How unlike Father Jeanotte and every other priest he had known! Looking up, he saw Father Wagner's eye fixed upon him with a little gleam of malice, and Bill stood up. Pale of face, but composed, at least in appearance, the boy returned the priest's look with apparent calm then, genuflecting to the altar, he turned and walked the length of the church and out the door in the stillness of the whole congregation. Even Father Wagner refrained from comment, realizing now that the boy's departure was inevitable.

CHAPTER FORTY-ONE

Creston, 1909

The naming of non-subscribers was not an unusual event in Creston, or elsewhere. Priests and ministers were forever beset by money problems, and sometimes, in desperation for basic needs, had to resort to tactics such as Father Wagner's. Some published lists of contributors, and the amounts given. Others, more gentle and less worldly, literally starved themselves into early graves, by refusing to put the facts of life before their complacent congregations.

Father Wagner himself had mixed emotions about what had occurred. Justification warred with a sense of shame, arising from an action which he knew in his heart was born of pique.

The aftermath of the Sunday episode took place in the middle of the following week. The priest, in all justice, had some idea of appeasing the editor's family for what could be considered indiscretion on his part. It was not in his nature to apologize, or admit that he had been in the wrong; on the contrary, reflection on the events had convinced him that he had acted properly. Nevertheless, he was prepared to go to the printing office and proffer the olive branch.

A handbill in the window of the *Review* office, which Father Wagner paused to read, ruled out any possibility of an armistice. There, for all the world to see and be scandalized by, was the announcement of *Arabian Nights*. The play was to be held that very week, Holy Week, in Lent! The cast of characters included the names of his two parishioners, the editor and his son, so any feelings of forgiveness or reconciliation that the priest might have nurtured flew out the window. Even the title of the play was an affront, suggesting something vaguely indecent; certainly not in keeping with the penitential spirit of Lent.

Since this was his first encounter with *Arabian Nights*, Father Wagner was unaware that other pastors in Creston shared his scandal at the play and its poor timing. Though merely an innocuous farce, the name was offensive to the clergy, and the date of its showing was an unfortunate mistake. As Alice had said that morning, "Really Joe, is it necessary to put it on before Easter?" Her husband, though, with the other actors, was ready, and nothing was to stop them. One reason given was that Bill was leaving town shortly, and there was no one to replace him.

Father Wagner took the contents of the handbill as a personal insult. He stormed into the *Review* office, and confronted a surprised Joe and Jack, who had been poring over a pageful of type. The priest's outthrust finger indicated the offending advertisment in the window, and he stuttered with rage, as he indicated the enormity of this new offence.

"Do you have no shame?" he thundered.

Uncle Jack was considerably taken aback by the the priest's words, and wondered what tack his cousin might take. Bill appeared in the doorway from the shop, with a look of concern upon his face. Joe would normally have done his best to calm his pastor by diplomacy, but this new attack, on top of the Sunday censure of his son, was a little too much for him.

"Ashamed of what, Father?" he enquired, deceptively mild in his manner. Jack ducked his head, as if aware of being in the line of fire.

"Attending, let alone taking part in, an entertainment during Lent! That's what you should be ashamed of, Joe Atherton." Now that he was on completely defensible grounds, Father Wagner pressed the attack. "You should be giving a better example than that; a man in your position," he said scornfully. "Furthermore, you allow your son to take part in a performance that is highly questionable, and give scandal by his participation!"

In the doorway, Bill's lips tightened, and his face went pale, but he said nothing, intercepting a look from his father that told him the editor would handle this in his own way.

"Do you know the play, then, Father?" asked Joe, still mildly.

"No, indeed I do not, nor do I ever intend to know it. It is enough that you have disregarded common decency, by engaging in a shameful performance during Lent."

Oh-oh, thought Jack, *you've torn it this time, Father.* While the priest could well criticize his parishioner for participating in a play during Holy Week, he was letting the title of the play misguide him. "Shameful performance" hardly described the silly little farce.

"Father," said Joe, misquoting an old joke, "I'm a great respector of the cloth, but I'll ask you not to interfere in a quite private decision." He knew very well he was acting atrociously, and that he should have been trying to pacify the priest. Instead he threw discretion to the winds. "While I'm about it, Father," he said, unconsciously slipping into a broad Irish brogue for the occasion, "I'll thank y' not to reprimand me family in public."

It was too much for Father Wagner. So much for *his* good intentions, all wasted on this unregenerate scoundrel. "Cancel my subscription to your detestable newspaper," he said. "I want no more of your or your son's nonsense." He was boiling with rage as he slammed the door shut behind him.

"Hoity toity!" said Joe

"Silly bugger," said Jack.

Bill stepped forward, his anger and resentment plain to see. "I'll never go to his damned church again!" he cried. Tears of frustration came to his eyes, as he slammed his foot against the door through which the priest had passed.

"Hold on there, Bill," said Joe. He realized that the boy was taking this a great deal more seriously than he had intended, and he put his hand on Bill's arm, as if to restrain him. "Don't blame the Church for Father Wagner's personality." He smiled at the angry boy to coax him out of his temper. "Don't fault Father Wagner too much, either. He was doing his duty as he saw it." He regretted that his own words had not set a good example. "I shouldn't have baited him," he said, more for Bill's benefit than with remorse on his part; and a suppressed chuckle came out with the words.

Jack grinned as well. "You're going to have to watch your p's and q's for a while, Joe m'lad." Remembering the look of loathing on the priest's face, Jack burst out laughing. "He . . . he, did take on though, didn't he!" he gasped, and for all their good intentions, he was joined by Joe in uproarious laughter.

Bill looked at his father and uncle with hurt and amazement. "How can you laugh?" His head shook in dismay at the light manner of his elders, after such a shocking confrontation. One showed respect to people in authority, and a priest was due a special reverence and esteem. His own rebellion, in the way of departure from the church on Sunday, and his angry words a few minutes earlier frightened him with the intensity of the dislike he had for Father Wagner. It was sinful to feel such hatred, and for the priest!

Joe saw the torment in the boy's face, and smiled reassuringly at his son. "Bill, Father Wagner's a man, just like you and me. He's subject to the same temptations and feelings as everyone else. Men are different, and priests are different. You know how dissimilar in temperament Father Wagner and Father Jeanotte are? That's because they're not from the same backgrounds, or the same kinds of parents; and because they had other teachers and superiors to mould them into the sort of men they became."

Bill could appreciate his father's words, and some of the tension drained away. "For all their differences," Joe went on, "Father Jeanotte and Father Wagner still have their priestly vocations, and that is what we respect in them."

Notwithstanding his philosophical explanation, Joe couldn't resist a footnote. With one last thought of the raging Father Wagner, he added, "Mind you, you don't have to respect any man who makes a damn fool of himself!" This time Bill, shakily, joined in the laughter.

Although Alice, when she heard of the scene in the printshop, was very put out with Joe, and could not see anything funny in the episode, at least one other person enjoyed the story of the angry cleric.

Colonel Lowery, the frankly irreligious editor of *The Ledge*, wrote in his newspaper:

> The *Creston Review* has lost the patronage of one parson. (And still there are people that say editors aren't lucky!)

The play was performed on Thursday and, due to the clerical boycott, with indifferent success at the box office. The players didn't care though; they'd had fun and their supporters told them they were wonderful. The effort had been worthwhile as far as the cast was concerned.

Ernie came home on Saturday, and was met by all members of his family, except his working brother.

He stepped down from the train steps with a new assurance. An early tan accentuated his good features, and his newly muscular frame was, he noted, earning the admiration of his younger brothers and sisters. He was studied by his parents with satisfaction, as well. Hard work on his uncle's farm had done him no harm, nor had it altered his goodnatured and lopsided grin. He suffered his mother's embrace with some embarrassment, Alice wryly experiencing a moment of disappointment, while acknowledging that diffidence might be expected in a fourteen year old.

The boy saw no difference in his mother, other than a fullness of figure which had no significance for him. With a little shock, he did see a difference in the others, the little kids having grown noticeably, and his father thinner and older somehow. Joe's strong handshake and the wide grin, so like Ernie's own, reassured the boy. The eight month absence had wrought changes in his family, most noticeably in Margie. He kissed her cheek with reserve, as he noted a figure filled out with the first evidence of womanhood.

The current baby was Teddy, now a toddler of two years. He, with Reggie and Winnie, hung back as their parents greeted the homecoming son. When it became their turn to welcome the new arrival, they did so shyly, almost as if they were seeing him for the first time. His grinning appraisal of them restored relations quickly, and they took over his few pieces of luggage for the walk home.

He did not see his brother Bill until that afternoon and, though their greeting reflected some of the old camaraderie of the Ferguson and Trout Lake days, it was evident from the outset that Ernie no longer looked to Bill for leadership. They were together for only a couple of days, but in that short time Ernie made it plain that he was his own man. They were headed in different directions anyway; Bill a working man, Ernie still in school, with Creston providing a secondary education he could utilise for two more years. New friendships would be made by the younger son in this new town, while his dependence on family ties lessened.

With the others of his family, Ernie made his Easter duties of Confession and Communion, but discovered the coolness that had developed between his family and their parish priest; heretofore an unimagined circumstance. Also, he learned of Bill's challenge to Father Wagner's authority, and his brother's resulting decision not to partake of the Sacraments. Bill went with the family to Mass for this last time before he left Creston, but his absence from the communion rail was noted, not only by Father Wagner, but by others of the congregation, as well.

Alice had, prior to Easter, asked Bill if he had yet been to Confession, and his quiet, noncommittal "No, mama," had worried her. When she spoke to Joe about it, her husband gave the answer which they both had to accept.

"If he's old enough to go out into the world on his own, mama," Joe said, with regret in his voice, "we haven't the right to tell him what he's to do anymore. If we insisted, I'm sure he would go to Communion for our sakes, but I'm not sure that's a good enough reason."

It was a distressing decision for Alice. She had been wise enough, over the years, to release the reins on her children as she felt their growth warranted, but this was the first time any real challenge to parental or church authority had been encountered. She grasped at the one straw that seemed to offer strength for her hopes.

"Surely his regard for Father Jeanotte and his early training will tell in time," and, as much for her own sake as to convince Joe, she added, "Under different circumstances, another pastor, Billy will come back to his duties, I'm sure. We'll pray for that anyhow, Joe."

"Amen!" was Joe's heartfelt reply.

Their goodbyes to Bill on Easter Monday were all the harder, under the circumstance. It seemed to Alice that it had only been yesterday that he had played with his brother and sister on the liner bringing them to Canada, and on the mountains and shores of the Lardeau country. She told herself that he would be only a few miles away, but it was a first parting, in any permanent sense, and stressful. Bill himself showed indecision, but rallied to comfort his mother.

"I'll come home as soon as possible, mama, and if you need me for anything, there's the telegraph," he said. "Don't you worry. I'll be fine, and I'll write as soon as I get settled."

His farewell to his father was typical of his responsibility within the family. "Take good care of mama, now, papa," and his father's answering rueful grin acknowledged the boy's right to make this demand.

CHAPTER FORTY-TWO

Creston, 1909

In the month that elapsed between Easter and the Victoria Day holiday, Alice adjusted to Bill's absence. Young Ernie gained a whole crop of new friends, and one close chum in particular. Joe recovered entirely from the attack of guilt that followed his fall from grace the previous November. His recovery was a little too quick and too complete, but his paper's success, the comfort of Alice's presence, and his enjoyment of new friends in this booming town, brought the old Joe back in full bloom. Alice could not fault him. She loved his sense of fun and mischief, and enjoyed the social things with which he entertained her; things like Creston's celebration of Victoria Day, which was to begin with achievement and acclaim, and end in a mellow haze of affirmation for a new loyalty.

The fairground, forlorn and empty for most of the year, was alive with people, horses, wagons, and even a few automobiles, on May twenty-fourth, 1909. Today was the town's annual Sports Day, so the rickety structure kindly called a grandstand had been given a new coat of paint, and had red, white and blue bunting strung across its entrance. The sports field in front of the grandstand was laid out in white powdered lines for the athletes, and various officials, marked by their badges and ribbons, moved importantly around the area. Across the track from the centre of the grandstand, the high judges' stand was garlanded with even more bunting, and a new Union Jack in the centre of the field.

Joe found good seats for his family well before one o'clock, after a meal provided by the Altar Society in the exhibition hall. The stands were rapidly filling for the juvenile events, and no seats would be left by the time the later, adult events would be run.

As if by arrangement, a small corner of the stands was avoided by the whites. It had long been filled with the native people from the Kootenai settlement on the flats. Joe recognized Chief Alexander and his good looking son and heir, whom the townsmen referred to as Buck Prince Dominic. Alice also saw, and caught the eye of an old woman named Sophie, receiving a toothless but delighted smile of

221

recognition. As a frequent visitor for tea and whatever sustenance came to hand on Alice's back porch, Sophie had recently been showing an increasing interest in Alice's noticeably swelling belly, with much guttural language and appreciative nods. She made Alice colour now, as she patted her own middle and nodded her head vigorously.

A few races for toddlers were run off, then the announcer called through his trumpet for boys six to eight years. Reggie needed no prompting from his father, and was down on the field before the official could complete his announcement. Young Reg, like all his family, was tall for his age. Moreover he had been trained by Joe in how to get a good start, and how to give his best effort at the finish line. He won the race handily.

People who knew the family turned to smile at them, and Joe and Alice waved their thanks. Below Alice and a little to her left, a man she did not recognize smiled and doffed his hat. Joe returned the man's smile and raised his hand in a gesture that acknowledged the pleasantry, and the man still smiling, nodded and turned away.

"Who is that?" asked Alice idly. "He's a nice looking man."

"Don't know," said Joe, his attention already elsewhere. "Guess he saw Reggie sitting with us."

In the girls' relay race, which Margie had anticipated with much eagerness, she and her partner were not even among the first five teams to finish. She could hardly hold back her tears, as she came back to the comfort of her mother's right arm, and the reassuring pressure of the fingers that held her shoulder.

In the fifteen and under foot race for boys, Ernie, and his friend Bobs Sholto Douglas, came second and third respectively. The winner of the race was a barefooted, lithe Indian lad named Tommy, who outstripped his nearest opponent by a yard and a half. The cheering section of Indians made little noise, but their glee could be seen in their nudges and knowing looks at one anther. It wasn't often that they had something over their white neighbours.

In the open relay race that followed, most of the participants were youths. This was the event Ernie and Bobs had practised for, and in the white community, they were odds-on favourites. Tommy was partnered with another Indian boy, and their supporters in the stands became more vociferous for this event; looking to their champions to outdo the white man's choice runners. The superior instruction and training of their opponents was the undoing of the Indian lads. Bobs and the younger Indian were well matched, but Tommy fumbled the baton as he took it, and Ernie gained three precious yards at the beginning of their run. Even so, Tommy's superior speed nearly won the race, for him and his partner. He gained steadily on Ernie, and the two breasted the tape only inches apart.

The highly partisan white crowd roared their approval, even before the judges could confer, and some muttering in the native section indicated disapproval of the final judgement. Once more Joe and Alice were congratulated, before the printer slipped away, to put on his singlet and knee length running shorts for the main events; the one hundred and two hundred yard dashes. As the runners came out from the change room below the stand, a gasp went up from the crowd, then a derisive and prolonged hoot of laughter.

Following the lead of the white athletes, Tommy had shed his trousers and appeared to be wearing only a shirt, its tails flapping against his slender thighs. If the boy's thin legs and bare feet seemed to make him an unlikely competitor against the grown men who were his opposition, Joe, at least, was aware of the speed, which he had shown in the earlier events, and knew the Indian lad was the one to beat. He was not one of those who laughed.

In the first race, the hundred yard dash, Tommy won, in spite of a superior start by the former championship runner. The crowd was momentarily silent in surprise; then applause, at first grudging, rose in a crescendo, as the spectators showed their appreciation of the boy who had won out against adult opponents, all properly shod and clothed for the event. Joe was a poor second.

The two hundred yard event was closer to Joe's particular forte in racing, and he was fairly confident of winning. He grinned at the serious young man beside him and got a glimmer of amusement back, before they both settled on their marks. The starter's cry of "Go!" saw them take off simultaneously, running hard. It was apparent to the crowd that the Indian was indeed wearing some tattered underclothes under the flapping shirt tails, which seemed not to hinder the boy's progress one bit. He was putting his whole heart into the race, and in the first fifty yards, pulled ahead of Joe and the other runners. He held the lead for another fifty yards, but was unable to increase it. Driving hard behind him, Joe could see that the boy had put too much effort into the race's beginning. Gradually, the older man overcame the boy's lead, and passed him with a yard to spare at the finish line. The crowd erupted in a jubilant roar.

Joe was badly winded and gasping, as he and Tommy slowed their pace after the race. The boy beside him, although he had put his best effort into the race, was beginning to breathe evenly and lightly again. It was evident to the former professional that his superior knowledge of racing tactics had won for him, and he had to offer his hand in admiration to his young opponent. "You're a great runner, Tommy!" he said, with smiling respect, and the boy ducked his head in pleased embarrassment.

An aftermath of that afternoon's events was grudging approval of the Indian youth by Creston's townsfolk. In some derision, mixed with real respect for his performance on that May twenty-fourth, he was known thereafter by a title he accepted with humour and pride; Shirt Tail Tommy, the running man.

Joe was greeted with loud hails of welcome and congratulation, as he entered the bar of Brock Moran's Creston Hotel.

"Ho there, Champ!"

"Nice going, J. J.!"

"Fast company, those Athertons!"

Usually well lit, the bar room, this evening, was dim with clouds of tobacco smoke. It was hard to make out faces in the crowded room, and the noise was deafening, as the holiday spirit carried over into the night. It was an all male crowd, and the men of the town and nearby rural areas were making the most of the occasion, to indulge in mannish talk and mannish pursuits, which in this conservative community were limited to drinking and wild conversation, and to some discreet card playing, available to the more venturesome.

The scene, the noise, and the odours of beer and tobacco smoke were welcome to Joe's senses; deprived since the arrival of his family in town four months ago. Certainly he had been more than content with his home life, after his long absence from Alice and the children. Still, it was nice to be with his friends. For her part, Alice appreciated the devotion he had shown to the family and to herself since Christmas, and felt that he was entitled to indulge himself in a little male company. She had urged him to join his friends this evening.

Acknowledging greetings and congratulations from the crowded tables, the editor made his way to the bar, where men were standing two deep. He elbowed a path to the side of Joe Carver, who was carrying on a conversation at the top of his voice with Gus Muller, the representative of the Moyie Brewery.

"Welcome J. J., my boy!" shouted Carver

August Muller, eyes twinkling in his round face, beamed at the printer. There was just a trace of an accent in his voice.

"Why should I argue, J. J.?" he said. "I agree completely that the Kaiser is a maniac, and that the German people are crazy to listen to him."

"How did you get onto that subject?" asked Joe, as Gus Muller signalled for a drink for him.

"It was a natural consequence of a discussion about Victoria Day, and King and Empire," declared Joe Carver indignantly. "When I stated that the British Empire was the finest institution since the beginning of time, I certainly expected a rebuttal from my Prussian friend here!" and, turning again to Muller, he demanded, "Where's your patriotism, man?"

"I am a patriot," said Muller, "but not of Germany, nor of Britain."

His good natured face showed his refusal to take offence at Carver's attack. Carver himself, was less than half serious.

"Would you listen to that!" he shouted, in apparent high disgust. "The man's deranged!"

"He's right, you know, Gus," said Joe, and he struck a noble pose, and declaimed, "My country, may she be always right. But right or wrong, my country!"

"Pagh!" said Muller; his turn to be disgusted. "What a sentiment!" Again he signalled for refills of his company's brew for his companions, before he said, "Nonsense aside, I'm no longer a German, Joe Atherton, any more than you are an

Englishman. It's time both of us thought of ourselves as Canadians." The thought caught Joe by surprise.

"I don't know," he said, as he pondered the idea.

He knew the brewman had been in Canada longer than himself, had married a Canadian girl and had several very Canadian young children. Joe's first reaction to the challenge was to deny that he had been in Canada long enough to consider himself a Canadian. Joe Carver put his views into the momentary pause in the conversation.

"My folks came from back east. I guess they were English or Scottish or something at one time, but we never thought of ourselves as anything but Canadians and citizens of the British Empire," he added as an afterthought.

"How long does it take one to adopt a new country?" Joe mused.

"How long since you thought of going back to England?" countered Gus.

"On that basis, I guess I'm a Canadian," chuckled Joe. It was the first time he had stopped long enough to consider any implication of nationality, yet in only seven years, he had come to fiercely embrace this land he had brought his family to. Its sheer immensity and the challenge of its variety enticed a free spirit in a manner foreign to class-conscious Britons, at the beginning of the century. "I'm not sure about Alice," he said. "I don't think she'll ever stop being a proper English lady, but the kids and I . . . I guess we're Canadian all right!" He finished his drink and called for refills all around, to toast his surpising discovery. "Here's to Canada, and us, or we Canadians, or whatever the hell it is!" he toasted enthusiastically, and drank deeply from the new tankard.

"To Canada!" echoed August Muller, while Joe Carver added the common sentiment," And the Empire!"

A new voice beside them remarked, "I'll say amen to that, if you keep England out of it!" The grinning face of the Irish hotel keeper, Brock Moran, was at Joe's shoulder.

"No problem there," said Joe Carver airily. "This limey here just renouced his birthright."

"I did not!" said Joe indignantly. "Joe Carver, you're a damned trouble maker."

"Isn't that what you understood, Gus?" Carver now was ready to make an ally out of his previous victim, but neither Gus nor Joe took his bait.

"Go to hell, Carver," said Joe, amiably. "Does anyone here feel like a game?" He cocked his eye at the host. "The back room empty, Brock?"

"Sure is," said Moran, and with the unspoken assent of the others, he led the way toward the private parlour behind the lobby desk. He stopped on the way to greet a guest of the hotel, who was chatting with the desk clerk. Joe recognized the stranger as the smiling man who had turned to congratulate them, after Reggie's race that morning. He nodded to Joe again in recognition, as he greeted Brock Moran.

"Do you know J. J. Atherton, then, Mr. Archer?" asked the hotel keeper.

"Haven't had the pleasure," said Archer amiably, "but I saw him and his family clean up at the races today. Congratulations, sir." He and Joe exchanged hand shakes.

"This is Conrad Archer, gentlemen," continued Moran. "Mr. Archer has been a guest here for a week. He reperesents the State of Montana, and is doing some studies on the Kootenay River system." Joe Carver and Gus Muller in turn shook hands with Archer, who supplemented the hotel keeper's introduction.

"I'm away from home quite a lot, so it's a pleasure to meet you gentlemen."

Joe glanced at the others, and offered, "We are about to engage in a few hands of poker if you'd like to join us."

"Maybe I'll watch for a while. Thank you!" Archer seemed genuinely glad to have company, and his smile was warm and ingenuous.

"Come along, then," said Moran, and pausing only to give instructions for refreshments to the desk clerk, he led the way into the private parlour. As the four ment settled themselves around the green baize-covered table, the American found an easy chair. Brock Moran announced the rules, as much for the visitor's benefit as for the regulars.

"Only stud or draw poker, with jacks or better to open. Joker limited to aces, straights or flushes. No freak games, except one wild card allowed on dealer's choice. Two bucks to buy chips, whites a nickel apiece. Two-bit limit. All agreed?" As the others nodded their agreement, he dealt the cards one at a time around the table. "First jack deals."

As the game commenced, a little desultory conversation was allowed. If the pots got high, the players were expected to keep their conversation and their minds on the game. "What sort of work for your state brings you to Canada?" Joe asked the American.

Archer smiled. "Well Mr. Atherton or may I call you J. J.?" and he continued without waiting for Joe's approval, "my employer is the Water Resources Authority of Montana. I'm up here with two young engineering students who do field work for me during the summer. The Kootenay is an American river too, you know," he added. "We do water sampling, record water depths at various seasons, that sort of thing."

Drinks were brought in by a waiter, and they all concentrated on filling their glasses from the foaming jug of beer, or from the bottle of whiskey deposited on a side table. It seemed years to Joe, since he had enjoyed the relaxation of convivial companions and strong drink. He took a generous serving of whiskey, and enjoyed its warmth in his mouth and stomach.

"Come on gentlemen, let's play poker," warned Brock Moran, and as they settled down the cards, the American brought his drink and watched the game at a discreet distance. He moved unobtrusively a couple of times, to see how an individual would react to a particular challenge, and obviously enjoyed a vicarious pleasure from the play.

At eleven thirty, Archer took his leave, bidding the others a pleasant goodnight, and the players agreed to a midnight deadline. Joe was the big winner, by about ten dollars, in spite of being pleasantly befuddled by the drinks he had consumed. He said his goodnights to the others, who made scathing remarks about his dubious playing methods and "damn fool luck." He went home with a fine sense of well-being. It had been a great day; a wonderful outing with his family, a change for Alice, Reggie's and Ernie's winning races, his own win against the fleet Indian boy, and finally this profitable evening in the company of fine friends. Not the least of his good feelings arose from his embracing a new allegiance. He was a Canadian now, by God, and proud of it!

CHAPTER FORTY-THREE

Creston, 1909

The newfound Canadianism was something to be savoured in the weeks that followed the Victoria Day celebrations. A new country with new rules. No confining patterns, as in outdated Britain. A heady realization! And good fellowship regained. Of course, he had a responsibility to his family. He would never forget that again, he thought fervently. At the same time, maybe he had been a little neglectful of his friends and his customers. One had to fraternize.

There was no sign of discontent; no indication that Jack was unhappy. At least, in considering the matter later, Joe could not recall any kind of clue to Jack's sudden burst of temper, or his out-of-the-blue decision. His greeting to Joe, one late afternoon in mid-June, was therefore the more shocking.

"Where the devil have you been?" he demanded with heat. Jack Atherton's usually phlegmatic disposition was absent today.

His mellow mood caused Joe to overlook his cousin's tone. "Why, as you can see Jack, old boy, I've been out."

Jack's simmering anger spilled over at Joe's easy answer. "Listen! I don't give a damn if you neglect your newspaper. You were quick enough once to tell me it was none of my business, but you're letting the brunt fall on me, Joe, and I won't have it!"

"Hey-y-y, what's up?" Joe was genuinely surprised by the complaint. He had been out all afternoon soliciting advertising, and had landed one order which seemed to call for a few drinks. For the past hour he had been in the Commercial Hotel, in the company of his client and a few drummers who had ended their work day early. He was quite unprepared for Jack's next bombshell.

"What's up? I'll tell you what's up, Joe. I'm leaving!" It had taken a lot of firing up of his temper to reach his present mood. Joe's mouth dropped open in amazement, and he looked in vain for a sign that his cousin was joking. Jack, though, was deadly serious, and he clarified his intention with his next words.

"I've taken a job with Western Printing in Calgary, and we'll be gone within a week." Joe was stunned.

"I don't understand."

Jack was calmer now, but his words were emphatic. "I don't like the way you're acting. It's too much like New Denver all over again."

"What do you mean?" He still did not understand.

"You're a good printer and writer, Joe, but you're not a good businessman. A little success goes to your head too quickly, and you do all the wrong things."

"What wrong things?"

Jack took a deep breath, and plunged on. "You know full well that you've been drinking too much for the past three weeks. I really thought you had straightened up at Christmas, and that's why Carrie and I agreed to join you here. But you seem to be at it again, hard and heavy, ever since you fell off the wagon on May twenty-fourth."

"Oh, come on . . . a few drinks!"

"It's not only the drinking. If you confined that to your own time I wouldn't mind, but you're playing poker two or three times a week and frankly I think you are heading for trouble."

"My God Jack, everyone plays a little poker, and takes a drink!"

"And if they have any sense, they know when to stop! Do you realize how many hours you have been away from the shop in the daytime, recently? Lord knows how many evenings you've put in that way as well. And I'll tell you another thing; it's not fair to Alice and the children."

He was about to make a hot reply, but caught his tongue in time. Maybe he had been thoughtless. Alice was ever forbearing, and he shouldn't take advantage. God knew he did not want to lose her again.

"But Jack, you don't have to leave. I'm sure we can work something out. Maybe we can share the outside work, as well as the printing."

"I'm sorry, Joe, I really am." He had spoken his mind much more plainly than he was prone to, and now he softened his tone. "I've always like you and wanted to work with you. But I feel uneasy about our future. I think it'd be best for Carrie and I to take young Florrie to Calgary. The city's bigger, and if anything happens to the job I've taken, there're others to be had." Jack's expression reflected both his resolution and his regret.

Joe did not fight the issue, nor did he lose his temper, as he had in New Denver. It was going to be difficult to put out the paper by himself, but he had done so before Jack and young Bill had joined him. Maybe his cousin was right, he had not been businesslike enough, and certainly he owed Alice more consideration. He couldn't fault the other, and he offered his hand.

"No hard feelings, then. I guess you're right in a way. And good luck to you in your new job!"

Jack accepted the proffered handshake with a sigh of relief. Lord, had he actually said all those sharp words to his older cousin?

While Joe was reflecting that he owed more thought to the feelings of his wife and family, Alice was examining her own feelings; and the thoughts that had been at the back of her mind for the past three weeks were coming to a head. Her pregnancy was now in its seventh month, and although she was not unduly uncomfortable, she tired easily and was content to stay at home. Possibly, she thought to herself, this was one of the reasons she had so readily sent her husband out to join his friends on the evening of May twenty-fourth. She had begun to regret that act, and could not help but think that her condition had something to do with Joe's restless behaviour.

Something else was troubling her. While he was not displaying the dark mood which preceded his departure from New Denver a year before, she could detect a change from the happy and carefree person she had enjoyed since Christmas. He was a little evasive about his movements, and vague about mealtimes and homecomings. He was obviously drinking more, and exhibiting a trait she detested: he was his most solemn and precise self when the drink affected his tongue, as he tried to present perfect sobriety. She was also aware that the good friends he had been with on Victoria Day, friends of both her and Joe, were not frequently his current companions.

She had put off discussing the subject with him. The months since their reunion had been wonderful, and it seemed petty to reproach him for a little recreation with male friends. It wasn't as if he could not afford it; business was better than ever, and she supposed social drinking was part of the pattern. Nevertheless, as he had continued to drink more during these weeks, and to stay later at night playing cards, her concern had increased. She had determined to speak to Joe that very day, but a letter, which Margie brought from the post office on her way home from school, drove every other thought from Alice's mind.

Joe hurried home after he had closed the shop, full of high resolve and anxious to make amends to his wife. He realized that she had been more than patient with him, and he intended to make it up to her.

She was sitting quietly at the kitchen table when he entered. Her back was to the door, and the usually chattering Margie sat silently beside her. Their unnatural stillness was unnerving, and his feeling of guilt returned. Before he could make any remark, they both turned to face him, and he saw for the first time tears in their eyes. Alice held up the letter Margie had brought home.

"Jinny's dead, Joe."

The flat statement did not begin to express Alice's depth of feeling over her sister's passing. For Margie's sake, she had kept her grief from spilling over until this moment. Joe's shocked look, and his gesture of concern towards her, broke the flood of emotion she was holding back, and she ran into his arms. Her racking sobs were upsetting to Margie as well as to Joe, and he held out one arm to the girl. She joined them, and the three stood with arms entwined as they cried out their grief for the sweet young woman whose sufferings were now ended.

Jinny's passing, coupled with Jack and Carrie's decision for departure, were difficult for Alice to bear. Joe not only cancelled all his business and social engagements, but gave close attention to his wife for the next few days, as she adjusted to these new facts. Ordinarily, Alice's strength of character allowed her little time to grieve over that which could not be changed; but her pregnancy had stolen some of her regular reserves, and Joe recalled her miscarriage of years before with misgiving. She suffered an agonizing bout of migraine, which began soon after the fateful letter arrived. The pain's intensity increased that night and throughout the next day, then as always, receded. Alice's general good health prevailed, and within another day she was able to cope completely with family responsibilities.

Joe was able to return to full days at the printshop, and to clean up, with Jack, the outstanding workload, before his cousin's departure for Calgary. The couple had qualms about leaving under the circumstances, but Joe and Alice assured them that they would be all right, and insisted that the compositor keep to his agreement with his new employer. In spite of the glad faces put on by everyone, it was not an easy parting. Jack, Carrie and little Florrie were family, and had become dear and close to the older couple, since their arrival in Canada a year and a half earlier.

They were seen off at the station by the "who-o-ole blamed fam'ly," as Uncle Jack put it. As he shook hands with Joe, he told him gruffly, "I'll miss you Joe . . . silly old bugger," and he looked more mournful than ever.

The familiar words put a rough edge on Joe's voice. "I'll miss you too, Jack." It was not going to be the same around the printshop without his cousin's easy presence, let alone his competent assistance.

Jack picked up his valise. "I'm glad you brought us to Canada, anyway, Joe. And don't forget, if you decide to chuck it here, we'll find a place for you in Calgary."

Joe nodded his appreciation. He and Alice embraced Carrie and kissed the baby, and the young Athertons suffered hugs and kisses all around. Trains and partings seemed to be becoming a regular part of their lives.

For two weeks after Jack left, Joe had to work ten to twelve hours a day, just to keep up. Ernie was pressed, albeit reluctantly, into after-school duties, sometimes involving his friend, Bobs Sholto Douglas, in the less skilled chores of the printshop. Over the years, young Ernie had picked up some printing abilities, and could run the press and mind the office, if necessary. For the two boys, the only redeeming factor of their jobs was that they were paid, allowing them to accumulate funds for the upcoming July first holiday.

This event was to be marked for the first time, by a small carnival coming to town to augment the speeches, band concert and Indian riding display that were the usual entertainment at the fairgrounds. In the more trustworthy weather of this holiday, over the last, the exhibition hall would be open, not only for the ladies' dining rooms, but for the prodigious displays of flowers, handicrafts, sewing, crocheting and knitting; and for the judging of jams, jellies, pickles, chutneys and other preserves.

On Dominion Day, Joe closed the doors of the printing shop at noon. He had engaged in two weeks of unremitting labour, and this afternoon took his family to the fairgrounds.

The carnival had set up its booths, carousel and side show in the area allotted to it behind the grandstand. It wasn't much of an operation, but since the show was not long into its season, the paint was fresh and the bunting clean and unfaded. People thronged its short street, and gathered before the platform of the sideshow, listening to the spiel of the barker. Over at the grandstand, a few people sat resting themselves after a tour of the short midway, and were attempting to listen to Creston's brass band. This group, on the stage in the centre of the oval, was vainly trying to outdo in volume the harsh racket of the calliope drifting over from the midway.

The printer's children were in a seventh heaven of delight. In return for a little extra advertising, the carnival owner had presented Joe with a sheaf of tickets for the use of the family, allowing them free entry to the sideshow, rides on the carousel, and even ice cream cones from the stand that travelled with the show.

In his professional foot racing days in England, Joe had often encountered the "carnies" at the race meets he entered, and had always felt at ease in the atmosphere of sawdust, glitter and ballyhoo. He knew the types spawned by the carnival; the con man and the shill, the barker and the freaks, the roustabouts and the grifters. He was also aware of the camp followers not directly connected with the show; the gamblers and pickpockets, the pimps and the easy women. The little carnival that appeared in Creston was too insignificant to rate the attention of any bigtime crooks, so its followers were limited to one gambler, one rather inexpert pickpocket and a seedy couple who offered some badly worn merchandise.

The family dined with the ladies of the Altar Society in the late afternoon, as the sun shone through the dirty windows of the exhibition hall, its slanty rays laying golden bars across the crowded tables. Alice and Joe were tired after taking in the local displays, as well as the midway, but it was a pleasant and relaxing tiredness. Alice was herself again, and Joe was able to ease up after a busy two weeks without his cousin. The children requested permission to leave the table and to spend the balance of their tickets, and raced away while the couple sipped a second cup of coffee.

"Hello, J. J." Joe turned towards the voice, and recognized the American engineer, Conrad Archer.

"Hello Archer." He stood up and shook hands. "May I present my wife, Alice?"

As before, Alice was taken with the appearance of the stranger. His ready smile and charming manner put one at ease with him immediately. "How do you do, Mr. Archer?" she said. "I believe we saw you on the Sports Day."

"I'm flattered, ma'am, that you remember," said Archer. "That was a great day for your family." He paused before adding softly, "I also heard about your loss of a sister, and I offer my condolences."

He was very observant, Alice thought, and kind to remember such things. She acknowledged his thoughtfulness with a small smile, and a murmured. "Thank you."

"Will you be in town this evening, J. J.?" It seemed to be an idle enquiry.

He was about to answer negatively when he caught his wife's eye. Imperceptibly she nodded to him.

"Well, I might. Haven't been down to see the boys for a few weeks. Too busy." Alice's encouragement was puzzling.

"Fine, I may see you then," said Archer heartily. "Good day to you, ma'am," and with a pleasant smile, the engineer raised his hat and left them.

"Do you think I'm trying to get rid of you?" laughed Alice.

He pulled back her chair and they sauntered out onto the midway. The children spied them and came running. "Well, I thought, really, that you preferred that I spend more time with you and the children."

She looked solemn for a moment. "I have no intention of tying you to my apron strings, Joe." She looked up at him earnestly. "You have your own life to live, and your own decisions to make. I don't want you to be something that really isn't you!"

Joe bent over and kissed her then, right in front of their wide-eyed children and the smiling crowds of the fairgrounds. "Alice, you're beautiful!" he exclaimed.

CHAPTER FORTY-FOUR

Creston, 1909

Again, as on Victoria Day, the taproom of the Creston Hotel was filled. Joe went to the bar, as on the other occasion, and found Brad Moran and Conrad Archer together.

"What will it be, J. J.?" asked the hotel keeper.

"A beer, I think."

For all that he was here with his wife's blessing, he intended to be careful. He recalled the May twenty-fourth evening and subsequent bouts with a little twist of discomfort, resolving to be more discreet in his drinking tonight, and to get home at a decent hour.

"Yes, a beer please, Brock," and, as Moran turned to give the order, he looked around the tables and up and down the bar. "Where is Muller?" he asked of the hotel man.

"Gus left town yesterday to be in Moyie with his family for the holiday," replied Moran.

"And Joe Carver?"

"He was here just before suppertime, and said he had promised his missus he'd be home early."

"I was hoping for a few hands of cards." Joe was disappointed. "Ah well ... " Changing the subject, he brought the American into the conversation. "Neither May twenty-fourth nor July first have much meaning for you, Archer."

"True, but I'm heading home the day after tomorrow for the Fourth of July in Havre."

"Havre?"

"Montana," explained Archer. "I'm looking forward to renewing acquaintance with my family. I surely envy you fellows who live where you toil." He looked tentatively at Joe and Brock Moran. "I wouldn't mind a game of cards myself, if we are not too late. Have to work tomorrow, you know."

"I'd appreciate a game, gentlemen." The speaker was a character of medium height and nondescript appearance. His face was narrow and his eyes small and mean-looking. An ingratiating smile was on his lips as he made his bid for attention. It was Archer who answered him in a cold voice that was shocking in its intensity.

"Take a powder, Mac! We don't play cards with strangers!"

The smaller man began to bluster, but a small light of recognition seemed to glimmer briefly, before he sidled away from the fury in Archer's voice.

"Rotten little gambler!" said Archer, not bothering to lower his voice. "Sorry, gentlemen," he said in a milder tone. "I know the type and despise it with all my being!" He laughed. "Guess I spoiled your chance for a game, though, J. J."

Joe was disappointed, but not for the reason Archer had indicated. His disappointment arose from the fact that his friends were not available this evening. He had looked forward to a hour or two of banter with Carver, Muller and Moran, whom he had not seen for several weeks. The prospect of an evening with only casual acquaintances was not half as promising, and it was with reluctance he made his response to Archer's last remark.

"Not necessarily," he said. "Brock, if you don't mind we'll try the Commercial, maybe the drummers didn't all go home for the holiday."

For a moment, it appeared that Moran was about to say something about the couple leaving his premises, but the pause was only momentary.

"Sure, go ahead, J. J. Have a good time, fellows," and nodding at them both, he took himself elsewhere. Archer looked at his watch.

"If there are a few fellows you know at the Commercial, I'll play for a while."

At the Commercial, three young mercantile travellers were playing a desultory game of blackjack. They welcomed Joe with loud and ribald remarks, even as they warily eyed his companion. As Joe introduced him, Archer's easygoing manner and the respectability of his professional project on the Kootenay River, impressed the young men favourably, and they invited him to join them. Now they had enough players for a good game of stud or draw poker, so they deferred to the printer.

"What's the game to be, J. J.?"

"Dealer's choice, straight draw or stud. Joker legit for aces, straights or flushes only. No other wild cards."

"What do you boys usually ante and limit?" asked Archer.

The young men looked at one another and shrugged. "How about ten cents ante and two bits limit?" one of them offered.

"A nice friendly game," approved Archer. "Okay with you, J. J.?" and Joe nodded his agreement while catching the eye of the waiter for drinks all around. The fellow holding the deck dealt the cards one at a time until the first jack was thrown. It went to Joe.

"Let's play poker, gentlemen," he said, and the game began.

Although he was not with his close friends, he enjoyed the game for the next hour. It was interesting to study the play of his neighbours. The young men were inclined to flamboyance in their styles, showing off with slick words and phrases, to indicate their familiarity with the game. Archer played conservatively, dropping out, as a rule, before the younger men, who usually stayed in the game, contributing to the pot until the best hand was revealed.

The printer played well, neither winning nor losing a great deal, but conscious of the erratic moves of the drummers, and the cautious play of Conrad Archer. It was Joe himself who suggested increasing the raise limit to fifty cents, and for the next hour he played skillfully, working the odds carefully and winning with some regularity. He ran two successful bluffs; one against the conservative Archer, and another against the youngest of the drummers, to rake in a pot of twelve dollars.

"What did you have?" asked the disgruntled young player.

"You'll never know, son," said Joe evenly, and grinned at the boy's discomfiture, ordering a bottle of whiskey to celebrate. As the cards were dealt again, he poured a more generous drink for himself, and felt the bite of the overproof liquor in his throat and stomach as he downed it.

Nobody had been hurt very badly so far, and Joe was the largest winner, with some twenty dollars in chips beside him. The young men wanted their revenge.

"I think your winning streak just ended, J. J." said one of them, "and I suggest we hike the limit to one buck."

His friends nosily endorsed the change, and as Joe glanced at Archer, that gentleman nodded, with a shrug. The dealer dealt the last card, and Joe opened for a dollar. His hand contained the joker and the ace of clubs, and he dropped the other three cards on the table. The move was a gamble, designed to draw the others into the pot. The best he could have was obviously a pair, but what they couldn't know was that, with the joker, he had a better chance of drawing a matching card than anyone else at the table. As he thought, the player next to him met the dollar bet, which was in turn raised to two by the next man. The others stayed in the game, so there were ten dollars in the pot before cards were drawn. The amount represented half a week's salary for any of the young men.

Joe picked up his three new cards, but watched the play until all the additional cards had been dealt. Two of the players, like himself, drew three cards. One, the man who had raised him, drew two new cards, and Archer drew one to the remaining four cards in his hand. It appeared that he was drawing to a straight or to a flush. Now Joe looked at his hand. He had drawn the extra ace, and he studied the situation. Archer's drawing to a straight or a flush with the joker unavailable, was an unlikely event. The two men drawing to a pair could not match three aces, and a drawn full house was not in the odds for them. The man who evidently started with three of a kind, couldn't beat his three aces, unless he bettered his hand to four of a kind or a full house.

"Come on, J. J.!" growled the man who had raised him. "You opened the pot."

"One buck," he said, pushing in the chips.

Next to him the young drummer hesitated, but put in his dollar. The second added his, and the third raised the bet to two dollars. Archer disgustedly threw in his hand, and the betting was back to Joe.

"And a dollar," he said, putting two chips into the pot. To his left the drummer slammed his cards down on the table.

"I'm out, dammit!" he said.

Across from Joe, the remaining travellers looked at him and each other. "Up a dollar," said the first.

"And another," said the second.

"And one more," said Joe. The others cursed and refused to raise any more, but stayed to see his hand. "Three aces," said Joe, displaying his cards.

"You're a lucky son of a gun, J. J; I had three queens," said one. The other player turned his cards down. "Beats me," was all he would say.

The printer raked in the chips. He had won about thirty dollars in the one hand, and another drink seemed called for.

By the end of another half hour, he had a hundred and twenty dollars in chips beside him; the most he had ever won in a game. His good fortune, together with the liquor he had consumed, brought an extra glow to his cheeks. After his hard work and the family problems he had experienced recently, it was a marvellous treat to be out again, pitting his wits against genial companions.

"What do you say to no limit?"

He turned in surprise. It was Archer, of all people, making this suggestion in his soft even voice. But an Archer with a new and harder look.

"You've won enough, J. J. I, for one, want an opportunity to win some of it back."

There was no indication of friendliness in his tone, and the fun went out of the evening for Joe at that moment. The young men, by this time, were more than a little drunk, and incautious as a result. At least two of them were quick to acclaim the no limit suggestion, and the third went along without realizing what it was all about.

Now the play began in earnest. One by one, the young men were eliminated as they lost everything they had. Joe won some, and a steely-eyed Archer won the rest. There was no caution in the American's play now, and the boldness of his moves was shocking to the printer. The pile of chips beside him dwindled, as Archer's grew. Only one of the drummers remained in the game when the last hand was played.

It was Archer's deal and he called again for draw poker.

Joe picked up his cards and kept a straight face as he fanned the cards one by one. He had been dealt three kings, a deuce and a five. "I'll open for ten dollars," he said.

"I'm out." The remaining drummer threw down his hand.

Archer looked steadily at Joe, as he tapped the five cards gently on the table surface. "Fancy your hand, do you?" he said. There was no humour in his question. He looked at his cards for the first time, and he allowed a grim smile to pass his lips. "Up twenty dollars," he said, putting in the required number of chips.

With misgiving, Joe added his twenty to the pot. He was now down to his original investment in the game, so he could honourably quit, but those three kings!

"Cards?"

"Two," he said and picked up the new cards dealt him by Archer. He saw the American draw one only, before he looked at his own new hand. He had done it! His hand now contained the four natural kings plus the ace of Hearts.

"Your bet," Archer had lost none of his confidence. The possibility that he was holding four of a kind from the beginning crossed Joe's mind, but it wasn't likely that he could beat four kings.

Drawing on his cash reserves now, he made his bet. "Fifty dollars," he said, throwing the bills onto the table.

"Up one hundred dollars," said Archer, without a minute's hesitation, and added one hundred and fifty dollars to the pot. It was apparent now that the engineer was trying to buy the pot, whether or not he had the hand to take it fairly. Joe did not have a hundred dollars left, but he believed that Archer had to be bluffing.

"I'll give you an I.O.U. and raise a hundred," was his response.

"No I.O.U.s," said Archer. The blue eyes, until this night so soft and friendly, were as hard as flint. "If you can't meet the bet, throw in your cards."

He couldn't believe his ears. The young drummers were silent, awed by the size of the stakes and the ruthless manner of the American engineer. But Joe was livid, and his voice almost a shout.

"You've sucked me in, Archer, but I'm not going to let you get away with it! I've got the means and credit to pay my way and I insist that you accept my I.O.U."

"No I.O.U. and no credit," said Archer again, and he looked at Joe with disdain. "Don't play with the big boys unless you can afford it!"

He felt like hitting him. "Goddamnit, I can afford it!" he yelled. "I have a business and property worth . . . "

"Ah yes," Archer said smoothly, his eyes lighting with a small gleam of interest, "your business and property, worth?"

"Hell, at a modest estimate, twelve hundred dollars!" he snorted, glaring at Archer. "I can back up . . . " He was interrupted by the American.

"I'll accept your evaluation, J. J., and I'll make you a sporting offer." His expression again changed. His gentle smile and winning manner returned. The three young salesmen held their breath at the drama they were witness to, while Joe was confused and alarmed, suspicious of Archer's proposition, whatever it might be, but fascinated by the other's bewildering change of pace.

"What kind of offer?" He saw Archer pause carefully to regroup his thoughts, before he spoke.

"I have sufficient cash in my possession to add twelve hundred dollars to the pot as it stands now. That's with my extra hundred that you couldn't meet." Now Joe could see what was coming, but was helpless to protest. Archer continued. "In other words, I'm betting thirteen hundred dollars, against your twelve hundred dollars in property, that I have a better hand than you."

"Showdown?" said Joe. His stomach was in knots, but he managed to say the words steadily, as he searched Archer's eyes for a sign of indecision, triumph, or recklessness.

"Showdown!" agreed Archer, inscrutable as ever. "These gentlemen will witness your signature on a note disposing of your business and property to me. In the event that I win, of course."

A silence fell on the group, as Joe's thoughts ran their course from despair to exhilaration and back again. Archer reached for his wallet. As the others watched with fascination, he carefully counted out twelve one hundred dollar bills, then fanned them on the table in front of him. The display of so much cash was as dazzling a sight to the editor as it was to the mercantile travellers.

Pent up breaths were expelled, as Joe said to the passing waiter, "Bring me pen and paper."

He was cold sober now and he poured another glass of whiskey while he waited for the paper. Archer was not bluffing, he knew. He had already passed up the opportunity to close Joe out for lack of cash. What did he have? A straight or flush? Four kings could beat either. A straight flush? Unlikely, as would be three aces with the joker. Joe was holding the odd ace. In all his experience at poker, both in England, on the race circuits, and in Canada, he knew the odds were with him. He had to win, and when he did, he would take home nearly fourteen hundred dollars in cash to his wife. Exulting within, he scribbled out the promissory note, and the solemn and silent young men each witnessed it. Archer nodded, as he read it.

"One more thing," he stated, holding up his money above the pot. "I'm leaving town on the third, that's the day after tomorrow. If I win, I'll expect you to present the deed to your property no later than ten that morning."

"Agreed," said Joe easily. Archer was a practiced gambler, but he was overconfident this time. The engineer dropped his bills and the promissory note on the pile of chips and cash in the centre of the table.

"Winner takes all." He looked at the four other players who nodded their agreement. "What do you have, Atherton?"

With a flush of confidence, Joe displayed his four kings and ace of hearts, and the drummers gasped and smiled. They were as sure as he that he had won; but the printer watched Archer's face with mounting apprehension. The American smiling broadly.

"Not good enough," he said. "A straight flush, ten high," and he laid the cards face up on the table.

Joe walked away from the hotel in a daze. The night was hot and sticky but he did not feel its discomfort, or the jostling he received from the revellers who passed him. The liquor he had drunk was just a sour memory in his mouth, and lacked any dulling effect upon the memory of his reprehensible action of the evening. A clock in a store he passed marked the time as eleven thirty. Had all that taken place in less than four hours?

He looked around in bewilderment when he reached Fleet Street, without conscious recollection of having made his way there. The sight of the small but neat bungalow centred on the large property, and the nearby printshop and office, brought him back to reality, and to a new stab of remorse.

He neared the house, and in the light that spilled onto the porch from the front room, could see that Alice was still up and waiting for him. Through the lace curtain window she was plainly visible, serene as always, with eyes upon her work and with sewing basket beside her on a low table. He flinched at the thought that he was about to destroy that tranquility, and even as he mounted the steps, she added to his torment. Lifting a shirt he recognized as his own, she gave it an approving pat before briskly folding and adding it to the other completed mending.

Alice looked up as he opened the door. The ready smile on her face faded as she saw his stricken look. Her eyes clouded for a moment as she searched for evidence he had been drinking, but the expression on his face was neither of foolishness nor befuddlement. Instead he was wearing a look she had only seen once before, and that in England; deep despair and misery were etched on his face as he stood looking at her.

"Dear Joe, what is the matter?" Fright gripped her, and her hand went to her throat as she rose. Her first thought was that he had had some bad news of Bill; all her other children being safely in bed.

The words which had been hammering at his brain all the way home came out in a rush. "I've gambled away everything we have, Alice, I've lost the business and our house, too!"

The shocking words were almost incomprehensible, and she did not react immediately to their import. Instead, the sight of his dazed face, his usually erect self stooped and forlorn, was her primary concern. His hands were hanging loosely at his sides and she grasped them, to find them limp and cold even in the warmth of the July evening. He was virtually in shock, and she drew him to the table, her eyes anxiously studying him and wondering if he had suffered some sort of breakdown, a loss of memory, perhaps. Her loving concern brought him to a certain resolve, and he gripped the hands that held him.

Looking directly into her concerned face, he said evenly and slowly, "Did you hear what I said, Alice?"

"Yes I heard, but it doesn't make any sense. Are you sure you are all right?" She was relieved to find his tone more normal. Nothing could be worse than illness, or, she shuddered to think about it, a death in the family. Firmly she patted his hand and said, "Tell me what this is all about."

Taking a deep breath, he began to tell her the events of the evening. He did not spare the details, and directed his anger at himself even more than at Conrad Archer. But when he reached the point of telling her how he had actually put up all their assets against the turn of a card, he couldn't resist the temptation to justify himself.

"Damn it, Alice, I had four kings. I should have won!" His rationalization faded as she looked at him with a sad expression harder to bear than reproach, and he was compelled to finish, "I'm sorry Alice, your husband is a tinhorn gambler, and a poor one at that!"

She was silent. As his story emerged the end was foreseeable, and she could not escape the rueful fact that she had encouraged him to go out that evening. When the shoddy ending came, the initial shock was over, replaced by a numbness that came of the full knowledge of Joe's reckless action. As always, her thoughts were for the welfare of the family.

"What do we do now, Joe?" The absence of any sign of reproof shamed him.

"God knows, Alice," he said with bitterness. "You would have been far better off if you had never met me!"

The words did not carry conviction. The actor in Joe felt they must be said, but in the absence of any outraged reaction on Alice's part, he was beginning to recover some of his ordinary aplomb. He still felt shame over his intemperate action, but he also placed more than half the blame on Archer's shoulders. Alice sighed as she listened to his lofty utterance.

"But I did meet you," she said quietly," and I fell in love with you, for better or for worse." The dignity of the simple words overrode the artificiality of Joe's speech and he was quick to appreciate the fact.

"Ah, Alice!" He expelled a deep sigh, and gathered her in his arms, as he felt the corresponding comfort of her own. Some strength returned to him, in spite of the shame he felt. He would have to make it up to her somehow. Now he thought of Archer with anger. There was no doubt that he had been a gull; but Archer had tricked him with a pleasant manner that had concealed complete ruthlessness, and had possibly cheated in order to win. Joe recalled now how positive Archer had been of the outcome of the final hand. It would be impossible to prove, though. Archer had allowed him a chance to escape, before he had trapped Joe into betting his entire worth.

There was little sleep that night. They talked the whole matter over until the subject was exhausted, without coming to any satisfactory course of action. Sleep, when it did come, was fitful, each of them waking wide-eyed at intervals as the enormity of the situation struck them.

CHAPTER FORTY-FIVE

Creston, 1909

"I'm sorry, Mr. Atherton, the bank could under no circumstance advance twelve hundred dollars with your holdings as security. The best we could do ordinarily would be to loan you half that amount, and we would require a mortgage on your property to secure the loan." The news of Joe's loss in the poker game the night before had spread rapidly through the town, as it was leaked by the commercial travellers. The bank manager coughed discreetly. "Since the . . . ah . . . promissory note for your property is held elsewhere, I'm afraid that even this latter option is out of the question."

The editor's shoulders slumped. The bank had been his last resort. His friends had been sympathetic, embarrassed and contrite, but pointed out that they could not jeopardize their own businesses to assist in what could be considered at best, a speculative venture. Newspapers were always coming and going, the least stable of undertakings in frontier country. It was just another blow to suffer. He could not fault his friends, or the banker either, for that matter.

"Thanks anyway," he muttered, and took his leave with the feeling that everyone in the bank was looking at him. He jammed on his hat at the door. *Damn tinhorn gambler*, he accused himself again bitterly, and headed for the printshop in despair.

At home, Alice poured a second cup of tea for Mrs. Rodgers, the friendly wife of one of Creston's leading citizens. She had not been ready for a casual visit and her mind was anywhere but on the chitchat they engaged in. It was the visitor who changed the direction of their talk.

"Forgive me Alice," Mrs. Rodgers set down her cup and spoke with decision. "We have been sitting here prettily, acting as if nothing has happened, and you must be in a turmoil."

She looked at her guest with resignation. It was the final humiliation. "So, you have heard, then?"

"My dear, I'm afraid the news of the game has spread around considerably." She patted Alice's hand and smiled brightly. "Don't look so forlorn. It is not the first time that *men* have acted stupidly in this town and this province." She sighed with exasperation. "They feel they must gamble and drink and carouse, to show how manly they are. It's the same throughout the West. I wouldn't want to live anywhere else, but sometimes I envy the women of Toronto and Montreal, whose husbands are God-fearing and respectable people, who would be horrified at the thought of gambling their fortunes, or drinking to excess." Mrs. Rodgers gave a little deprecating laugh. "I guess the women of the East must get awfully fed up with their sanctimonious husbands on occasion, though!"

Alice joined her laughter shakily. She had been put more at ease, exactly as her guest intended. Mrs. Rodgers was being more than kind. Her own husband, Charles, enjoyed an impeccable reputation in the town.

Briskly she continued. "It's time we women took a hand. It isn't the end of the world, my dear, and I suggest that you decide to take some action of your own, starting with a visit to my husband."

Alice's mouth fell open. In all her life, it had never occurred to her to usurp the male role of decision-making, or to question male omnipotence in business matters. Only once, in New Denver, had she questioned Joe's business insight. Looking back now on their six moves in as many years, she realized with new conviction that she was going to have to play a less passive role in the economic factors of their life. She clasped the older woman's hands. "Thank you, Mrs. Rodgers! I don't know exactly what I'm going to accomplish, but whatever it is, it will be better than sitting around here, moping about it!"

"Atta girl!" said Mrs. Rodgers inelegantly. "Go after some of those foolish and self-satisfied men and show'em we women have spunk, too!"

Whether or not Mrs. Rodgers had forewarned her husband to expect a visit from Alice, she was received with punctilious good manners by the dignified Charles Rodgers, in his sawmill office, early that afternoon.

"How can I help you, Mrs. Atherton?" Chas Rodgers was a well-dressed man of middle age, every inch the business executive. His personal office was large and impressive, with heavy walnut furnishings and tasteful pictures on the walls. Alice quelled the panic that threatened to overcome her, and came directly to the point.

"Mr. Rodgers," she said, clasping her purse tightly so her hands would not tremble, "I'm sure you have heard of the unfortunate incident that involved my husband last night?" Her voice strengthened as she got over this first hurdle. Rodgers looked at her with respect.

"Yes, I have heard of J. J.'s misfortune, and deprecate the means of its doing. I don't hold your husband entirely responsible, ma'am."

"Thank you." She was encouraged to go on. "My husband is an excellent printer and writer, don't you agree?"

Surprised by this tack, the sawmill owner nodded his agreement. "Indeed he is, ma'am. The *Review* is well-written, and technically equal to some of the larger dailies. It is a credit to your husband's professionalism."

She drew a long breath; the interview was progressing as well as she had hoped. "Are the other services provided by the *Review*, that is, the printing of handbills and stationery and so on, are these services of value to the community?"

"Of course they are," he agreed, openly admiring of this lady's appeal on behalf of her husband.

"Mr. Rodgers," said Alice, "don't you think that some of the leaders of this community might offer a hand to save my husband and keep the *Creston Review* alive?" Now that her purpose was accomplished she felt the resolution draining out of her. She was aghast at her own temerity, and wished desperately that she could be anywhere but in the office of Mr. Charles Rodgers. Her face burned, as she wondered what he might think of her outrageous cheek.

The sawmill operator looked at her with a grave expression. "You speak well on your husband's behalf, ma'am." He looked down, and straightened the already meticulously placed articles on his desk. "You understand of course, that business decisions are correctly devoid of any sentimental considerations, and one cannot help but recognize the personal aspect of your appeal." Alice's heart dropped. "Nevertheless," he continued, "you have presented some very good points for consideration. There is no doubt this town would be the poorer if the *Review* were to cease publication." A smile broke out on the usually dignified, if not severe, features of the businessman. "If others will join me in a consortium, I will buy the assets of the *Review* for twelve hundred dollars from Conrad Archer, and we will employ J. J. to operate the newspaper and plant for us!"

His statement was almost as stunning as Joe's revelation of the night before. "Do . . . do you really mean that?" she asked faintly.

"Certainly!" he smiled, "and I'm almost sure I can interest two others." He looked serious for a moment. "The transaction of course depends upon Archer's accepting our offer. He could be difficult, but we will cross that bridge when we come to it." He was smiling again as he rose to offer Alice his hand.

She got to her feet as well and released her grip on the purse long enough to clasp his hands with grateful pressure. "I don't know what to say except, thank you!" She could feel tears pressing at her eyelids, and added hastily, "You are a kind man, sir!" Turning quickly, she made for the door before she became completely undone. As she glanced back, he nodded and smiled his farewell.

After his noonday meal of sandwiches in the printshop, Joe had gone to the office of the lawyer Mallandaine to arrange the detail of the transaction with Conrad Archer. Afterward he had headed home, in little better mood than when he had ended his appointment with the banker.

He was amazed and gleeful at her news. He praised her and got her to repeat again everything that had transpired that morning and early afternoon.

"You're marvellous, Alice!" he crowed, shaking his head in wonder at her temerity. His change of mood was so pronounced that she couldn't help thinking wryly that he was rebounding very fast from his astounding loss and humiliation of the night before. She reproached herself; this was what she wanted as well of course, but his contrition might have lasted a little longer.

He had a second appointment at Mallandaine's office for three o'clock. The probability of the buyout by Charles Rodgers and company now added a new dimension to the legal transfer. While he busily conjectured how this might come out, she returned to the mundane world of wife and mother, picking up Winnie and Teddy from the neighbour who had kept them in her absence. Her brief appearance in the arena of commerce was over.

Sharp at three o'clock, Joe entered Mallandaine's dusty office once more. Charles Rodgers was there before him, and was deep in conversation with the lawyer. They looked up as he opened the door, and beckoned him to come behind the railing that marked the lawyer's private domain. A young man opened the gate for Joe, and then discreetly withdrew to some inner room. Joe shook hands with Rodgers. "Thanks for your interest, Chas. You won't regret your decision!"

Rodgers's reserve had returned. "I'm sure, I'm sure," he said briskly. He was all business again and showed by his manner that the arrangement was to be purely on a commercial basis. "I have asked Guy Constable and S. A. Speers to join me in this venture, and they are agreeable, J. J. We will sit down with them later to discuss the terms of your employment, if that is agreeable with you?"

"Of course," he said. The three had the reputation of being fair men, and the printer trusted them to provide a decent wage. At this time, moreover, he had no other choice and was glad to accept the opportunity for a continued livelihood for his family. "Whatever you say, Chas."

Mallandaine gestured him to a chair and asked, "What were the exact terms of your promissory note to Archer, J. J., as you remember them?" He evidently did not think highly of such a loose arrangement, but with the signatures of the witnesses the note was quite binding upon the printshop owner.

"Well, let's see," Joe pondered, "I wrote that I would deed my business and property to Conrad Archer, about as simple as that."

"You own two lots," said Mallandaine, "and your house straddles the centre line." He could see what the lawyer was getting at as he continued. "Did you specifically mention your house to Archer?"

Joe thought for a moment and said excitedly, "No, I'm sure I used the phrase 'business and property' when I spoke of it, as well as when I wrote it!"

"I don't see what difference it will make," said Mallandaine drily. "You can hardly give up half a house, and there is no doubt you are legally commited to deliver the lot occupied by the business, as well as the printshop and everything in it."

"It doesn't matter to me what solution you find, if any," put in Rodgers. "Speers, Constable and I are committed to purchasing the newspaper and its assets for twelve hundred dollars, providing, of course, that there is no hitch with Archer. If he's smart, he'll take the money, but I don't know what his motives may be."

An idea was growing in the printer's mind, and the answer to his next question was critical to his plan.

"Has this buyout arrangement been discussed with Archer or anyone else yet?"

"Only with Speers and Constable."

"Can we keep this private then, and ask the others to do so?"

"Until when?" asked Rodgers.

"Until tomorrow morning," said Joe. "I have until ten o'clock to deliver the deed to Archer."

"I have to prepare the deed and register it," protested Mallandaine.

"You open at eight-thirty in the morning, don't you?" asked the printer, and as the lawyer nodded, he asked, "Can you prepare the deed and register it by ten o'clock?"

"Barely," admitted Mallandaine.

"Then I'll be here at eight-thirty!" he said, with something like his old enthusiasm. His grin was infectious, and the others had to smile.

"What are you up to, J. J.?" asked Mallandaine, but added hurriedly as he held up his hand. "No, no. Don't tell me. God knows if it is legal or not!" He wagged his head in despair at the printer.

He was positively joyous by this time. "Gentlemen, you have been most kind, and thanks for giving me such a good idea."

"We did?" blinked Rodgers.

"Yes, you did!" cried Joe, "And now I have things to do. See you tomorrow morning," and he left, with a springing step and upright bearing. Behind him, the lawyer and sawmill operator shook their heads in disbelief.

"Did you ever see anyone like him?" asked Charles Rodgers.

CHAPTER FORTY-SIX

Creston, 1909

It was eleven-thirty, and the night was still. Alice sat quietly, with only the moon giving dim light to the room. One of the children, Reggie, she thought, whimpered some gibberish in his sleep; the small outcry startling her as she strained to hear the other sound. It shouldn't be long, surely. He had been gone for an hour now.

She had overcome her initial worry, and now found herself curiously alive and savouring the experience. At first, she had been sure the outlandish idea would put her husband in jail, or at best, result in some terrible confrontation. Now she was accepting the plan with calm, even looking forward to it. There was much of the Wonderland Alice in her still, and surely this adventure was every bit as bizarre and outrageous as anything that had happened to the other Alice. *I'm mad as the Hatter,* she thought giddily. *Here I am, Mary Louise Polly Alice Atherton, thirty-six years of age and mother of six children, acting like a thirteen-year-old.* Being married to a madman helped, she supposed. Well, whatever the outcome, she was in this thing as deeply as her husband. In the meantime she refused to worry, and intended to enjoy her part in his crazy scheme.

The children had been allowed to stay up until ten o'clock, to ensure their eventual sleepiness. For the time being, Ernie was not in his cot in the living room, but in his parents' room, as was usual when they intended to be up after his bedtime. The light shining underneath his door indicated he was still reading. Never mind, he of all the children would likely be the first to awake.

Winnie called out sleepily for a drink of water, and Alice took a cup to her. The four year old was sitting up in bed, drowsily rubbing her eyes. "Is Papa home?" she asked, as she took the water.

"No dear, but he will be shortly." The girl gave her mother the cup and lay down again, with an expelled breath of sleepiness.

"G'night, mama."

"Winnie." She should warn the child.

"Yes, mama." Winnie's eyes were closed and she was nearly asleep again.

"If you hear noises, and feel bumps, don't be afraid. I'll be right here."

"All right mama, g'night." Alice wasn't sure the child had understood. *Good Lord, how could anyone understand, let alone a little girl,* she thought.

Now she heard it. The clop of many hooves and the jangle of harness seemed unnaturally loud against the quiet of the sleeping neighbourhood. It would be a marvel if the whole town didn't wake! The sounds came nearer, and she opened the door to see the wagon, piled with timbers and tackle, roll into the yard, three men sharing the narrow spring seat. Two extra horses were harnessed and tied to the back of the wagon. Joe jumped down, as the McBeath brother driving the rig called a soft "Whoa!" and the clattered ended abruptly. Only the occasional snort of one of the horses or the creak of their harness broke the silence. The McBeaths didn't waste any time. With Joe helping, they unloaded the timbers and unhitched the lead team from the wagon.

Shortly afterward, the beams and timbers that were to shore up the raised house were at hand, and the mechanical cranking sound of jacks began to be heard, as the house shuddered and creaked to a new level.

Ernie was the first to open his door.

"What's going on?" he asked, round eyed.

"We're moving," said Alice, reasonably enough.

"Moving!" said Ernie, then he comprehended, as the whole house gave a lurch. "They're moving the whole place!" he yelled, with a mingled look of surprise and glee. "Hey, what do you know. We're *really* moving!"

"That's right," said Alice airily, as if this was a perfect normal procedure. "We're moving about two feet up and twelve feet away."

Margie joined them, her eyes blinking in the light. "Is everything all right?" she asked. She was reassured by the smiles on her mother's and brother's faces.

"Everything's just fine, dear. Ernie, you tell her about it," and Alice calmly set about making coffee on the still hot cook stove for her work crew.

The actual transfer of the house to the lot adjoining the printshop took no more than fifteen minutes, once it had been raised and the rollers placed in position. When the house began to move, its racket disturbed Reggie, who joined the others in some apprehension, then was reassured by their excited laughter. Through all the screeching of rollers, the groaning of wall partitions, and the clatter of crockery, the three young ones slept the night away. It would not be until the following morning that they would find their house astonishly moved from its original position, and still raised off the ground by supporting timbers.

It took a while to get to sleep after the house movers departed, but sleep, when it did come, was deep and peaceful. Gone was the despair of the previous evening, replaced by an air of comedy and excitement that was still with the couple when they woke the following morning.

Joe was at the law office on the dot of eight-thirty. It was obvious from his broad grin that the mood of devilment, which accompanied him from the office the afternoon before, was still with him this morning. Mallandaine was more than a little apprehensive of learning why.

It didn't take long to tell the story, and by the time Joe was finished the lawyer was hooting with laughter and triumph, and the clerk pretending to work in the background was grinning his head off.

"By George, J. J., I believe you've got him!" Mallandaine directed Joe to a seat across from his desk. He sat on the edge of his own chair and leaned towards the other excitedly. "That 'business and property' phrase should stand up in court as meaning the printshop and the land it occupies. Mind you," he warned, "a good lawyer might successfully argue original intent, but we have another trick up our sleeves that should keep this matter out of court," and he sat back with a smug smile on his face; now he was the one with the surprise.

Joe looked at him quizzically. At least it was not to be bad news. "What have you got, Mr. Mallandaine?"

"We've been making some enquiries. You are not Archer's only victim, Joe."

He was dumbfounded. "How did you find that out? There's been no breath of scandal about Archer. He's been a model of virtue. Every woman in town approves of him."

"Well, we've found out that he's played cards often since May twenty-fourth, and won some pretty substantial amounts. Nobody was anxious to boast about it."

"Do you mean he's cheating?" A new hope began to build in Joe. Maybe he could recover his whole loss.

Mallandaine shook his head regretfully. "We'll never know. He's covered himself very successfully, if that's the case. In each instance, he allowed his card partners an early out, just as he did with you. The worst we might find is that he plays cards very well and wins without cheating."

"If we could get the others to testify, couldn't we take him to court?"

Again Mallandaine shook his head. "I wouldn't advise it. There's only a fifty-fifty chance of winning, and win or lose, your legal fees would eat up most of the worth of your property." He looked at Joe in sympathy. "I'm sorry, J. J., but as far as the law is concerned at this moment, you gambled away some of your worth. Be content that you have salvaged your house."

Joe grinned. His stunt of last night was a victory in itself. "Guess I'll have to be satisfied with that," he agreed.

The American showed up at Mallandaine's office sharp at ten, just as the lawyer returned with the registered deed from the courthouse. Archer was suave and courteous again. "Morning, J. J."

"Good morning!" was Joe's terse answer. "Do you know Mr. Mallandaine?"

"My pleasure, sir," the engineer replied but, as the lawyer did not offer his hand, Archer contented himself with a nod. "Well, I presume you have the deed ready for me?" and he took the document offered by the lawyer. While he scanned it, Mallandaine told him, "I have the transfer documents for both of you to sign."

Archer stiffened. "What is this!"

"You find something wrong, Mr. Archer?" asked Mr. Mallandaine pleasantly.

"The property I won consists of two lots and a house as well as the printshop."

"Oh? How do you know that, sir?"

"I searched the property of course."

"Before or after Dominion Day, Mr. Archer?" purred the lawyer.

"That's of no consequence," shouted Archer. "You are wasting my time, gentlemen. I was assured that the transfer of property would be ready for me at ten this morning."

"And so it is," said Mallandaine. "May I see your promissory note, sir?" and Archer produced Joe's handwritten promise. "This note says nothing about a house or two lots. It does say "business and property," which is exactly what you are deeded."

"By God, I'll take this to the courts!" shouted Archer, his eyes blazing with fury. "There is a house on my property, and I intend to have it."

It's not on your property anymore, Archer," put in Joe for the first time. "I was a damn fool to get into the poker game with you, and even a bigger fool for gambling away my property. Nevertheless, I did do that and I'm going to stick to my part of the bargain!" He met the glare in the engineer's eyes and wagged his finger under the other's nose. "You tricked me into staying in the game, and forced me to either lose a considerable amount of cash, or to bet my property against you. I don't have any qualms at all about moving my house last night onto the second of the two lots."

"You moved the house?" Archer stared at Joe with astonishment. For the first time he was completely nonplussed.

Mallandaine came again into the conversation. "I am authorized, Mr. Archer, by a group of local businessmen, to offer you twelve hundred dollars for the property described in this deed, the amount that represents its value."

Archer snorted. "Even the printshop and its lot are worth more than that. No thanks. I'll dispose of the property as I see fit. And I assure you that I won't accept your attempt to trick me out of a house and lot!" He glared contemptuously at Joe. "I told you not to play with the big boys unless you could afford it."

Mallandaine spoke softly but his words got through to the American engineer. "Mr. Archer, you have played cards incessantly, since your arrival in this town, and usually have won. Altogether you have taken a considerable amount of money out of the pockets of our citizens."

"Are you accusing me of cheating?" asked Archer. There was contempt, as well as menace, in his voice.

"Not necessarily," said Mallandaine, unperturbed by the other's tone, "but the businessmen of this community will not stand by and see a professional gambler fleece our citizens, whether it be fairly or unfairly." Archer started to protest, but the lawyer overrode him. 'Furthermore, Mr. Archer, if you don't accept Mr.

Atherton's fair offer, I will take it upon myself to advise your employer, the State of Montanta, of this and other gambling incidents you have been involved in."

The lawyer had spoken quietly and clearly but the words carried an emphasis which Archer studied.

"A little gamble, Mr. Mallandaine?" he asked with a little smile on his lips. "All right, you have played a strong card." He gave Joe a mocking little bow of congratulation. "I'll take the twelve hundred," he said.

They lay on the old Ostermoor on their own bed, in what was still their own house on the single lot on Fleet Street. They were drained by the initial shock and uncertainty, then by the frenzied activity of the past two days, but were still too excited by the final curtain event to get to sleep.

Alice was heavy with the child she was to bear in September, and she was content to lie in the curve of his arm, as he excitedly went over each detail of the game, the house move, and the confrontation with Archer. She never ceased to be amazed at his resiliency. There was no room for regret in his thoughts. In his mind, he had won the final victory. For a moment, she thought of the lost business, then assured herself that Joe might be better off without the financial responsibility of a newspaper. At any rate, they had a house and an income assured, and their condition was not a great deal different than at any other time during the fifteen years of their marriage.

Fifteen years! she thought. So much had happened. Happy memories of the Kenyons, Annie Pipe, Father Jeanotte, Jim Murray and his wife, Alice Jowatt and the Andy Daneys. What fine friends they had been. And now in Creston, how kindly and resolutely the townspeople had supported them!

And the children. *Six and a half of them,* she thought whimsically. If, back in Beccles, she had ever envisaged that many, it surely would have been a cause for dismay. But here they were, all healthy, all intelligent and goodnatured, and possessing their father's great capacity for nonsense and wit.

Ernie; he would be fifteen next month. More like Joe than any of the others, he lived for a good time, good companions and fun. Like his father, he could put his mind and his efforts to work if aroused by an idea; but his impetuosity might be his undoing some day.

Margie; changing from child to young woman. An intriguing blend of stateliness and whimsical humour seemed to be emerging each day. Her features were handsome, and her bearing in keeping with her taller than average height. Her blue eyes were startling in her dark complexion, and the promise of a very attractive woman was in her narrow frame.

Reggie; even at eight showing a tendency to fight for causes and justice. In school he had already confronted his teachers over matters that the other children were ready to shrug off. Alice's little sigh for her third son went unnoticed by Joe, as he continued his excited resume of the day's events.

The others, Winnie and Teddy, were still too young for one to predict their adult dispositions, but like their elder siblings, they were secure in their positions in a happy and well adjusted family.

Alice allowed her mind to turn to the one never far from her thoughts. Dear Bill. How she missed his strong presence and reassuring love. What was his future to be? His letters home revealed his progress, and the esteem in which his new employer held him. Bill would be just fine but oh! how she missed him! She began to be aware of what Joe was saying.

" . . . and automobiles and lorries and even aeroplanes are going to make a big difference in the way we live and the opportunities we will have. By God, Alice, we're just entering into a whole new world!"

She was getting sleepy at last, but she responded obediently. "Opportunities for you and the boys?"

"That's it Alice. All sorts of new occupations, and new ways of doing business. It won't matter that the boys didn't have the opportunity of higher education. The new industries will conduct their own training." Alice struggled to keep herself from drifting off.

"Moving pictures!" Joe exclaimed. "Can you imagine what they are going to do? I'll tell you what. They're going to bring good acting and great plays within the reach of everyone. Maybe world news as well!" Alice's thoughts were scrambled but she saw that Joe's forward-thinking was, as always, sound, lacking only the resources to carry the ideas through to success. She came wide awake at one frightful word.

" . . . the war, if it does come, won't last long. Europe is not going to put up with the Kaiser's nonsense, and it will be over before we can get into it." There was a certain wistfulness in Joe's last words. At thirty-seven, it was not likely that he would be drawn into any conflict between Britain and Germany.

Alice shuddered. "I pray it won't come. Billy and Ernie would surely be of an age . . . "

For a moment, Joe's excitement and preoccupation with his own thoughts vanished, as he looked down at his wife. "Don't you worry, love," and he squeezed the shoulder he was holding. "Everything's going to be just fine from now on."

Sleep was overcoming her now, and driving away the thought of horrible conflict that might affect her family.

"Just as long as we have one another, and the children are all right, I won't worry." She was asleep and unaware, as her husband gently withdrew his arm and kissed her cheek, and carefully drew the covers over her shoulders.